IN THE NAME OF LOVE

There was a sound outside. Fleur flew to the window but it wasn't Michael. She began to worry, he was seldom late. Normally he would be waiting for her already undressed and propped up in bed.

Fleur blushed at the thought of his smooth, young body. He was so different from Noble who was large and muscular and from Benoit who was too soft. Even his lovemaking was very different. At times he would be gentle and tender. At other times, he would be a violent fury. But no matter what he did to her she always came back. She needed him like no other man she had ever known.

She had almost made up her mind to leave when he walked in the door. In two strides he was in front of her, grasping her chin with one hand and caressing her breast with the other. She sighed and leaned against him feeling his hardness against her leg. He stood up and unbuckled his trousers. When he was naked he turned back to Fleur who was still fully clothed.

His eyes commanded, and she obeyed—and slowly began to unbutton her robe . . .

BLAZING CIVIL WAR SAGAS

MEMPHIS (807, $2.95)
by Shana Clermont
When Southern belle Melanie Beresford met Yankee officer Blake Townsend, she never dreamed she'd fall in love with the enemy! While the Civil War rages, so does Melanie's passion—does she dare risk loyalty for love?

VICKSBURG (789, $2.95)
by John T. Foster
Palatial Lightfoot Landing burns to the ground, the nation erupts in a bitter war, homeless Nora Lightfoot flees to Vicksburg. In peacetime, she had known love and passion—and Nora is determined to survive the war and find true love again . . .

RICHMOND #1: THE FLAME (654, $2.75)
by Elizabeth Fritch
Amidst the rage and confusion of the Civil war, Melissa Armstrong fights a personal battle for an ominous goal: to maintain loyalty to her family—without losing the one man she loves!

RICHMOND #2: THE FIRE (679, $2.75)
by Elizabeth Fritch
Now, in Richmond, Melissa knows a passionate love for a Cavalry lieutenant who helps her forget the only home she's known. But will she ever truly forget—or do their destinies lie on opposite sides of the flag?

RICHMOND #3: THE EMBERS (716, $2.95)
by Elizabeth Fritch
If time could heal a nation stained with the death and blood fo the Civil war, perhaps Melissa's heart would mend one day also. But she never really believes it—until she rediscovers love.

Available wherever paperbacks are sold, or order direct from the Publisher. Send cover price plus 50¢ per copy for mailing and handling to Zebra Books, 475 Park Avenue South, New York N.Y. 10016. DO NOT SEND CASH.

New Orleans

BY MIRIAM PACE

ZEBRA BOOKS

KENSINGTON PUBLISHING CORP.

ZEBRA BOOKS

are published by

KENSINGTON PUBLISHING CORP.
475 Park Avenue South
New York, N.Y. 10016

Printed in the United States of America

One

"Aurore! Where are you, Aurore?"

Aurore shrank down behind the green leaves of the towering magnolia. One slender hand clenched a narrow branch. Two firmly planted feet were jammed in the valley of two intersecting branches swinging up and over her.

"Aurore! Please come out." Maman's voice faded as she searched another area of the courtyard, her shoes beating a tattoo on the faded red brick.

"I cannot find her, Luce," Maman said unhappily. "Where can that child be. You find her, and find her quickly, or I shall order you whipped."

Maman's threat was a hollow one. She could not have Luce beaten. Luce was not a slave. She was free as were all the slaves Papa had inherited after the death of Maman's parents in the yellow fever epidemic in 1853. Papa did not believe in slavery, not for any noble reason, but because slavery was unsound as a business. Few plantations operated at a profit, all their money being in slaves. Papa always operated at a profit. He believed in money in the bank, not in human flesh.

"I will find her, Madame," Luce said, nodding gravely to Maman's stricture against her daughter's disobedience. She was a tall, Barbados negro who towered over Maman's petite form. Luce was broad-shouldered, yet slim. There was a hint of power in her straight back and proud face. The other servants were deeply afraid of her.

"She is here in the courtyard, hiding from me. She is a very naughty child to worry her Maman this way," Marie-Odile complained weakly. Her pretty face pouted, her dark eyes filled with self-pity.

"I will find Aurore, Madame," Luce said again, her deep voice filling the courtyard. Luce never yelled or shouted, yet she was always heard.

Marie-Odile turned on her heel and left the court-yard, her wide blue skirt rustling over the brick. The sound of carriage wheels outside the house quickened her footsteps. She hurried through the open door, slamming it behind her.

Aurore climbed higher. She peered over the high wall of the courtyard which shielded the house from the street. It had rained in the early hours of the morning leaving the stones in the street sleek and black. Aurore loved the clean smell of the wet street. She sniffed it delightedly. Soon the morning would grow warm and the water on the street would evaporate into the already steaming air of humid New Orleans.

The carriage door opened and closed with a slam. A young man stepped out onto the pavement. He had wavy brown hair, and was slim and tall. To Aurore's young eyes he was very handsome. Her breath caught in her throat as she gazed at him. A young negro in blue and gold livery stood next to him, arms raised to take the luggage tossed down by the driver.

"I see him, Luce," Aurore whispered excitedly. She climbed higher for a better look. Luce looked up into the tree at her young charge seeing the round bottom of her hoops with two lace sheathed legs dangling within. She shook her head in frustration. Mademoiselle Aurore would never learn to be a lady. "He is very handsome."

The front door of the de Champlain house opened revealing Persia, the butler, standing in the shadows. His graying head was bowed respectfully. The young man swept regally past without a nod at the old negro. Persia stepped aside quickly, the corner of the young man's coat flicking him on the hand. The boy in livery followed with the luggage. The carriage pulled away from the curb, turning down the street toward the dock to collect the next fare.

Aurore jumped agilely from branch to branch. There were wooden pegs pounded into the tree at intervals to make her descent less precarious. It was not easy climbing trees in billowing skirts and layers of petticoats over a hoop. Luce held her hands out to the little girl, swinging her down the last few feet. Aurore giggled. Luce's face softened as she brushed magnolia petals from the folds of her skirt.

"Do you think Marget will be happy with him?" Aurore asked innocently. Her young world was still inhabited with fairy tale princes and princesses who always lived happily ever after. The seeds of realism had not yet been planted in her ten-year-old mind.

Luce shrugged. It was not her place to say whether or not Marget would be happy with the young man. Privately, Luce did not think she would. She remembered Benoit de Ville as a little boy from the

7

neighboring plantation and she had not liked him then. She drew a comb from one of her many, spacious pockets and tugged it through the gleaming black curls forcing them back into place.

"Ouch!" Aurore squealed. "That hurt!"

"*Pardon, ma petite*," Luce murmured. She grinned at Aurore who grinned back. They were good friends. If it had not been for Aurore, Luce might have left long ago. But now that Aurore was on the threshold of womanhood, the youngest child, three-year-old Thérèse, was tugging at Luce's heartstrings.

Luce brushed a smudge of dirt from the hem of Aurore's ruffled pink dress and fluffed up the huge apple green bow at her waist.

"You don't think Marget will be happy, do you, Luce?" Aurore said with uncharacteristic maturity in her dark brown eyes.

"You must go in to your Maman," Luce said, leading the child to the door. "Hurry."

Aurore kissed Luce and skipped into the house.

"Walk like a lady," Luce commanded. Aurore obediently slowed to a sedate walk, but not even Luce would still the excited jiggle of the blue-black curls. Luce shook her head, smiling. She seldom smiled, but she always did for Aurore.

The last ten feet to the drawing room door were the longest in Aurore's history. Her feet dragged reluctantly at the thought of facing Maman. She was sure to be extra angry on the special day.

The sound of voices filtered into the hall. Aurore stopped, listening. There was Maman's high tinkle of laughter. She only laughed that way when she had company or was being unreasonably flattered. A lower voice joined with hers in laughter, but there was a note of artifice in it. It could only belong to Monsieur de Ville.

She turned to the tall, hall mirror checking her neatness. Despite Luce's combing, a few curls were already springing back into rebellious non-conformity. Aurore twisted them around her finger forcing them back into position. They stayed. She tugged at her gown of pale pink. She hated pink. It was her newest gown presented to her a few weeks before to replace the one she had irreplaceably torn. Aurore would have preferred a new doll with a painted china head, but Maman had decreed her too old for toys the Christmas before. From now on she would get clothes. Aurore wrinkled her nose in disgust. Pink! Always pink!

"When I grow up, I will never wear pink again," she told her reflection in the mirror.

Someone cleared their throat behind her. She whirled around to find old Persia regarding her with a bright twinkle in his old eyes, and a quiver of merriment pulling at the corners of his mouth.

"Talkin' to yore self again, Missy Aurore," he grinned. "That ole mirror is goin' t' break with all the sorrow you heap on it. You'd best go in, yore Mama will be mighty angry if you don't."

"Thank you, Persia," Aurore said in her best English with barely a trace of an accent. Persia was the only servant in the house who did not speak French. Aurore was always careful to speak English around him. It was impolite to chatter in a language someone else did not understand. Aurore might be a hoyden, but she was never impolite.

Persia opened the double doors of the drawing

room and beckoned to Aurore with a bent finger. She slipped past him, trying to enter the room unnoticed. The door closed silently.

Thirteen-year-old Fleur looked up, a hint of malice in her dark eyes. What a pity to see Aurore getting away again with her unruly behavior. She deserved a thrashing, and Fleur wished she were old enough to give it to her.

Aurore ignored Fleur with head held high, careful to stay out of reach of her older sister's hand. Fleur liked to pinch, and she pinched unmercifully when she thought no one was looking.

"Aurore," Maman's voice was sharp with anger. "Make your curtsey to our guest. Monsieur de Ville, this is my third daughter, Aurore."

"Lovely," M. de Ville said softly. His dark brown eyes surveyed her intimately from head to toe bringing a blush to her already healthy cheeks.

"Good day to you, Monsieur," Aurore said awkwardly. She did not like the familiar way in which he looked at her. She curtseyed clumsily, then turned to sit down next to fifteen-year-old Marguerite, more affectionately known as Marget.

On closer inspection, Aurore did not like Monsieur de Ville at all. There was a handsomeness in his long, narrow face and pursed lips, but his eyes were too close together and his nose was too long for his already long face. His chin was short and already receding. With age it would disappear altogether. No, Aurore did not like him at all. She stole a glance at Marget who sat next to her, eyes modestly on the floor, hands clasped tightly in the folds of her white gown. She was pale, and trembled slightly. Aurore reached out and

10

slid her fingers between the ice-cold palms of her sister's hands. Marget looked at her little sister, smiling sweetly.

"As I was saying, Monsieur," Marie-Odile continued. "Ocean travel is remarkably improved since I was young. I went to Paris as a young bride with Monsieur de Champlain and the ship was horrible and smelly. I was ill most of the time, but Paris was wonderful though not the Paris of today. My cousin writes me that the Empress Eugenie is a lovely person. Paris rings with her laughter."

Marie-Odile chattered. Benoit made the appropriate responses though he was not truly listening. His dark eyes kept wandering around the opulent room. Wealth was apparent in every corner from the Dresden figurines in a rosewood cabinet to the plush velvet on the furniture. It made Grandeville look like a country cottage with its tattered barrenness. Even the gowns on the children were of the finest Paris silk. He was beginning to like the thought of marrying into this powerful family. The girl, Marguerite, was pretty, too, though a trifle colorless. He studied her, taking in the smoothly parted black hair over the exquisite oval face. Her small breasts strained against the low-cut bodice of her gown. She was only fifteen, maybe she would fill out. He preferred women with a little more substance to them under the bodice, but her great dowry would compensate for her lack of bosom. He moistened his lips thinking of the hidden delights of her body. This marriage meant giving up the delights of Paris, but he would survive. Before coming to the de Champlain house, he had spent a few moments looking over the women on the slave block. An older, full-bodied woman had caught his eyes and he had bought her and then sent her upriver to Grandeville. If Marget proved cold, he could always take Serena to his bed.

Marget could feel his appraising eyes on her. They made her hot and flushed, then cold and shivery. She stared at the Oriental carpet under her feet, trying to lose herself in the intricate design. She did not want to marry this man with his calculating look as though she were a filly to be sold. She did not want his clammy hands touching her.

"Marget," Marie-Odile said, finally breaking into her daughter's absorbed thoughts. "Monsieur de Ville has asked you a question. Twice!"

"Pardon," Marget said, reddening in embarrassment. Her eyes met his and dropped quickly to the floor. "I was not listening."

"You are forgiven, Mademoiselle," he said, smiling. Aurore was reminded of a cat studying its prey. "I was requesting permission to accompany you to Mass tomorrow morning. Your maman says you go every morning. May I go with you?"

It was on the tip of her tongue to deny permission, but she saw the angry glance her mother tossed at her. "If you wish," she replied faintly. She hated the thought of him invading the only sanctuary of peace she had. Mass was her special joy. She did not want to share it with anyone, least of all him.

"May I come, too?" Aurore asked brightly. Marget suddenly looked happier. Fleur reached out to pinch Aurore, but Aurore skillfully evaded her sharp nailed fingers.

"Of course," Marget answered. There was no deny-

12

ing the relief on her face.

"It is getting late," Marie-Odile announced. "Would you care to freshen up for luncheon, Monsieur? I will ring for Delphine to show you to your room. Aurore, Fleur, it is time for your lesson on the pianoforte. Go along. No, Marget, stay. I wish to speak to you."

Marget sank back on the sofa weakly. She did not want to talk to her maman. But she stayed, head meekly bowed. Aurore was pulled from the room by Fleur who dragged her impatiently into the hall.

"You are so slow," Fleur hissed. "Come on."

Delphine walked quickly down the hall. She opened the drawing room door, bobbed a short curtsey and stood patiently while Monsieur de Ville raised first Maman's wrist to his lips, then Marget's. He straightened and left the room, following Delphine and eyeing the sway of her hips under her skirt.

Aurore shrank against the bannister as he went past, horrified when his hand reached out to touch the smooth rump of the maid. Delphine giggled, then hurried up the stairs.

"Will you stop standing there, gawking," Fleur said, giving Aurore's arm a savage pinch.

"That hurts!"

"I'll do it again if you don't hurry."

"Did you see what he did to Delphine?"

"What did he do?"

"He pinched her. Right here." Aurore demonstrated on her hip.

"Monsieur can pinch any maid he wants to."

"If Papa knew, he'd . . ."

"Don't be so dumb. Papa pinches the maids, too."

Fleur grabbed her sister's arm and tried to pull her up the stairs, but Aurore pulled free.

"I'm hungry. You go, I'll be up after I get a snack in the kitchen."

"You'll ruin your luncheon. You know how Maman feels about snacking."

"I'll be up in a little while."

Fleur clattered up the polished stairs. Aurore watched her go out of sight, then crept down the stairs and over to the closed door of the drawing room. She leaned against the wood, her ear pushed against the grain.

Luce's hand on her arm was as tight as a vise.

"You add eavesdropping to your many sins," she said severely, her face pulled down in disappointment and disapproval.

"I was just listening to Marget and Maman," Aurore protested.

"Go to your room," Luce commanded. "I am ashamed of you." Her turbaned head nodded toward the stairs.

"But . . ."

"Eavesdropping is unacceptable behavior. Go to your room immediately. We will speak of this later."

Aurore turned to the stairs, head down, feet dragging. She turned one last time, but Luce's face was stern and forbidding.

Marget sat in her chair trying not to cry. She listened to her maman extolling the virtues of the young man who was shortly to be her husband. Now was the time to tell Maman she did not want a husband.

"He is a fine young man," Marie-Odile said quickly. She saw the rising protest in her daughter's eyes and hastened to point out how acceptable the match was. "He comes from one of the finest families. His maman was a Charpentier before her marriage and a fine woman. You could ask for no better mother-in-law." Privately, Marie-Odile had never liked Monique de Ville. She was bold and immoral, always casting her eyes at other women's husbands, seducing them when she pleased. She pitied her daughter, for her husband would prove spineless when standing up to his mother.

Marget opened her mouth to speak. Now was the time to tell Maman, but her lips refused to shape the words, her thoughts dying unborn as her father opened the drawing room doors and stepped into the room.

Renault de Champlain was fifty years old, eighteen years older than his tiny wife. He looked barely forty, his face still firm and unlined, his body still slim and muscular. He was a tall man. He held himself erect with great pride. The de Champlain name was one of the most powerful in New Orleans.

"How do you like de Ville?" He asked his daughter as he kissed her on the cheek. He turned to his wife and kissed her lips. "He will make a suitable husband."

"I . . ." Marget tried to force the words out.

"Of course, he has no money, but I have arranged for your comfort. Marrying you is a great honor to his family." And an excellent investment for me, he added silently. Renault pictured the fine plantation, Grandeville. It was on the river, and would be important someday. Especially now with the war coming.

Renault had no doubt there would be a war. Slavery was too controversial an issue to be solved by peaceful debate. Secession had been talked about for years, and it might come to pass if Abraham Lincoln was elected to the presidency.

"Papa . . ." Marget said. He looked at her, delicate eyebrows raised in anticipation of her words. ". . . he seems very nice, Papa, but . . ."

"But . . ." Renault prompted.

"I do not wish to marry him," she finished faintly.

There was little change in Renault's face though his manner rapidly chilled. He sat down in his favorite chair.

"If you do not wish to marry, what do you want?" he asked with mild interest. He pronounced each word with deliberate clarity.

"I wish . . . I wish . . ." Marget faltered timidly, ". . . to enter the convent and give my life to God and holy works."

"I see," Renault replied calmly. He opened the newspaper he carried in his hand, the pages rustling dryly as he turned them.

"Please, Papa," Marget cried. She fell to her knees in front of him, her small face raised to him. A blur of tears shone in her dark eyes. She looked at her maman, surpressing a look of understanding and sympathy. "Please, Papa."

Renault scanned a page and turned it leisurely. "You will marry Benoit de Ville one month from today. There will be no further discussion on the matter."

Tears spilled from Marget's eyes, trickling down her pale face. "Please, Papa."

"No more discussion. The matter is closed." He turned another page of his newspaper, scanning it quickly.

Marget began to sob, her face a well of misery. She rose numbly to her feet, stumbling to the door. She opened it and closed it quietly.

"Renault!" Marie-Odile said tentatively. "Why do you not arrange the match between Monsieur de Ville and Fleur instead? Fleur would be a much better match for him. I know she is only thirteen, but what will two years matter?"

"I do not wish to discuss it," Renault said mildly. "Would you pour me some sherry, my dear? It has been a very difficult morning. Thank you." He returned to his study of the newspaper, leaving his wife bending mutely over her embroidery.

Two

Marget stood in front of her mirror, pinching color into her cheeks. She felt tired and listless after a night of crying. Her eyes were puffed and red, her skin blotchy pink. She wore a pale green walking dress and a dark green sash and knew she looked horrible in it.

Aurore waltzed into the room, pink flounces flying. She carried her hat in one hand, a brush in the other. Her black curls were a wild tangle about her face.

"Will you comb my hair, Marget? Luce is helping Maman who does not feel well this morning, and I cannot find Delphine."

"Such a tangle," Marget said. She was always in despair over her straight hair. It was always the fashion for curly headed girls to admire straight hair and for straight-haired girls to admire the more curly-headed. Marget took the brush and pulled it through her sister's ragged mop.

"Someday, I will cut my hair and be a boy," Aurore announced solemnly. Marget burst into laughter.

"You can't turn into a boy just by cutting off your hair."

"Why not?"

"It doesn't work that way."

"Well, why not? Cannot Luce make me a charm or

18

chant a spell that would make me a boy?"

"No, she can't, and don't ask why not again, because I don't know. There, you are done. Now come here and let me retie your bow. It looks awful."

"Fleur did it. Isn't it right?" Aurore turned to look over her shoulder at the offending bow.

"It is not right. Fleur has never learned to tie a bow properly."

"You look very nice, Marget. You should never wear green, though. It makes you look sick." Aurore observed as she stepped in front of the mirror to check her appearance. She looked neat enough, despite her pink gown. Pink again! There was nothing in her wardrobe that was not pink, except her crinolines and petticoats which were white. She hated crinolines, too.

"I'm ready to go, Marget."

They went out of the room, hand in hand, to encounter Monsieur de Ville leaning against the wall.

"I've been waiting for you," he grinned, looking Marget up and down. "We shall have to hurry, or we will be late for Mass."

Persia let them out. Delphine scurried down the steps hurrying to catch up. She dropped into step a few feet behind, Aurore's hand clasped firmly in hers.

Aurore loved New Orleans in the morning before the heat set in and everyone went indoors to nap away the afternoon. She loved the sights and the smells. She loved the close-packed houses with their high walled courtyards, and she loved the people. Nowhere on earth was there a people as full of charm and laughter as the Creoles of New Orleans. This was her home, and she adored it.

Marget did not like the feel of Monsieur de Ville's

hand on her arm. It was hot and sweaty, moistening her skin and leaving it sticky. She tried to disengage her arm only to have his fingers tighten peremptorily. She quickened her pace. There were other people walking to early Mass, mostly women with children. After the service, the older children would be dropped off at the Ursuline convent school and picked up again in the early hours of the afternoon. Because of the importance of Monsieur de Ville's arrival, Fleur and Aurore had not attended school the day before. But they would today, and Aurore looked forward to it. She did not much care for the strictness of the nuns, but she did enjoy the learning. She liked reading and devoured anything she could find. Sister Marie-Anne was appalled at the obvious thirst for knowledge, but was powerless to stop it. She had been ordered by Renault de Champlain to encourage it.

"Your maman tells me you are very religious," Benoit said in a voice so low only Marget could hear. "I am sorry to say, services are a bit irregular at Grandeville. A priest comes every few weeks to say Mass. I hope the lack of religious propriety does not disturb you when you come to my home as my wife?"

Marget murmured something under her breath. She clutched her missal in much the same way a drowning sailor clutches at a piece of driftwood to keep from drowning. Her heart ached as they approached the cathedral and realized the comfort of the place was soon to be denied her.

Inside, the dim cool interior met Marget. She hurried to the confessional and slipped inside. At least here, Monsieur de Ville could not follow her. She knelt in peace until the grate slid open and Pere

Buiron whispered to her. Outside she could hear the Mass beginning. She whispered her few sins and hurried out of the confessional feeling a peace. Tomorrow she would confess her momentary rebelliousness against her father, but for another day she would nurse her hesitant anger.

Marget slid into the pew next to Aurore. Aurore looked up from her less than pious contemplation of the little boy seated directly in front of her. She grinned merrily. Marget returned the smile, but immediately bent her head over her missal hurrying to catch up with the Mass. She murmured the prayers, beat her breast, and fingered her rosary. She prayed to God for guidance, asking his forgiveness for forsaking the holiness of religious life, and rose to take Communion. Monsieur de Ville rose with her and when she took her seat again, he shoved Aurore aside and knelt next to Marget. She tried to pull away from him, but he slid an arm around her waist and pulled her close.

"Do not be shy, *Cherie*. You have beautiful eyes."

"Monsieur, this is the house of God!" Marget struggled to pull away, but he tightened his grip.

"God does not frown on love, *mon cher* Marget. He is joyous for us." He nuzzled her ear while he whispered to her, his lips nipping delicately at her lobes. "Do not struggle so much. Enjoy our love as I do."

"Monsieur," Aurore tugged on his cuff, "Monsieur, the priest is looking at you."

Benoit looked up to find the eyes of the priest on the altar staring at him, commanding him to pay attention. Benoit dropped his arm from Marget's waist and moved away from her. His face flamed with anger.

Marget sent a look of gratitude to the priest. He looked away and continued solemnly with the Mass.

Benoit fumed during the final prayers of the service. He glared angrily at the priest, and at Aurore who shrank away. When the Mass ended, he stalked past Marget, hurrying from the church as though trying to outrun the reason for his embarrassment. He would never come again and when he was married to Marget, neither would she.

Aurore giggled uncontrollably. Benoit ignored her. He stalked ahead of them. A carriage passing too close to the curb, accidently splashed him with water from the gutter. Benoit spluttered in rage.

"I think God is angry with him, Marget," Aurore giggled.

Marget felt answering laughter trembling on her lips. She sternly forced it down, but not before Benoit turned and saw the amusement in her face.

"We must not be unkind to Monsieur de Ville," Marget said firmly. "Come, it is time for school."

Sister Marie-Anne tapped her desk with her long stick. The little girls, giggling and squirming in their seats, stopped and turned wide eyes on her. Sister Marie-Anne was very tall, and very thin. Her habit never seemed to fit her, always looking as though it had been made for a shorter, heavier person. Her pale face was framed by a snow-white wimple giving her a look of serene peace and ageless beauty. Only her mouth destroyed the illusion. It was hard and firm, a long slash across her face that was in perpetual disapproval.

"Come to attention, girls," she called. She never shouted or yelled. She preferred to let the universal fear of her stick do her justice for her. "Aurore, sit up straight. Marie-Claire, straighten your stockings. Untidiness is unbecoming to a lady. Fleur, your ribbon is undone. Retie it at once."

The girls put themselves in order to Sr. Marie-Anne's instructions. Then with feet together and backs straight, they stared straight ahead waiting for the nun's next signal. With a savage tap of her stick on her desk, the girls rose in unison, made their formal curtsey, and wished the black clad nun a solemn good morning. At her next tap, they crossed themselves, pulled out their rosaries and began their prayers. At the end of their prayers, they all sat down obediently and waited for the next command.

Fleur hated school, but she loved Sr. Marie-Anne. At night she often dreamed of the composed face of the nun and wished for those cool lips to kiss hers. Fleur loved the nun passionately though she felt no desire to enter the convent. She was content to adore from afar. She was the best pupil in the mixed class of ten to fourteen year old girls. She worked hard at being the best student in order to receive the praise she thirsted for from her teacher. Still she hated school and the constant repetition of reading, writing, and math. A woman of her station did not need such accomplishments. She would marry a man who would do all for her. Yet, Fleur still continued to reach out and outshine all the other girls.

"Attention, girls," the nun said, rapping authoritatively. She gave her orders for the day, breaking the students into groups and assigning

23

various assignments.

Aurore was bent over her paper, her pen moving laboriously over her paper. She was pleased with the flowing style of each letter. Sr. Marie-Anne came up behind her and dealt her a sharp blow on the back.

"Sit up straight, Aurore. You will grow up with a crooked back," the nun ordered sharply. She did not like the pert de Champlain child anymore than she liked the father. "You have splotched your paper. Your A's are terrible and your Z's are sloppy. Start again and remember to sit up straight."

Aurore did as she was ordered, careful to keep the pain from her eyes. She straightened her back and took another sheet of paper. She dipped her pen in the ink bottle and started again. She was angry. She had not splotched her paper until Sr. Marie-Anne had hit her.

"That is better, Aurore," Sr. Marie-Anne commented before she passed on. She patted Fleur approvingly and walked to the next girl. Fleur turned and stuck her tongue out at her sister. Aurore ignored her and concentrated on her letters. There were only two days of school left, then the family would be leaving New Orleans to spend the summer at their plantation upriver. Aurore enjoyed going to the country and the huge plantation called St. Angele. There vigilance would be relaxed and she would grow brown and strong from riding every day on her pony.

A pinch from Fleur recalled her to her surroundings. She looked up startled, expecting to see the nun standing over her again, but she was on the other side of the room castigating some other poor girl who sat with head hung low in shame.

Only two more days, Aurore said to herself.

School was out. Aurore flew out the door ignoring the calls of the nun who commanded her to walk decorously. Today was Wednesday, the day she went to her father's office and watched the huge riverboats coming and going, loading and unloading.

"Wait," Fleur said, grabbing her sister's arm. "Maman said you were to come straight home today. She said I was to see that you did."

Aurore twisted out of her sister's grasp. This was the happiest day in the week for her. She would go to the dock no matter what Fleur said. She ran down the street, dodging Fleur among the groups of people, easily eluding her among the crowds. Through the market she ran, no longer hearing Fleur's frantic shrieks.

"Papa," Aurore cried, running up the steps to his office over the giant warehouse which stored his merchandise. "Papa." She flung open the door, ran breathlessly into the dim interior.

"Aurore!" Renault said, sternly. "You must learn to conduct yourself in a manner appropriate to a Creole woman. Go down to the bottom of the stairs and walk up in a proper manner."

"Papa!"

He waved her toward the door. She reluctantly stepped out and walked down the rickety stairs. She forced herself to pause at the bottom and then walk sedately up the old stairs and knock politely on the door. The door opened and Renault opened it. He stood aside, gesturing her in and politely arranged a chair so that she could sit facing him. Aurore sat down, arranging her skirts around her.

"Good afternoon, Papa," Aurore said pleasantly.

"Good afternoon," he responded gravely. He sat down at his desk. "I trust you had a good day in school today."

"Yes, Papa. I practiced my letters and Sr. Marie-Anne made me do it again because I spotted my paper when she hit me with her stick."

"Why did she hit you?" Renault frowned. He did not like the nun. Over the last year Aurore had come home more and more often with tales of being switched for offenses he considered triflingly minor. He had once questioned her, asking if the other girls in the class were beaten as often as she, and she had answered no, but then the other girls were not as naughty as she. Renault did not consider her naughty, high spirited maybe, but never naughty. He did not understand the cruelty being dealt out to his daughter. In a boy's school, brutality and cruelty were the accepted thing, but not in a girl's school. He was seriously considering removing Aurore from school especially since the beatings were increasing rapidly.

"I was not sitting straight, Papa. Truly, I was being disobedient." Renault did not consider slouching a reason for being switched. It increased his determination to remove Aurore from Sr. Marie-Anne's savagery.

"What else did you do today?"

"Sr. Marie-Anne has a very fine new book from France, but she would not let me look at it. But I sneaked a look anyway. It has beautiful poetry in it and the loveliest pictures. I am the best reader in the class, but she gave it to Fleur to read and Fleur made the poems sound ugly." Her voice reflected her disappointment, Renault resolved to find out what book it was and find a copy for her.

"Would you be my guest for coffee? The *Sophie Sutter* has docked. Afterward, you may go and watch the unloading."

"The *Sophie Sutter* is very beautiful, Papa. Capitaine Alexander said I might come aboard next time to look at her. May I go aboard?"

"Only if you stay out of the way."

"I will, Papa. I promise." Aurore jumped up and kissed him fervently on the cheek. Of all her papa's riverboats, the *Sophie Sutter* was the most beautiful.

"You must promise to act a lady."

"I promise, Papa."

In the coffee shop, Aurore was given a place of importance. She was the only child among a group of roughly dressed seamen. A few of the men were more finely garbed like her papa, but most of them were fresh from the sea looking for a cup of good coffee, a hot meal, and a fancy woman in that order. Several greeted Aurore and she waved back at them. She was well-known in the shop.

As they sipped their coffee and nibbled at their donuts, Aurore chattered about their summer at St. Angele. She coyly asked him if she was old enough to have a larger horse than her old pony, but her father only frowned at her. She switched to the scene in church that morning where Monsieur de Ville was rebuked by the priest for causing a disturbance during the Mass. Renault did not like what he heard. He disapproved of Benoit de Ville interfering with his daughter's faith. It gave her solace. Who was he to deprive her of it?

When their coffee was finished, Renault went back to his office while Aurore skipped off toward the bustling activity of the docks. A few feet behind her slouched an old sailor in a worn jacket and patched pants. He followed discreetly as the nimble Aurore skipped ahead of him.

Out of sight of her father's office, Aurore waited for Patrick Callahan to catch up with her. Then she took his gnarled hand in hers and skipped along beside him.

"Papa says I may go aboard the *Sophie Sutter* today, Monsieur Patrick," Aurore told him. Years ago, Renault had assigned the old sailor to chaperone his daughter on her jaunts into the less refined world of the docks. He had not known her sharp eyes had picked Patrick out immediately, causing them to be friends long ago giving up the pretense of being strangers.

"You stay out o' the Captain's way, girl," Patrick said as they walked up the gangplank. "You go on and explore, I'll wait here for ye."

"I will not get in the way. I already promised Papa," Aurore said. She skipped away toward Captain Horace Alexander who leaned against the rail directing the unloading of the hundreds of bales of cotton he had picked up on his journey downriver. Many of the bales were stacked neatly on the dock, but many others still inhabited the deck of the *Sophie Sutter*.

"*Bonjour*, Capitaine Alexander," Aurore said merrily. "Papa says I may come aboard today."

Horace Alexander swept the little girl up into his arms and kissed her soundly on the cheek. "And how is my favorite darlin'?" There wasn't a man on any riverboat on the de Champlain line Aurore did not know by name. A couple of roustabouts waved at her, and she waved back.

"I am fine, Capitaine," she said, dimpling happily. She kissed him back, savoring the smell of his fragrant tobacco clinging to the fabric of his shirt.

"I've no time to play today, child. Go on with you and play your games. But stay away from the men, they've enough to worry about without having to be careful of a little girl." He set her down on the deck and watched her skip away.

The *Sophie Sutter* was a glittering palace to Aurore. She imagined she was a beautiful princess in a fairy tale castle. In the grand saloon, she caressed the magnificent velvet drapes of royal blue and walked over the deep plush matching carpet. The tables were empty, but during the dinners Aurore knew they would be covered with white damask tablecloths and table settings of the finest china and silver. She imagined seeing the hundreds of beautifully gowned women with their hair piled high on their heads and diamonds around their necks. Someday she would grow up and be one of them. She executed a few dance steps on the shining parquet floor, ghostly music whirling in her head. The glittering chandeliers with thousands of candles glowed softly on her gown of rich red. When she tired of the saloon, she tiptoed through the court staterooms with their Louise XIV furniture, and massive state beds. She imagined herself grown and occupying one of these staterooms with a man whose image was only shadowy at best.

Leaving the staterooms behind, she walked around the deck peering into the galleys where one of the cooks gave her a tart which she munched as she walked around and wiped her sticky hands on her hem.

The room that fascinated her the most was the huge gambling saloon. A hundred tables with smooth wood tops and straight-backed chairs greeted her. She ran her fingers along the satin wood top of the bar, stumbled over a brass spittoon, and gazed in awe at the painting of a voluptuous woman adorning the wall. Aurore was endlessly fascinated with the painting. She was completely naked except for a scarf coyly hiding her private area. Her breasts were full and large with rosy tipped nipples that seemed to thrust out of the scene. Her eyes were closed and her mouth slightly parted. She looked deliciously content. Aurore thought of how horrified Maman would be if she knew what her daughter was looking at. Maman considered it improper for even a stray ankle to accidentally show. Aurore wondered how she would react at seeing this painting. A glance down at her own pitifully flat chest made her wonder if she would ever look like that.

"Aren't you a little young to be in here?" a voice drawled.

Aurore whirled around to find herself staring at the belt buckle of a man. She looked up and up to see him. He was so tall. She stared open-mouthed at the handsome, blond stranger. He smiled at her revealing even white teeth.

"Were you speaking to me, Monsieur?" she asked politely.

He looked around the room with exaggerated care, even peering under two tables. "I would assume I am speaking to you, young lady," he said. He slid his hands under her arms and swung her up on the bar to sit facing him.

"I am Aurore de Champlain. My Papa owns this riverboat. I am allowed to be on it," she said with all the dignity she could find. His deep blue eyes laughed at her, crinkling at the corners. An answering smile tugged at her lips.

"I am Mr. Gayle Courtland, late of the riverboat *Sophie Sutter*, and presently the heir to Grey Lawns, the family estate."

Vaguely, Aurore remembered seeing him a few times. She knew he was one of the many professional gamblers who made their living playing cards on the riverboats.

"Did you like living here?" she asked curiously. She wondered what life was like living on the river day after day. She felt excitement fill her, instinctively knowing she would love that kind of life.

"Yes, I did," he answered gravely, his eyes sweeping around the room sadly.

"Do you like being a gambler?"

"Oh, so you do know what this room is?"

"But of course, do you play cards?"

He picked her up and deposited her on the nearest chair, seating himself opposite her. He pulled a deck of cards out of his pocket, expertly shuffled them, then began to teach a ten-year-old to play poker.

"It is so exciting," Aurore said, jiggling in her chair when she won.

He dealt another hand smiling when she won again. He dealt hand after hand, patiently teaching her and enjoying it.

31

"You're very lucky with cards," Gayle said. He noticed the growing dark outside the wide windows of the saloon. He put the cards back in his pocket ignoring Aurore's protests over the end of their play.

"Is it good to be lucky playing cards?" she asked as he pulled out her chair and took her hand.

He shrugged.

"Can I ask you a question, Monsieur Courtland?" She looked up at the painting of the naked lady as they passed the bar. "Why is she unclothed?"

"Because men like to look at ladies with no clothes," he answered chuckling.

"But Maman says a lady must always be modest and demure. She must never show herself to any man, not even her husband."

"Don't tell your maman, but I think she is very wrong. Most of the men I know not only like looking at ladies in paintings, but also real ones who are undressed."

"Really," Aurore glanced at the picture. She pulled the bodice of her gown out and looked down at her chest in despair. "No one will like looking at me. I do not have big things like the lady in the painting."

Gayle burst out laughing. "Don't worry. When you grow, they will grow."

"How wonderful," she said, clapping her hands, dancing around the room. "When I am grown, will you like looking at me?"

"Enough of this," he said sternly. "You are just a little girl and it is time you were home and in bed with all the other little girls of this world." He led her down the gangplank, hailing a carriage.

"Will I see you again?" she asked as he swung her

up into the carriage. She saw Capitaine Alexander on the dock and waved to him. Patrick Callahan ran puffing across the dock quickly.

"Someday, little girl. When you grow up."

"I shall grow up fast for you, Monsieur," Aurore said, gazing at him with growing adoration.

"I'll see the girl home, Mr. Courtland," Patrick said reaching the carriage and jumping in. He settled across from Aurore with a sigh. "Her Pa would never forgive me if I let her go home alone."

"Good-bye, little Aurore," Gayle said, taking her hand and kissing it. Aurore felt a chill travel up her arm. Never had she felt like this before. He stepped back, slammed the door and signaled to the driver. The carriage jumped forward.

When Aurore reached home, she went to her room and locked the door against intrusion. She flung herself on her bed and dreamed wide-eyed about the day when she would be grown. The shadowy figure of her dream man developed into a full picture of Gayle Courtland. She sighed, not understanding the fluttering of her young heart, but she knew she would be inconsolable if she never saw him again.

Three

"I must protest," Marie-Odile said. She sat in bed, her legs modestly covered by the light quilt. Her body was encased in a long, voluminous nightgown decorated with lace and ribbon. A wide frill fell from her shoulders showing the long, proud column of her neck. Renault thought of how exceedingly pretty she was with her hair tumbling about her shoulders and her slightly slanted eyes staring up at him. At thirty-two, she looked little different from the winsome sixteen-year-old he had taken to Paris as a bride. Her excessive modesty had amused him then almost as much as it did now. It amused him to play with the flames of passion she kept carefully under control.

"Protest what, my dear?" His gaze caressed her as he neatly hung up his coat and started to unbutton his shirt baring a smooth, muscular chest.

Marie-Odile turned her eyes chastely away. It was improper to look upon a man's unclothed form. For the thousandth time, she wished Renault would use the connecting bedchamber instead of sharing a room with her. It was considered indelicate for a man to share his wife's room, yet he continued to ignore custom by refusing to move. He had once told his wife he liked sleeping with her which had brought a blush of confusion to her pale cheeks. He had also told her he liked making love to her which had sent her in a flurry to her prie-Dieu to offer prayers of forgiveness for hearing the word sex. Her intense religiousness amused him. He tolerated it as long as she did not force it on him or bring it to bed with her.

"I must protest Aurore's wandering around the docks every week. I told Fleur to see her home today, but she refused to come, running away instead."

"She likes the river," Renault said mildly. He liked the river. The Mississippi had proved continuously fascinating for him as a child and as an adult. It gratified him to see Aurore with the same intense fascination. He encouraged it, the same way he encouraged her voracious appetite for knowledge. It upset Marie-Odile that he insisted on talking politics with her, but he felt that no one can live in the South in these turbulent times without understanding the political situation. Aurore, with her uncluttered mind, was often quick to understand things he often puzzled over for days.

"But she disobeyed me, Renault," Marie-Odile cried. She forgot herself and looked up to encounter his undressed body standing proudly at the foot of the bed. She gasped and lowered her eyes immediately, fighting the temptation to look again and admire his still young looking body. She castigated herself for her impure thoughts, saying a few prayers to drive the devil out of her mind, yet still she felt the first faint stirring of her own body betraying her again as always. She sank down in the bed, pulling the quilt tightly around her as though denying her sudden excitement. If only he would wear a nightshirt, she

35

mourned. But he adamantly refused to entangle his body while he slept. He had done without a nightshirt for fifty years, he would continue to do without one. He slid into bed picking up a book from the side table and opening it. Marie-Odile pulled away from the feel of his leg against hers.

"She is a child, Marie-Odile," Renault said. "Let her enjoy what little time is left to childhood. I guarantee she will grow fast enough when this war starts."

"There is going to be no war," she cried. "Why must you always persist in this argument about a war? Everyone says the South is too strong for the North. It would be foolish of them to start a war."

Renault sighed. He had explained over and over again the situation, but she refused to believe with the same deafness of her many friends. He had purposely married her when she was sixteen in order to shape her thinking. He had not counted on the rigid limitations her parents had imposed on her. Still he loved her and tolerated her inability to understand politics.

"Go to sleep, Marie-Odile," he said quietly. He closed his book with a snap, leaned over and extinguished the lamp. He slid into the bed, stretching as he did so. Of late, he had been feeling the heat more. He was fifty years old. One could not stay young forever. He turned on his side, reaching out to touch his wife. She would never come to him willingly. He ran a hand down the smooth length of her leg, pulling up the hem of her gown. He could feel the velvet sleekness of her skin. He caressed it. She shivered. His other hand reached for the ribbons around her neck. He tugged till the front of her gown fell open to the waist. He pushed the corners off her shoulders revealing small, firm breasts. After seven pregnancies, she was still slim. He admired that slimness, letting his fingers wander down the angle of her hips as he pushed the gown down to her feet. She continued to shiver, but already she was opening to him, responding to him. He did not know who she feared more, herself and her faithless body, or him with his ability to rouse her to those delights she considered sinful. He kicked the nightgown off the bed, watching it sail through the air to puddle near the wall. Then he pulled her to him, thinking that tonight might be the night they would conceive the son he eagerly wanted.

Marie-Odile woke first in the morning. The sun peeked through the louvered windows making stripes across the floor and her body. She gasped to find herself naked. Renault's leg was thrown across hers, one hand lay lightly across her thigh. She moved slightly, trying to disentangle herself and reach for her nightdress, but his fingers tightened on her leg. His eyes opened to survey her lazily. A blush rose on her body as he studied her. He cupped her breast, but she pushed it roughly away.

"If we are to remove to St. Angele in two days, I must see to the packing." She struggled to get away from him.

He smiled contentedly, wrapping one arm around her and drawing her back. She look horrified, but he did not release her.

"But it is daylight," she moaned, feeling his expert hands finding all the little places that roused her quickly.

"Who is to know we are not sleeping. I am your husband. You are my wife. There is nothing wrong in taking our pleasure when the fancy strikes us. Be it in the dead of night or in the light of morning."

"But the packing!"

"If we do not leave on Saturday, we shall leave on Monday."

She opened her mouth to tell him of the problems of packing, but he stopped her with his lips. She groaned, as her arms crept around his shoulders and she held him tight against her.

Aurore and Fleur were at school by the time Marie-Odile finally walked downstairs to the dining room for her breakfast. Long before she reached the room, the tantalizing odors of the food reached her reminding her of her hunger. She thought of her Maman who deplored the fashion of taking breakfast in bed. No mistress of a large house ever idled the morning away in sloth. She was the mistress, and the mistress was up to oversee everything almost as soon as the servants.

Marie-Odile walked into the dining room surprising Monsieur de Ville on his knees before a reluctant Marget. She strained away from him, her face dreadfully pale.

"Bonjour, Madame," he said winking at her and glancing at the clock.

Marie-Odile's eyes widened in shock. He leered at her as though he knew what had detained her in the early hours of the morning. He rose calmly to his feet and walked to her. He pulled out her chair and seated her, though she avoided his touch.

"I trust you slept well?" Again the leer that made

Marie-Odile gasp. She wished Renault were here. He would never be so bold as to hint at the private relations existing between her and her husband. She found herself slowly disliking him. She picked up a small bell and rang it curtly. A young maid appeared.

"Bring a fresh plate of food for Mademoiselle Marget," she ordered, noting the congealed grease on her daughter's untouched plate. The girl bobbed and took the cold plate of food and returned with a fresh one. Then she handed a second plate to her mistress.

"I am not hungry, Maman," Marget said in a low, strained voice.

"Nonsense," Marie-Odile said. "You must eat to keep up your strength for your wedding."

Marget obediently picked up her fork and put some food on it. She raised it to her mouth and put in the food, but Benoit de Ville smirking at her made it impossible to swallow. Her fork clattered to the plate as she hastily jumped up and ran out of the room.

"Your daughter is very sensitive," Benoit said smoothly. He ate with relish. It would not be long before the already tight waist of his breeches would grow tighter.

"You must be patient with her," Marie-Odile responded.

"I shall be very careful with your daughter, Madame. She is a prize worth winning."

Benoit attacked a second plate of food hungrily. He eyed the de Champlain dining room between forkfuls of food. The chandelier was imported from France, the drapes were of the finest velvet. The furniture was like none he had ever seen before. Madame de Champlain had excellent taste, he hoped her shy daughter had inherited it. Grandeville was sadly in need of refurbishing.

He congratulated himself on making such a smart alliance. No matter that Marget was so retiring. Every man recognized an act when he saw it. Her shyness would evaporate as soon as they were wed. He could bet she would have a few things to show him about marriage that even the many experienced women he knew in Paris didn't know. He smiled to himself, glancing at Madame. He would bet anything she was a real wanton in bed, too. He wished he had the nerve to sample of her, but he had not the courage.

Aurore did not want to go to school. She stood in front of the forbidding walls of the convent hesitating. Fleur tried to drag her in, but Aurore refused to move. Then Fleur pinched her, but in a show of uncharacteristic hostility, Aurore pinched her back as hard as she could.

"That hurt," Fleur screamed.

"It hurts when you do it to me."

"I'll tell Maman."

Aurore shrugged. Threats failed to move her. Finally Fleur went to school by herself thinking of how she would tell Sr. Marie-Anne of her sister's mutiny.

Aurore continued to stand on the sidewalk staring at the school. Several other girls arrived and waved to her, but she did not wave back. She was uncertain on how to go about running away. She was certain to be caught and punished. She wondered if the punishment was worth a day of freedom. She decided it was and set off down the street skipping happily. When the convent was out of sight, she turned on Rue St. Philippe past Chartre to the market. She had a few pennies in her pocket. She stopped at a stall, bought some fruit and wrapped it in her handkerchief, stuffing it in her pocket. Then she wandered among the stalls listening to the strange mixture of languages. There was English, loud and strident, from the servants from the American homes in the Garden District. There was rapid Italian from the vendors in the markets. And there was French in its many forms, from the pure musical sounds to the patois of the mulattoes and negroes. She listened to it all, loving it.

She moved around the stalls watching the people. She smiled at the many children, and bumped into an elegant woman gowned in rich gold silk with a brightly colored tignon about her head proclaiming her a free woman of color. There was nothing negroid in her beautiful features as fine as any highborn Creole woman. Her hair was a rich, lustrous brown, falling about her shoulders in luxurious waves through the open back of the tignon. Aurore gasped at the beautiful woman even while her mind whispered *placée*. No matter how sheltered a young girl was, she still heard whispered references about the free women of color who lived in the rows upon rows of demure white cottages beyond Rampart Street.

"Are you all right, *ma petite?*" A strange expression swept over her fine features as she righted Aurore with one elegantly gloved hand. Aurore decided her protector was very rich.

"Yes, thank you," Aurore said, curtseying respectfully. A smile appeared merrily on her lips and her eyes brightened. The woman felt an answering smile quiver on her lips. "I am sorry. I was not looking where I was going, Madame."

"It is all right," the woman chuckled. She automatically straightened Aurore's dress as though she were her own daughter. She pushed her curls out of her eyes and resecured them in the bow at the back of her head. "There you are all neat again."

A boy peered around the woman's skirt. He was older than Aurore, but Aurore was immediately struck with the feeling that she knew him.

"Hello," she said brightly, and was shocked to see a startling change sweep over his face. One moment there was open curiosity, and the next he radiated extreme hate. He pursed his lips and spat at Aurore, a large blob of mucus landing on her bodice. She jumped back, hurt and unreasonably frightened. The woman turned on her son cuffing him on the side of the head. He moved away sullenly. Then the woman turned back to Aurore, using a fine cambric handkerchief to rub away the stain.

"I apologize for my son. He has not yet learned his manners." She shook her head sadly. "Now, why are you not in school?"

"I am being the naughty girl today," Aurore said, her good humor restored when the woman handed her a sweet cake thick with icing and fancy candied flowers.

"Be careful of where you go, child. There are some places in New Orleans that are not safe for a little girl alone."

"I promise to be careful," Aurore said. The woman gave her one last smile, then picked up her basket and disappeared into the crowd. Aurore stood for a long time trying to figure out where she had seen the boy's haughty face before, but the familiarity eluded her.

Soon she forgot them as she turned to wander around the stall, biting delicately into the cake, savoring the sweetness.

Tiring of the market, she walked along the docks, careful to avoid her Papa's warehouse. She watched the huge paddle-wheelers being loaded or unloaded. She found a seat on a huge crate and ate her fruit when she became hungry and watched a huge, fat lady in extremely wide crinolines berating a tiny negro girl for some offense. Aurore felt immediate sympathy with the other child who looked to be her age or younger. She could picture Marie-Odile giving her the same type of tongue-lashing for her naughtiness. Finally the woman grew tired of her yelling and snapped her fingers at the porter who stood waiting patiently. The porter picked up her heavy trunk and walked behind her up the gangplank of the riverboat, the little girl trailing along, tears running brightly down her dark face.

Aurore slipped down from the crate and walked to where the *Sophie Sutter* was still at her moorings. She was loading passengers which meant she would soon be leaving for her trip upriver. Aurore thought of stowing away on her, but chided herself for such cowardice. It was not her maman she was as afraid of, as her father.

Brilliantly dressed women and soberly clad men walked up the long gangplank with servants and slaves following with their luggage. There were loud cries as people from the docks waved to their friends on the deck. There were hasty farewells, and soon the *Sophie Sutter* swung her gangplank away from the dock and secured it at her side. As the paddle-wheeler edged away from the dock, Aurore thought of the trip upriver she would be taking in another day. She thought with longing of the plantation and the cool summer nights and the wide lawns of green grass. She thought with longing of her pony and the days she would spend getting brown in the sun.

Suddenly she thought of home, realizing that it was long past the time when school was out. She turned around and ran along the docks, turning down one alley and then down another. Suddenly she found herself on a street where she had never been before. The garbage piled on the sidewalks was incredible. New Orleans was not the cleanest city in the world, but this street was far dirtier than any other Aurore had ever seen. She was appalled to find people sleeping on the garbage. One was a woman who wore no clothes, her flat breasts exposed to Aurore's shocked gaze. Next to her was a man who snored open-mouthed and clutched at her breasts. She heard loud laughter coming from one of the open doors. When she peered in, she saw women in various stages of undress sitting on slatted back chairs with men walking around looking at them. Some reached out to touch and Aurore shrank away afraid to look at more. A window above her opened and a woman tossed out the contents of a chamber pot not bothering to look if there was anyone below. Aurore sidestepped, but still some of the filth splashed on her shoes. She shuddered, suddenly very frightened. She looked up at the street sign to find the word Gallatin Street staring down at her. This street was the worst area in New Orleans. It housed the very dregs of society. Aurore turned to run, but a hand gripped the collar of her gown and jerked her back. She turned around to find a man holding her. He reeked of filth and rum. Aurore shrank away from his awful smell.

"What 'ave we 'ere, matey?" he asked, holding her securely. He studied her, his rheumy eyes taking in her expensive silk gown and the small pearl necklet about her neck. He fingered the silk appreciatively. " 'Ave a look, will ya." He grabbed at the necklet and it broke. He stuffed it into his pocket. "No you don't, matey," he said when Aurore tried to break free.

"Please let me go, Monsieur. I took a wrong turn and . . ."

He lifted her skirt to look at her long legs encased in dainty pantalets. "These should bring a few pennies," he chuckled, ripping them away from her and holding them to the light.

"Oh!" Aurore cried. She struggled, but he gripped her with fingers of steel that bruised her tender flesh. He picked up the hem of her skirt again, after stuffing the lace pantalets in his pocket and eyeing her immature body. "There's a big price for little virgins," he said, chuckling evilly. He reached out and touched her with a dirty finger. Aurore screamed desperately. "You are a pretty one. Got spirit, too. Old Mag'll break you o'that."

"No! No! No!" Aurore jerked and pulled, but he would not let her go. She didn't know what was happening to her. No one had ever touched her in her private parts. She screamed again. The man smiled showing the black stumps of rotting teeth.

Suddenly he twirled around and fell on his back in the dirt.

"Wha' ya doin', matey?" he asked. "I was just 'avin'

a spot o' fun wi' 'er. Do you like em little? Go on, take 'er."

Gayle dragged him to his feet, and planted his fist on the man's nose. Blood spurted out, darkening the front of Gayle's shirt. He hit the man again and again. Finally the man slumped to the ground, his face in a pile of garbage.

Aurore was lifted into his arms and carried away. She felt shudders shaking her body as she clung to Gayle. Her fright gave way to tears and she sniveled on his collar.

He patted her, wiping her face with his handkerchief.

"It's all right. You're safe now."

Her sobs gradually quieted, but still clung to him, trying to still her shaking.

"What were you doing there?"

"I was going home and I took a wrong turn. The alleys were so confusing and I was late. I was trying to hurry because Maman will be worried about me." The tears started afresh, rolling down her dirt-streaked cheeks like bubbles. "I didn't mean to come this way."

Gayle soothed her the best he could while looking for a carriage. There was none to be had. He walked into the nearest, respectable looking coffee shop and ordered *café au lait*.

"I'm sorry," Aurore gulped as she blew her nose noisily.

Gayle shook his head in frustration. "Calm yourself," he said gruffly. "You're lucky I came along. It's all right. You're safe."

"I'm sorry," Aurore wailed again.

"Don't tell me, you'll have to explain to your

Maman when you explain how you lost your pantalets."

"Oh!" She had forgotten about that. She looked at him, the tears drying on her face while her fertile brain constructed a lie that would explain away a pair of lace pantalets. Obviously, they were lost in the confusion of packing and unpacking. "I thank you for rescuing me, Monsieur. How can I ever repay you?"

"By staying away from Gallatin Street. I don't believe you live so quietly, you have never heard of that place. It's notorious. No person in their right mind goes there ever."

"I shall never go there again," Aurore promised sipping her coffee.

"It's time to get you home," Gayle said. He watched her returning calm, marveling at the healing powers of children. The horror was passed and now she was preparing herself to enjoy her few minutes with him. She was charming, though, he told himself. He wondered what she would be like when she was grown. Probably a difficult little minx making life hell for some unsuspecting man.

Aurore looked up. She smiled at him and he was struck with the beauty of the smile. There was a spot of cream on her mouth. He wiped it away with her napkin.

"Let's get you home."

They left the shop. Gayle found a carriage depositing a fare near the shop. He hailed it and shoved Aurore into it. He climbed in after her.

"It is not necessary . . ."

"I'm seeing you home just to make sure you get there," he said grimly. "Give the man your address."

She shouted it to the driver and the carriage lurched into motion.

"If I ever catch you somewhere you don't belong, young lady, I'll spank you," Gayle said when he dropped her off a half block from her home. "Do you understand me?"

"Yes, Monsieur," she replied managing to look contrite and angelic at the same time. She reached up and kissed him on the cheek, her arms snaking around his neck. "I am sorry. I promise to be good."

"At least until tomorrow," Gayle chuckled. "Go on now."

"I don't want to leave you."

"We'll see each other again."

"When?"

"Probably this summer. You must know St. Angele borders on the north with Grey Lawns."

"How wonderful! I shall see you soon," Aurore gasped with pleasure. She kissed him again, liking the feel of his smooth shaven cheek.

"Soon," Gayle promised wondering if he were soft in the head for being so enchanted with a child. "Go on, your family is probably worried to death."

"I did not go to school today," Aurore said suddenly.

"Playing hookey, you little rascal," he grinned, remembering the countless times he had done the same thing. "Good-bye, Aurore."

"*Au revoir*, Monsieur." She waved to him and ran up the street, happy to be home again.

Four

Aurore was not punished. Marie-Odile was too engrossed with the packing to bother with her third daughter's indiscretions. She simply sent Aurore to her room to say twenty prayers and memorize three passages from the Bible. Aurore escaped gratefully, aware that her fall from grace was being treated with unusual tolerance.

With Aurore out of sight, Marie-Odile forgot about her in the sudden panic of finding three-year-old Thérèse ill with a fever. All her children were dear to her, but little Thérèse with her angelic smile and consistent good humor was Marie-Odile's favorite. By the time Renault came home, Aurore had been completely forgotten in the rush to get the doctor and make the baby comfortable.

Renault was as concerned as his wife. He loved Aurore best, but he was more strongly attracted to his youngest child because she looked so like his mother with her golden blonde ringlets making her look out of place in the family of black haired, brown eyed people. Renault never heard of Aurore's misbehavior, though she spent several days in fear of him and going through the worst mental agony she had ever known.

Benoit de Ville watched the hustle and confusion

with a jaundiced eye. Sick children bored him. In the late afternoon, he took himself off to place and places unknown. Much to Marget's relief.

Marget stood in the window of her bedchamber watching Benoit climb into a coach. She was afraid to leave her room with him around the house. Always, he was at her elbow whispering words of love and trying to touch her in places she knew to be improper. He tried to wear down her resistance by telling her they would soon be married. If it was all right then to do these things, it should be all right now with the wedding less than four weeks away. Marget continued to resist, and took to hiding in her room. She yearned to walk to the cathedral, but Benoit had followed her again this morning and made another scene earning the wrath of Pere Buiron and a stricture to mend his manners.

Marget did not know what to do. Her bedchamber was no longer sacred because he stood outside her door for hours waiting to pounce on her the moment she came out. She found she was dreading this forthcoming marriage. She longed constantly for the serenity of the convent. This was denied to her. She took to spending more and more time at her *prie-Dieu* praying for guidance through the hellish life she knew was to come.

Finally the day arrived when everything was packed and sent on ahead in the huge lumbering wagons with the servants. They left early in the morning, leaving only Luce and Delphine to help with the last minute packing. They would accompany the family on the riverboat that would make its leisurely way up the river arriving at St. Angele late in the morning on the next day.

"There is no more school, Luce, for three whole months." Aurore cried as she waltzed around her bedchamber. Her imaginary dance partner was Gayle Courtland. She flirted with him and laughed softly. She wished she were grown so that she could marry him. She had decided this in the night following her escape from Gallatin. He had to wait for her. She found herself praying harder than she had ever prayed before.

"Stop, Aurore," Luce said sharply. In the last two days Aurore had been unusually docile. That docility irritated her. "If you must prance about the room, go do it in the courtyard. I cannot concentrate on your packing."

"Could you make me a charm, Luce?" Aurore asked suddenly.

"What kind of charm would a little girl like you want?"

"I want a charm to make me grow up fast and be a woman with big things on my chest to please a man."

For a moment, Luce was so shocked she couldn't speak. She stared in amazement at Aurore.

"Where do you get such thoughts?"

"But it is important. Very important."

"Come here, *ma petite*," Luce said, sitting down in the only chair in the room not yet in dust covers. She held out her arms to Aurore, who slid into them and leaned against her knee. "Growing to womanhood is a wonderful thing. You cannot hurry it to satisfy yourself. It must happen gradually. A good wine must season and mature, so must little girls."

"But I am not a wine."

51

"You are like a wine, child. You must grow slowly, and learn as you grow. In the end, the more time you take, the better you will be."

Aurore bit her lip, turning the words over and over in her mind. "Then there are no charms to help me?"

"No, my sweet," Luce chuckled.

Aurore looked disappointed. Luce set her down and shooed her off to play in the courtyard.

Fleur giggled as Benoit poured her another glass of wine.

"I have never had so much wine before," she said, sipping the berry-colored liquid greedily. She felt light-headed and vague, but the feeling was not unpleasant.

"Think of all you have missed in the past," Benoit replied thickly. Fleur leaned over. He stared down the gaping neck of her gown at budding breasts, feeling a massive swell of desire consume him. Her body was shaped little differently from her older sister, yet he was more attracted to her. Or was it because he was so frustrated over his unsuccessful campaign to entice Marget to the spot Fleur now occupied on his bed? He had grown tired of Marget's continued chastity. He had been surprised when it was Fleur who sought him out, knocking boldly on his door with two wine bottles hidden in the folds of her skirts. He had been willing to invite her in, knowing she would never be missed in the last-minute bustle of preparation before leaving for the docks.

He left the chair and seated himself next to Fleur who giggled and leaned against him. She smiled coyly as his arm slid around her narrow waist.

She drained her glass. Benoit refilled it. She sipped casually, feeling giddy and disoriented. She was not surprised when his fingers moved to the fastenings at the front of her gown and fumbled at her buttons. She turned to make it easier. Her bodice fell away, then her chemise was slipped down over her shoulders. The feel of his fingers brushing against her sent tremors of delight through her entire body. She lay back on the bed, invitingly.

Benoit fell on her eagerly. His lips fastened hungrily on her tiny breasts. His hands pulled her skirt down over her hips, then reached for the tape of her petticoats. He pulled hard, and when they loosened, he pushed the petticoats and skirt down around her knees, surprised to find her without pantalets.

He smiled at her, his fingers finding those secret places on her body that sent shivers through her. She parted her legs eagerly.

"You're beautiful," he breathed, his breath warm against her belly. She was smooth and hairless, he was fascinated.

The knocking on the door was furious. They both stiffened. Benoit rolled away from her, one last lingering, regretful glance.

"Monsieur de Ville," Marie-Odile called. "We are ready to go to the dock."

"I shall be down immediately," he replied, turning to help Fleur into her gown, struggling to button her bodice. "Later, in my stateroom," he told Fleur. She nodded, tiptoeing to the door, still buttoning the last few buttons of her bodice, clutching her chemise in one hand. She heard her mother walk rapidly down the hall, then fainter steps as she descended the stairs.

She opened the door and flitted across the hall to her room, where she hastily took off her gown and re-donned her chemise. She adjusted the tape of her petticoats, pulled on her gown and quickly brushed her hair. When she stepped into the hall, she looked calm and unruffled.

She was eager to find out the mysteries of men and women. She and her girl friends had speculated on these mysteries often. So far, they had only whispered and wondered, but Fleur thought of how much a coup it would be if she could return at the end of the summer and report to her little group. They would admire and respect her daring. She walked sedately down the stairs smiling at her mother who told her to hurry. She allowed Luce to fasten her bonnet securely and then walked out to the carriage, her eyes delicately avoiding Benoit's.

The trip to the dock was short. Aurore enjoyed it immensely, occasionally waving at her friends as they walked on streets. Once on board the riverboat, she ran around to find her stateroom, pleased that she would have it all to herself. She had been afraid she would have to share it with little Thérèse, but her small sister's recent illness kept her separated from her sisters.

The *Lady Marion* was a much smaller riverboat than the *Sophie Sutter*. She carried five hundred passengers to the *Sophie Sutter*'s two thousand. The *Lady Marion* was old and shabby, but Aurore was fond of her. She was one of the first riverboats Renault had purchased twenty-five years before. She was kept running more from sentiment than from any reason of business. The staterooms were small and cramped, the decor was threadbare. Aurore did not care. She was on the river and happy. She stared at the huge paddle-wheel going around and around. She leaned far over the rail to watch the muddy waters of the Mississippi churn under its slats. She was in danger of falling overboard when a hand clamped down on her arm and dragged her back to the safety of the deck.

"Am I doomed to spend the rest of my life rescuing you?" Gayle Courtland asked sternly, though there was a faint twinkle in his eyes.

"Monsieur Courtland!" Aurore cried. She threw her arms around his neck and kissed him sloppily. "I just knew you would be on the *Lady Marion*. I prayed hard to God and he answered my prayers."

"Imp!" Gayle chuckled fondly. He tousled her curls.

"Mr. Courtland! Yoo-hoo, Mr. Courtland!" a young female rushed up to him breathlessly. "I told Mama it was you. Imagine seeing you again after all these years. You do remember me, don't you. It's Arabella. Arabella Moore. I was just a little girl when you went away."

"Of course, Miss Moore. I seem to remember a little girl with blonde curls," Gayle said, his eyes sweeping over her admiringly. She blushed prettily.

Arabella Moore was no longer a little girl. She smiled up at him wide-eyed, her graceful head coming just to his shoulder. Her blonde curls were confined to a snood, but a few escaped, coiling coquettishly about her ears and throat. Aurore hated her on sight. She wore a fashionable traveling suit of pearl gray broadcloth that matched the shade of her eyes exactly. Her skin was pale and fashionably soft. She had long, narrow hands with long nails, one of which rested possessively on Gayle's arm.

"Who is this?" Bella asked, leaning over, determined to be pleasant to the grubby child Gayle had set down on the deck.

"Allow me to introduce Mademoiselle Aurore de Champlain," Gayle nudged Aurore, recalling her to her manners.

"Bonjour, Madame," Aurore said not all together pleasantly.

"Not Madame, Mademoiselle," Bella said, fluttering her long pale lashes at Gayle. She hid her acute dislike for the child, recognizing in her the superior beauty that would never be hers.

"Bonjour, Mademoiselle," Aurore said again, dimpling prettily.

"Come along, Mr. Courtland, and say hello to ,ama. She will be so delighted to see you again. It has been years." Bella slid her arm through Gayle's. She was a little annoyed when he grabbed the child's hand and pulled her along.

"Do give her back to her mama," Bella pouted sweetly.

"Can't," Gayle replied. "She's my ward for an hour or so."

Mrs. Moore was an older, fading version of her daughter. She wore an overpowering scent that tickled Aurore's nose and made her fight to control her coming sneeze. The sweet scent curled around her, exploding in her nostrils until she could barely breathe. She felt herself becoming ill. After several minutes' dull conversation, Gayle looked down to find Aurore slowly turning green. He suddenly cut off the

56

conversation, picked her up and rushed away.

"I must get her outside," he yelled over his shoulder at the two astonished women. He ran out the doors of the grande saloon and pushed Aurore toward the rail. Slowly her green tinge faded and she regained her normal color though somewhat paler than normal.

"Are you all right?" he asked supporting her gently as she leaned against the rail breathing in great gulps of air.

"I'm feeling better," she said weakly, though her stomach continued to heave and boil. "It was Madame's scent."

"Aurore, are you all right?" Marie-Odile rushed up to her daughter. "Are you seasick?"

"No, Maman," Aurore said. Suddenly her stomach heaved and she leaned far over the rail with Gayle holding her tightly.

"A lady in the saloon's perfume was extremely overpowering," Gayle said tersely. He held Aurore until she was finished retching, then he set her down on the deck, drawing out his handkerchief and wiping her soiled mouth.

"It made me queasy in the tummy, Maman," Aurore complained. She was beginning to feel better. Her color returned and Gayle sighed in relief.

"I am glad it was only that," Marie-Odile said, fussing over her daughter. "I was afraid you had caught what little Thérèse has." The worry cleared from her face as she hugged her subdued daughter. "Thank you, Monsieur, for your quick thinking."

"Maman, this is Monsieur Courtland. He owns Grey Lawns right next to us. Is it not exciting to meet a neighbor?"

"How do you do, Madame," Gayle said bowing correctly. He saw the resemblance between mother and daughter.

"Bonjour, Monsieur," Marie-Odile said politely.

"I rescued your daughter earlier. She was in danger of falling overboard."

"And now you have saved the hem of some lady's gown. I am doubly in your debt," Marie-Odile grinned. "My husband would be delighted to meet you. Would you join us for dinner?"

"I would be honored," Gayle said.

"Until later, Monsieur," she replied. "I must take my daughter back to her stateroom and change her gown."

"Until later." Aurore and her mother hurried down the deck with Gayle gazing after them. He was about to re-enter the saloon when he saw Arabella Moore's face coming toward him. He turned hastily down the deck, turning firmly into the men's saloon, ignoring the trilling tones of her voice as she called after him.

"He is very nice, Maman," Aurore chattered as Marie-Odile buttoned up the bodice of her clean gown.

"Yes, he is," Marie-Odile said, dreamily remembering how handsome he was. Even she was not immune to his immense charm. "You are finished. Go find your sister Marget and wait with her until dinner. Do not get into any more mischief, please."

"I won't, Maman. I promise." Aurore threw her arms around her maman's neck and kissed her soundly on the lips. Marie-Odile smiled affectionately and left the room to go change for dinner.

Fleur took out the only gown she owned that was

not pink. The dressmaker had mistaken the fabric Maman had chosen and made it up in a soft-hued blue that turned Fleur from a child to an almost grown woman. She slid it on and hooked up the front, looking at herself critically in the mirror. She pulled the lace fall over the hooks and fluffed it, eyeing herself in the mirror. She pinched color into her cheeks, liking the effect. She added a bow to her hair, then took it out. She wadded two handkerchiefs into balls and placed them under her bodice, then took them out. She added a third petticoat, and smiled in satisfaction. Finally she dropped cologne on her handkerchief and slid it up her sleeve. It gave off a marvelously subtle scent. She hoped Benoit appreciated what she had gone through to please him. When she was satisfied with her appearance, she sailed out of her cabin heading for the dining room.

Aurore was pleased that her parents liked Gayle Courtland. She sat next to him, feeling very grown up. She held her head proudly, very much aware of the dark looks Arabella Moore tossed at her parents' table.

Dinner progressed slowly while they all chatted and drank more wine than they should.

Fleur sat next to Benoit acutely conscious of his leg pressed against hers. Occasionally he would reach down with his hand and pat her thigh. The tremors she had felt earlier in his bedchamber returned to her as she remembered the feel of his fingers on her smooth skin. Long before the meal was over, she ached with emotion she only partly understood.

Marget picked miserably at her food. The smallest trip on the river made her ill. Finally she stood up and excused herself, telling her mother she felt ill. Marie-Odile nodded her dismissal, then returned to her conversation with Gayle Courtland. He was charming and she could not help but fall under his spell.

"I knew your father," Renault said over his port after he and Gayle had retired to the smoking room. He lit a fat, fragrant cigar after offering Gayle one. Gayle refused and took out a long, thin cheroot. "His death was a great shock."

"Yes, it was," Gayle agreed. Gayle offered a cheroot to Benoit who refused, preferring to drown himself in a glass of brandy, thinking drunkenly of little Fleur and her sweet, hairless body. He wondered how long he had to endure this boring conversation while anxious to be away.

"I did not know him well," Renault continued. "My business interests are in the city. I seldom get to stay long at St. Angele. Though we did meet from time to time and share a drink. I understand your brother also died in the accident."

"Yes," Gayle said. Pain washed over him. He and Grant had been very close. "I shall miss my brother."

"Wasn't there a wife?"

Gayle thought of Fay Courtland who waited for him at Grey Lawns. "Grant and Fay were only married a few months. As far as I know there was no issue."

"That makes you sole inheritor," Renault mused. He thought about what he knew of Grey Lawns. The elder Courtland was heavily invested in cotton.

"Sole inheritor of an estate nearly $100,000 in debt," Gayle replied bitterly.

Renault looked up. He saw a great deal on the young man's face. One of the things he saw was a reluctance to take up the reins of responsibility of an estate heavily in debt.

"After you settle in a bit, why not get together with me and we'll talk it over. I might be able to do something."

"I doubt it, sir, but thank you for the offer."

"Don't be so hasty, Mr. Courtland. There are few problems that have no solutions."

"Mr. de Champlain, the only solution I can see is to sell out and let the creditors haggle over the spoils."

"Never sell, Mr. Courtland. Land always has value. Go home and look the situation over, and then come over and we'll talk about it. I think you'll manage all right even if it means letting your fields lie fallow for a few seasons."

"How would I live during that time?"

"Sell your slaves. There aren't many years left to slavery. Get rid of them now while they still have a value."

"Who would I hire later? Cotton takes a big labor force."

"Not cotton, Courtland, but rice and sugarcane. For that you don't need such a big labor force, yet the profits are better."

"I'll think about it. You have a few things to say that sound interesting."

"We'll talk it over again," Renault promised.

"If you will excuse me," Benoit said, stumbling to his feet. "Think I'll go to my cabin. Getting late." He fell over his feet as he turned around. Gayle caught him before he could fall, then released him as the young man shrugged and weaved his way to the door.

"If you will excuse me, Mr. de Champlain," Gayle

said getting to his feet. "I think I'll join that card game in the corner."

"You'll think over what I said?" Renault asked.

"I'll think it over, and I'll consult with you before I do anything rash, sir," Gayle said. For the first time since he had heard of his father's death and of the heavy debt overhanging the plantation, he felt a glimmer of hope. He walked over to the card table, feeling lighter than he had in weeks.

Fleur bid her mother a chaste good-night and ran to her stateroom. She pulled off her gown and hung it neatly on a hook, then unfastened her chemise and tossed it in her valise. She dropped her petticoats and hoop to the floor and stepped out of it, standing in the middle of the room naked while she laid out three different nightgowns, trying to decide which looked less childish. Finally she decided on the embroidered lawn that was faintly transparent. She kicked her petticoats and hoop into a corner and flew into her bunk just as Luce opened the door and walked in. Luce tidied the room, then kissed Fleur good-night and extinguished the lamp. Fleur offered a sleepy good-night and snuggled down in the bed, pretending to fall asleep. Luce closed the door softly and walked to the next cabin where Aurore was. Fleur waited for a long time before she felt the riverboat settle down for the night. There was distant laughter from the smoking room, but eventually all the people around her settled in for the night. When she was certain it was safe, she jumped out of her bunk and slid into her robe. She threw her coat about her shoulders and opened the door cautiously. Benoit's cabin was only four doors from hers. She darted into the hall and ran to it, knocking quickly. He opened it and pulled her in.

He wore a brocade dressing gown and looked very mature. Fleur felt her breath catch in her throat as she looked at him. They had never gotten to the part where he had undressed earlier that day, and she was intensely curious as to what he looked like under his robe.

"I was afraid you wouldn't come," he said in a low voice. He locked the cabin door with a loud click. He drew her to his bunk, slipping her coat from her shoulders. He ran his hands through her soft, black hair, pulling it teasingly. Then he kissed her, a long, lingering kiss, parting her lips gently with his tongue. "Would you like some wine?"

"Yes," she answered thinking of the warm glow it had given her that morning. She smiled at him as he filled a glass and handed it to her. His fingers caressed hers as she took it. She downed it nervously, and he refilled it.

"I am so glad you came, Fleur," he murmured, untying the belt at her waist and slipping her robe from her shoulders. He gasped at the hint of shadow under the sheer nightdress. He caressed her lightly. She finished her wine, and he took the glass from her cold fingers and set it down on the small side table. Gently, he untied the ribbons at her neck, pushing it aside to reveal her budding breasts. "Ah!" he said softly, fingering each nipple.

Fleur leaned against him, unable to believe she was finally here. She remembered his flicking tongue on her. She pushed his head down, and leaned back on her hands, her lips parted. He pushed her nightgown down her legs. She raised each one for him, waiting for his fingers to find the root of her desire. He reached out to turn off the lamp, but she stopped him. She untied his robe and slid it off. She gazed at him, not feeling the least bit frightened. Then she leaned back, pulling him on top of her, parting her legs.

"I won't hurt you," he whispered. "Don't be frightened."

"I'm not frightened," she said, softly, her eyes gleaming. She nodded at the lamp and he turned it out.

Five

Fleur sat in front of her mirror staring at her reflection. From outside her stateroom came the sounds of the roustabouts casting off from the landing where the paddle-wheeler spent the night. They sang in low undertones as they worked, their bare feet padding up and down the deck. The river was a treacherous lady by day; by night, villainous witch waiting to snare over-confident captains with sandbars lying almost invisible under the surface of the swiftly churning water. Frequently dense fog floated over her, making it dangerous to travel. Storms blew up quickly producing massive cyclones. The Mississippi was a dangerous place to be after dark. Few captains were foolhardy enough to travel the river at night. The captain of the *Lady Marion* was not one of them. With the descent of darkness, he made for the nearest landing and made secure for the night.

Fleur touched her eyes, her cheeks and her full lips. She outlined her lips with a finger. She pulled her ears forward, and checked the line of hair framing her face. She lifted her chin, frowning at the long column of her neck. She looked worried, but her search produced nothing. Nowhere on her slender body was there the faintest mark to proclaim her fall from grace. The threats of the nuns at school with their horror stories of lost virginity and disfiguring bodies had all been lies. There were no marks anywhere on her body. She had committed the ultimate sin and was thrilled to find that she was not disfigured. They had lied to her. They knew nothing of physical love. She drew her robe over her shoulders and cinched it tightly about her waist. She smiled at her reflection wondering how such a monumental change in her body could show little. She ran her small pink tongue over her lips remembering the sweet love words Benoit whispered fervently in her ears. He likened her lips to the color of red carnations, and her teeth were the lustre of matched pearls. She treasured those beautiful endearments even if she did not treasure the man who whispered them to her.

Overnight she had changed from a girl's innocence to a woman's awareness. Never again would she be a child. For the first time in her life, she was aware of the power she wielded with her body and her beauty. She was pleased with herself and her discovery.

The piercing whistle of the riverboat disturbed her thoughts. The huge craft was slowly pulling away from the landing and maneuvering into the middle of the river. The pilot of the *Lady Marion* knew his business.

The first stop of the morning would be Grandeville where Benoit would depart. Next was St. Angele and finally Grey Lawns where the handsome Mr. Courtland was going to live. Fleur caught her bottom lip between her teeth thoughtfully. In the darkness of the night as she lay in Benoit's arms, she had already planned her next conquest and that was to be Mr.

Courtland. Her new discovery of her body now demanded the sureness of a man, not the fumblings of a boy. Let Benoit fumble with Marget. Fleur would be forever grateful to him for lifting the veil of mystery surrounding sex, but even in her inexperience she recognized his limits. Benoit thought of nothing but the gratification of his own pleasure. Fleur instinctively knew that a woman was made for more than just the satisfaction of a man. She had felt those faint stirrings within her. Benoit had not satisfied them.

She glanced out her louvered window. Mr. Courtland stood at the rail watching the river. Fleur was disconcerted to find Aurore with him chattering with easy familiarity. That association would have to end, she thought. She would not share his attentions with her ten year old sister. Gayle moved off flicking his cheroot into the river. He glanced down at Aurore and smiled a particularly tender smile. She gazed back at him, adoration lighting her face. Fleur snorted in disgust as she turned away from the window. She dropped her robe on the floor and grabbed the nearest chemise. If she was to catch his attention, she would have to hurry before Maman and Papa were awake. She stepped into her hoop and petticoats, pulling the tapes taut around her waist and knotting them. She flung a gown over her head, wrestling impatiently with the buttons. She hurried, but even as she stepped out on the deck, Monsieur Courtland and Aurore had already disappeared from view. Fleur looked up and down the deck, but they were gone. She stamped her foot in disappointment, turning back into her cabin and slamming the door.

Marget was not overly sad to be saying good-bye to Benoit. Another three weeks would see them wed. She allowed him to kiss her hand, feeling vast relief well in her as he hurried down the gangplank to the waiting arms of his Maman. From the distance of shore to riverboat, Marget could feel the powerful personality emanating from Monique de Ville.

Monique de Ville embraced her son, happy to see him home from his many years abroad. He had changed much, growing from sullen boy to man. She was glad to have him back with her. The plantation was badly in need of man's guidance. She waved to the de Champlains enthusiastically. Once, she had contemplated marriage to Renault, but he had shown little interest in her. She was strong-willed and outspoken. He had wanted a soft and pliable wife. Monique had wanted him badly not only because of his fine position in the city, but because of his vast fortune. Monique craved money. She had none, her only possession being a broken down plantation run to ruin because of her father's insatiable gambling fever. She married Georges de Ville because he said he had money. He had none, but he did have land. Vast tracts of land. Georges had been a man of advanced age. Monique decided she could stand a few years with him as long as she was compensated by his land. But he died within the first year of their marriage, two months before the birth of his first and only child.

Monique waved until the paddle-wheeler was out of sight around a bend in the river. She kept Benoit at her side, pleased with him now that he was twenty-one and ready to take up the reins of responsibility. She viewed his alliance with the de Champlain family as a wise and intelligent move. They had money, and were bound to settle a great deal of it on their oldest daughter. Her dowry would prove useful in making the improvements Grandeville had never had. As she planned for the use of the dowry, her eyes running over the neglected plantation, she linked arms with her son and started walking toward the house. She had no idea that her silly son had already signed away his control of Marget's dowry as well as giving his father-in-law a controlling interest in Grandeville for little more than a half bottle of wine and a night in the most famous bordello in New Orleans. He had nothing but a verbal promise of forthcoming monies to pay his outstanding debts and provide for a moderate income to keep him in the life to which he was accustomed to leading. Benoit was well pleased with himself. He thought he had gotten the better of the deal. He hurried his Maman toward the house, full of his shrewd bargaining, unaware of the storm that was yet to come.

An hour later, the *Lady Marion* tied up at the landing at St. Angele. Marget walked off the gangplank happy to have firm ground under her again. Aurore ran down the gangplank looking forward to renewing her friendship with her pony. And Fleur thought of how she could concentrate on her plan of attack in seducing Gayle Courtland. He had proved surprisingly elusive and immune to her flirtations. It piqued her to realize that he preferred the inane chatter of ten year old Aurore to the mature promise of Fleur. She had fluttered her long lashes at him and brushed against him suggestively, yet he ignored her. She considered the ways she could get him alone and was deciding on how to do it when she stepped off the gangplank onto the lush, green lawn of St. Angele.

Marie-Odile smiled tenderly when she realized that a close friendship was developing between Monsieur Courtland and Aurore. She saw nothing wrong with it, even going so far as to issuing an invitation to him for Marget's wedding. She then informed her husband that little girls often conceived these passions when they were on the threshold of womanhood, further informing him that she would eventually grow out of it. Renault had frowned. He was not as certain about the innocence of the relationship. But then again, Monsieur Courtland was twenty-five, and would be long married by the time Aurore was of an age to be thinking about marriage. Renault was willing to extend the hand of friendship to the man and even help him out of his difficulties, but he did not want an alliance with him. Besides being a notorious gambler, he had killed two men in two separate duels, and had once been accused of murder. His past was unsavory, and was not a suitable match for any of the de Champlain daughters. Besides, Renault wanted a Creole for Aurore.

The gangway swung away from the dock and was secured along the side of the *Lady Marion*. The captain shouted a final farewell and disappeared into the wheelhouse. Everyone watched as the steamboat pulled away from the landing and nudged its way into the middle of the swift-flowing Mississippi. Aurore waved till she thought her arm would fall off, then turned to jump into the carriage that would take them up the hill to the house. She ripped a flounce in her haste, and was gently scolded by her maman. The horses jumped into a trot and waltzed up to the huge house dominating the hill overlooking the river.

St. Angele was a huge plantation. The house was breathtakingly beautiful. As a young man, Renault studied and traveled extensively in France. Returning home to take over the family business on his father's death, he had bought the land and proceeded to build himself the most magnificent plantation house in Louisiana. St. Angele was a masterpiece.

Perched high on a hill out of the way of the annual flooding, the house overlooked the Mississippi River. Looking like a page out of French history, the house was comprised of a main building and two wings. The main building was large, housing the formal rooms used only on formal occasions opening to an inner courtyard of flowering gardens and high fountains. The north wing held the private quarters of the family. The south wing was reserved for visiting guests. It consisted of nineteen bedchambers.

Aurore's favorite room was the immense ballroom with its adjoining picture gallery. On hot summer afternoons, she would steal into the dim coolness of the vast room and dance waltzes with imaginary lovers to the ghostly strains of an orchestra. During intermissions they would stroll through the picture gallery and stare at the many works of art her father had been collecting for thirty years. As the carriage drew up to the wide front steps, she was wriggling with excitement at being at St. Angele and thinking ahead to her reunion with the ballroom and picture gallery.

Persia bowed elegantly as he stood on the wide steps signaling for a footman to open the carriage door and help the ladies out. Nothing on his face showed his fatigue at the long journey he and the other servants had taken to St. Angele the day before. A journey that lasted past dark, after which they were committed to readying the huge mansion for their employers' stay. He had exchanged his formal black of the city for less formal attire normal for the country. During formal occasions he would change again. He grinned as Marie-Odile nodded approvingly at his attire. The maids had exchanged dark blue for pale gray striped uniforms. They looked cool and comfortable.

"The roses are looking extremely well, Ben," Marie-Odile commented to the head gardener as she walked past. Ben grinned broadly. He had come from Marie-Odile's childhood home. There he had been a field hand, but Renault had recognized his particular genius for plants and growing things. Ben had ten gardeners under him who devoted their time solely to the outside work. He had taken over the long, low greenhouse behind the stables where he grew an infinite variety of flowers to be brought into the main house and arranged in every room. The greenhouse was his pride, no other gardener was allowed in it. No other gardener was allowed to touch the many plants Renault had sent to him from all over the world.

Marie-Odile stepped into the house through the formal entry and into the drawing room. The members of the staff assembled quickly, each one to be formally greeted by her. She knew them all even though she only saw them once a year during the summer. She commented on new faces and asked about families. There was nothing beneath her notice. She was the mistress of St. Angele. When the many greetings were done, she went down the long, cool hall toward the master suite to change from her traveling gown into a summery gown of pale green lawn. She would partake of a light refreshment, then she would inspect the house. She did not believe in leaving everything to be seen to by servants.

Aurore slipped away from the group. She ran down the hall, through the kitchens deserted with the staff still greeting her mother, and out into the shade of the garden. She paused once, to look back and admire the sparkling clean windows of the ballroom as she looked over her shoulder. Then she skipped happily toward the stables.

"Hello, Silas," she screamed, throwing her arms around the ancient, grizzled man sitting in the sun whittling. There were no slaves on St. Angele plantation. Silas was proud that his ancient age had given him the distinction of being the first person to receive his papers.

Silas was old. He remember dimly a childhood in a blazing hot land living in a small hut and hunting the same animals that easily could have hunted him. He dimly remembered a fearful crossing on a dark, foul ship over a huge body of water that drove terror into his soul. He dimly remembered the auction that gave him body and soul in ownership to another man. He remembered many things including a few isolated memories of America's War for Independence. Some memories were good, but mostly they were bad. But one of the brightest things to come into his old life was Aurore de Champlain. If he had the choice, he would have died for her.

"Growed some, ain't you, child?" was his only greeting. He held her at arm's length to study her. He shook his head over the torn flounce and the dirt on her white patent leather shoes. "When you goin' to start bein' a lady?" he asked, fingering the torn flounce.

"Never," Aurore laughed heartily. She planted a second kiss on his worn face.

"It's been awhile," he said, smiling a toothless smile. He held up the object he had been whittling, a delicately carved horse with arched head and slender legs.

Aurore pulled up a stool and sat down at his feet, taking the offered horse and running her small fingers over it. He had taught her to carve when she had been five, but her creations had yet to match the master-piece of the dainty horse in her hands.

"I missed you," she said simply. She laughed a little, turning the horse over and over in her hands. She lived her life with laughter and joy, mixed with daring and mischief. She surrounded herself with people like herself. But only Silas had been privileged to share her fantasies. They had lived them together, the old man and the girl child.

"Go in and see your pony," Silas coaxed. His ancient eyes twinkled. "Been waiting for you, too." He pushed himself up slowly, shaking the kinks from his gnarled body. "Well, come along, girl."

Aurore followed reluctantly. Last summer she had reached the monumental decision that she was too old for fat Jolie. She was ten, soon to be eleven. It was time for her to move to a larger animal. She dragged behind Silas, petting each horse as she went. She loved the feel of their velvety noses against her palm. She called each one by name, apologizing for not bringing each a treat. They seemed to forgive her, nuzzling her hair. When she reached Jolie's stall, she found it occupied by a tall graceful mare with limpid brown eyes.

Aurore stared. Her mouth dropped open. She stood at the door and stared. The mare pranced coquettishly over to her. She nickered softly against Aurore's outstretched hand, her warm breath blowing across Aurore's fingers. She was golden brown with four stockinged feet and a large white slash across her forehead.

"Her name is Belle," Silas said.

"Is she for me?" Aurore asked, hardly daring to breathe for fear he would say no. He didn't.

"She is beautiful," Aurore whispered, her eyes wide with growing love.

"Your Pa thinks you too big to ride old Jolie," Silas said in deep satisfaction. "He buy you Belle."

"I love her," Aurore said. She opened the stall door, slipping inside her voice crooning to the beautiful creature. She examined her carefully, admiring the breeding that flowed through every inch of her frame. "I shall always love you." She kissed Belle. She kissed Silas, and ran into the house to kiss her papa.

Fleur waltzed around her room in delight. Over the winter, her maman had ordered her room to be redecorated, banishing the girlish ruffles for more mature lines. This was the first sign of womanhood. Maman had done the same for Marget when she had been thirteen. She would do it for Aurore and Thérèse.

Fleur was well pleased with the new decor of cool greens and blues. Gone was the perpetual pink and white deemed proper for a girl. She threw her arms out and laughed.

"Escuse me, miss."

Fleur came to a sudden halt, her feet slipping on the smooth floor. As she went down, muscular hands and arms reached out to her and caught her as her feet crashed into dark trousered legs. Her breath was knocked out of her and she stood for several minutes, her small chest heaving violently.

"I'm sorry, miss," he said. "I didn't mean to startle you." He righted her, watching to see her normal color flood back into her cheeks. He was surprised when her hand lingered a moment on his arm.

Aurore stared at the man standing before her. He was the tallest negro she had ever seen, and the blackest. He wore a white shirt, but it hardly concealed the bulging muscles rippling under it.

"Who are you?" she asked, craning her neck to look up into his dark, sober eyes.

"I'm Noble, miss," he answered. "Just bringing up your luggage." He indicated her trunk and valises on the floor with a huge hand. Aurore wondered how his hand would feel on her body. Her eyes widened at the thought.

"You're new here," she said, tilting her head flirtatiously.

"I'm the new blacksmith, miss," he said, grinning. He interpreted her saucy look. He let his eyes roam deliberately over her slim body, liking what he saw. He chuckled.

Fleur moved close to him, her hand brushing the inside of his thigh. He reached out and touched her breast. It swelled and grew under his finger.

"You're mighty pretty lady," he said softly.

"So are you, Noble," Fleur responded. She leaned against him, her lips parted. She rubbed against him as he kissed her deeply. She stepped back sighing.

Steps sounded behind them. Fleur turned away. When she looked, he was gone.

Six

Renault sat at a large, wood-topped desk. The desk was ornately carved with scrolls, and inlaid with finely set veneer. He liked the desk because it was large, yet not pretentious. It was the desk of a wealthy man who was not obligated to intense display of wealth. The whole room reflected Renault's feelings. He used it as an office, yet it looked more like a large drawing room with long wide sofas surrounded by large, overstuffed chairs to stimulate conversation. The floor was bare of rugs and highly polished. Renault liked the room, he felt comfortable here.

He glanced up from the ledger book laid across the desk. John Miles, the estate manager sat across from him, a glass of excellent brandy in one hand and a cigar in the other. His legs were crossed at the knees, one foot dangling. His eyes openly admired the huge marble fireplace surrounded by beautifully bound books in floor to ceiling bookcases. Renault was a reader, but John Miles was uninterested in the hundreds of years of knowledge in them. He was more impressed by the gold embossing on the leather covers. As he sat in the chair, he pretended he was master of this vast plantation unaware of Renault's eyes on him, measuring him.

John Miles thought about the many changes he would make if he were master here. One of them would be to re-institute slavery. Another would be a return to cotton as the main crop. He turned away from his scrutiny of the fireplace to look out the open french doors behind Renault. The white curtains billowed slightly in the breeze framing the open expanse of lawn stretching for several hundred yards before meeting the tall trees of the forest. Aurore de Champlain flitted back and forth across his vision, galloping around the park on her new horse. Admiration leaped in his eyes at the sight of her, small and straight on the pony. Her dark hair had fallen loose and spread around her shoulders in dark waves. Miles watched until she was out of sight before returning his gaze to his employer. He liked young, innocent girls. It as a pity that one of the prettiest he had seen in a long time had to be the owner's daughter. Still, he would not mind finding her in a remote part of the forest.

Renault tapped his finger against the ledger while his keen eyes ran down the long rows of figures expertly. Everything appeared to be in perfect order, yet there was a feeling of something subtly wrong that nagged at the back of his mind. The figures added up, the amounts appeared correct, yet the feeling increased as he turned page after page. He looked up at Miles lounging in the chair. Was it only his imagination, or did the man seem unusually tense.

John Miles had worked for Renault for little less than a year. He had come highly recommended after Renault had lost his previous manager to a crippling accident. In a hurry to return to the city because of business, Renault had hired Miles without a thorough investigation into his background. Now he was beginning to regret his lack of efficiency.

On the surface nothing seemed terribly wrong, yet it was the little things that disturbed him. Like the way the women in the house hid their daughters when Miles was around, and the sluggish way the men went to their work in the fields. There had always been a feeling of gaiety around the plantation before that was now conspicuous by its absence.

"Is there anything you wish to discuss while you are here?" Renault asked. He closed the ledger with a thud. Miles relaxed, tension draining out of him in a flood. A small smile played around his thin lips. He brushed a finger over the curled ends of his mustache. Renault did not offer to give the ledger back, thinking to keep it a few days more.

"I'd like to talk about your niggers," Miles replied. Renault nodded. "You need slaves for this work, not free men. Free men don't do their work right. They give themselves airs."

"Are you saying the workers on this plantation are not doing their jobs?"

"That's what I'm saying," Miles grinned. "They give me more trouble not doing their work. I ain't got no way of disciplining them."

"I see," Renault said softly, his dark eyes never left the smoothly handsome face of the manager. "Is there anything else on your mind?"

"Yeh! I think you should forget rice and sugar cane, and go back to cotton. There's no market for anything but cotton in the South. That's what you should be growing," Miles said forcefully. He warmed to his subject, flattered that his employer thought enough of him to ask his opinion. He praised cotton enthusiastically, then turned to the supremacy of the South and the logic of slavery. Renault watched him closely.

"You overlook the fact that rice and sugar require a much smaller work force than cotton, yet the profits are nearly as good," Renault said mildly when Miles was finished.

"Buy yourself some niggars. That's about all they are good for, slaving away in the cotton fields. I know a bunch that can be had cheap." Miles leaned forward confidently. His chest puffed out at the thought that Renault was listening to him. He winked suggestively. "There's a couple of gals at Arundal that are mighty good lookin. Got themselves bosoms out to here and legs as long and slim as . . ."

"You are straying from the subject, Mr. Miles. It costs me less to pay my workers a wage, than it does to feed and clothe them under slave conditions. With the money I pay them for their work and the land set aside for growing their own food, they are self-sufficient, and I am not responsible for them."

"You don't know nothin' about the slave business," Miles scoffed. "You just put all this in my hands and I'll have this plantation running like clockwork in a year. Cotton will make you so rich you won't know what to do with all your money. You'll be a king."

"What about the war?"

"What war? Even if there is one, the South will whip those thievin' Yankees in less than a month."

"That remains to be seen. Until the time comes and I change my mind, we will continue under the present system."

"Can I have my . . ." Miles gestured at the book as he rose to his feet.

"I have some entries to add. I'll return it tomorrow. Good day, Mr. Miles."

Miles was dismissed in a manner he did not particularly like, but he swallowed his resentment and walked past Renault out the french doors to the lawn. He paused on the edge of the cobbled walk to watch Aurore walking her horse up and down while old Silas looked on. That's another thing, Miles thought. He'd get rid of that old darkie. He didn't do nothing but whittle and carve, yet he still got full wages. Miles stepped onto the grass walking swiftly to where his horse stood patiently in the burning sun. He leapt aboard, spurring the animal cruelly as he galloped toward the fields.

Renault opened the ledger again, looking at the neat rows of figures. He was still unable to get the strange feelings of foreboding out of his mind. He did not like John Miles. He bent over the book to concentrate. Suddenly the door to his office flew open with a bang. Monique de Ville stalked in angrily.

"I want to talk to you," she stormed.

Renault rose to greet her, nodding at his anxiously hovering wife who followed Monique into the room. He smiled faintly watching the tension leave Marie-Odile's eyes. She left the room, closing the door silently.

"Sit down, Monique," Renault said gesturing towards the group of chairs near his desk. "It has been years since we last met."

"What are these?" Monique screamed. She tossed some papers on the desk. Some of them landed on the floor forcing Renault to pick them up. Monique stood in front of him, glaring, her arms akimbo and legs apart.

"Please sit down, my dear. May I offer you some brandy? Sherry?"

"I want nothing but an explanation," she snapped viciously at him.

Renault glanced down at the papers. He didn't have to look at them to know they were the contracts Benoit had signed releasing him in his authority over Marget's dowry, and the turning over of control of Grandeville. Renault straightened them, laying them neatly on a corner of his desk.

"What is there to explain?"

"Look at them," she shrieked. "How could you do this to my son."

"I did nothing to him. He signed the contracts of his own free will."

"You cheated him," Monique screeched. She gestured wildly, a strand of hair catching on a button from the sleeve of her riding jacket. She pulled a length of hair loose to float across her face. She shook her head angrily and the rest of her blonde curls fell to her shoulders. Renault smiled at her. He always did have a fondness for women in a temper. Though dear Monique had more of a temper than he liked, she was still very lovely in her anger.

"Sit down, Monique."

She fell abruptly into a chair surprised at the steel in his voice and the glint in his dark eyes.

"Stop screeching like a madwoman and let us discuss this like two rational adults."

"You tricked him," she wailed. The top button of

her riding habit had come undone giving promise of rich, full curves and skin the color of porcelain.

Renault's eyes strayed to that open button, a heat of desire rising in him. He remembered a young Monique enticing him with her tender body twenty-two years ago. He had seriously contemplated marriage with her, but he was not certain he wanted to spend the rest of his life with a fiery demanding shrew. Looking at the disheveled Monique grown plump with the years, he was surprised to find he preferred the cool, slim beauty of his wife.

"I have neither tricked nor cheated your son," Renault said mildly.

"Then what did you do?" she stormed. The old attraction for him stole over her. Her breath came in ragged gasps and she felt a melting in the bottom of her belly. She recognized the appreciative gleam in his eyes. She casually reached up and released another button.

"I have done nothing, but insure that my daughter's future is safeguarded."

"You don't trust my son."

"You were never one to mince words, Monique. You are quite right. I don't trust your son." Anger leapt once more in her eyes, but he held up his hand asking for silence. "He came to me begging that I settle the most staggering debt he incurred while he was in Paris. He could hardly go to you, you have no money, I did. As I investigated his affairs, I found your son to be not only a braggart and a liar, but an irresponsible child. I do not intend to turn over my daughter's fortune to someone unable to control it. I refuse to allow her money to be squandered, nor will I allow you, or him, to continue to mismanage your plantation with the gross stupidity you have displayed over the last twenty years."

"I am not a business woman," Monique said faintly. "I did the best I could."

"I understand, but I wish to make you both secure and solvent."

"By assuming control of Grandeville? That is a strange way of helping, Renault."

"I will only exercise my control until Benoit shows himself capable of assuming it himself. Then I will relinquish my interests."

"And the girl's dowry?"

"And Marget's dowry."

"But there are so many repairs to be made. The roof leaks, half the rooms on the second floor have been water-damaged almost beyond repair. The barns are falling down, and my stock is less than perfect. You should see the nags Benoit and I must ride. Three of my slaves have run off in the last year, and must be replaced."

"Everything will be seen to. After the wedding."

Monique relaxed in her chair, her anger evaporating now that she was certain Renault meant no harm. It was for Benoit's own good, and she would no longer be in the state of constant worry over the many problems that had plagued her over the years.

"I think I will have a little sherry after all," she said smiling, thrusting away her disappointment over losing control of a fortune as big as Marget's. Even she was not blind to her son's many faults. After three days with him, she was beginning to doubt more than his abilities to run the plantation.

Renault rose and poured sherry into two glasses offering one to Monique.

"Shall we sit where it is more comfortable," he indicated the group of chairs away from the desk. She stood and he caught a glimpse of whiteness under the jacket of her habit. Twenty-two years ago she had been an excellent bed partner, he wondered if she still was. He guided her to a chair. As she moved past him, his fingers brushed the skin of her neck softly. She turned around to face him. She stood almost eye to eye with him, being much taller than average. He could not help but compare her with Marie-Odile.

"You feel it, too," Monique murmured. She pressed her body against him, feeling his response.

"Do you still know how to please a man?" he asked huskily. His fingers strayed to her jacket, unbuttoning button after button until her breasts were fully revealed. His hand slid down to caress her warmth.

"I still know how to please a man," she whispered, her lips covering his.

He pushed her toward a wide sofa. He went to the door and locked it, then walked over to the french doors, closed them, and pulled the curtains across them throwing the room into darkness. When he turned around, Monique was stepping out of her skirt and petticoats to reveal her full formed body. He hurried to her, his pulses racing.

She undressed him slowly, her fingers caressing him into a heat of desire that he had not known in a long time. When he was undressed, they stood facing each other, gazing at the other's body.

"Beautiful," Renault whispered, reaching out to stroke her breasts into erectness. "Absolutely beautiful."

Benoit sat on a wicker chair on the veranda, legs crossed, idly hitting his booted calf with his riding crop. He was in the height of fashion in fawn colored trousers and jacket with silk ruffled shirt and flowered waistcoat under his jacket. He felt very elegant indeed, and was surprised to see Marget walk out of the house in a riding habit that was only two shades darker than his suit. He nodded approvingly at her, thinking what an attractive couple they were together.

"Thank you for consenting to ride with me," he said, standing. He bowed in a courtly fashion, thinking of the secluded glade he would take her to and gently seduce her.

"It was kind of you to ask," Marget replied. She had been reluctant, at first, but Fleur's offer to accompany her had made her feel easier.

"I enjoy a stimulating ride with stimulating company," Benoit said. Anything was better than arguing with his Maman over the fatal signing of the contracts. It had suited him to have her announce her desire to ride to St. Angele and confront Renault de Champlain. Benoit decided to use the chance to further his relationship with Marget, and perhaps catch a glimmer of Fleur.

Fleur came running out of the house dressed in a dark gray habit. For the first time, Benoit noticed two horses being led around the house. He frowned, but brightened at the seductive look Fleur tossed at him. He thought again of the glade and having two women with him to fulfill his desires.

"Good morning, Monsieur de Ville," Fleur trilled.

Benoit swallowed fitfully as he glanced at the slim body of the girl he had so successfully deflowered only a few days before.

"I can hardly ride without a chaperone," Marget said gently, seeing his frown.

"Of course not," he replied. He tossed her into the saddle, then turned to Fleur who tossed him a seductive look over one shoulder. Behind the body of her horse, he brushed his fingertips across her neck and bosom. He apologized in a whisper, but Fleur only laughed. She fluttered her long lashes as he bent and tossed her into the saddle.

"Where are you going?" Aurore demanded. She swung Belle into step next to Marget. "May I come, too?"

"No!" Fleur and Benoit cried in unison. Benoit looked ashamed at his outburst as he thought longingly of the isolated forest glade. Fleur looked sullen.

"But, of course, she must come," Marget replied. "Have you no love for your sister, Fleur?"

Fleur said nothing, sullenly looking away.

"Let her come," Benoit said, glaring at the child.

"Let her come," Fleur said angrily.

"Thank you," Aurore said. She puzzled at the antagonistic attitude of both her sister and Monsieur de Ville. "It is much nicer having someone to ride with than just trotting about the park with Silas."

"I'll race you to the trees," Fleur called, jabbing her horse savagely with her spurred boot. "Last one there is a rotten egg."

The other three riders jumped into action with Aurore pulling ahead of Marget and Benoit. Belle stretched her neck out, leveling out into a mile-eating run that swiftly overtook Fleur. Though Belle was smaller than Fleur's horse, she was built for speed, and Aurore was lighter.

"I won! I won!"

"So, you won," Fleur snarled. "If my horse had not stumbled, I would have won."

"Stop quarreling," Marget admonished her sister. She came in last, but was unperturbed by it. She was not the horsewoman of the family, preferring more amiable horses to the fiery spirits her sisters rode. "You cheated, Fleur. You had a head start, so Aurore won fairly."

Fleur stuck her tongue out at her sister and would have pinched her, but Aurore moved out of range briskly.

"Which way shall we go?" Benoit asked, unfamiliar with this area. His remote glade was south. His heart sank to realize there was nothing he could do to get either Fleur or Marget there without making a scene.

"This way," Aurore yelled.

"This way," Fleur said. "You won the race, I get to choose where we're going." She turned her mare stubbornly north, not looking to see if anyone followed.

Marget shrugged helplessly, trotting after. Benoit scowled, but fell into step next to her.

Fleur skirted the field keeping just inside the line of trees. She had a purpose in going north. North was Grey Lawns and Gayle Courtland.

"We've gone too far," Marget protested an hour later. She was tired of riding and longed to return home for a soothing glass of lemonade. "Maman will be worrying about us."

"Just a little further," Fleur pleaded.

"But . . ."

"Please!" Fleur dimpled at Benoit.

"What harm, Marget," he said. "A few miles more won't make much difference."

"Good morning, ladies," Gayle Courtland said, riding out of the shadows. "Good morning, Mr. de Ville." He was astride a magnificent black stallion that moved restlessly under him. He wore stark white trousers and a white silk shirt open at the throat revealing a few blond hairs curling slightly against the dark bronze of his skin. The ends of a scarf fluttered around his firm chin. He smiled at them, removing his hat.

"Monsieur Courtland," Fleur squealed. She whirled her mount about and trotted toward him. Her eyes devoured him hungrily from the tanned skin at his throat to the shiny toes of his black boots fitting snugly against his legs. "What a surprise. We have been riding."

"Good morning, Monsieur Courtland," Marget greeted him warmly. She eyed her sister suspiciously, wondering how much of an accident this meeting was. "I am sorry if we are trespassing on your land. We came further than we intended."

"No need to apologize, Mlle. de Champlain," Gayle said, replacing his hat on his head. The action startled the stallion into a head shaking snort. He pulled the reins firmly. "Grey Lawns enjoys visitors as much as I. Would you consent to be my guests for a glass of lemonade and a short rest in the shade before you return?"

"That would be delightful," Marget said softly. She had to confess to a certain curiosity about this man whom her mother labeled a notorious gambler.

"And pray tell me, where is your delightful sister, Aurore?"

"Aurore!" Marget said. She turned around and looked behind her. "She was with us a moment ago."

"She can't be too far behind," Fleur said. She nudged her mare close to the stallion, who laid his ears back and bared his teeth.

"Careful," Gayle warned her. She dropped away. He stood in the saddle trying to pierce the shadows for a glimpse of Aurore, but there was none. "Go up to the house. It's straight through there," he said, pointing. "I'll go back and try to find Aurore."

"I'll come with you," Fleur offered.

"No," he said. "Go on and instruct my sister-in-law, Fay Courtland, that you are my guests. I shall be along directly."

"Thank you for your hospitality," Marget said. She turned her mare, forcing Fleur to accompany her.

"Do find little Aurore," Fleur called solicitously. She was annoyed. He had barely looked at her. She tugged at the buttons of her habit, opening the top two to expose the line of her throat. Let him ignore this, she thought pushing the corners under and fanning herself. It was daring, but calculated to catch his attention.

Seven

Aurore stopped to adjust her stirrup which had caught on a branch. Belle stood under her, completely still, ears cocked forward toward the shadow. When Aurore sat up, she saw the doe.

The creature was small and brown. It stood poised for flight as it watched her. Aurore touched Belle's neck. As though sensing the need for stillness, the mare did not move. Aurore watched the creature, her eyes alight with the gracefulness of the animal. She felt rather than saw Gayle come up behind her. She touched her finger to her lips, then pointed at the still form of the doe.

The doe bent down to touch something on the ground, she raised her head to sniff the air. Gayle moved his stallion until he was next to Aurore and watched the wild animal. He calmed the stallion who touched noses with Belle and snorted.

The doe jumped and was gone, her white tail a blur in the underbrush that quickly disappeared.

"Oh!" Aurore cried. "She ran away. She was so pretty."

Gayle smiled at her. "I wonder what she was looking at?" He dismounted and walked into the shadows with Aurore on his heels.

"It's a fawn," Aurore cried. The small animal on the ground tried to get to its feet, bleating in terror at the sound of Aurore's voice. "What's wrong with it?"

Gayle knelt down next to the tiny creature and touched it. It struggled to get away, but fell back rolling on its side, its legs tangled in a snare. Gayle gently took the snare off the fawn. He ran his hands expertly over the spotted coat and down each of the spindly legs.

"Its leg is broken," he said grimly. The fawn bleated in terror, its huge eyes rolling in fright. At the edge of her vision, Aurore could see the mother. The doe stepped up to her fawn, crying. The infant struggled to its feet, but fell awkwardly. Suddenly the doe jumped high in the air and was gone, crashing through the brush until there was silence.

"She's abandoned her baby," Aurore cried. Tears glistened in her dark brown eyes. She stood up and looked after the fleeing doe. "It will die."

"There's nothing she can do for her young," Gayle said gently. He watched the trembling fawn, trying to think.

"Don't kill it," Aurore cried. "Please, don't kill it." The tears splashed down her cheeks and Gayle took her in his arms tenderly wiping away the tears.

"I won't kill it. I promise. What should we do with it?"

"I don't know," Aurore sobbed. "But don't kill it. It's so pretty and it's only a baby."

"Hush," he said holding her close. "Get on your mare and I'll hand the fawn to you. We'll take it back to the house."

"Thank you." Aurore grabbed Belle's reins. She

found a large rock and climbed on it, jumping into the saddle, hooking her leg over the saddle horn. She arranged her skirts about her feet, then held her arms out to Gayle who scooped the fawn up into his arms and laid it in Aurore's lap. She soothed it, running her hand lovingly over the soft, spotted coat. The fawn cried piteously. She held it close to her small, flat chest and cradled the head against her shoulder.

"Hush, baby," she crooned. "Don't cry. We won't hurt you. We'll fix your leg. Don't cry." She stroked the smooth head, gradually quieting the animal. Its head sank against her, trust bubbling into the huge eyes.

Gayle took up the reins of his stallion and vaulted into the saddle. He took one of Belle's reins and led her while Aurore continued to cradle the tiny creature in her arms. Belle fell into step with the stallion. Gayle led Aurore through the forest and across the green expanse of lawn leading to Grey Lawns.

Gayle loved Grey Lawns. It was a two story structure with huge round pillars across the front. Ten steps led up to a wide, cool veranda that was shaded by several oak trees. Inside there were dozens of rooms in which he and his older brother, Grant, had played hide and seek as children. Those had been the days of innocence and youth before he realized that the plantation would never support both he and his brother. At the age of sixteen, he left home forever for a life on the riverboats as a roustabout. Before long, he was working in the barroom and soon after that he was dealing cards with the sharpness of many gamblers twenty years his senior. Gayle had a feeling for cards which he rapidly turned into a living. It was an exciting living. He had been loathe to leave it when he first heard of his father's and brother's deaths in a boating accident. But he had returned home anyway, taking up the reins of management with reluctance. Now that he was home, he never wanted to leave it again.

He glanced back at Aurore who still held the fawn in her arms. When she saw Grey Lawns, her eyes widened with instant love.

"Is this your home?" she asked.

"Yes," he answered, drawing the horses to a standstill to watch the morning light bathe the white stone in beauty.

"It's so pretty. It's much prettier than St. Angele," she said. "Can I see the inside?"

"After we take care of your new pet."

"Thank you."

"Boston," he called. "Where are you, Boston?"

"Comin', Marse Gayle," an old negro called. He came running out of the house. He was dressed in butler's livery and the fond expression on his face showed Aurore the depth of his devotion for his master.

"Boston, this young lady found a fawn in the woods. Is there anyone around who has a feeling for wild animals?"

"Maggie's gal likes the wild creatures," the old man said. "I'll fetch her."

"Fine, then order lemonade for Miss Aurore and wine for myself."

"Yes, sir." Boston hurried back into the house.

"What do you have?" Fleur demanded, running up to her sister, her arms out-stretched.

"I found it in the woods," Aurore said, hanging on to the fawn tightly. She petted it, her narrow hands moving down the long, satiny neck.

"I want it," Fleur commanded. "Give it to me."

"Its leg is broken," Gayle said, sliding down from his stallion. He moved Fleur away from Belle and took the fawn from Aurore. She jumped down to stand next to him, her dark eyes smiling sweetly at the creature.

"Will you kill it?" Fleur asked. She licked her lips in anticipation. If the fawn were dead, Aurore could not have it.

"No," Aurore cried. "I'm going to fix its leg and make it better."

"When you make it better, you can give it to me. I've always wanted a fawn for a pet."

"It belongs to your sister," Gayle broke in. He favored Fleur with a frown. She took a step back, then smiled sweetly.

"Of course it belongs to Aurore. I only meant we could share it."

"It belongs to your sister," he repeated firmly. Fleur's smile fled. She pouted, eyeing the small animal, coveting it. She drew her lips together into a straight line thinking of how to get it, but the piercing glance Gayle leveled at her stopped the tumbling thoughts in her mind. She smiled at him. How foolish to quibble over the stupid animal. She strolled away, swinging her hips suggestively.

Marget hurried up with Benoit following her. Marget was filled with sympathy for the fawn. She stroked it and murmured to it until Benoit pulled away saying how foolish it was to form an attachment to something that would only grow up to be someone's meal. His comment frightened Aurore who put her hand on the fawn's neck protectively, and refused to be comforted by Gayle's assurances that the fawn would never grace anyone's table.

A young negro girl ran around the corner of the house, her sack dress billowing behind her. Her hair was braided into two thick braids falling over immature breasts. She was twelve and one look at Aurore, who looked back happily, made them firm friends.

"I'se Maggie's gal," she said, her beautiful eyes on the fawn. "I'se Jewel."

"I'm Aurore. I found it in the woods. Its leg is broken."

"You speak English funny."

"I am Creole. Normally I do not speak English. I speak French."

Jewel's eyes widened in amazement. She had never been off the plantation in her life, much less met someone who spoke with such a strange accent.

"Can you fix the fawn?"

A smile flashed across Jewel's face, lighting it to mature beauty.

"I can fix it," she said, taking the animal from Gayle and cradling it. Aurore moved close to stroke the fawn. Then they walked off, disappearing around the corner of the house.

"Will she be all right?" Benoit asked, looking worried as the two girls bent their dark heads over the animal.

"Why shouldn't she be?" Gayle asked, curiously.

"You know how niggers hate us white folks," Benoit answered.

A look of contempt crossed Gayle's face. Without bothering to answer, he turned on his heel and stalked toward the house.

"Boston," Gayle called. He walked up the steps and stood in the shade of the veranda.

"Yes, sir."

"Send a message to St. Angele and tell Mr. de Champlain that his daughters are safe at Grey Lawns and staying for dinner."

"Mr. Courtland, please," Marget interrupted. "If your man will bring pen and paper, I will write the note."

"Boston!"

"Yes, sir. Comin' right up, sir." He disappeared into the house, returning with a tray and pen and paper.

"Maman will be relieved to know we are not lost," Marget said. "She worries over us constantly."

"I can understand why. She has three very beautiful daughters." Marget blushed prettily.

"Gayle!" a voice called. It was soft and musical.

"Fay, our guests are staying for dinner."

"How nice," Fay said, stepping out onto the veranda. She sank into a fan-shaped wicker chair gracefully. Her lavender voile skirts floated daintily about her ankles and settled across the tops of her matching kidskin slippers.

Fay Courtland was a beautiful woman with generations of grace and delicacy bred into her. She was medium tall and slim with huge blue-gray eyes and soft auburn hair. Her skin was flawlessly white and smooth. She was acutely conscious of the fragile beauty of her hands which she fluttered constantly.

"It is so nice to have guests," she drawled. "It does

get lonely here sometimes." She lowered long lashed lids over soft eyes. From under the thick veil of her lashes, she studied her guests carefully. Marget she dismissed immediately as no rival. She was as gray as a mouse and twice as timid. Fleur gave her a moment's pause, but the girl was terribly young and no match for the vibrant beauty Fay owned.

"Thank you for having us to dinner," Marget said sweetly. She admired the cool grace of the other woman, watching the long-fingered hands dance in fascination.

"It is Gayle's home," she said. Her voice was low and husky of a timbre that made men shiver when they heard it. Benoit stared at her unable to take his eyes from the oval of her face, and the rise and fall of her generous bosom. "It is hot today. There is nothing as hot as Louisiana in the summer."

"It is the steamy air that makes it so hot," Marget said. She sipped from her frosty glass of lemonade. "Everything feels so damp."

"I like the heat," Fleur said. "Because when I get too hot, I can go swimming in the pond." She laughed childishly.

"I am afraid my pond swimming days are over," Fay said. She fluffed up the lace over her bosom to emphasize the fully developed curves. Fleur blushed and turned away.

"Look," Aurore said, bounding up the steps. "She's all fixed." She pointed with pride at the wobbly fawn, standing on long spindly legs precariously. The broken leg had been tightly splinted. Aurore found a length of ribbon and tied it around the animal's neck looping it into a bow. "Jewel says in a few weeks, she'll be completely healed." Aurore grabbed Jewel who hung back shyly. "Jewel knows all about animals. She has a squirrel and a raccoon in her home. There's even a tiny bird in a cage."

"The wing is broken," Jewel offered in a whisper.

"What are you going to do with the fawn now?" Gayle asked. His face was curiously tender as he smiled at the two girls.

"Jewel is going to take care of her, and I'm going to visit every day. Jewel says she is a baby girl. We're going to call her Sally."

"Sally's a nice name," Gayle chuckled.

Fay wondered if she were the only person there to see the change come over her brother-in-law at the approach of the beautiful child. She frowned thoughtfully, wondering if she had anything to fear from this incredibly beautiful Aurore.

"Would you like some lemonade?" Gayle asked. He poured it into two tall glasses and gave one to Jewel and the other to Aurore. Jewel drank hers thirstily, then slipped down the stairs. She waved good-bye to Aurore who waved back.

"I'll come tomorrow," Aurore promised as Jewel led the fawn away. "We'll play together."

"You can't play with her," Benoit objected.

"Why not?" Aurore looked at him.

"Because she's a nigger."

Aurore looked puzzled.

"If Aurore and Jewel wish to play together, there is no reason why they can't," Marget interrupted. "Our Papa does not have slaves, and we have all been brought up to look upon negroes as people like we are. Papa says there is nothing wrong with having one of them for a friend."

Benoit gasped.

"I don't like your attitude, Marget," he said. "When we are married, I will trust you to keep your treasonous thoughts to yourself."

"My Papa did not bring up daughters to accept blindly the opinions of others," Marget said softly. "I have been taught to think and speak as I please. Not even my husband will tell me how to conduct myself."

Benoit gasped.

So the little mouse has claws, Fay thought, her eyes narrowing.

"Shall we go in to dinner?" Gayle asked, breaking through the unease filling the air around them.

"When will you show me your house?" Aurore asked. She skipped into the house at his side.

"After our meal," he replied.

"I'm so hungry."

"Aurore!" Fleur suddenly screamed. "Ladies are not supposed to talk about being hungry, and they don't skip."

"Then I'm not a lady because I'm hungry and I'm skipping."

Fay pursed her lips in annoyance. How could he possibly be attracted to such a rude child? She watched Gayle lean over Aurore as she sat down at the table. He spread her linen napkin across her lap. She giggled. He straightened and turned to Fay to assist her in seating at the long table.

Fleur tapped her foot impatiently. She tried to catch Gayle's eye, but he was not watching her. Benoit turned to her after Marget was sitting at the table. Fleur could have screamed her anger. How was she ever going to get him to seduce her when he never even thought of her.

Two maids walked in, carrying huge round platters. The platters were set on the table and the lids removed. The heady aroma of baked chicken, sausage, and meat pies filled the air. Soon everyone was eating hungrily, forgetting their animosities.

"How beautiful," Aurore cried breathlessly. She held the vase up to the light. Around the edges she could see the subtle shades of blue and lavender. She turned it slowly marveling at the beauty of it.

"Put it down before you drop it," Fleur said sourly. She had been forbidden to touch anything after dropping an amber crystal goblet and chipping the rim. She was angry that Aurore was encouraged to touch every piece presented to her.

"I won't drop it," Aurore said, her voice low and filled with awe. Gayle pointed out the scene cut along the bottom for decoration.

Fleur resisted the temptation to gently bump her sister's arm encouraging her to drop the vase, but the look Gayle turned on her told her he was anticipating her action. She backed away from her sister to stand at a window to observe the peacocks on the lawn.

"I like this best," Marget said. She held a small cranberry wine glass etched with flowers. It matched seven other glasses and a tall decanter positioned on a silver tray.

"My father brought that set back from Germany when he traveled there as a young man," Gayle said. He enjoyed watching the admiring looks on Marget's and Aurore's faces. He could see they appreciated the beauty of the glass collection as much as he did. Marget carefully returned the wine glass to the tray, her fingers lingering over the delicately cut flowers. Gayle decided to present the set to her as a wedding gift. He knew she would treasure it always.

Fay Courtland yawned.

Benoit walked idly around the room peering into the huge glass doored cabinets decorating every wall. He decided he would start a collection of his own. It would not be glass. It would be . . . It would be . . . His eyes alighted on a shelf of small porcelain snuffboxes. His decision was made. He would collect snuffboxes, and be the envy of every man in Louisiana.

Gayle showed Aurore every item he personally treasured. He watched her reactions, enjoying her delight. He found himself trying to imagine what the adult Aurore would look like. But he could not smooth the childish planes into a woman's mature angles. He could only see her as she was, soft and round, her heavily fringed lashes closing over dark brown eyes surrounded by the wild disarray of her blue black curls. She looked up. Their eyes met. The feeling that passed between them was intense and personal. Aurore looked away blushing, conscious of a hunger possessing her. The threshold of womanhood yawned before her. She could feel the beginnings of a yearning filling her, consuming her, accompanied by the pain of knowing she was still a child. She stepped back from the chasm retreating into the safety of childhood.

Gayle was shaken. He moved away from her to the other side of the room pretending an interest in his treasures he no longer felt. Never had he felt this way before. Never had he seen such intense emotion as he had just witnessed in the eyes of the girl-child across the room. He recognized the woman struggling to emerge, but why did he react so strongly. He fought to regain his composure.

"She is only a child," Fay murmured. She stood close to him, her head bent to brush his shoulder. "What is it in her that fascinates you so much? Is it her innocence? Her vulnerability? She is a child, Gayle. Why do you hunger for her when there is a full-blooded woman willing to comfort you," She took his hand and laid it against her breast. He jerked it away.

"You are the wife of my dead brother."

"You must know I never loved your brother. I love you. Always have I loved you."

"But you married Grant."

"It was arranged. My father was destitute, your father was willing to advance him a small amount to keep his plantation running."

"And you wanted a rich husband, not a second son, didn't you." Gayle said bitterly.

"I love you."

"You didn't love me enough to give up your comforts. The woman I marry will have to love like that." His glance flickered over Aurore. Would she give up everything to be with the man she loved? Gayle thought she would. She would give up everything and more.

Abruptly he walked away from Fay. He would never give his love to her again. He would never give her the chance to play him false as she had before. Never. He glanced back at her. She was smiling at him.

Fleur was angry. Not once during the afternoon had she managed to get Gayle alone. As she mounted her horse, she tried one last time to catch his attention, but he did not notice. His smile was reserved only for Aurore as he swung her up on her mare, kissing her cheek. He bowed to Marget and Fleur. Her rage increased until she was unable to sit still. She spurred her mare savagely, not waiting for the others. She heard Marget shouting, but refused to stop. She disappeared into the woods, the cool shadows closing in on her, shielding her from the others.

"What is wrong with Fleur?" Marget asked, puzzled.

Fay knew. She had watched the looks of open desire fill Fleur's face each time she looked at Gayle. She understood that all-consuming need to have a man.

Fay waved her guests out of sight, then walked slowly into the house. Inside the cool grayness, she realized she was tired. A headache began to pound at her temples. She yelled at Boston, ordering a decanter of brandy be sent to her room. She walked up the stairs, ignoring the sniggering looks the slaves exchanged with each other. Could she help it if she had such miserable migraines. Brandy was the only thing that eased the awful pounding. She turned down the hall, a maid coming after her with the decanter and glass on a tray. Inside her room, the maid set the tray down on a table, then hurried away. Fay locked the door, and closed the drapes. She poured herself a glass of the fiery liquid and prepared to drink the afternoon away.

Eight

Marie-Odile bent over the trailing gown draped across her lap. With quick sure strokes, she put the last stitches through the fabric, securing the lace ruffle to the bodice. She smiled a little remembering her own wedding gown. It had been as beautiful as the one she held.

She shook out the folds, holding it up to look at. It was a pity white was the traditional color for weddings. Marget did not look good in white. For this reason, Marie-Odile daringly stitched deep blue forget-me-nots around the neck, hem, and narrow cuffs. It would be frowned on, but on her special day, Marget had to look her best. In a second defiant act, she dispensed with the bridal veil and coronet. Instead, Marget's hair would be braided with brightly colored ribbons and threaded with flowers from the greenhouse. The brightness would take away from the dreadful pallor in her daughter's face. A pallor that increased with each passing day. Marie-Odile was concerned over her daughter's listlessness and lack of appetite. There was nothing she could do. After all, she had been bartered and sold in the same manner and her marriage had not turned out too badly except for, Marie-Odile blushed scarlet, her husband's voracious appetite for the intimate side of marriage. Like Marget, she wanted to retreat behind the high walls of a convent. Like Marget, that refuge had been denied to her.

Many families were honored to have children enter the religious life, but Marie-Odile had been the only child of extremely wealthy parents. Her choice for her future had been brushed aside because her family's honor had been more important than her own desires. Marry, she did. As Marget was about to do. In two weeks she would be the bride of Benoit de Ville, all for the sake of honor. If it had been in her power, Marie-Odile would have allowed her daughter to enter the convent and achieve the peace her heart desired. But Marie-Odile did not have the power. She was a woman, in a severely limiting role.

"Maman?" Marget opened the door and sailed into the room. She wore her newest gown of lavender crepe with white daisies embroidered on the bodice and cuffs. It was a pity she could not be married in this gown, it suited her as no other ever had, accentuating her slim waist and creamy complexion.

"It is perfect," Marie-Odile said. "Turn around, child. Luce, the last length of lace on the hem is not straight."

Luce fell to her knees, picked out the basting thread and pinned the lace correctly.

"Thank you, Luce. Turn around again, Marget. That is much better. Run along and change. You have been very patient with all these fittings. I know how boring they can be. Get your horse and go for a ride. It will put the bloom of color into your cheeks again."

"Yes, Maman," Marget said obediently. She curtseyed, then ran from the room.

"She is not well," Luce said in her low, carrying voice. "She loses weight and cries much."

Marie-Odile looked up helplessly. "There is nothing I can do, Luce. I have tried to talk to her. I have tried to tell her it will not be as bad as she fears."

Luce said nothing. Her heart was heavy as she looked at her young mistress. They both understood that the marriage was to happen regardless of their wishes. Marie-Odile ached with her daughter's unhappiness, but there was nothing she could do. She would pray for an easing of the pain, but she could not pray her child out of this dreadful union.

There was no peace in Marget. She felt as though there were a whirlwind in her. It made her head ache and turn dizzily. She took off the lavender gown, tossing it on the bed. She stared at it in hatred, appalled at herself for her hate. She wanted to rip the gown into shreds, but the many hours of loving work Luce had put into it, restrained her. She covered her face with her hands. Never in her short life had she known such misery.

Luce drew the girl into her arms, holding her tightly. Marget clung to her, listening to the steady beat of her heart.

"The marriage will happen," Luce said gently, her French strangely accented with her Barbados lilt. "You cannot stop what was set in motion before your lifetime."

"I hate him. I hate his hands on mine, his breath against my face. I don't know what to do. I have prayed for guidance, but there is none. I hate him,

108

and I am ashamed of myself for the hating." She began to shake, her teeth chattering in her head, her hands twitching.

"Stop it," Luce commanded sternly. "You can change nothing. Your only hope lies in acceptance."

With Luce's warm arms around her, Marget's trembling finally stopped.

"Two weeks! Two weeks!" she cried. "I have only two weeks."

"Enjoy them. Make yourself enjoy them. Ride, swim in the pond, do all the things that make you happy. Live for the next two weeks, live like you have never lived before."

Luce scooped up the lavender dress, leaving the room. Her face, hidden from Marget, was twisted with the depth of her emotions.

Marget pulled on her riding habit. She would survive. She had the strength to survive. She ran out of her room, determined to make these last two weeks count.

Luce dropped the gown on her bed. She went to the window to watch Marget race across the lawn to stables. Old memories popped unbidden into her head. She saw herself as a child running free on the warm island where her parents had lived. She ran through the jungle and along the beach, the sand hot on her feet. She ran and ran until she was exhausted. Then the raiders caught her, when she had no more strength to run. They had laughed at her pitiful struggles to get free, thrusting their dirty, bearded faces at her.

The hold of the ship had been evil and smelly. She

remembered the groans of her parents from the chains that bound them making sores on their ankles and wrists. She remembered the burly sailor who was not content to violate her mother, but had violated her own ten-year-old body. Then she remembered the day her mother died and was thrown overboard to feed the hungry sharks.

Luce turned away from the window, the shame of the slave block stealing over her as though it had been only yesterday. The men who had poked and probed in her privates to see if she were virgin, or pulled open her mouth to stare at her teeth. Never would she forget that shame. She still ached with that shame. She understood Marget. Marriage was another kind of slavery.

Luce drew the drapes, throwing the room into darkness. She locked her door with a click. She took from the last drawer in her bureau a small bundle wrapped in a black cloth. She sat down in the middle of the floor, opening the bundle reverently. A copper bowl, two thick candles, two firmly sealed jars, and several closed pouches were revealed to her. She spread the black cloth smooth and set the copper bowl in the middle. From one of the jars, she poured some water, swirling it around and around. She opened two pouches, the fragrance of their contents flowing out and filling the room. Luce breathed deeply of the scent. She took a pinch of each pouch and tossed it over her left shoulder. She lit the candles and set them on either side of the bowl. The bowl gleamed brightly in the candlelight. Luce's lips moved in a chant, centuries old and handed down from mother to daughter. She had never forgotten it, nor any of the other things her mother had taught her. She opened two more pouches letting their scents mingle in the already heavily scented air. Her head felt light. She was staring down a long tunnel, and at the end was the copper bowl. She picked up the bowl with arms ten miles long and carefully swirled the contents. The smoke from the candles filled her nostrils. Her lips moved automatically in chant after chant, invoking little known gods for a glimpse into Marget's future. She stared at the bowl, concentrating on the swirling water.

Luce had not done this in many years. The harder she concentrated, the more the vision slipped away from her. She put the bowl down. Sweat poured down her face.

She stared into the settling water, but it remained stubbornly clear. No look at Marget's future was to be allowed her. She took a deep breath, cleared her mind, and picked up the bowl. She built Marget's face in her mind and smiled when the water started to cloud with shadows. She stared at the slowly forming picture.

It was not Marget, but Aurore who stood in the depths of the bowl. She wore a dark gown. Her black hair was pulled into a chignon at the base of her neck, a sharp little hat perched on her head. She held the arm of a man who was a stranger to Luce. He was young and dark with wavy black hair and bright blue eyes. He looked at Aurore with tenderness and she smiled back at him with love. The vision widened. Luce recognized the street in New Orleans where the de Champlain town house stood. A carriage was parked at the curb, its fare in the process of stepping

111

down. A brindle dog approached the carriage and lifted his leg. The vision faded.

A blackness crept into Luce's head. She set the bowl down carefully, and lay down on the floor. Gradually the blackness receded and she was back in her room at St. Angele. When her strength returned, she sat up. Carefully she poured the water back into its jar. She closed the pouches and blew out the candles. She dried the bowl with the corner of the black cloth. Then she bundled everything up again in the cloth and put it back into the bottom drawer of her bureau. She unlocked her door and threw open the drapes. The sun streamed into the room startling her. What had seemed like hours had been little more than twenty minutes. With an aching head, she picked up the lavender gown, sat down in her chair and began to fix the lace ruffle. She was bitterly disappointed that she had not seen anything of Marget's future. She had thought to offer a tiny crumb of happiness to the girl, but it had been Aurore revealed to her. Aurore, grown and mature, standing with a strange man who loved her as much as she loved him. Luce sighed. She put the vision from her. Her heavy lids dropped over tired eyes. She leaned her head against the back of the chair and slumped in sleep, the lavender gown slipped out of her hands and fluttered to the floor.

The pond was cool and refreshing. Fleur climbed up on the huge rock in the center and dived in, parting the water smoothly and coming to the surface a few feet away. She laughed as she paddled in circles. She did a surface dive, then headed back toward the rock.

It was glorious, she thought, climbing once more on the rock, water dripping down her body. There was no Marget to be scandalized by her swimming in the nude, or Aurore tagging along wanting to be included. It was marvelous being able to sneak away, to swim and frolic by herself until she was wrinkled and cool. She dived again coming up in the deep part of the pond. Her dark hair hung over her face, she flipped back with a practiced flick of her head. She swam back to the rock and was poised to dive again when she saw him.

He stood at the edge of the pond, arms on his hips grinning at her. His black body gleaming in the rays of the sun.

"Why don't you come in and join me. The water is cool," Fleur said.

"Dive off the rock again," he said.

"All right." She jumped, streaking through the air like a graceful swan. She hit the water and came to the surface a few feet away from him. He was pulling off his trousers, tossing them on the ground next to her gown and turning around. Fleur gasped. He was beautiful. His shoulders were broad and muscular, his waist slim. His legs were long and powerful. Here was the man she wanted, she thought, staring at him, thinking how much larger he was than Benoit.

He stepped into the water. It rippled around his ankles, then his knees. Fleur's eyes followed him hungrily. Already she felt a growing warmth deep in her that ached to be satisfied. The water reached his hips, then his waist. Finally he stroked out to her, the water glistening on his dark body like little drops of crystals.

"Catch me," she challenged, kicking off in a powerful sweep toward the middle of the pond. She was slim and lithe, her strokes long and powerful, but he was stronger than she, catching up easily. One hand encircled her waist. His fingers moved up to cup her small breasts, erect and rosy from the chill of the water. He caressed her until she moaned with excitement. Suddenly he pushed her away.

"Now, you catch me."

Fleur giggled. She followed him easily, but he pulled away circling around the rock and disappearing from view. She changed direction going the other way around the rock. As he came into view looking over his shoulder, she pounced on him. One arm slipped around his massive shoulders, while the other ran over his smooth belly to nestle intimately between his thighs.

"You're beautiful," she told him. "I love you."

He pulled her close, arms around her, dark eyes smiling mockingly down at her. His lips covered hers, parting them. She moaned again, clinging to him. The minute she saw Noble, she knew he was going to be hers. They slid under the surface, their lips still locked. Then Fleur broke away and headed for shore. Noble followed her slowly, his dark eyes studying her white body.

How different he was from Benoit, Fleur thought as she stroked his dark skin. Her fingers teased him until he pushed her down on the ground and lay over her. This was a man who would fill her and bring the pleasure Benoit had managed to awaken, but not satisfy.

Noble parted her legs with a huge hand. His lips

nibbled at her and she squirmed under him. He felt a moment's guilt over taking his pleasure with his employer's thirteen-year-old daughter, but then again, she wasn't protesting. He wasn't surprised to find she was not a virgin.

The afternoon sun slanted over them as they lay on the grass idly caressing each other. Noble had performed more times that she had expected, yet while he was spent, she was ready again. She pulled him toward her, but he rolled away gathering up his trousers.

"Don't leave yet," Fleur cried.

"I got work to do," he told her regretfully. "Someone will notice I'm gone, if I don't get back soon."

"Will you come again?"

"Can you get away tomorrow night."

"No, we're having a party for Marget and Benoit," she said, her voice filled with disappointment.

"The night after tomorrow," he said. "I'll wait for you here."

"I'll be here," she said. She jumped to her feet, kissing him and pressing her body against his. She felt a stirring in him, but he pushed her away and slowly put on his clothes.

Noble disappeared into the forest. Fleur fell to her knees in acute disappointment. She wanted more of him. She touched her breasts, caressing them in the manner he had used.

"Don't tell me that big buck niggar didn't satisfy you, girl?"

Fleur looked up to find John Miles standing over her. His fingers fumbled at the buttons of his trousers. For a long second, she studied him, her fingers still caressing her breast.

"Let me help you," she whispered sweetly. She stood up and walked to him, rolling her hips. He stared at her, his mouth falling open. She reached up to unbutton his shirt and push it off. Then she reached down and unfastened his trousers and dropped them down his hips. He had nothing of the athletic build that Noble had. He was flabby and soft, but he was big in the area most important to Fleur. She fell back on the ground inviting him with her lips. His mouth crushed hers hungrily as he fell on her. When he was through, she gathered up her clothes and pulled them on. She looked at him sadly. He wasn't nearly as good as Noble. Then she hurried home.

Aurore sat on the grass with Jewel. The fawn lay between them, curled into a ball. They watched the river, the swift moving Mississippi with its dangerous eddies and sandbars. Aurore longed to be on it, traveling from one city to the next, meeting new people and seeing new places.

"Someday, I'se goin' upriver to Chicago," Jewel sighed. Her dark eyes followed the twisting river as far as they could. "I'se goin' to fine me a place where's I be free."

"Aren't you free now?" Aurore asked curiously. Her father owned no slaves. It had never occurred to her that his many friends did.

"No, I ain't free. I belong to Marse Gayle."

"My Papa has no slaves," Aurore said slowly.

"Everyone knows your Pa don't hold with slave ownin'," Jewel said. "But that don't mean they is free."

"What do you mean? They are free."

"They still work for your Pa, don't they?"

"He pays them wages. And they have land to grow food on. How do you want to be free?"

"I want to live in a big house like you do and go to balls all the time and find me a handsome man to love me."

Aurore frowned. She never thought of living in a big house and going to balls as being free. Her life was being spent in learning all the little things that it took to run the house, and the hundreds of details that came up every day, and the dozens of problems that always seemed to need solving. To her it wasn't freedom. She started to tell Jewel about how she felt about it, but Fay called from the veranda.

"Aurore, come and have some lemonade."

"Can Jewel come, too?"

"Not today, dear," Fay replied, annoyed that such a question was asked. No one asked a nigger child to sit for cookies and lemonade on the veranda. It irritated her to see Aurore playing constantly with Jewel. Jewel was supposed to be learning housework, but Gayle had freed her for the summer to be Aurore's companion.

"I guess I got to go," Aurore said with a sigh. She stood up and brushed loose grass from her skirt. She did not like Fay Courtland. She exchanged looks of mutual dislike with Jewel. Jewel did not like Miss Fay either, but she was still a Courtland slave and did not have the freedom to express her feelings.

"You go on and please Miss High and Mighty Courtland. I'll see to Sally. It's time for her milk."

"I'll see you tomorrow."

Jewel nodded. She jumped up and helped Aurore

brush the grass from her skirt. Aurore brushed off Jewel. One good thing had come of Jewel's association with Aurore, had been the change in her wardrobe. No longer did she wear the rough cotton sacks deemed proper for her by Fay, but rather similar gowns to Aurore's. Today she wore a fine beige cotton broadcloth embroidered with yellow daisies. She looked very pretty in it with her hair pulled back and tucked into a chignon at the back of her head. Gayle had brought about the transformation saying that Aurore could not have Jewel looking like a grub if they were going to be playmates. Jewel smoothed her gown down and took the rawhide rope tied around the fawn's neck.

"Come on, Sally. Ain't you hungry yet? I'll see you tomorrow, Miss Aurore."

The fawn jumped up and stood looking indecisively between Jewel and Aurore. Finally she ambled after Jewel, her rumbling belly winning out.

Aurore turned to the house, walking with dragging feet across the lawn.

"You are going to get all brown sitting in the sun like that," Fay scolded. "Your mama will be vastly displeased to see you going all brown and dark like a nigger." She had decided to be nice to the child, but it was difficult. Everywhere Aurore went, Jewel went. Fay could not abide seeing them together, though she had to be grateful to the child for keeping Gayle at the house more. It gave Fay a chance to practice her charms on him though he proved to be unusually immune.

Gayle walked out of the house and sat down. He held a book in one hand frowning over it. He put the

118

book aside and accepted a glass of wine punch thankfully.

"I think tomorrow I will go over and have a talk with your father, Aurore. When you go home tell him I'll be in around nine in the morning."

"Are you planning to accept his offer of help in saving this place?" Fay asked in her affected drawl. It grated on Gayle's ears.

"He did offer to give advice. I can't make heads or tails of these ledgers. I think Pa and Grant were keeping a chicken farm instead of a cotton plantation."

"When are we going to play poker again?" Aurore asked.

Fay shuddered delicately. A child playing poker, how unladylike. She would have spoken her disapproval, but her words would be ignored by her brother-in-law. He took great pains to encourage the child with her unusual thinking.

"Not today, pet," Gayle answered absently. He took up the book again, drawing a pencil out of his pocket and marking the ledger in the margin. "I have to do some work on these accounts before I take them all over to your father."

Aurore's face fell in disappointment. The highlight of her day was being near Gayle with his masculine smell. She ached to grow to adulthood so that he would look at her with more than a tender smile that told her she was nothing more than an amusing child.

"I should go," she said with a sigh. When he was this preoccupied, there was no interesting him in anything else.

"Look who's coming," Fay said as a horseman walked out of the forest and across the lawn. It was

Marget, come to escort her sister home. It was becoming a habit of hers. Like Aurore, she was turning brown with the rays of the sun. She wore no hat and her dark hair showed bright strains of red as it bleached out.

"Come have some lemonade, Marget," Aurore called. Marget jumped down handing her horse over to a groom.

"Thank you," she said. Marget looked serene and peaceful. Her days of freedom were rapidly drawing to a close, but she found herself enjoying them more and more. Her small tanned face, smiling, looked at Gayle. It was amazing how wonderful the light tan looked on her. For the first time in months she actually looked healthy. "I came to say thank you for the wine goblets and decanter, Monsieur Courtland. They are so beautiful."

"I'm glad they please you, Mademoiselle Marget," Gayle said looking up. He thought how pretty Marget looked today in her deep blue riding habit edged in ecru lace. "I remembered how you admired them the day I showed them to you. I thought it would make a fine wedding gift."

"It is a beautiful wedding gift, Monsieur, and I came to thank you in person." She dimpled sweetly. "But we cannot stay for lemonade. Maman has Luce fitting everyone for their gowns for the wedding and Aurore is next. I must take her back immediately."

As on signal, a groom stepped around the corner of the house leading Belle. Aurore kissed Gayle and curtseyed to Fay. Soon she and Marget were cantering across the lawn.

Fay relaxed. Another day with the child was over.

She was alone with Gayle.

"It has been so hot, Gayle," she said, fanning herself with her handkerchief. The handkerchief wafted delicate scents of lavender over her nose. "I should like to see the weather break and turn cool for a few days."

Gayle grunted, not really listening to her. He was busily trying to pay debts without money.

"I do think I shall go up and change into something cooler, Gayle dear. You will wait for me here."

He nodded, but didn't see her go.

Fay had been planning this moment for days. She ran up to her chamber and tossed off the gown she had been wearing. She unhooked her chemise and pulled at the tapes of her petticoats. She untied her hoop and dropped it to the floor. Naked, she padded to her wardrobe and pulled open the doors to gaze at the brightly colored display of her clothes.

She drew out a white gown edged with Brussels lace. She held it up and studied herself in the mirror. She smiled. She pulled the gown over her head, pulling it until it molded itself to her slim body. The neck was indecently low, barely covering her breasts. She pulled it lower until both nipples showed slightly. This should get his attention, she thought. She pulled on one petticoat, then pulled it off again. She turned around liking the way the skirt clung to her legs. She slid her feet into matching slippers, grabbed up a light shawl and left the room.

She sat down opposite Gayle, dropping the shawl over the back of the chair. She arranged the skirt about her ankles, unaware that her fussing had drawn Gayle's look. His eyes widened at the sight of her body outlined by the sun through the transparent skirts of her gown.

"I was so hot, Gayle," she said sweetly. "I just had to change into something cool. You don't mind, do you?" She flirted coyly, shrugging her shoulders and exposing totally the tip of one breast.

In a second he was standing over her, his eyes raking her figure. She stood up offering herself.

"Shall we go in?" she coaxed.

Gayle stared at her, desire flooding through him. It had been weeks since he had last had a woman. He pulled her into his arms, his lips crushing down on hers, his breath warm and vibrant against her cheek. He swung her up in his arms and carried her into the house.

In her room, he threw her down on the bed, then tore her gown away from her and tossed it to the floor.

"You haven't changed, have you, Gayle?" she whispered when he lay with her. His fingers roamed over her coaxing into flames the passion she had for him.

"Aurore," he whispered in her ear when he climaxed. He rolled away and fell asleep.

Fay stood up staring rigidly at him. She had expected a return of the love they had once shared, but all he did was call the name of another woman. She pulled on her robe and ran in search of her brandy decanter.

Nine

Today! Marget flung away the mosquito netting and jumped out of bed. She ran to the window to find the arbor the servants had built still decorating the lawn. Tables and chairs had been set up with huge arrangements of flowers on the tables. Marget had helped, but to keep her peace of mind she had convinced herself it was for someone else's wedding and not her own.

"Good morning," Marie-Odile said, still sleepy-eyed and yawning. She wore a long robe over her crinoline, belted tightly around her waist. Over one arm, she carried Marget's wedding gown. She folded it over the back of a chair, arranging the folds so that they would not crease. "Did you sleep well?"

"Yes, Maman." The words sounded choked and faint. She was aware of a dry, parched feeling in her throat.

"Luce will be here shortly to help you bathe. Delphine is bringing you breakfast. Remember to eat lightly. All this excitement will make you ill if you eat too much. I should know, I was terribly ill at my wedding, but your Papa was very thoughtful." Marie-Odile blushed, remembering how she had disgraced herself in the privacy of her room after the ceremony

123

with Renault holding her head over a basin with understanding.

"I'll be very careful, Maman," Marget promised. She didn't think she could eat anything, her stomach was all tied in knots with tension.

Delphine arrived, her giggling face peeking around the door at Marget. She set the tray down on the bed and Marget sat next to it. Delphine uncovered the dishes.

"It is a beautiful day for a wedding, Miss," she said.

"Thank you, Delphine. That will be all," Marie-Odile said briskly. The little maid curtseyed and disappeared from the room, shutting the door silently behind her.

Aurore skipped into the room in her nightgown and sat next to her sister.

"Where are your slippers, Aurore," Marget scolded gently. "Your feet will get cold."

"They won't get cold," Aurore said lightly. She took a piece of toast from Marget's tray and wolfed it down. "Maman won't give me a proper breakfast. She says I will get sick all over my new dress. But I won't, Marget." Aurore whispered, peering at her mother's back as she fussed in Marget's wardrobe drawing out an armful of petticoats and a fresh chemise. When she left the room Marget thrust the tray at her sister.

"Here," she said, viewing the poached eggs and toast with distaste.

"Aren't you hungry?" Aurore asked, eyeing the food greedily.

"I'll just have some of the cocoa. Help yourself to what you want." Aurore attacked the food as though she had not eaten in a week.

"Maman says I can't go to Grey Lawns today to see my fawn. I wish I could go, Sally will miss me. And she grows so fast. I won't recognize her tomorrow."

Marget laughed. "She will not grow that fast."

"And I am not allowed to play with Jewel today even though she is coming with Miss Fay."

Marget frowned. She felt Aurore to be altogether too friendly with the Courtland slave. It was all right to have her as a friend, but not such an intimate one. Marie-Odile disapproved more than anyone.

"You shall have friends to play with today. And tomorrow you can visit your fawn and Jewel."

"I can't tomorrow either. Papa says I have to stay around and help clean up the house. Ugh! I hate cleaning."

"Aurore, come along." Marie-Odile called. She poked her head into Marget's room to find Aurore calmly finishing the last of the food on Marget's tray. "What are you doing?"

"I was hungry, Maman," Aurore said whiping her mouth with a napkin. "Marget did not want her breakfast, so I ate it."

"Go back to your room. Luce is waiting to give you your bath. Hurry! And don't you dare be sick today or I shall be extremely angry." Marie-Odile disappeared, her shoes clicking imperiously on the polished boards of the hall floor. Aurore gave Marget a sloppy kiss and ran out of the room.

Marget gazed sadly around the room that had been hers for fifteen years. Her dolls sat abandoned on a shelf in the corner. All her books were on another shelf, some of them fallen over on their sides. She picked up one of the books, thumbing idly through it,

125

reading the childish words she had learned so many years before. She felt a desire to return to childhood, to return to the innocence she no longer possessed. She found herself sinking on her prie Dieu, clasping her hands together in prayer. She beseeched God to help her, but there was no answering flow of strength. She stood and looked sadly at her Bible and missal sitting neatly on the edge. She would have to find her own strength, she thought sadly. She turned back to her bed and climbed under the blanket. She pulled the blanket over her head and burrowed down in the comforting darkness. Her problems would still be there when she climbed out, but for the moment she could pretend she was still a child.

Aurore hated having her hair washed. It tangled and was difficult to comb. But Luce attacked her ruthlessly, scrubbing and rinsing, ignoring Aurore's protests. When her hair was finished, Luce then washed Aurore, scrubbing and rinsing until her skin was a rosy red. Finally Aurore was let out, wrapped in a blanket and set in the sun to dry. Then Fleur was called in and just as ruthlessly shoved in the tub.

"I don't want to be washed like a baby. I'm not a baby," Fleur wailed as she was dunked into the water and then soaped all over. She glared at Aurore who sat on a shelf next to the window, the sun streaming over her dark hair. "And I'm too big to share the bath with Aurore."

Luce grabbed a fistful of hair and dunked Fleur again. She came up sputtering and angry. Luce was less gentle with Fleur than she had been with Aurore. Aurore may not have liked the scrubbing she got, but she was less vocal about it.

"Ow!" Fleur screamed. Luce dunked her again. "You're hurting me."

"I'm getting you clean," Luce announced stolidly.

"I'm clean. I swim in the pond every day."

"I know," Luce replied. The look she favored the girl with struck terror into her heart. "Today you will get clean with my help and no one else's."

Fleur sank back into the water, her eyes glazed with terror. She saw the knowledge in Luce's eyes and would have fainted if Luce had not pulled her hair savagely.

"Ow!" Fleur yelled. Luce yanked her out of the tub and pushed her toward the window, wrapping a towel around her. Then she advanced on Aurore with brush and comb. She was gentler in brushing the blue-black curls than she had been in washing them. When the strands lay glossy and curling around Aurore's shoulders, Luce advanced on Fleur who shrank away from her.

"Fleur's body is different than mine," Aurore said, observing curiously her sister's body when the towel was dropped on the floor.

"You will develop soon child," Luce said, running practiced eyes over her favorite. Already the small breasts were swelling out from her chest. Soon her monthly courses would start and Aurore would be a woman. Hopefully, she would not be as quick to experiment with her body as Fleur had been.

Aurore smiled happily as Marie-Odile brought her gown into the bathroom and spread it over a chair. For once, it was not the eternal pink of her mother's choosing, but a brilliant blue with white lace

127

decorating the bodice. For the first time in her life, she was to wear a gown that fell all the way to the floor. It made her feel very grown up and mature. Fleur's gown was of a lighter blue with a different arrangement of lace around the bodice.

Delphine came into the room and started to arrange Fleur's hair while Luce turned to Aurore. Both heads were braided and threaded with colored ribbons. Then the braids were pinned high on their heads and small tendrils of hair were brought down to curl around their ears. Then they were put into chemises and crinolines. White silk stockings were rolled up their slim legs and secured with satin garters. Dainty kid slippers were laced around their ankles and finally the gowns were dropped over their heads to settle over their modest hoops. Aurore's eyes kept straying toward the mirror. She could not help but watch herself as she twirled around and watched the billowing folds flow around her and settle back around her ankles. She did not feel like a child, but like a woman.

"You must act modestly today," Luce warned her. "You are a lady and a de Champlain. If you disgrace your family, I myself will take a willow stick to your back. Is that understood?"

Aurore hung her head subdued. She glanced fearfully at Luce, knowing full well she meant every word. Aurore nodded and Luce smiled. Luce kissed her lightly and then pushed her towards the door. Already the sounds of carriage wheels on the drive sounded throughout the house.

"Marget?" Renault said to the bundle under the blanket. "I wish to speak to you. Won't you come out and see me?"

The bundle stirred and Marget peeked out at her father. Her eyes were red-rimmed with unshed tears. Her face was puffy with sorrow.

"Tears are unbecoming," he said oddly moved by the sadness in her face. "Benoit will not mistreat you. I will not permit it."

"Even fathers have limits, Papa." she responded. "If he wishes to mistreat me, he will do so and you will be unable to interfere."

"Such a lack of faith in me, child. I am sorely grieved."

Marget turned her head away. "Papa, I am more sorely grieved that you force me into a marriage I do not want."

"I have said before, child, the matter is ended," Renault said more severely than he intended. The unshed tears spilled over her cheeks and trickled down her face and neck. "Look, I have brought you a gift to wear at your wedding."

He held out a long slender box. When she did not take it, he sat down on the bed, snapping it open to reveal a necklace of pearls. He waited for her approval, but she looked at him with such pain that he turned away.

"Did you think to buy my acceptance, Papa, with this gift?" she asked softly. "I will wear it, but it does nothing to ease the loathing I feel for what you are doing to me. The slaves in the field have more freedom in choosing their mates than I. You say you do not believe in slavery, yet you have sold me as easily as you would any slave."

"I did it for you, Marget."

"You did it for yourself, Papa, and the honor of

your family. My feelings were never discussed." She pulled the blanket over her head and slid down under it, curling her body into a ball. Renault sat staring at her still holding out the box of pearls. He stood and walked to the dresser to lay the open box where she would see it. He left the room, heavily. He had arranged this match for his daughter for her own good. No child of his would languish in a convent beating her chest and punishing herself for thousands of imagined sins. He would force Marget to live in the world he understood. He forgot his daughter as Persia announced the first guests. He hurried down the stairs to greet them.

Marie-Odile thought she looked exceptionally well in the mulberry striped silk. It was plainly designed to show off the elaborateness of the diamonds about her throat and in her ears. She looked at herself critically knowing that she looked truly elegant. She looked cool and calm, no one was to know that her palms were sticky with sweat and perspiration trickled down the insides of her thighs. She reached for some powder and pulling up her skirts, ran the puff over her thighs. she looked at herself again, thinking no one would know how nervous and tense she was. She patted her hair and tucked a single magnolia blosson into her tightly woven chignon. She took it out and replaced it with a spray of carnations. She took the carnations out deciding she looked more mature without the flowers. She tugged her gown into position, then turned around and left the room heading for Marget.

A tub had been wheeled into Marget's room though Marget's bath was long over. It had not yet been removed. Marget sat at her dressing table dressed only in a robe while Luce combed her hair and arranged it. Then she helped her into her chemise and crinolines.

"Why did you ever let yourself get so tanned?" Marie-Odile sighed in frustration though she had to admit the tan was very attractive on her daughter. Marget stood and allowed her mother to drop her gown over her head, then Luce fastened it. "It looks much better than I expected." Marie-Odile commented as she pulled the skirt into becoming folds over the wide hoop. "You look enchanting, Marget. Your groom will think you the most beautiful woman here."

Marget stood unresisting as Luce and her Maman fussed over her. If truth be known, she would have preferred to crawl back into her bed and pull the blankets over her head. In a few short hours she would be Madame Marguerite de Ville. She would then take up her duties as hostess and mistress to a large plantation. There would be no one to rely on but herself.

Luce skillfully arranged the flowers from the greenhouse in Marget's hair. The ribbons and the flowers made Marget look so beautiful, Luce's breath caught in her throat. She turned the girl toward the mirror, but Marget's eyes were dull and unseeing.

"It will be over soon, chèrie," Luce whispered.

Marget said nothing.

"I do think the forget-me-nots around the neck are a perfect touch. What do you think, Luce?"

"They are perfect, Madame," Luce said. She wished Marget would show some sign of life. She looked as though she were going to her death.

"Sit down, Marget. Carefully. Do not wrinkle your

131

gown. Wait here. I will call you when it is time."
Marie-Odile pecked her daughter lightly on the cheek
and left the room. Luce sat down next to Marget,
preparing to share the vigil with her.

Marie-Odile dearly loved a party. She moved
among her guests, her wide-hooped skirts rustling im-
portantly. She was pleased to note that Aurore was on
her best behaviour for a change, and Fleur was equally well-mannered. Marie-Odile laughed and chattered
as she greeted the guests. Maids were assigned to
watch over small children. Grooms hurried forward to
lead horses and carriages around to the stable. Those
people invited to spend the night were steered towards
their rooms. Delphine passed by with Therese tod-
dling along next to her, her hand securely grasped in
the hand of her maid's.

"When are we to see the bride?" Bella Moore asked.
Her eyes moved over the crowd looking for the tall,
blond head of Gayle Courtland. She was disappointed, but then she saw Michael Slaughter hovering
over Fleur de Champlain. Bella moved purposely forward and engagingly disentangled the young man
from the child and walked him away.

Fleur wanted to shout angrily at Bella Moore. She
had been enjoying the flowery flirtations of Michael
Slaughter.

"The ceremony starts at eleven," Marie-Odile told
Mr. and Mrs. Moore. They nodded and drifted away,
following the distinct laughter of their daughter.

Gayle Courtland bowed over her hand. He introduced his sister-in-law to Marie-Odile, then left
them together. He walked into the house, carefully
avoiding Bella Moore. In the study he joined the knot

of men gathering around the bar, whiskey glasses in one hand and aromatic cigars in the other.

Marie-Odile disliked Fay Courtland immediately. Fay said all the right words in the right tone of voice, but Marie-Odile could not help noticing the bold looks she tossed at the men. Daniel Niven approached and was promptly snared by Fay. He was three years younger than Fay with ginger shaded hair and freckles over a pug nose. But he was wealthy in the right amount to suit her. She walked off with him to Marie-Odile's relief.

Monique de Ville arrived in a handsome new carriage with Benoit in tow. She stepped out of the carriage bending too low and revealing too much of her bosom. Marie-Odile gasped, more upset as Monique righted herself to show a bodice much too low and revealing. The rosy tips of her breasts were not only partially visible by the low bodice, but were also fully outlined by the clinging silk of her bright red silk. She wore no chemise and had even dispensed with a wide hoop, preferring several petticoats that did little to hide the long, sensuous line of her hips. Marie-Odile came close to asking Monique to leave. Her gown was in no way suitable for a wedding.

Renault walked up to greet Monique, his eyes flickering over her and showing acute distaste. He looked at his wife in her prim gown of elegant simplicity. He decided it was much more attractive and subtly inviting than Monique's. He reached over a chair and borrowed a white lace shawl from a passing woman and slipped it around Monique's shoulders.

"Your gown is very indiscreet," he murmured to her.

"I wore it especially to please you," she whispered. "Don't you like it?"

"It is inappropriate for so solemn a ceremony as our children's wedding. Wear the shawl. I will find you another shawl shortly, and you may return this one to Miss James."

"But . . ." Monique darted angry eyes at him.

"And pray tell me where you found your new carriage?" he asked, studying the gleaming new vehicle with its polished silver trim. It also sported two perfectly matched black geldings.

"I purchased it," Monique answered. She dimpled at Renault coquettishly. "You will be receiving the bill tomorrow."

Renault felt an uncontrollable impulse to thrash her. First she shows up in a gown unsuitable for the occasion and then has the effrontery to sport a new carriage and team. He supposed he would also get the bill for the gown in a couple of days, as well. He sighed inwardly and turned his attention to his future son-in-law who gazed at him hazily. It didn't take more than a second to realize that Benoit de Ville was drunk. He swayed against Renault who grasped him tightly under the arm and led him firmly into the house. Silently, Renault cursed both Monique and her son, seriously thinking of canceling the wedding. But the thought of Grandeville being in his control stopped him. He propelled his future son-in-law toward the kitchens, turning him over to a footman with instructions to sober him up as quickly as possible.

The young footman was a freedman in Renault's employ. On more than one occasion he had been commissioned to sober up a guest of his employer. He looked at Benoit with relish, steering him to the nearest unoccupied bedchamber and forcefully ministering to him.

Renault walked into his study and found himself downing a glass of wine. He had a second to fortify himself, then returned to the lawn to help his wife greet their guests.

The lawn was filled to overflowing. Many people had come from as far away as New Orleans while most others were friends and neighbors. A riverboat stopped at the landing and off-loaded a large party. A group of children ran to the levee and waved at the remaining passengers who cheerfully waved back. Governesses, nurses and maids ran after their charges to see that they did not fall into the river.

Marie-Odile found Aurore and Fleur, dragged them into the house and sent them up for a last minute wash. She cornered a maid and sent her along to make sure they washed properly. By eleven o'clock, the guests were settling down in the rows of chairs in front of the makeshift altar. Pere Buiron arrived and was ushered into the house to the room set aside for his use.

First there would be a Mass, then the wedding ceremony. Afterward, the guests would eat at the long tables set up under the shade of the towering oak trees. During the heat of the afternoon, the women would be invited to retire to the nineteen guest chambers to rest. Then there would be an early buffet followed by the grand ball and supper at midnight. Those guests who had come the furthest would stay the night at St. Angele and return to their homes in

135

the morning.

Marget watched the bustle of the crowd with disinterest. She was hot and sticky as the morning cool evaporated. For weeks she had dreaded this day, now she wished it over. She waved at Aurore who waved frantically from the lawn. She saw Fleur flirting busily with a reed-thin boy a few years older than she. He followed her about like a puppy on a leash. Even from this distance, Marget could see that her sister was treating the boy cruelly. It saddened her. She turned away from the window to find a maid arriving with a cool pitcher of water and Luce advancing on her with a wet cloth.

"It's nearly time," Luce said. She bathed Marget's face and neck. The cloth was cool and refreshing. She adjusted the billowing gown, fluffing up the lace and pulling the folds into place. She poured scent on a handkerchief and touched Marget's pulse points before pushing it down her bodice where it continued to give off delicate wafts of scent. "You look lovely, Marget."

"Thank you, Luce." She stood on tiptoe to kiss her old nurse, feeling already lost with the ending of their relationship. From now on Marget would be Madame de Ville to Luce.

"It's nearly time," Marie-Odile said walking into the room. She looked flushed and happy. "Aurore is dirty and tore a flounce on her gown."

"I didn't tear it, Maman," Aurore protested, following her mother into the room.

"I told you to go to your room and wash," Marie-Odile began angrily.

"I didn't tear my gown, Maman. Please don't be

angry. This ugly little boy stepped on my hem because I wouldn't play tag with him. He was very mean, Maman. I'm sorry, truly I am. I tried to be a lady so you would be proud."

The anger drained away from Marie-Odile's face. She hugged her daughter.

"It's all right," she said, seeing the tears in Aurore's eyes. "I didn't mean to be angry. Luce will fix it for you. Now go to your room and wash. Your hands are dirty and there is a smudge on your cheek."

Within minutes the small party was ready. Marie-Odile gave them all one last critical glance, then hurried downstairs to find her husband and give the order to start.

"Where do you stand, Renault?" Marcus Slaughter demanded. He was a big man. In his youth he had been trim and muscular, but the years had turned his bulging muscles to bulging fat. The elegant cut of his clothes shouted his prosperity, but could not hide the rolls of excess which tipped over his waist. He always felt out of place among those men, slimmer and more elegant. He tried to make up for his lack of equality with a booming laugh and jovial good humor. Among all else, the Creoles appreciated good humor, and Renault was no exception. He had invited Marcus Slaughter because of that and because he was Renault's closest neighbor. Marcus liked Renault, though he had no clear idea of how Renault felt about him.

Renault was completely indifferent. He admired his neighbor because of his business abilities even if he did not admire his profession. Marcus Slaughter was a

137

breeder, one of those men whose business grew as less and less slaves were imported from Africa. With unusual shrewdness, Marcus recognized that eventually governments would ban the importation of slaves. Denmark had been the first country to do so in 1792. The United States and England followed with their own ban in 1807. In 1845, the practice was nearly abandoned. But by then, Marcus had built a solid business of breeding his own slaves and selling them at higher and higher profits. His stable consisted of two hundred prime breeding bucks and four hundred and thirty-two women. There were countless children usually sold off in their early teens. The more promising he educated, though most were sold as field hands. He boasted the finest specimens in Louisiana and often invited his many male friends to come and watch the breeding whenever they felt the need to observe something different. Marcus had built himself a fine business. There wasn't a plantation in the state who had not bought slaves from him at one time or another. If one of his slaves had slightly lighter skin than another, who cared. A man had to have his pleasures and with four hundred and thirty-two wenches to choose from, Marcus had been indulging his pleasures for nearly fifty years. Now in his mid-seventies, he called for a woman less and less often, but he still indulged as did his son, and four grandsons. That was the privilege of being the owner and having an unlimited choice.

"With the South," Renault replied. He would always be a southerner.

"Even on the question of slavery," Marcus persisted. Everyone in the room knew Renault kept no slaves on

138

any of his three plantations. Every man disapproved of his actions and condemned him for it without understanding the economics of it.

Renault looked around the room at faces friendly, eager, or hostile. They had no compunction of partaking of his hospitality while hating him. Ten years ago, the questions Marcus raised would never have been asked. Despite his business actions, Renault would never have been questioned. But slavery was an emotional issue, growing more and more heated with each succeeding day. The dividing lines were sharply drawn, and these men were judging him.

Renault surveyed them lazily. Except for him and Marcus Slaughter, there was not one man in the room who wasn't up to his ears in debt. That was the advantage slavery passed on to them. They lived from one crop to the next, praying for a good year, devastated when there was a failure. For money, they mortgaged next year's crop before it ever went in the ground. Renault wanted to make them understand that he had no slaves because he was a businessman. He did not gamble on next year's harvest, nor did he sink his profits into human flesh. Slavery was an unprofitable business. When a crop failed, a man with slaves was still responsible for them. Freed, they were only responsible for themselves.

"Most of you men have known me for over twenty years. Have I ever shown the least disloyalty to the South?"

"You freed the niggers you inherited from your wife's estate when her parents died. You educated them, gave them land, and paid them when they worked for you." John Wright was fiftyish and balding. Dissipation showed in the curled droop to his mouth and in the lines scoring his forehead. It was barely noon and already he was drunk, his large hands ready to pinch any maid who came within his reach. Wine had splotched down the front of his frilled shirt and his dark gray suit was none too clean.

"It was strictly for business reasons," Renault said mildly. He had been explaining himself for twenty years. "I simply could not afford to support all those extra people. Yes, I freed them and gave them the means to support themselves, but I benefited from the action, as well."

A few men stirred uneasily. It was easy to see that Renault was a wealthy man. In his own closed circle of Creole friends, he was highly respected. Any man knew that in times of deep trouble, they could go to him for a loan. He was more fair than any bank and he cultivated their trust. He did all this not for any feelings of friendship, but because these men all had crops to be transported downriver and Renault had the steamboats to transport those crops. When the cargoes reached New Orleans, they were transferred to one of the ocean going vessels Renault also owned to be distributed to various foreign ports where he sold it and then brought back the luxuries his customers demanded. He would do nothing to endanger the delicate relationship he enjoyed with these men.

"We know you stand with the South, Renault," Jean Mahieu said softly. He was young and inclined toward idealism, but his sincerity broke the tension in the room.

Suddenly everyone was laughing and joking, refilling their empty glasses and lighting up fresh cigars.

They slapped each other on the back, their spirits rising with the consumption of liquor. Over their heads, Renault saw his wife peer into the room, anxiously searching for him. Their eyes met and she nodded briefly.

"Gentlemen! Gentlemen!" Renault called. "Shall we join our ladies on the lawn. The time has come for me to give the bride away."

Ten

On July 26, 1860, Marguerite Marie-Anne de Champlain became the unwilling wife of Benoit Edmund de Ville. Benoit swayed drunkenly during the entire Mass and the brief ceremony that followed it. In order to build up his courage, he had consumed more liquor than he was able to hold. Despite the ministrations of the footman assigned to sober him up, he was still very, very drunk. A few times he grabbed at Marget to keep from falling. Once he grabbed her gown and ripped a flounce of lace.

Marget was embarrassed beyond tears when Benoít slurred his words and could not find the proper finger to place the diamond and ruby encrusted band he presented to her to seal the ceremony. With uncharacteristic boldness, she took the ring out of his hand and placed it securely on her finger. She ignored the astonished gasps of the guests and the disapproving glare of Pere Buiron. When the organ struck up the chords of the closing hymn, she grasped her new husband firmly under the arm and led him down the aisle and across the lawn toward the arbor erected for them for the greeting of their guests. Midway across the lawn, Benoit stumbled on the hem of her gown. She heard an ominous rip, but managed to ignore it.

With head held high, she entered the arbor and turned around to be kissed by her parents, then congratulated by each passing guest. She felt Luce enter the arbor and kneel down next to her, her nimble fingers repairing the damage Benoit had wreaked on her gown.

When the long line was ended, they all sat down at the long damask covered tables to be served their dinner by a horde of grey clad servants. Persia and Luce oversaw the serving of the meal and then the cleanup when the meal was completed. Marie-Odile conducted the ladies to the bedrooms for their afternoon rests. Maids divested them of their morning gowns and hung them up before drawing forth the elaborate ballgowns to be donned for the evening. The women lounged in robes or chemises, their great crinolines and hoops relegated to distant corners. They laughed and chatted, catching up on gossip and news while eating sweets and drinking lemonade and wine punch.

Marie-Odile lay on the huge canopied bed in her darkened bedchamber. She had discarded all her clothes for a short-sleeved peignoir of embroidered lawn. It was a touch too sheer for comfort, for she daringly wore no nightdress under it, but she knew Renault to be safely ensconced with his male guests in the study drinking away the afternoon.

The door opened. There were light steps across the floor. Marie-Odile sighed. At the feel of warm hands on her breasts, her eyes flew open.

"We have guests, Renault," she said as he undid the sash about her waist. "You must return to them, they will wonder."

"Let them wonder," he replied, pushing the robe

off her shoulders.

"But it is day!" she protested. His lips covered hers, then moved down her neck nibbling and biting. Her body responded as it always did. He opened her robe fully and sat back to smile at her, his eyes roaming up her legs and chest. She flamed crimson. Would she never get used to this. She tried to cover herself, but he pushed her hands away.

Renault undressed, tossing his clothes carelessly over a chair. Marie-Odile started to protest, but he lay down next to her, drawing her lips to his. His hands moved over her, teasing her into throaty moans. Never once in their sixteen years of marriage would he allow her to shelter herself in passive indifference. He expected her to respond, nursing her into a passion which frightened and shamed her. She would have made a terrible nun, Renault thought in wry amusement. Even if she did not recognize the natural passion in her, he did. For sixteen years he had nurtured her until their lovemaking left them both satisfied. When would she recognize that she was a very passionate woman. His lips teased each part of her body until she groaned with desire, pulling him to her demanding that he satisfy her.

Is this what the rest of her life held, Marget asked herself. Was she to spend the rest of her days lying in bed next to a drunken, snoring husband. She hated him. She hated him with an intensity that frightened her. She thought she should pray for forgiveness for her hate, but how could God forgive her today when tomorrow she would still feel the same.

She edged away from Benoit, drawing her robe around her as she walked across the room to the window. She opened them to clear the room of whiskey fumes and vomit. Then she walked to her dressing table and poured water into a basin to sponge away the smell of Benoit on her body. She winced uncomfortably as the cloth went over the dark blue bruises already showing on her body. One bruise high on her neck would need Luce to make it invisible for the evening's entertainment.

She had been nearly asleep when Benoit stormed into the room, pouncing on her. Her cry of fear had been muffled while he pulled away her chemise and grabbed at her. Then he collapsed on the bed gagging with the sickness he had tried to hold down during the ceremony. Marget had grabbed a basin and held it under his face while he vomited into it. His sickness did not decrease his ardor. As she emptied the basin into the chamber pot, he tore off his clothes and was on her before she could get away.

Marget had been stunned. All her life she had been taught to respect men and their authority. Now she felt her respect for him draining away. No man who understood the nature of womanhood would have treated her as her new husband just did. Rape was not a word in her vocabulary.

Her tortured muscles suddenly collapsed. She stumbled to the lounge and fell on it, falling asleep instantly.

John Miles sat in his office, a fat cigar held between his lips. He wore dark trousers and a white shirt open at the throat. His exposed skin was tanned from many hours overseeing the vast St. Angele plantation. He considered himself an overseer, not a manager. He preferred slaves, not freed men. He knew and understood slaves. He glanced at the long black whip coiled over a nail next to the open door. He was proud of his prowess with it. He knew how to make it sing for him. He knew how to curl it delicately around black flesh without breaking the skin while administering the maximum amount of pain. Badly scarred slaves didn't bring much on the block. Scarred backs shouted rebellious slaves. No one wanted a troublesome nigger. John Miles was an expert on protecting his masters' investment.

He puffed contentedly on the cigar. It was rich in aroma, firm in texture, and filched from Renault de Champlain's office. Miles amused himself by blowing rings into the air before he tired of it. There was little to amuse him today since the field niggers had been given the day off to celebrate the master's daughter's wedding. John did not approve of that action. Renault was too soft on his niggers. If John Miles had his way, they would all be working today. He swiveled in his chair to look out the window. His office was situated so that he could just barely see the lawn. Most everyone had gone inside, the women to rest and the men to drink. He could see the servents cleaning the tables and taking them down. They moved languidly in the afternoon heat.

A young black girl scooted across the lawn. He recognized Jewel, brought over from Grey Lawns to attend Miss Fay, and given a few hours freedom to play with Miss Aurore while her mistress slept away the afternoon. John Miles wondered if she really were sleeping. Before her marriage to Grant Courtland, Miles had been overseer on the plantation next to her daddy's. He had sampled the hot, flowing passion concealed under her voluminous skirts. That was a mighty pleasing woman. Miles smiled. He remembered the nights she had sneaked away from her daddy to spend a few hours in his cabin learning some mighty pleasant things. She had been a willing learner.

Jewel drew closer. Her young laughter mingled with the childish tones of Aurore. White skin against dark, black hair against deep brown. Miles admired the way her dress stretched across her budding chest. He liked the way she walked, long and fluid like a man.

"Let's go to the pond and skip rocks across it," Aurore suggested. "We could take off our shoes and stockings and go wading."

"Yes, lets," Jewel agreed happily. A few hours freedom from the imperious demands of Miss Fay were like heaven to her. She took Aurore's hand and skipped with her into the woods.

Jewel was going to be a tall girl, Miles observed. He liked tall girls. He thought of the cook's daughter, Sylvie. She was tall and slim with skin the color of ebony. She was good in bed, too, now that Miles had shown her who was master. She was willing because he threatened to turn her whole family off the plantation if she didn't do as he told her. Thinking of Sylvie and watching the two girls skip past him made his belly ache with desire. It took great effort to turn his thoughts away from the pretty Sylvie and the childish Jewel and return to his work. He went back to the open ledger on his desk. On it was a sheaf of papers. On each paper was a tally. He carefully counted each tally, setting the figure at the bottom of the sheet and

147

deducting five for himself. He entered the lesser number in the ledger and wrote the deducted number in a small book on the edge of his desk. Renault de Champlain would never know if his supplies were short, or his crops a little less than normal. If he should notice, Miles could always say the niggers were cheating him. Miles grinned. He did not consider cheating his employer cheating, but rather his dues for a job well done. After all, he was allowed his pound of flesh and if he couldn't take it out of the slaves, he would take it away from his employer.

He added his personal totals, nodding his head in satisfaction. The day would come when he would not have to work for snobs like Renault de Champlain. He'd be his own boss on his own plantation with all the slaves he needed to do the work and see to his personal needs. He thought fleetingly of Jewel and Aurore. He did like little girls. He thought he might sample Jewel later, but it was a pity Aurore was beyond him. She had such beautiful black hair.

Jewel and Aurore moved silently through the forest. Occasionally Jewel would point out a squirrel on a branch, or a raccoon disappearing through the underbrush. Jewel knew a lot about the forest creatures. A knowledge she delighted imparting to Aurore. They came to a patch of ground broken by bright splotches of sun. They giggled as they jumped from one patch to the next, careful not to step on the shadows. It was a game they had thought up. Aurore seldom won. Her legs were not as long as her friend's. Jewel affectionately let her win as they approached the clearing.

They heard muffled laughter. They stopped, looked at each other curiously. The laughter sounded again.

Silently they approached the clearing, stooping down behind a bush and peering around it.

Jewel was the first to see them. They lay in the shade, their clothes strewn around them on the grass. Her eyes widened. She backed up trying to drag Aurore back from the scene in front of them. Aurore jerked away, peering curiously around Jewel. She gazed, puzzled, at her sister, Fleur, who lay beneath the new blacksmith, Noble. Her pale legs were spread and he lay between them, his dark haunches rising and falling rythmically. They laughed and grunted.

Jewel grabbed Aurore and pulled her away from the clearing. She went unresisting, looking back curiously.

"Fleur had no clothes on," Aurore said in a low voice. She frowned at Jewel. "Why? What was she doing?"

"They's playin'," Jewel said. She wondered if she should explain what the two lovers had been doing. She had grown up with a clear understanding of sex, but Aurore had been carefully shielded.

"Why was she playing with Noble?" Aurore was confused. The image of her sister on the ground with her legs wrapped around the huge Negro danced before her eyes. "He's a man and Fleur is a little girl. Men don't play with little girls."

"You're friends with Marse Gayle," Jewel said. "He's a man and you're a little girl."

"We only play cards," Aurore said, "and he lets me visit my fawn. Fleur had no clothes on." She tried to understand the complexities of what she had seen, but she was young and innocent. Unbidden, the picture of a naked woman hanging over the bar on the *Sophie Sutter* entered her mind. There was a connection with that picture and with Fleur and Noble playing. She thought of Gayle telling her how men liked looking at undressed women. Did Fleur take her clothes off so that Noble could look at her?

"Listen, Miss Aurore," Jewel stopped suddenly. Aurore bumped into her. "Can you keep a secret?"

"Of course I can," Aurore replied haughtily.

"Don't say anything about what you seen Miss Fleur doing. It's her secret and we got no right to tell on her. Do you understand?"

"I'll keep her secret for her," Aurore promised, feeling strangely frightened. "I won't tattle. I promise."

Jewel was relieved. She led Aurore out of the forest, starting a game of tag. Aurore allowed herself to be manipulated into forgetting, but the picture of her sister and Noble would remain with her always.

Jewel was still troubled when she left Aurore in Luce's care. She saw Gayle standing on the lawn with a group of men. She went to him standing silently. After awhile the men drifted away leaving him behind.

"What is on your mind, Jewel?" he asked sensing her unease.

"You tole me to watch out for Miss Aurore," Jewel said, raising worried eyes to her master. In them was love and devotion for both him and her young friend.

"I told you that," he said gravely. "Can you tell me what is wrong?"

Jewel hesitated, then launched into a description of the scene she and Aurore had witnessed at the pond. Then she painstakingly repeated their later conversation. Gayle listened, frowning.

"Did Miss Aurore know what her sister was doing?"

150

"No, sir," Jewel said. "And I didn't tell her. She promised to keep it secret."

"Thank you for telling me," he said. He looked across the lawn to see Fleur skillfully merging with a group of children playing blind man's bluff. "You go to Miss Fay. She'll be up soon and needing you. I'll take care of Miss Aurore."

Jewel curtsied and ran to the house.

Gayle continued to watch Fleur. Sensing his stare, she looked up and waved. He turned away. He found he could not look at her without feeling repulsion. He headed toward the house, hearing the laughter of the men in the study. He felt no inclination to join them. Finally he sat down on a chair in the drawing room, staring out over the lawn with the river winding in the distance. He had to do something, he thought, something that would set to rest the turbulent thought in Aurore's head. He did not doubt they were there. Aurore was not a person to forget a worrying thought. When he decided what to do, relief spread over him. He suddenly felt like company again, and got up to join the men.

The buffet supper was set out in the long dining room adjoining the ballroom. In their best finery, the ladies wandered down as the heat of the afternoon waned to find their husbands and sit in the cool garden until supper was announced. When they finished eating, the five piece orchestra struck a note and the ball was formally started. Renault led his wife onto the polished marble floor twirling her around and around in a stately waltz. Soon other couples joined them, and the floor was crowded with people.

A sober Benoit held his new wife tightly. She had discarded her wedding gown for another gown of pale lavender. Regally she ignored the twittering stares of the other women. Let them think what they pleased, she told herself. What they thought was hardly flattering. Benoit complimented her on her attire, but she coolly ignored him. He whirled her around for a turn searching her face. Under the pale sheen of the make-up on her neck, he could see the faintly blurred edges of the bruise he had inflicted on her. There were other bruises, as well.

"I want to apologize for hurting you this afternoon," he said stumbling over his words charmingly. He assumed a look of innocence and guile thinking how easily other women were swayed by his enchanting manner.

Marget raised cold eyes to him, remaining silent.

"How was I to know you were still virgin," he said suddenly. She seemed to look straight through him. He felt the first shiver of uneasiness. His apology was going wrong. He was not influenced by his winsome charm.

"I was until this afternoon," she said in frigid tones. "Most women are who marry for the first time."

"None of the ones I knew were ever virgins." He had not meant to hurt her. It was too late to relive the afternoon, but there was no reason not to start over. "I am truly sorry." He hung his head in despair, peeking at her from the corners of his eyes. The waltz ended. She stopped so suddenly that he danced several steps beyond her. When he turned she had disappeared.

Aurore stood at the edge of the dance floor watching the people twirling around. She had been given permission to remain up for one whole hour past her bedtime to watch the dancing and to dance a few of the country sets. She had also been given permission to dance one waltz with Gayle because he had petitioned her mother nicely. Fleur had also been given permission to stay up. Several of the other children had gathered in a corner forming their own sets, Fleur danced in the middle on light feet. Aurore watched her still troubled over the afternoon scene. Aurore's father claimed her for a waltz, admiring the lightness of her feet. She blushed, thanking him prettily when the dance was over and going to stand by a pillar. She watched a country set, then a quadrille before another waltz was announced and Gayle approached her.

"May I have this dance, Mademoiselle Aurore?" he asked gallantly. He bowed over her hand and drew her out onto the floor. He was so tall and she was so little. People looked at them curiously. Heads turned, but faces reflected no disapproval of the man and child who looked as though they belonged to each other. A few women whispered behind their fans at the unusualness of it, but even they offered no censure over the oddly matched couple.

Fay Courtland stood on the side of the room staring angrily at Gayle. How could he dance with that child and treat her as though she were the person he was madly in love with. Her foot tapped impatiently as they glided past her. Aurore's face was animated and happy. Gayle seemed to glow with a contentment that infuriated Fay. Marcus Slaughter edged close to her asking for a dance. She curtly refused him.

"You are a fine dancer, madam," he coaxed. His

eyes were drawn openly to the low neck of her sage green gown. She shrugged delicately, one pink-tipped breast briefly revealed by her gesture. She could not picture herself waltzing with this grossly fat man. "If you do not wish to dance, may I take you for a walk in the garden? It is warm in here and the garden is cool."

She accepted, taking his arm and allowing him to escort her through the open door. There were other couples in the garden strolling along the paths and scurrying into dark arbors.

"It is much cooler out here," Fay said, fanning herself briskly and watching Marcus out of the corner of her eye. He repelled her, yet attracted her. He led her down a shadowed path deeper and deeper into the garden until the strains of the music were distant and muted. He guided her to a dark arbor and settled her on a stone bench, sitting heavily next to her.

"Your gown, madam, is an excellent choice for you," he said, running a pudgy hand up and down her arm. She shivered.

"Thank you, sir," she said archly, flirting boldly. "This has always been a good color for me."

His hand wandered to the neck of her gown, moving down the warm flesh of her bosom. His thumb caressed her lightly through the silk. She sighed. His other hand reached behind her for her buttons, undoing them with a rapidity that surprised her. The bodice of her gown fell away freeing her to his touch.

"Ah, beautiful," he cried softly. He took each round breast and fingered them into erectness. Fay gasped. "Incredibly beautiful."

Fay was melting. She moaned, pushing her body into his. Never had her husband been able to rouse

154

such intense feelings in her. There was a burning in her, a fire that spread from her breasts to the inner softness of her thighs.

"You must know, madam, my wife has been dead for twenty years." He said breathing hoarsely in her ear.

"Do not tell me you lack feminine companionship," Fay said, her laughter a soft tinkle in the secluded arbor. "You have over four hundred black wenches to choose from."

"That I have, but none stir my blood the way you do." He pushed her away slightly, one hand reaching for her skirts. He pulled them up searching for the soft flesh hidden under them. She gasped when he found the innermost part of her that blazed with passion. He pushed her pantalets down around her thighs while this thick fingers sought her. She cried out slightly. Fay wondered what it would be like making love to him. His enormous weight was a disadvantage, but there were ways.

"How lovely you are, madam," he moved against, guiding her hand to his sensitive throbbing manhood.

"You mean how lovely I feel," she whispered huskily.

She writhed and groaned in his arms while her fingers pleasured him at the same time his fingers pleasured her. They both reached their climax at the same time, falling back breathing heavily. When they were rested, he helped her to dress, neatly buttoning her bodice with the expertise of a maid.

"My home is a bachelor establishment," Marcus said when they had left the arbor and reappeared along the better lighted paths. "My wife has been

155

dead for twenty years and my daughter-in-law died five years ago. My home could use a woman's touch."

"Are you asking me to marry you?" Fay asked, shaken. Besides Renault de Champlain, this man was one of the richest in the state. She thought of debt ridden Grey Lawns and the poverty she had endured after she thought she had been marrying into a wealthy family. She hungered for riches.

"If you would have me," he said solemnly. "I am fifty years older than you are. My needs are few. I would be willing to settle a handsome sum of money on you that would be totally yours when I die. I'm seventy-four, madam, and haven't long to live. But when I go, I shall make you a very rich woman if you would marry me."

"You say your needs are few. I am young, yet, my needs are great. I cannot be content with a few fingerings and an occasional coupling whenever you can find the strength." Fay replied.

"I have a lusty son and four lusty grandsons," Marcus said. "We've shared women before. They'll stand in line outside your door until you are satisfied with yourself. If you do not wish my son or grandsons, I have two hundred black bucks who like to service wenches black or white."

"Oh!" Fay's breath caught in her throat. In all the years she had been sexually active she had never had a black lover. She had thought about it, but never had the courage to try. She stared at Marcus Slaughter, her mind turning his words over and over again. A smile lit her face when she realized she would be rich and could have any man she craved. She pressed her body to his. "It does look like there's goin' to be another weddin'," she drawled.

He took her back into the ballroom leaving her in the arms of her next partner. Then he went to look for his son and tell him of their good fortune.

Aurore listened unhappily to the closing strains of the waltz. Her one hour was nearly over. She was loathe to see it end. She thrilled in dancing with Gayle. His masculinity excited her in a way she did not understand. She smiled at him her eyes soft with love.

"Thank you, sir. It was the most wonderful dance I have ever had," she said. She curtsied formally. He bowed.

"Will you come to Grey Lawns tomorrow?"

"Yes," she answered. She saw Luce out of the corners of her eyes. She beckoned to Aurore, but Aurore did not want to leave Gayle and the feeling of heaven she felt in his arms.

"Someday," he said, tilting her face up to his and planting a light kiss on her lips, "you'll be a woman. I hope you will reserve a waltz for me then."

Luce approached and took Aurore. She smiled at Gayle who strolled away. He stopped to talk to Bella Moore and Aurore felt the stirrings of jealousy in her. After all, she was still a little girl.

"I want to hurry up and grow into a woman, Luce," she said impatiently as they walked down long deserted halls to her bedchamber.

"Why?" Fleur asked crossly. Young Michael Slaughter had just asked her for a walk in the garden when Luce appeared to take her to bed. She had been horribly embarrassed at being shown up as a little girl in front of a man who was nearly twenty. As she

157

walked past him, he had whispered for her to meet him at the deserted cabin that bordered their properties. Fleur had been unable to answer, but the look she had thrown him seemed to satisfy him. He had smiled briefly as Luce led her away.

"Because I want to grow up fast," Aurore replied. She was tired. She yawned widely. "I'm tired of being little. You have to be old and grown to have fun."

"You'll grow up soon enough," Luce said gently. She was becoming tired of the child's constant chatter about growing. She opened the door to Aurore's room and pushed her inside. Delphine approached from the hall to take Fleur.

"Make me a charm, please, Luce!" Aurore pleaded sleepily. Luce shook her head as she pulled the blankets over the child.

"Not tonight," Luce said softly, but Aurore was already asleep. Luce bent over the child and kissed her on the lips, then slipped quietly from the room.

The ball was a great success. Marie-Odile looked around happily at the other dancers feeling great pride swell her bearing. She could not have hoped for a finer wedding and ball. Gayle Courtland saw her self-satisfied smile and commented on it. She blushed prettily, bowing her head. Out of the corner of her eye she saw Renault waltz past with Monique clinging to him. His eyes met his wife's and he smiled. Her own light smile was suddenly tight and strained. She wished Monique would find someone else to chase. It frightened Marie-Odile to see the open desire so apparent on Monique's face when she looked at Renault. The scarlet gown of the morning had been discarded for a stark gown of black satin. It was as low and revealing as the other, but somehow the black changed Monique from corner harlot to high paid courteson. Marie-Odile did not like the disturbing thoughts that chased around and around in her mind. She could not help but wonder if her husband desired Monique as equally as she desired him. The music trailed into silence. Gayle bowed over her hand politely, complimenting her on her wonderful ball, then was replaced by Renault.

"Do I detect jealousy in your eyes, my dear?" he asked teasingly.

She turned her head away.

"Don't be ashamed, my love," he murmured. He expertly maneuvered her through an open door away from the crowd of milling people and into the soothing darkness of the night. "Shall we walk a bit? Would you dally with me in the garden?"

Marie-Odile allowed him to lead her down a shadowed path. When they were out of sight of the house, he pushed her into a dark arbor, pulled her into his arms and kissed her passionately.

"No, Renault," she said, pulling away, "wasn't this afternoon enough?"

"I never get enough of you, my darling," he whispered, his lips pressed against hers. He pulled her deeper into the dark, his hands insistent and demanding.

"We must go back," Marie-Odile protested feebly.

"Later," he whispered. He sat down on the grass, pulling her after him. Monique de Ville was a slut, he thought, comparing her with his wife. There was little excitement in her bold enticement. Renault much

159

preferred the gentle sweetness of his wife. He had enjoyed the encounter with Monique, but it would never be repeated. She was too bold, too suggestive. His arms tightened around Marie-Odile. No one would ever replace her in his affections.

It was a night made for love, Gayle thought as he wandered restlessly around the ballroom. The high chattering voices of the women fell harshly on his ears. He looked at a few of them, speculation in his eyes, but their vapid faces and insipid manners turned him away. He could not ask one of them to walk in the garden with him. Unbidden the picture of bright, vivacious Aurore crowded into his mind. How could he ask any of these women to walk with him when it was her he wanted.

"Mr. Courtland," Bella Moore called, hurrying toward him. "You haven't forgotten our dance, have you?"

"Your pardon, Miss Moore," he said, "I was thinking how close it has become in here and wondering if you would care for a refreshing stroll in the garden instead of a dance."

"Oh, Mr. Courtland," she drawled, snapping her fan open and waving it briskly in front of her face. "You would think me terribly forward if I agreed to go, but it wouldn't be proper. My mama would consider my reputation totally ruined, and my papa would be forced to seek a settlement . . ."

Gayle turned abruptly away from her. She stared after him, her mouth hanging open.

"Dumb Bella," Thomasina Niven hissed. "You should have just gone."

Bella turned on her friend, fury raging in her eyes. "You mind your own business, Thomasina." Then she hurried quickly across the ballroom after Gayle. She couldn't find him anywhere though she searched the ballroom, picture gallery and the brightly lighted lawn in front of the house. She could have stamped her foot in anger, Thomasina was right, she should have just gone.

At midnight, Benoit and Marget departed to the loud farewells of the guests. Marie-Odile could not help noticing the haunting look of dread in her daughter's face. The brand new carriage recently purchased by Monique glided over the drive and stopped at the foot of the stairs. Marie-Odile kissed Marget who resisted the desire to cling to her mother. Then Renault gravely kissed her and shook hands with his new son-in-law and clapped him heartily on the back. Benoit stumbled.

Bella Moore caught the bouquet joyously. She searched fruitlessly for over an hour for Gayle Courtland before Thomasina Niven told her he had left and gone home early. Bella sought out her mother and indulged in a tantrum to which her mother quietly called for their cloaks and hurried her daughter home. Mrs. Moore told Bella over and over again that she would not be allowed to waste herself on a notorious gambler who had nothing to recommend him except his good looks, but Bella stared stonily at her mother who finally gave up with a tired sigh.

It was nearly dawn before the last of the guests departed for their homes. Marie-Odile stood on the veranda feeling wilted and drained. It had been perfect, but tiring. She smiled shyly at her husband who sent her to bed telling her to sleep as long as she wished and promising to see to the departure of their overnight guests.

"How long will Monique de Ville be staying?" Marie-Odile asked.

"Only until Benoit and Marget leave for New Orleans to catch their ship to Nassau," Renault answered. "It would hardly do to have a mother interfering in a honeymoon."

Marie-Odile sighed. She silently walked through the house to her bedchamber to allow herself the luxury of sleep only to be tormented by dreams of her husband bedding Monique de Ville.

Eleven

Aurore was up early. The morning sun had barely risen above the horizon before she was dressed and running out to the stables, her hair flying around her shoulders in a wild tangle of knots. The house was very still. No servants stirred, even Luce did not appear to scold her for not buttoning her jacket correctly. She ran through the ballroom. Persia did not even glance at her as he ordered sleepy-eyed maids through the business of cleaning up. His eyes were red-rimmed and puffy, but he was immaculately dressed as though it was an ordinary day.

The ballroom was a mess. Burned out candles lay in a pile in the middle of the floor waiting to be picked up for reuse in the servants hall. Napkins, smudged with dirt, had been dropped in a pile on a sofa. Punch glasses were on tables and under chairs, some empty, some half-filled. Aurore sipped from one, grimacing at the sharp alcoholic taste. Then she ran back to the dining room to grab some food to stuff into her pockets. She ran out of the house nibbling on a piece of dried ham with fat congealed around the edges. The roll left a greasy smudge of butter on her face and collar, the chocolate eclair left a trail of custard on her cheek, fingers and skirt where she wiped her hands. By the time she reached the stable she had devoured a half-dozen bon-bons leaving her sticky and a target for greedy flies who attacked her en masse.

The stable hands were up and seeing to the comfort of the dozens of extra horses crowded into the stalls. Silas offered to saddle Belle for her, but Aurore declined graciously seeing the load of work he was forced to attend to this morning. She saddled her horse herself knowing Maman would be angry to know her daughter had soiled her hands with manual labor. She led Belle out to the mounting block and slid into the saddle. She adjusted her skirt over the horn and kicked Belle into a swift trot. As her horse turned toward Grey Lawns, Aurore pulled her handkerchief out of her pocket and opened it with relish to view the piece of cake in it. Letting Belle pick her own course, Aurore gulped down the crumbling mess with her fingers leaving sticky tracks on her reins and skirt.

Gayle had never seen such a dirty little girl before. He walked out of the house to stare at Aurore grinning broadly at him as she pulled Belle to a stop. Dust had blown over her face and hands to add another layer to the layers of custard and chocolate. He laughed at her.

"When I invited you to come today, I didn't expect you to arrive at seven in the morning."

"Is that too early?" she asked sliding down from her horse to stand in front of him. She wiped her dirty palms on her skirt adding to the cake, chocolate and custard already there. She had forgotten her gloves, her face was regrettably tanned and her hair had not been combed.

"Have you had breakfast?" he asked viewing the

stains on her skirt and guessing at the foods she had already consumed.

"I had a piece of ham, a roll, an eclair, cake and some bon-bons," she answered brightly.

"Come inside," he ordered. "Mandy!" A plump black woman hurried across the hall.

"Lordy, Miss Aurore!" Mandy cried when she saw the girl. "Who let you go this morning looking like that?"

"Luce wasn't up yet," Aurore explained politely.

"Good heavens, child. Come on along upstairs and we'll clean you up proper. What's this on your skirt? Cake! What you done have for your breakfast?"

"She had a piece of cold ham, a roll, an eclair, cake and candy," Gayle answered, swallowing a chuckle at the woman's stricken face. "Find her something to wear and see what you can do about the gown."

"Yah, suh," Mandy said. She grabbed Aurore's sticky hand and pulled her up the stairs.

An hour later, Aurore descended the stairs dressed in a white cotton shirt and fawn colored breeches that had belonged to Gayle when he had been a boy. The breeches fit her tolerably well, the shirt was a little too large. Her hair had been combed back from her face and tied into a ribbon. She had been bathed and scrubbed until her softly tanned skin glowed with cleanliness.

"Here she is, Marse Gayle," Mandy said, shoving the child into his study. "That's all I could find for her to wear. I hope it's all right."

Gayle looked up from his book to stare at Aurore who danced up to him. She blushed feeling vulnerable and strange in the boy's clothing.

"Thank you, Mandy. Send breakfast in here, please." Mandy left the room quickly. "Come closer and let me see you."

Aurore didn't look like a little girl anymore. Gayle stared at her in astonishment as she walked toward him her hips swaying slightly. They were rounding hips, showing the beginnings of womanhood her childish gowns had not yet revealed. He could see the slight darkening against the shirt and the gentle contours of its lines as it molded itself to her budding breasts. The start of womanhood hidden in full skirts and tight bodices was startlingly visible in boy's clothing.

"You're staring at me," Aurore said, a bright blush crept down her cheeks and neck to disappear in the open collar of her shirt.

"I'm sorry," Gayle said.

"Do you like my clothes?" Aurore twirled around gracefully.

"They're fine. Sit down. Mandy will bring you something more appropriate for breakfast than cold ham and sweets."

"I like these clothes. I bet I can run faster and climb trees better in them than in my old skirts."

Mandy reappeared bearing a huge tray which she set down on a table. She shoved the table in front of Gayle and Aurore then lifted the lid to reveal steaming hot coffee, deliciously fried eggs and hot slices of ham.

"I tried cleaning that old gown of Miss Aurore's," Mandy said as she deftly set plates in front of Aurore and Gayle and poured the coffee. "But most of them stains won't come out."

"Do your best, Mandy. She can hardly go home in what she is wearing so she will have to return home in what she came in."

"Yah, suh!" Mandy replied. She picked up the empty tray and left the room.

"Go on! Eat!" Gayle ordered. He didn't have to tell her twice. In a second she was digging through the pile of food on her plate as though she had not eaten in months. In between bites, she calmly told him of the tree she was planning to climb as soon as she had finished her breakfast.

"Who is that with you, Gayle?" Fay asked as she walked into the room. She looked pale and wan. Her night of dancing had left dark shadows under her eyes and pale hollows in her throat. She also knew she looked exceptionally attractive this way, so she had chosen a deeply frilled gown of indian gauze that fluttered and flounced around her as she walked.

"Aurore," Gayle answered.

"What is that stupid child doing here at eight o'clock in the morning," Fay cried sharply.

"Eating her breakfast."

"What is she wearing? Breeches! Gayle, how could you allow her . . ." Fay was left speechless as Aurore jumped up to show off her new clothes. Then her eyes narrowed as she took in the budding womanhood in the rounded hips and breasts. "It is indecent!" she exploded. "You come here, child, and I'll find you some decent clothes to wear."

"Leave her alone, Fay," Gayle said, a growl starting in his throat.

Fay backed away, gasping. "Look at her! Why you can almost see her bosom through that shirt. No girl can go around dressed like that especially when she is . . . when she is developing." Fay stuttered in fury and horror. "I insist you allow me to find her a proper gown. Where is the gown you came in, child?"

"Mandy's cleaning it. It has cake all over it." Aurore sat down again after pulling up a third chair to the table for Fay to sit in.

"I'll see the gown is cleaned immediately so that you can put it on," Fay said, ignoring the chair and sailing out of the room.

Aurore forgot Fay immediately, but Gayle sat staring at the door. He had just about made up his mind that Fay had to go. He enjoyed using her body though he had no particular fondness for her anymore, but she disliked Aurore and made Aurore's visits impossible.

"Let's hurry," he said. "Then we can be gone before Fay returns."

Aurore bolted down the last scraps on her plate. She gulped down her coffee and was standing and waiting for Gayle at the door as he pushed the table away. She ran ahead of him down the hall and out the front door. At her horse she came to a halt staring at the sidesaddle still on Belle. She looked down at her breeches then up at Gayle as he approached.

"Gayle!" Fay's voice came distinctly from inside the house. "Where are you, Gayle?"

"Up you go, Aurore. We'll trot around to the stable and put a proper saddle on Belle." He tossed her into the saddle and chuckled as she automatically reached out to settle her non-existent skirts around her ankles. She stopped and blushed.

"Toby," Gayle said to the man holding his horse.

"Take a horse and ride over to St. Angele and tell Luce or Persia Miss Aurore is with me and that I'll send her home in time for supper. They'll probably be glad to have you out from under foot with all the work to be done cleaning. Hurry, Toby, before Luce starts worrying."

Toby ran toward the stable happily contemplating the joy of a few hours freedom from the tyrannical eyes of the head groom.

"Gayle, you come back here with that child," Fay yelled furiously. She ran out of the house as Gayle and Aurore spurred their animals. "Bring her back, Gayle!"

A quick stop at the stable and Aurore's saddle was changed. She sat astride feeling very strange as she and Gayle thundered out of the yard toward the fields. Aurore felt good without hampering skirts. She felt wild and deliciously free.

"Where are we going?" she asked when they slowed their horses to a walk. She was supremely happy when she was with Gayle. She smiled at him broadly. He realized he had forgotten a hat. Then he wondered why bother with a hat, she was already burned to a golden tan.

"To the meadow beyond the field. I want to oversee the mating of one of my mares to my black stallion." he said. She looked mildly curious and he wondered if he were doing the right thing. The facts of life were best left to her mother, but then her mother did not know what he knew about Fleur.

They rode in companionable silence. Aurore looked at her breeches in wonder. She touched them with her hands, running her fingers down their softness. It was wonderful riding astride. She devoutly hoped her Maman never heard about this transgression from femininity, Aurore knew she would be severely punished. They approached the meadow to find a pure white mare prancing shamelessly across the grass.

"Come here, my pretty," Gayle coaxed. The mare danced up to his outstretched hand, nipping at the green apple he held out for her. She took the apple delicately, then nudged his hand for more.

"She's beautiful," Aurore said reverently. The mare turned liquid brown eyes on her, then breathed gently on her face.

"Her name is Sulie."

"Can I pet her?"

He nodded. Aurore stretched out her hand to touch the velvety neck. The mare nickered against Aurore's ear.

A groom from the stable rode up leading a nervous black stallion who snorted and pulled his head. The groom dismounted and led the stallion to the gate.

"Let him loose, Daniel," Gayle ordered.

The groom opened the gate. The stallion shouldered past eagerly.

"What's going to happen?" Aurore asked. Small shivers crept up and down her spine. She watched the mare, prancing and flirting with the stallion who nipped playfully at her neck. Suddenly the mare jumped and started racing across the meadow, the stallion following her. She stopped and the huge black skidded to a halt next to her. The mare squealed and raced away again.

"When they are finished, next spring a foal will be born." Gayle said. He watched her face. There was no fear in it. She watched curiously, her eyes going wide as the stallion mounted the mare.

When it was over, the stallion left the mare to browse while Daniel walked across the meadow speaking softly to him. He clipped the lead to his halter and led the stallion out of the meadow. The mare trotted regally to the fence, her white mane and tail flowing behind her. She stopped at Gayle who presented her with a second apple, then she approached Aurore who reached out a trembling hand to stroke her smooth neck. As she touched the mare she remembered Fleur laying on her back with Noble on top of her. She looked at Gayle. "Jewel told you, didn't she."

He nodded.

"I'm glad." Aurore sighed. The mare nibbled at her fingers, then suddenly wheeled away racing to the other end of the pasture to browse. "Noble and Fleur weren't playing were they?"

"They weren't playing."

"After I saw them, I remembered the painting of the woman on the *Sophie Sutter*. She had no clothes on and you said men like looking at women who have no clothes on."

"There's more to it than that," Gayle said gravely. "It's hard to explain and even harder to understand when you're young."

"Will I understand when I'm old?"

"Probably, but I want to tell you this. What Fleur and Noble were doing can be very, very beautiful when it is between the right man and woman. It can be very ugly when it's between the wrong man and woman."

"It's wrong for Fleur and Noble, isn't it."

"I'm afraid it is."

"Because she is still a little girl?"

"Yes, and because it is something normally shared only between a man and his wife. Will you promise me something?" Gayle fell to his knees in front of her taking her by the shoulders and holding her firmly. She nodded. "Don't be like Fleur. She was so anxious to find out all the mysteries of life that she has given herself away to Noble because she was curious. I don't want you to be the same way. Grow up a little more and wait for the right man who will love and cherish you. Then it will be beautiful and filled with love. Do you understand what I am saying?"

"No!" Aurore said softly, "but I will do as you say. I won't be like Fleur. I won't let the wrong man touch me. I'll wait for as long as it takes for the right man to come. I promise, Gayle. I don't understand, but I promise to do as you say. Pere Buiron says a girl must be chaste and pure. Is that what you want me to be?"

"Yes," Gayle said. "You'll understand some day." He wanted to smooth the bewildered look from her face.

"Should I still keep Fleur's secret?"

"It may be wrong for Fleur to act the way she does with Noble, but it is not up to you to tell your parents. Now, I think that is enough schooling for one day."

"When I grow up can we talk about this again?" Aurore asked shyly as Gayle lifted her into the saddle.

"Maybe!" Gayle replied noncommittally. "Let's go back to the house. Jewel looks forward to being with you."

"I haven't seen my fawn for three whole days," Aurore said, bubbling with laughter again. The

172

serious moments were forgotten as she spurred Belle and was racing across the field before Gayle had mounted his horse.

Back at the house, Aurore was careful to stay out of Fay's way, fearful that she would be forced to don her wide-skirted gown again after enjoying the freedom of breeches. She and Jewel ran into the woods to play before Fay could object and force her to change.

"If that child's mother knew what she was wearing, she would have heart failure," Fay said signaling to Mandy to clear the dinner dishes from the table set up on the veranda to catch the early morning breeze off the Mississippi.

"You are not going to tell her," Gayle said firmly. "Childhood is too brief to be spent hampered in those silly hoops you women wear."

"She'll find out one day on her own. I don't have to tell her." She flipped open her fan and waved it languidly in front of her face. "Before you go, Gayle, there is something I wish to discuss with you."

"Another new gown, Fay. I haven't the money right now."

"It is not about a gown. Marcus Slaughter asked me to marry him. I have accepted."

"What!" Gayle in the act of standing fell back into his chair with a thud.

"I said Marcus Slaughter proposed to me and I accepted."

"That old lecher!"

"What's wrong with that. It is an excellent match."

"He's over seventy and you're just a girl."

"There are a great many marriages that are widely spaced in age. It is nothing new to have an older groom for a much younger bride."

"Not fifty years, Fay."

"It isn't any of your concern. I will marry who I choose."

"But you're Grant's wife!"

"Grant is dead. I'm tired of posing as the grieving widow and wearing weeds that are shabby and old. I want parties and new gowns, not old ones that have been turned so many times I can't remember which side was the original. Marcus is rich and powerful. My position in the parish will be much envied. Besides, he hasn't long to live, and when he dies I'll be rich. I'm tired of being poor, Gayle. I've been poor all my life."

"What about your father? How will he feel having a son-in-law ten years older than he is?"

"I thought you knew, Gayle. My father died two weeks after Grant and I were married. I wouldn't care how he felt, anyway.

"You're determined to marry Marcus."

"Yes, I am."

"I'll go to New Orleans in the morning and have control of your dowry returned to you. You can't go to your bridegroom empty-handed."

"Keep the land, Gayle. I don't want it. Marcus won't care."

"No, I guess he wouldn't. He has all the land he needs for the business he's in," Gayle replied sarcastically. He rose from the table to the sounds of carriage wheels on the drive. Fay jumped up and ran down the steps.

"It's Marcus," she cried over her shoulder. The carriage pulled to a stop, the horses snorting.

Marcus stepped down from the carriage, puffing

174

from the exertion. By the time he stood on the veranda and sank into a wicker chair which groaned under his enormous weight, his face was red and swollen.

"Have you told him yet, my dear?" Marcus asked. Mandy offered him punch which he downed in one gulp and held out the glass for more.

"She's all yours, Marcus," Gayle said with all the graciousness he could find. In a way, he was glad Fay would be soon leaving. It had been in his mind to set up a modest place for her in New Orleans, or to send her back to her father. In a way he was relieved, because he could hardly afford to set her up in the grand style she would expect now that he knew her father was dead.

"Thank you, Gayle. I do think we'll rub along tolerably well. What do you think, my dear?"

Fay sent a coy look to him over the edge of her fan. The heat of desire flared in his face. She suddenly wished Gayle would leave, but he didn't. He reseated himself across from Marcus and deftly turned the conversation to business matters.

"Renault de Champlain tells me that in order to save my plantation, I will have to sell off some of my slaves." Gayle said watching the frustration leap into Fay's eyes with amusement. "He also tells me that you're the best man to set up an auction in New Orleans and dispose of my slaves for the best money."

"If he says that, it must be true," Marcus said preening at the compliment from such an unexpected source. Renault seldom offered compliments to anyone.

"Then I hope you will do me the honor of seeing to the arrangements of the auction. Renault says you are honest and the most you will accept is a six percent fee for the handling of the matter."

"Six . . . six percent!" Marcus gulped.

"Is that too high a percentage," Gayle asked innocently, knowing full well Marcus seldom dealt in auction arrangement for less than ten.

"No! No! Six percent is a fair charge," Marcus cried, wondering how he had allowed himself to be led into this like a lamb to slaughter. That damned wily Creole! Marcus would pay him back somehow. Renault knew his usual fee was ten percent of the profits. "How many slaves have you got?"

"About two hundred and fifty people, but I only want to sell two hundred. And I would prefer it if you would try to arrange for families to stay together. I don't like separating men and women and children."

"I can try, but sometimes you can get more for a single slave than a family."

"Do your best," Gayle said. He allowed the conversation to drift into other channels. After an hour, Marcus pushed himself out of the chair and signaled to his coachman.

"It is a pity, but I must be on my way. I'm attending a dinner party at Avalon tonight."

"Oh!" Fay said, suddenly interested and wondering why she had not been invited.

"I thought we might have a ball and announce our engagement in a few weeks. How do you like that, my love?"

"Oh! A ball! I would love that, Marcus," Fay sighed through parted lips.

"I almost forgot." Marcus reached into his jacket pocket and pulled out a small box. "I thought you might like this. To seal our agreement." He handed the box to Fay who opened it and found herself staring at the largest ruby she had ever seen. It was surrounded by large, sparkling diamonds. She slipped it over her finger and held her hand out to admire it. Gayle thought it was in vulgar taste.

"It's beautiful, Marcus," Fay cried. She threw her arms around his neck and kissed him, pressing her body against him. "Isn't it beautiful, Gayle?"

"Very nice, Fay," Gayle said, hiding his distaste for the gaudy bauble.

Marcus took his leave, climbing into his carriage and watching Fay admire her ring. She was such a pretty child, he thought. He tapped the roof of the carriage. It lurched and he was soon on his way home contemplating the evening's entertainment which he was providing. Ten lovely little girls from his stable all to be sampled by the gentlemen at this evening's party.

"How can you think of marrying him?" Gayle snorted when the carriage was out of sight. "He's a pompous old goat. Look at that atrocious ring. No woman of breeding would ever wear it."

"What does it matter whether or not the ring is tasteless? It is something I can sell someday and have money instead. As for Marcus, I can marry him. I can marry any man for money."

"Why did you marry Grant?"

"I thought he was rich," she said, smiling sweetly. She walked gracefully into the house, ordering a decanter of brandy as she went up the stairs. She had to celebrate.

Gayle watched her go, wondering if she really

thought she was keeping her drinking a secret. Her father had been a drunk and she was following in his footsteps. He walked to the door to watch her walk up the stairs still admiring the huge ring winking tastelessly on her finger. Behind him he heard laughter as Jewel and Aurore ran out of the forest. He turned smiling at them. The fawn hopped awkwardly behind them. It was growing quickly. Jewel fed him well with all the delicacies she could find, including fresh milk from the cow.

Aurore waved at Gayle. He waved back. Under a spreading oak tree, she flopped down on the grass with Jewel falling down next to her. The fawn curled into a ball against Aurore's back. There was fresh laughter and loud giggles. Gayle couldn't help the fond smile that spread over his face. Aurore was a beautiful girl. Someday she would be a beautiful woman. He turned and went into the house, heading for his study and the ever-present worry of bills and debts. Renault de Champlain was right. He would have to sell his slaves in order to save Grey Lawns, though he hated doing it. They were like children looking up to him for protection. They trusted him and he would have to betray that trust. He shrugged. There was nothing he could do about it. Grey Lawns came first.

Laughter drifted in from the lawn. There was one slave who he could never sell. Through an open window he saw the dark head of Jewel bending over Aurore as she tickled her. He would never sell Jewel. He sighed as he walked into his study and closed the door.

Twelve

Renault lounged in his chair, the ledger open before him on the desk. His keen eyes ran up and down the figures. Each figure was neatly entered, but the uneasiness consuming him would not leave. The books looked too perfect. Even his former manager made mistakes occasionally. Renault was even guilty of a rare mistake, but John Miles' figures added up perfectly on page after page. He continued to look through the book, the problem tugging at his brain refusing to let go. He would solve it eventually. He suspected Miles of cheating him, but Renault was a fair man. He would not dismiss his manager without proof. Tomorrow he was returning to New Orleans. He would take the books with him and turn them over to his accountant. If there were any problems, Edmund Vernay would find them.

Renault stood up stretching and rubbing his eyes. The beginnings of a headache pounded at the back of his eyes. He poured himself a brandy forcing himself to relax. John Miles had been in the office earlier to protest the appropriation of the ledgers. Renault had carefully explained to him that he always took them back to the city at the end of each fiscal year to be entered in the master books kept in New Orleans.

That way there were two sets of books in case one set was accidentally destroyed. Miles had not liked that. Since then, he had been alternately uneasy or overconfident. That manner by itself convinced Renault there was something wrong with the ledgers.

He looked out the window to see Aurore and Silas standing on the lawn. Belle waited patiently, her reins looped over Aurore's arm. Recently an old journal from England had surfaced praising the joys of foxhunting. Silas had read it with interest, more attracted to the jumping of fences and obstacles than the hunting of the fox. It had made him determined to turn Belle into a prime jumper and Aurore into the best horsewoman to rival any woman in England. Several low hurdles dotted the lawn. Silas pointed at them. Aurore nodded patiently. Renault smiled thinking that the servants were as determined to make a tomboy out of Aurore as Marie-Odile was determined to make a lady of her. It was amusing to watch the struggle and see his wife steadily losing. In a way, Renault felt sorry for her and her singleminded campaign to turn their children into ladies of the first order. Several times, Renault had thought to step in and turn her away from her campaign. The world was changing. It wasn't going to need ladies as much as it was going to need survivors. Aurore was a survivor and Renault preferred her that way. A knock on the door distracted him.

"Come in," he said, still watching Aurore. She mounted Belle and approached the first of the small hurdles taking it easily and cantering to the next.

"Thank you," Monique purred.

Renault groaned inwardly. Here was another of

180

life's little irritations. A week after the wedding, Monique was still in residence at St. Angele even though Benoit and Marget had departed for Nassau three days before.

"And yes, I would like some brandy, Renault. Thank you."

Renault automatically poured for her. He handed her the glass, their fingers brushing against each other. Renault withdrew hastily. A moment's dalliance with this woman had resulted in his being unable to rid himself of her. For some reason she had read more into their encounter than had actually been there.

"You must be anxious to return to Grandeville," he remarked casually. She wore a gown of dull gold lawn embroidered with brown daisies and bordered with matching brown ribbon. It looked enchanting on her full figure, yet Renault found he was unmoved by the blatant sexuality it suggested.

"I'm in no hurry," Monique replied airily. "What is at Grandeville for me now that Benoit is on his wedding trip and you control the place. I have no reason to return."

"There are repairs to be seen to. I was hoping you would consent to overseeing them and some minor redecoration of the house."

"Your daughter is mistress there," Monique said, shrugging.

Renault refilled his glass wishing Marie-Odile would suddenly open the door to look for him. The door remained stubbornly shut.

"I am returning to New Orleans in the morning," Renault said finally, aware that his wife was not going to look for him and it was up to him to get himself out of this delicate situation. It insulted his sensibilities to have her dogging his footsteps, pursuing him like a hunter. The only time he was safe was at night in his wife's bed.

"How wonderful," Monique trilled coyly. "I was thinking of taking a house in the city for a few weeks. I have a need for the city lights and the entertainments."

"Let me know when you plan to arrive. I shall arrange for a house and provide you with an escort."

"An escort! I was certain you would see to my pleasures personally, Renault." She fluttered her lashes.

"I doubt I shall have the time," Renault said, willing her to understand there would be no repeat of their pleasant afternoon.

"Why not?" she asked bluntly.

"I'm a busy man, Madame de Ville. I've little time for entertainments."

"A few weeks ago you called me Monique. Can't you call me Monique again." She tugged at her bodice. Renault averted his eyes as the dress fell lower and lower. How could he explain his momentary attraction for her? She had been beautiful and angry that day, filling him with a desire to touch her pride. Today she was only fat with little lines around her face she unsuccessfully tried to hide with powder.

"Madame, a few weeks ago was a few weeks ago. Today is today."

Her eyes narrowed angrily. She had thought he had been avoiding her to spare his wife the insult of having his mistress under the same roof.

"Are you telling me that I mean nothing to you? That the delightful time we had in this room has no meaning for you?" she asked shrilly.

"Madame de Ville, I love my wife dearly. I would do nothing to hurt her if I could possibly avoid it."

Monique recoiled from him. For weeks she had built a lovely dream around the importance of their encounter. She had thought nothing of the shadowy wife who seemed to hover on the edge of his life. Never once had she considered that he loved that pale creature who flitted about his house like a ghost. Monique was stunned.

"I see," she said faintly. Her voice was dry and harsh. It didn't seem to belong to her. "Do you love your daughter?" she asked casually.

Renault had been preparing for an attack against Marie-Odile. He had forgotten Marget who was married to this woman's son.

"I have an affection for my daughter," he replied calmly. It took great effort to remain calm. He forced himself to relax, not wanting her to know how much her question shook him.

"I could make life miserable for her," Monique continued offhandedly.

"You could, but if you did your son would never regain control of Grandeville or Marget's dowry."

Monique seemed to crumple like a piece of paper crunched up and discarded. She stared at him blankly, defeat filling her. She was only a woman. What defense did she have against a man like Renault. She walked slowly to the door, her body slumped like an old woman. She had planned and schemed for this marriage and the money it would bring. She had not reckoned on the stupidity of her son, nor the wiliness of Renault.

"I'll be packed and gone this afternoon," she said.

"Thank you," Renault replied. He watched her leave the room, pushing away any feelings of pity he had for her. He finished his brandy then went to look for Marie-Odile who would welcome the news that their guest was departing.

Early the next morning with the mist still curling around the house, Renault kissed his wife and each of his daughters, lingering over Therese who clung to him charmingly. He told her he would return in a few weeks, but when he boarded the riverboat, she started to cry. Marie-Odile hushed her and waved good-bye to her husband. Aurore stood on the levee long after the riverboat was gone feeling suddenly lonely for her father. Finally she grew tired of watching the river and ran toward the stables thinking of the breakfast awaiting her at Grey Lawns and the secret change of clothes hanging in a wardrobe in an upstairs bedroom.

Renault headed for the men's saloon. The room was smoke hazed and smelled of whiskey, perfume and sweat. A beautifully gowned woman approached him, the long curling plumes on her head swaying to the grace of her walk. She looked tired and haggard. Soon the saloon would empty and she would be able to retire, preparing herself for the next long night of coaxing men into drinks they did not want or stirring them toward one of her more available girls who kept a room in a discreet section of the ship in which to entertain those customers who preferred privacy. Renault waved her on. She smiled at him and he was struck with the unusual beauty of her face. She had slightly slanting eyes and wide arched brows over a small straight nose and full, sensual lips. Her chin was small, but firm and her fingers had an unusual grace. He almost called her back, but she had gone to another customer, stirring him toward the bar and pouring a glass of whiskey for him.

"Renault," a voice hailed him. He turned to find Marcus Slaughter pushing his way through a group of men. His belly arrived at Renault's side a full half second before he did.

"Going to the city, are you," Marcus boomed. He clapped Renault companionably on the shoulder.

"I have business to attend to. There's a ship due to arrive next week from France. I wanted to be on hand when it did. What takes you to New Orleans? You seldom stir from your plantation."

"Marriage, old friend," Marcus winked slyly. Renault led Marcus from the smoke-filled room for the cooler, cleaner air of the deck. A young woman with a black mammy trailing her was taking her early morning promenade. She eyed Renault curiously while her mammy coaxed her away from the evils of the men's saloon. Renault smiled at the sight of a trim ankle as her skirts slounced when she disappeared around the corner of the deck.

"The ladies still like you, Renault," Marcus said with a slight leer. A faint scent in the air was the only reminder of the young woman's passage. "Never saw so many gals give a man the once over the way they do you. How do you do it? You're no spring chicken any more, like me."

"I don't know, Marcus. What do you mean by marriage?"

"That beautiful ceremony and ball for your gal inspired me to propose to Mrs. Fay Courtland. She has done me the honor of accepting me."

Fay Courtland to marry Marcus Slaughter! Renault stared at the corpulent man. He quickly averted his eyes, concentrating on lighting his cigar and drawing on it while his stomach churned in disgust. Fifty years separated Marcus from his intended bride.

"There's been no woman in my home since my daughter-in-law died," Marcus continued. "I thought it fitting to go to New Orleans and order new furniture and the like to please my bride."

"I hope you'll be very happy, Marcus," Renault said.

"Don't care much if I'm happy or not," Marcus shrugged, "I just want my last days to be comfortable. I'm not long for this world. Fay will lead me a merry dance, but I don't care as long as she's in her bed where she belongs when night comes. Fine gal, that Fay. And while I'm in the city, I'm arranging for an auction of two hundred of Grey Lawns' prime slaves. Seems you advised Gayle to sell out and pay his debts to put the place back on its face by selling his niggers."

"I was not certain Courtland would follow my advice." Renault said, mildly surprised. He approved of Courtland's decision. It was the only way.

"I don't hold with selling off niggers," Marcus said, frowning. "He could mortgage next year's crop if he had to, but sell his niggers? I don't like it."

"Courtland is entitled to do as he pleases."

"I still don't like it. And I don't like you telling him I only work for a six percent commission."

186

"Six percent commission! I told him that!" Renault chuckled. Courtland had more sense than Renault had given him credit for. It took guts to face Marcus Slaughter with an offer of six percent when he usually got ten. And to think he used the de Champlain power to get it.

"You didn't tell him that!"

Renault shook his head. Fury mounted in Marcus to think he had been outsmarted by a kid hardly old enough to shave, or was he. For near ten years, Gayle Courtland had supported himself as a professional gambler. Gamblers knew how to bluff. He had bluffed Marcus out of a good ten percent commission. Suddenly the humor of the situation struck him. He started to laugh with Renault joining in.

"I was bested by a kid forty-five years younger than me. I must be getting old, Renault."

"We're all getting old."

"Still I don't hold with his selling his niggers. Why don't he sell that glass collection his pappy collected on all those tours he took around the world?"

"The glass collection has sentimental value," Renault said mildly. He did not approve of attaching sentiment to anything, but he could understand Gayle's desire to preserve the few achievements of his father.

"I'm going back in for a drink and some cards," Marcus said indicating the saloon. "Care to join me?"

"No, thank you, Marcus. Call for me at my office tomorrow night and we'll go out on the town. I understand Esther Nye has a couple of new girls who are very pretty and very good at their jobs. I can arrange for you to take one up to your room at the hotel."

"Thanks for the dinner invitation, but no thanks on the girl. I'm saving what little I got left for my bride," Marcus winked broadly and sauntered back into the saloon, his voice ordering a drink.

It was late afternoon before the riverboat pulled into New Orleans and disembarked her passengers. Renault stopped briefly at his office then went to a restaurant for dinner. It was dusk when he approached the white cottage, its lines blurred in the gathering twilight. He paid the carriage driver and watched as it rolled away heading for the downtown center of the Vieux Carre for its next fare.

Vegetation had grown wild and untrimmed around the small cottage making it isolated in the middle of a busy city. Even as he walked up the path, the city noises seemed to dim and disappear, falling to silence as he approached the cottage.

"Good evening, Renault," she said as she opened the door. She smiled at him, her beautiful face soft with longing. She stood aside, gesturing for him to give her his valise. She wore a gown of pale yellow taffeta that rustled pleasantly as she walked. The bodice was cut very low, yet seemed to cover her completely. Her long chestnut hair, caught in a matching ribbon at the back of her neck, curled seductively over one shoulder settling in the hollow between her breasts.

"Good evening, Victoire," he said. He looked around the small, but comfortable room in appreciation. It was tastefully decorated. Over the years the appearance had changed as she had arranged and rearranged things to suit herself, but the original furniture was still there. The original furniture he had purchased for the cottage after he had contracted with her mother for the future of the daughter.

She was slim and beautiful. Her chestnut hair was her glory and she lavished care and attention on it. Her next most attractive asset was her beautiful eyes, wide and warm brown, the only part of her reflecting her negro heritage.

Victoire took his jacket, replacing it with a smoking coat. She took it into the bedroom. Through the open door, he watched her hang it neatly on a hook in the wardrobe. When she returned she carried his slippers.

Renault sat down in his favorite chair, his newspaper across his lap. She untied his shoes and replaced them with the soft slippers. Then she got a cigar out of the humidor and placed it on the table next to him in exactly the spot he would have to reach for when he wanted it.

The click of her heels sounded on the flagstone floor of the hall, as she walked to the kitchen. He heard the distant tone of her voice, then she was back carrying a tray in her hands which she set down on a table and poured him steaming, hot coffee.

"Dinner will be ready in a moment," Victoire said, sipping her hot coffee delicately. The light from the lamps danced on her hair. Over the edge of his newspaper, Renault watched her.

"I trust you are well?"

She looked up to smile at him. It was a tender smile, filled with love and longing.

"I am well, thank you," she answered in a voice that was low and sweet.

"And the children?"

"They are well. They have gone to visit a friend for a few days. Have you been well?"

"Yes, I have. I've missed you, Victoire."

"It has been months. I have longed for you every night we have been apart." Between them hung unspoken thoughts of his other family. His legitimate family. It was not unusual for a man in New Orleans to have two families. One lived in his home, the other hidden away in the area beyond Rampart Street. Marriages were made for power, money or convenience. Mistresses were taken for love. Renault considered himself luckier than most. He had love with his mistress as well as his wife.

His liaison with Victoire Olivier went back twenty years, long before the gentle Marie-Odile had captured his eyes. In their own ways, Victoire and Marie-Odile were very much alike. They were gentle, tender and sweet. They loved Renault with an adoration that was single-minded in its intensity.

A tall, slim mulatto woman walked silently down the hall. She had come to serve Victoire at the beginning and had stayed over the long years showing a devotion and love seldom found in servants. She quietly announced supper accepting Renault's presence as though he lived at the cottage every day of the year.

"The meal was excellent, my dear," Renault complimented his mistress.

"It is Sylvie you must thank," Victore said. She blushed prettily.

"Then I shall compliment her. But I will do it later." He stood up. He had eaten too much, the food was excellent enough to excuse his lack of restraint. He went to stand behind Victoire, caressing her lovely sloping shoulders lightly. She shivered delicately. He

190

picked up the long curl of her hair and lightly tickled the back of her neck with it. She laughed sweetly. She stood up and turned to him, her dark eyes devouring him. His arms slid around her. He kissed her, then led her into the bedroom.

Early in the morning, Rampart Street was quiet. Not even the early morning chatter of the birds disturbed its serenity. Renault let himself out of the cottage and walked down the densely shaded path and into the already hot and humid air of the city. Steam rose from puddles that had collected in the gutters during the night. The morning air was dense and heavy with humidity. He hailed a cab, giving directions to his warehouse. He sat down in the carriage, the plantation ledgers across his knees.

Few people stayed in the city during the heat of the summer. Many of them left more from fear of infection than fear of heat. Summer was the time for epidemics of yellow fever and cholera. Renault clearly remembered the great epidemic of 1853. It had taken the lives of Marie-Odile's parents because they had stubbornly refused to leave the city even when the dead were piling up in the streets. Renault and his family had survived because he always insisted on their leaving in the first week of June. But the epidemics had not left him completely untouched. The two month old baby son Victoire had given him had died. Even now after seventeen years, he still felt the sorrow of that death. The death of his first son. Some of the sorrow had been erased a few years later when Victoire had presented him with another son as well as the boy's twin sister. Renault was very proud of

Etienne Olivier. He intended to take him into the business someday. And as for Ursule. No daughter of his would live the life of a placee. Renault already had a bridegroom picked out for his beautiful daughter.

The pulse of New orleans was the busy levees. Here ships from a dozen European countries tied up to unload the precious luxuries the New Orleanians loved. When the holds were empty of their trade items, they were then slowly filled with the bales and bales of cotton brought downriver on the massive paddle-wheelers. Renault did not believe in the sovereignty of cotton, any more than he believed in the importance of rice or sugar cane. What he did believe in was diversity. He kept his fingers in many pies. Besides the plantation, St. Angele, he owned two others that grew modest quantities of cotton. He owned a fleet of twelve riverboats which traveled up and down the river transporting cargo and passengers. He also owned three ocean going steamships to ship his cargoes to England or wherever. From the little office on the second floor of his warehouse, he continued the business of his small empire including not only his riverboats and steamships, but his two saloons, one coffee shop, and one boarding house. He also owned a far different three-story house off Chartres that boasted the finest clientele in all New Orleans. The girls there were the most beautiful to be found who loved their jobs. He hired only women who were good at their profession and enjoyed it as well. There were no reluctant whores in his pleasure house.

"Good morning, Renault," Esther Nye said as he walked into his office. She was modestly veiled, but not even the heavy veiling could disguise her graceful body or the excellent cut of her sky-blue gown. Renault demanded class from the women he hired. They gave it to him or were dismissed.

"Good morning, Esther," he replied, dropping the ledgers on his desk and sinking into the chair next to her. "What brings you here at this hour of the morning?"

"There was a brawl last night," she said softly. Her voice reflected an education in England at one of the best ladies academies. It had culture and poise, attributes seldom found in her business. "The main salon was damaged. I shall need to draw more than normal on my account for repairs."

"Were any of the girls hurt?"

"Thankfully, no," Esther sighed. She was protective of the girls she hired. She moved in her chair, her gown rustling. She insisted they reflect her tastes. There was not one woman in the house who wasn't a lady even if she was a harlot at heart.

"Draw what you need," Renault said.

"Thank you."

"Sherry? Brandy?"

"Thank you, I seldom drink these days. I find more and more that what I eat and drink eventually ends up on my hips." She laughed mildly. Under the heavy veiling was a plain woman who understood the meaning of beauty. She was forty-two years old and looked barely thirty. She had worked for Renault for twenty-five years rising from barmaid to proprietress in only a few years. Her taste was impeccable and Renault trusted her completely. "Another thing, Renault. There is to be an auction today. There is a girl who looks very promising." She stood up, gathering her handbag and slipping gloves over fingers a shade too stubby to be called elegant.

"How much?"

"Five hundred dollars."

"I'll see the money is added to your account this morning. Is there anything else?"

"No." Her smile was faintly outlined under the veiling. She walked to the door and let herself out.

Renault leaned back in his chair and sighed. Five hundred dollars was a bit more than he liked to pay for a girl, but she must be extra special or Esther would never have looked at her.

"Good morning, Monsieur de Champlain."

Edmund Vernay, Renault's accountant, walked into the office. He looked coolly elegant on the hot day.

"Good morning, Edmund. I have the ledgers from the plantation here. Take them please and go over them. I suspect my manager of cheating me, but I can't find anything. Take a look and see what you can come up with."

"Very good, Monsieur," Edmund picked up the ledgers and hesitated. "You once asked me if I knew of a strong man who could do some work for you and remain discreet. I have found such a man."

"Go on," Renault prompted.

"A few days after you left for St. Angele, a man came to my door claiming to be a distant cousin of my wife's. He had letters to verify his distant connection with the family. A branch of it moved to Texas sixty years ago. The man needs work and appears to be someone you could trust."

"Is he here now?"

"He waits at the bottom of the stairs. He had been

working on the docks to support himself while waiting for your return."

"You sound like you do not like this man, Edmund."

"I shall bring him up, sir. And as for liking him, let us just say I would like him out of my house."

The person Edmund ushered into Renault's office looked to be eighteen years old. The stubble of beard on his face was still soft. He was tall and slim with large hands and feet which seemed to move independently of the rest of his body. He stumbled slightly over the edge of the rug as he walked into the office. Edmund's lips tightened in annoyance. Renault decided that Edmund had forgotten what it was like to be eighteen and in a strange city with no friends. Renault liked him immediately. There was an open honesty in his darkly tanned face and light blue eyes.

"I'm Cole Taggert," he said, offering a work-roughened hand to Renault. Edmund looked at the hand with distaste, but Renault grasped it firmly pleased to find Cole Taggert responding with equal firmness. His voice was deep and pleasing with the melodious accent so peculiar to Texans. Renault nodded dismissal to Edmund who withdrew from the office.

"You and Edmund do not seem to be getting along." Renault said. He noticed the swift tightening of Taggert's lips and the sweeping coldness that filled his eyes.

"We've our differences, sir." Cole said. He sat down in the chair Renault indicated, catching the subtle scent of a woman's perfume. "Edmund tells me you've been looking for someone to do a job for you. Someone who works well and can keep his mouth shut."

"I am looking for such a man. The job is no ordinary job." Renault surveyed the man sitting in front of him. Traces of a hard life showed in the sharp angles of his face. Renault knew instinctively he could be trusted. "Nor is it easy work."

"I'm not afraid of hard work, sir," Cole said with muted dignity. He wished he could take off the stiff clothes Edmund had insisted he purchase and dress in his old worn jeans and faded flannel shirt. He felt naked without his old Colt revolver strapped to his side. He rubbed a toe of one shoe on the back of his trousers. It was still shiny and new. He thought with longing of his boots sitting in the back of his closet banished from his attire because Edmund had insisted they were not worn when meeting with a man like Renault de Champlain. "I've been kicking around a played out dirt farm for most of my life. The last three years, I've been working on the Santa Gertrudis ranch out of Corpus Christi. Cattle ranching's no picnic."

"There might be a war. How would you feel about it?"

"There's no 'might' about it. A war is coming and it's a foolish man who says it isn't. It won't be no glamourous three month war like some of these fancy Southern boys think who want to dash away on their white chargers and defend the South against the evils of the Yankees. It's going to be a long, hard war. And I think the South will lose, but before it does it's going to see a lot of death and a lot more suffering."

"Which way will you go when the fighting starts?"

"I'd rather stay out of the whole thing, but I won't be able to because people will force a man to take

196

sides. I'll go with the South, not because of slavery. I don't hold with slavery, but I don't like the way the North is trying to dictate to the South what it can or can't do. In Texas a man minds his own business or gets his head blown off."

"I have a plantation north of here that is unusually remote. It almost completely surrounded by bayous. Until last year I grew a cotton crop on it with a small crew in residence. This year I let the crew go, but not before they built me a good, hardy warehouse deep in the swamp."

"You planning to store cotton in this warehouse until the war is over?"

"Not cotton, wheat, corn, sugar, and anything else a beleaguered city like New Orleans is going to need when the North gets its blockade into full working order."

"Privateering?"

"Call it what you want. I don't want the war anymore than you do, but I'm a businessman first and a patriot second."

"What do you want from me?" Cole was intensely curious about this elegant Southerner sitting opposite him calmly discussing how he was going to make a profit out of the war.

"I need a good man to go up to this plantation and store the supplies my riverboats are going to start dropping off at the landing in a few days."

"People are going to get suspicious."

"No one knows I let my crew go. Most of them were free negroes I transported North. Any supplies that are dropped off will naturally be thought of as for my crew. Who is to know that every boat I own will be dropping off cargo every couple of days."

"Sounds good enough. What do I get?"

"How about enough money to set yourself up on a good ranch with enough left over to stock it. The war won't last forever. A man is going to need something to come home to."

"That sounds fair. But two can do more work than one."

"You have a friend? Edmund said nothing about a friend."

"Rico came with me from Texas. He wouldn't be welcome in Edmund's home. He's half Mex and half nigger, sir."

"I'm sure he could be useful."

"If there's two of us, the money should be double."

"If you take the job, the money will be double." Renault said.

"We'll take it."

"Good. My paddle-wheeler, the *Golden Girl*, leaves Friday. I will arrange for your passage. Captain Lester will be told you are my new manager."

"We'll be ready."

"You do understand that this conversation is strictly confidential."

"I understand, sir. I'm your new manager going north to handle your cotton crop." Cole stood up knowing the meeting was at an end. He put his hand out unhesitantly. Renault grasped it. They looked at each other, liking what they saw.

"Good luck, Mr. Taggert."

Cole nodded. He left the office, the sound of his cheerful whistling drifting up the stairs as he descended it. He had come to New Orleans seeking his fortune. It was turning out better than he ever expected.

Thirteen

Cole Taggert had been born on a farm in West Texas. He remembered his mother, a tall, slim woman with beautiful blonde hair and soft, musical laughter. He remembered his father was sturdy and well built. That had been before the failure of their first crop. With each succeeding failure, they both grew older and grayer. His father grew stooped and his mother forgot the sound of her laughter. Cole had loved his parents deeply. They instilled in him a thirst for learning and a respect for land. They died when he was thirteen. In respect for their memory, he tried to run the farm by himself. For a year he endured the loneliness and the work, but he was a restless boy. He dreamed of other things. He yearned for a different life. Finally, he sold the farm to a passing German and his family. He used the money to buy himself a good horse and saddle, then started east. Along the way he stopped at his grandmother's home who told him about his fine Creole cousins in New Orleans. She insisted he go there with a letter of introduction from her. Cole promised her he would go there but as he drifted farther and farther east he ran out of money and was forced to take a job. In Corpus Christi, Texas, he signed on as a hand for the Santa Gertrudis ranch.

There he met Rico.

"So we have a job, *amigo*." Rico Hernandez Lewis said.

"We go upriver Friday."

Rico nodded. He was a tall man, towering over his young friend. He was a curious blending of his runaway slave father and his Mexican mother. His skin was bronze, his hair black and curly without the wiry texture of his father's people. He was slim with a fragility that belied his enormous strength. He wore traditional Mexican clothing consisting of tight-fitting trousers, bolero jacket and snow-white shirt of linen decorated with tiny ruffles at neck and wrist. Rico was a handsome man with a square face, but with the sensitiveness of his mother. He sported a pencil-thin mustache over his upper lip and his high-heeled boots and spurs clinked as he walked down the street. He was a strange sight in exotic New Orleans.

"I like thees city," Rico said in the exaggerated accent he affected to impress the ladies. "The senoritas!" Rico rolled his eyes to heaven. "They are like angels in the church. What you say we visit Señora Esther again?"

"After what we did to her parlour last night?" Cole said. "She'll kill us."

"Not that woman," Rico grinned. "She has the eye for Rico."

"Later. Right now, I'm hungry. My cousin, Celeste, doesn't serve much of a breakfast."

"And you are a growing boy, *si!*"

Cole laughed. They passed a courtyard restaurant, the smell of fresh seafood filling the air. Cole had grown up on plain, wholesome food, but nothing could compare with the delicate couisine of New Orleans. They had evolved a style that was uniquely their own. He urged Rico into the restaurant where his friend went into his act of strutting like a rooster. His spurs clanked commandingly while his eyes devoured the ladies. Sensitive to the force of his charms, the women pressed fragile hands to generous bosoms.

"We'll have the money we've dreamed about for our own ranch." Cole said, watching one honey-haired beauty send languishing looks at Rico. Rico smiled at her flashing pure white teeth.

"That we will, *amigo*. A ranch of our own." He ran a finger over his mustache winking suggestively at the woman. She turned away in assumed confusion fluttering her fan. "Have you ever seen so *magnifico* a figure?"

"Don't you ever think of anything besides women?" Cole asked. The honey-haired woman had turned thoughtful eyes on him. He felt his face growing warm with the unaccustomed boldness in her look.

"Never, my friend. You should think of the ladies more often. Maybe then you will lose the virginity you guard so zealously."

Cole's blush intensified. He glared at Rico who threw back his head and laughed.

"Maybe tonight." Rico continued. He smiled at the woman who pretended she did not notice. "We will try it again, eh! Señora Esther will find you a sweet willing girl. One who will not flirt with every man, but the one she is with." Rico winked broadly at the woman. She fluttered her fan violently, a tinge of red staining her cheeks.

When they finished their meal, they parted. Cole to return to his cousin's house and Rico to take up a determined pursuit of the honey-haired woman.

Cole had been reluctantly admitted to the Vernay home in the middle of the Vieux Carré. One look at his rough clothes and ungainly build had immediately prejudiced Edmund against him. Family ties were highly respected in Creole circles, so Edmund could not actually refuse him shelter, yet did not welcome him either. Cole was treated with civility, that and nothing more.

As he approached the home, he could hear the whispered laughter of his cousin's children. They peeked at him through the elaborate wrought iron gate that separated them from the world. Cole smiled at them, but the two little girls and toddler boy scampered away. Cole liked children. At the Santa Gertrudis ranch, the Mexican children had followed him around constantly.

"Good afternoon, cousin," Celeste Vernay called to him. She sat in the shade of a large, fragrant magnolia with an embroidery frame balanced on the large roundness of her stomach. Unlike her husband, Celeste felt sorry for the youth who called himself her cousin. It was a feeling kept carefully hidden. Edmund did not like him.

"Madame," Cole said, "I came to pack my bedroll. I have a job."

"I am pleased for you," she said softly. The sun formed patterns on her coal-black hair. He would be leaving. She was touched with sadness. Cole always treated her with the respectfulness Edmund had abandoned two days after their marriage. "Won't you sit

203

with me for awhile?" She touched the stone bench next to her. Cole sat down.

Celeste would have been an attractive woman if not for the overwide mouth and too thin nose. Yet she had an air of sweetness about her that made up for her lack of beauty. Cole liked her despite the hostility of her husband.

"I shall be sorry to see you leave," she said.

"Edmund will not be," Cole replied wryly.

Celeste shrugged. She had no answer. She could have explained that Edmund was seldom pleased about anything. He was a disappointed man who took his disillusionment out on his wife and children.

An old slave walked out of the house carrying a tray with two glasses of lemonade. Cole took one gratefully. Celeste took hers, but set it down next to her on the bench. She was not thirsty. The baby inside her moved energetically and she sighed with discomfort.

"I best be packing," Cole said finally, breaking the silence. The children were hiding behind the tree, giggling. "Not that I have much to pack."

"There are the two new shirts I made you," Celeste offered shyly.

"Thank you for them." He grinned that merry, boyish grin that Celeste was going to miss.

"I should thank you for all the wonderful stories you have told me. You have brought a little of the outside world to me. Will you write and continue to share?"

"If I can. There's a lot of world beyond the gates of your courtyard."

"But I shall never see it," she said smiling. She glanced over her shoulder at her children. They were sturdy and healthy, but there was a war coming. How long would they survive deprived of their comforts?

"I'll write when I can," Cole promised. He walked across the courtyard, a little of the afternoon sun going with him.

Celeste sighed. She understood how much of Edmund's dislike of her cousin was rooted in envy. Envy for a man unhampered by family ties, able to travel where he pleased and when he pleased. She picked up her glass of lemonade growing warm in the heat and sipped it. For a few short weeks her life had been enriched. She would always look forward to those letters.

Esther Nye was delighted to see Rico beaming at her as she opened the door. From behind her drifted the sounds of music and laughter. Thick, blue smoke hung from the ceiling and filled the foyer, but the scent Esther wore was stronger than the smoke. It reminded Rico of the sea, vast and mysterious.

She wore a gown of blue-green silk opening over a frilled petticoat of aquamarine edged in vanilla lace. Diamonds were screwed into ears and hung in long icicle formations from her throat and wrists. Her golden brown hair was piled high on her head with thick sausage curls falling over one shoulder. She had the aura of a high-born Creole woman giving a dinner party instead of a madam operating a famous bordello.

She smiled at Rico, her china-blue eyes sweeping over him, widening in appreciation of the tight cut of his trousers and the bolero jacket straining over muscular shoulders. She let them in.

The fight of the night before had not been their

fault. It had been hers for not recognizing the almost painful shyness of the younger man. She should have known he would never have been able to handle Minette properly.

"We wish to apologize for the misunderstanding of last night," Rico said. He bowed to her while presenting a bouquet of summer flowers.

"I have already forgotten last night," she said, accepting the flowers graciously. Her voice was soft and husky. Her eyelids lowered demurely over her blue eyes. "I am glad you returned."

Rico forced Cole into the foyer and closed the door. He took Esther's arm lightly caressing the tender inner flesh under his fingers. She looked up at him. He was so attractive that her heart lurched painfully in her chest. She leaned close to him, savoring his man smell. She had known many men in her life, but none had stirred her the way Rico Hernandez did. He bent and kissed her expertly, nibbling briefly on her ear. Then they walked into the drawing room.

Cole drew away from them, uncomfortable during the moment of their intimacy. He had had little experience with women. He found them confusing.

"Cecile!" Esther called, catching the attention of a dark-skinned woman with curly black hair cut close to her head.

Cecile approached Esther, her printed gown of Italian silk clinging to her body in such a way that Cole felt a blush starting on his face. She was a little plump, but still pretty with dark eyes slightly tilted in an oval face.

"This is Mr. Taggert," Esther said, introducing him to the girl.

The dark eyes surveyed him shrewdly. They saw the dark color staining his cheeks and the immature face embarrassed and confused. She smiled revealing several uneven teeth. "You will see that Mr. Taggert is well cared for," Esther warned. Cecile caught the warning in the words and nodded.

"Come, Monsieur," she said, sliding a gloved hand under Cole's elbow and drawing him into the room. Her voice was surprisingly deep. Cole shivered. "May I offer you a drink?"

"Wine," he said hoarsely. She led him to a sofa partially hidden in a recessed alcove.

"Then we shall have wine." She snapped her fingers at a hovering waiter.

He nervously swallowed the lump in his throat.

"He's in good hands," Esther said to Rico. "Cecile understands the young and innocent."

"Hmmm!" Rico commented watching Esther. His eyes strayed to the bodice of her gown. It was very chaste, yet excellently revealing. It was hard to keep his fingers from her.

"Come along, I shall see you settled with a bottle of wine. Then I must resume my duties as hostess. You do understand, I cannot take my pleasures until I have seen to the comfort of my guests."

Rico understood. He followed her to a quiet corner acquiring two very handsome women as he walked. He allowed them to stay, flattering them and caressing them boldly, yet his eyes never left Esther Nye.

Esther's taste was faultless. The drawing room was decorated in muted tones of grays and blues with chinese silk on the walls. The usual ornamentation for brothels was missing. There was taste and elegance in the room without misleading the occupants as to its true purpose. There were no suggestive paintings on the walls, yet there was a mural on the ceiling of nubile numphs and well-endowed heroes, but a person had to crane his neck to see it. There were several marble statues in corners, yet each one was chastely covered. There was a lack of promiscuous overtones in the room that made the sensual undertones twice as exciting.

There was not a woman in the room who wore anything less than a gown that was in the height of fashion. Necklines were low, but not indecent. All the girls were pretty, but they were more than companions in bed. There were courtesans in the highest sense.

Rico sat back. His two companions had disappeared to be replaced by two more. The redhead pouted sourly when he refused to go upstairs with her. She glared at Esther sullenly. Esther looked up from across the room where she stood near the bar. She smiled at Rico who saluted her with his wineglass. She mouthed the word soon to him and he smiled his understanding.

Cecile was soft and sweet. She pressed herself into Cole's side like a kitten. She turned warm brown eyes on him in invitation. A few glasses of wine loosened him. He felt bold enough to put an arm around her and kiss her. She giggled and pulled his head down gently.

"You must learn to kiss properly," she whispered into his ear. She repeated the kiss.

A need flared in Cole. Cecile smiled at him, as she stood up and took his hand drawing him to his feet. He followed her out of the room and up the wide curving staircase in the foyer. She teased him slightly allowing him to touch her breast. His breath caught in his throat. He wanted to explore her further, but she stopped him.

"In here," she said, opening a door at the top of the stairs. The room was dark. She lit candles until it was bathed in light.

The suggestive paintings missing in the drawing room were plainly evident here. Men and women in varying forms of undress and intimacy stared at him. He looked with interest until he realized what they were. Then he drew back embarrassed.

"Do you like them?" Cecile asked. She came up softly, wrapping her arms around him.

Cole didn't know what to say. He stared at the painting unaware that Cecile was undressing him expertly. He tried to draw away from her, but her hands followed him easing him gently out of his shirt.

"We should be comfortable," she said.

A knock on the door interrupted them. Cecile went to it and opened it to a maid pushing a cart with a bottle of iced champagne and two glasses on it. There were two covered trays which told Cole they were food by the rich aroma emanating from them.

"I have heard that Texas men have large appetites," Cecile said. She served food on a plate to him. "I'm not very hungry. You go and eat." She smiled coaxingly. It was all Cole needed to dig into the food.

Cecile disappeared into an alcove Cole had not noticed before. When she returned she wore nothing, but a deep blue robe which clung to every part of her body.

"I won't eat you," she whispered. "Have some more wine."

"I . . . uh . . . never . . . had . . ."

". . . much to do with women before," she finished for him. She pulled the wheeled table away from him and opening the door shoved it out into the hall. "I understand. It must have been very lonely for you in Texas." She sat on the arm of his chair, the robe gapping slightly as she leaned over him. He could see the dark outline of her breasts under the robe. A throbbing heat filled him and intensified. His hands felt damp, his knees trembled. Cecile slid from the arm of the chair to his lap, pulling his head close to hers and kissing him deeply. She caressed his lean chest allowing her hands to wander close to the band of his trousers.

"You are a handsome man, Cole Taggert," she whispered, putting his hand inside her robe.

Her skin was soft and fragrant. With coaxing, Cole found himself exploring, his fingers probing into the dark shadows of her body. He began to enjoy what he was doing, and the fervor of his kissing increasing.

Cecile laughed a low, throaty laugh. She stood up and drew him with her into the alcove. She undressed him quickly and left him standing in the middle of the floor while she lit several more candles. Then she turned to him, untying the sash around her waist. With a fluid movement, the robe fell to the floor.

"Don't look away," she whispered huskily. She placed his hands on her. "A woman is made for pleasure as much as a man. First I will pleasure you, then I will teach you to pleasure me." She drew him into an embrace. Their lips met hungrily.

Cole started to blow out the candles, but she stopped him.

"No," she said softly. "It is good to see what you are doing before you learn to do it in the dark." She fell back on the bed drawing him with her.

The trip upriver was leisurely. Cole spent his first day on deck watching the shore passing swiftly by. The succession of stately mansions caught his interest, but he found himself growing bored with their sameness. They were mostly the same, huge two-storied houses with long verandas and white columns. He idly thought of the house he would build when he returned to Texas. It would be low and square in the Spanish style with all the rooms opening on a central courtyard. It would be a grand hacienda.

A wave of homesickness came over him for the lush plains and the waist-high grass. Louisiana was just a stopping place in his life. It did not compare to the simple beauty of Texas.

Renault de Champlain had arranged for first class staterooms for Cole and Rico. Cole felt surprise, then amusement, everytime he walked into the huge stateroom with its polished brass bed bolted to the floor. It looked strange on this boat. It was a different world from the simplicity he had known in the past.

"Mr. Taggert!" The voice was high and sweet. It belonged to Jane Borden whose dark good looks would attract any man.

"Good morning, Miss Borden," he said politely. There was an air of gentility about Miss Borden whose voluptuous body promised more than her subdued manner.

"Good morning, sir. Mama was asking about you. We thought you might join us for lunch later. Mama so enjoyed your company last night." Jane lowered thick, curling lashes over bright blue eyes. She brushed against Cole invitingly. Cecile's training had been thorough. She woke in Cole an awareness of his masculinity and its attractiveness to women. She also taught him the difference between a woman who offered a sincere invitation and a woman who was a tease. Jane Borden was a tease.

"I would enjoy sharing luncheon with you, Miss Borden. Last night was enjoyable for me as well," Cole replied.

"Mama will be so pleased," she gushed, brushing against him a second time. She liked this tall, quiet Texan. He offered none of the flowery conversation she was used to receiving, yet she was still drawn to him. She smiled at him, admiring the firm line of his jaw and the sharp eyes that sent delicious little shivers down her spine. He made her feel quite daring in a way no other man had done.

"Would you care to stroll about the deck, Mr. Taggert?" she asked prettily. She pouted when he said no.

"You go on without me," he said never taking his eyes from the distant shore. A child was playing on lush, green grass. Her dark hair flowed behind her in wild abandon. She waved at the riverboat and Cole found himself waving back. The black child following the girl caught up to her and Cole could hear the sound of their laughter flowing across the water. He grinned to realize some doting mother had even been allowed to dispense with long skirts for the girl. She looked free and cool in her buff-coloured trousers and knee high boots. She continued to wave at the steamboat. Cole responded until she would was out of sight.

"You have angered a lady, *amigo*." Rico said, startling him.

Cole was still thinking about the pretty child on the shore. He turned puzzled eyes on his friend. "Not the child, but the Señorita Borden." Rico grinned in amusement. "Does the lovely Señorita not please you? Such a figure." He traced an outline in the air with his hands and whistled through his teeth. "And such a bosom. I spent the night with a woman who would give anything for such a bosom as the Señorita Borden."

"Women and sex," Cole said shaking his head. "Don't you ever think about anything else?" For four years he had lived, walked and worked with this tall man. Never had he known such an intense pre-occupation with women in anyone else.

Rico shrugged. He had inherited his immense charm and extreme handsomeness from his mother's Castilian ancestors. He had inherited the erect bearing and style of his mulatto father's African heritage.

"I like the women. They like me. What else in life provides a man with such pleasure?" He shrugged philosophically.

Cole chuckled. He felt a child next to his older friend's experience.

Mid-afternoon saw the steamboat tying up at the de Champlain landing. Cole and Rico departed the ship for a rundown, two-story house completely hidden from the river by a tangled overgrowth of bushes and trees. The plantation was private and isolated. Deep bayous surrounded it making it impossible to reach or to leave except by the river.

"Here we are, Rico," Cole said, dropping his

bedroll and valise on the ground. He stared at the old house. Roustabouts were unloading supplies from the ship. Their laughter penetrated the heavy undergrowth. Cole approached the house warily. Windows had been broken and boarded up. Plaster had chipped from the outside walls and lay in piles on the ground. Mice scampered freely through the weeds.

"The *patrón* shows no interests in this fine home." Rico walked inside to pock-marked hardwood floors and moth-eaten carpets.

"I think he has a special reason for not being interested.

"Why so, *amigo?*"

"There's war coming. What enemy would be interesed in a derelict place like this?"

"No enemy would glance at it when there are far richer *haciendas* around."

"Where would a man hide something he does not want found?"

"In a place such as this. No?" Rico replied. "This *patron* is a very smart *hombre*."

"Very smart. We must be careful he does not outsmart us."

"Very careful," Rico agreed. He had gotten the impression that the Señor was basically an honest man, though an honest man who would be quick to take advantage of others.

They took the spacious kitchen at the back of the house for their living quarters and spent the remainder of the day cleaning it. In the early dusk, they went to the landing with an old wagon found in a barn, hitched to two old dray horses sleek and fat from idleness and grazing. They moved the stacks of boxes from the landing to store in the barn for the night. In the morning, they located the cleverly hidden warehouses and unloaded the wagon. When they returned to the landing, they found another steamboat tying up and the Captain hailing them. They spent the rest of the day moving the newest shipment to the warehouse.

Cole was satisfied. It was the beginning of a shared dream with Rico in owning their own land. Rico was less happy. There were no women and he preferred his work from the back of a good horse. But they managed, thinking of the money that would be theirs in the end.

Fourteen

"Renault!" Victoire said softly. She looked very pretty with the glow of candlelight on her face. Her dark hair was piled high on her head with several diamond encrusted pins securing it. She wore a gown of apple green silk with dark green velvet trim. Her large eyes were shadowed with sadness. "You will be returning to your wife soon. Before you leave we must speak of the children."

Renault folded his evening newspaper, laying it neatly on the table next to him. He had been expecting this conversation for days. He glanced at the dark heads of his twin son and daughter as they sat quietly on the floor reading a book though their sharp ears were attuned to the conversation between their parents.

They were thirteen, three months older than Fleur. They had wistful looks in their eyes that reminded him of Marget. There was a maturity in their slim faces that none of his other children possessed. It was as though the words bastard and nigger had aged them into maturity long before their time.

Renault was proud of them. He loved them dearly.

"It is time for them both to be sent away to school." Victoire said. She smiled tenderly at her children.

Victoire had been nearly twenty-two when she went to her first quadroon ball. Not because she wanted to go, but out of necessity. The small pension her mother had been given by her father was not enough for two. The only course available to her was the ball where she would contract an alliance with a wealthy man and live the rest of her life in comfort.

Renault de Champlain, young and wealthy, had seen her and fallen in love. In a short time, Victoire had been established in her discreet cottage off Rampart Street. She was surprised when the liaison was a happy one. She was even more surprised when it continued after Renault had married.

"Have you decided where you wish to send them?" he asked.

"Etienne is to go to Paris to the academy where my brother would have gone if he had lived. Ursule is to go to the South of France to the convent I attended."

"It will be arranged immediately."

"Thank you." she said simply. She kissed him, then called the children to him. They thanked him gravely and were sent to bed. Renault picked up his paper. More and more of the paper was filled with news of the coming elections and what the South would do if Lincoln were elected president. It was preparing itself for a firm stand on the right to secede and gearing itself for war with the North. Renault shook his head. War was a folly committed at any time. It would crush the South.

Victoire returned. She had changed from her gown to a robe of dusty rose silk. It clung to her body showing off her slim curves. With her dark hair tumbling about her shoulders, Renault was reminded of the proud beauty she had been in her youth. He had been attracted to her pride. It was seldom that a man continued his association with his mistress after his marriage. The arrangement between man and placee was usually a short one, pensioning the woman when the man had gone on to marriage with a woman of his class. But Renault had loved Victoire deeply and had been unable to give her up. Though their children were late in coming, he was doubly glad he had them especially his fine son. He had found he could not step out of their lives as casually as some men did. They were his responsibility and he could never have deserted them.

Victoire brought coffee. The rich aroma filled the room.

"Thank you, Renault," Victoire said.

"For what, my love?"

"For sending them away." she replied. She did not add that it was a relief to her to have them out of the city with the danger of war threatening.

"They will be safe in France," Renault said, accurately guessing the thoughts in her mind.

She gasped, looking at him, but there was no reproach in his look. She had not meant for him to know how she felt. She could not justify sending away her own children when his legitimate children remained.

"Do not worry, *ma chère,*" he said, drawing her close. She sat down on his knees, her robe gapping slightly. He slid cool fingers through the gap to caress her warm flesh. She undid the sash at her waist and allowed the robe to fall off her shoulders. Renault ran his hands over her. "My other family will be sent to

218

safety if they are endangered." He kissed her lightly and she swayed against him. He nodded at the bedroom and she smiled. Her robe fell to the floor as she stood and walked across the room to the bed-chamber.

Renault unbuttoned his shirt. As he turned to Victoire a great explosion sounded in the city. The little cottage shook, pictures fell from walls, clattering to the floor. Glass broke into thousands of fragments. There was a second enormous blast. A candle fell over and Renault dived to put it out. Victoire screamed at the third explosion. Then there was silence before the air was split with the sounds of slamming doors and running feet. Sylvie poked her head into the bedroom while she tried to shush the frightened children.

Victoire ran out of the room, pushing Sylvie out of her way. She grabbed her robe and pulled it on. Then she flung open the front door and raced outside with Renault right behind her. A great glow filled the sky over the levees.

"What has happened?" Victoire cried, crossing herself.

Renault did not answer. He ran down the path to the street hailing a passing cab. He was at the levee before he realized his shirt was unbuttoned and he still wore his slippers.

A crowd was already gathered helplessly watching the huge paddle-wheeler adrift in the middle of the river completely encased in flames. There were high screams. People were still flinging themselves from the burning decks into the water, their clothes on fire.

Small boats were being launched to search for survivors. They waded through the wreckage of steamboat and bodies.

"Monsieur de Champlain!"

Renault stepped back from the edge to face Edmund Vernay waving wildly. "You have come, Monsieur. It was the *Lady Marion*." Edmund had to shout to be heard over the confused babble of the crowd.

Renault felt ill. His old, trustworthy *Lady Marion* was gone.

"How many aboard?"

"She had just docked." Edmund's eyes were glazed with hysteria. "Captain Monroe handed me the manifest and then the boilers blew. One moment he was standing with me on the dock and the next, he was gone."

"Stop it, Edmund," Renault shouted, shaking the man roughly. Edmund stared at him unseeing. "How many passengers?"

"Two hundred and twelve," Edmund finally mumbled.

"Go home, Edmund. There is nothing you can do."

Edmund shuffled off dazed. Every few seconds he would turn around to stare at the fire.

Survivors floundered in the water. Boats pulled them aboard. Women screamed and cried begging their rescuers to find missing family members. Renault stared at the water. An unattached hand with two missing fingers bobbed on the surface. These disasters always happened, but they never failed to make him ill.

A woman grasped Renault's hand. Tears trickled down her face. The force of the blast had torn away the bodice of her gown exposing her. She seemed uncaring. She stared at Renault as he stripped off his

220

shirt and wrapped it around her.

"Please, sir," she pleaded in a whisper. "My children!"

Renault knew no words to comfort her.

"They were standing next to me on the deck. I can't find them. Will you help me look?" Her eyes were dazed with horror.

Carts and wagons from the hospital clattered across the dock, the rumble of their wheels drowning the groans of the injured. A passing doctor took the woman from Renault and led her gently away. It was only then that Renault saw that she was missing a hand. The doctor put a tourniquet on her arm and pushed her down with the other injured.

Nuns walked toward the docking boats taking the injured into their capable arms. Renault wanted to shut out the horror of the picture before him, but it would be engraved in his memory for the rest of his life.

A small boy wandered aimlessly about the dock. His clothes had been ripped away leaving him with one shoe and the collar of his shirt dangling from his neck. A nun came up and wrapped a blanket around him, picking him up and carrying him to a cart.

The flames of the steamboat lit the dock casting long, eerie shadows. Renault helped a man who had stumbled and fallen. A shard of wood stuck out of his back. A doctor was found to take the man.

Renault stayed on the dock for hours helping with the wounded and watching helplessly as the *Lady Marion* continued to burn. Gradually the bodies were recovered from the river and laid on the ground to await identification and burial.

When the last of the wounded was finally removed to the hospital, Renault returned home. As he drove away in the carriage, he watched the still smoldering wreckage of his ship. The flames grew less and less as the boat sank into the greedy river. In the morning, she would be towed away and abandoned in some bayou where nature would eventually remove any trace of her.

Victoire stood at the front door. She still wore her robe though it was wrinkled from her long hours of waiting. She smiled at him through trembling lips. She realized with a shock that Renault looked like an old man. When had he grown old? She led him into their bedroom. She undressed him and pushed him into bed. Then she crawled in next to him falling into an exhausted sleep.

Marget stood at the rail of the steamship, *Inheritance*. It was one of her father's ocean-going ships, sleek and beautiful. She enjoyed looking at it. She enjoyed looking at its captain.

"I hope you are feeling better, Madame de Ville."

"I am not a good sailor, Captain Quinlan," she replied looking into smiling gray eyes. He was a young man, barely thirty, with sandy-colored hair and a sprinkling of freckles across the strong bridge of his straight nose.

"I am sorry you do not like sailing." He came to stand at the rail with her.

She was conscious of the warmth of his body so close to her. He felt so different from the clammy coldness of Benoit.

"I wish to thank you for sending the doctor to see

me," she said. Benoit had refused to comfort her. He had insisted she would recover.

"It was my pleasure. I love the sea."

"I am happy for you." Marget smiled gently. He turned a sun-weathered face to her. There was a quickening in her heart that was echoed in the sudden darkening of his eyes. She turned away in confusion. When she looked up, he was gone, striding across the deck nodding politely to the other passengers.

"What was he saying to you?" Benoit demanded harshly, his face twisted with jealousy. The smell of brandy reached Marget long before he did. She turned away from the staleness of his breath.

"He was inquiring after my health." She started to move away, but Benoit pulled her back.

"You are my wife," he snarled. "I do not like other men talking to you. I can be a very jealous man and will not tolerate any indiscretions on your part."

"I will be a faithful wife. I have been taught to honor the vows of marriage."

Florence Sanderson pranced across the deck swinging her wide hoops and exposing her ankles. She had pale gold hair piled under a hat decorated with bright red cherries. Marget thought the little hat ridiculous though Florence maintained it was the latest from Paris. Florence stopped a few feet from Benoit and beckoned him with one long, carmine tipped finger. Benoit left Marget for Florence. Without a further word to Marget, he placed Florence's hand on his arm and led her for one last promenade around the deck.

Marget waited patiently for Benoit to secure a carriage to take them to the hotel. She looked about her half expecting to see her father, but there was no sign of his thin, erect figure. She swallowed her disappointment. She looked up and encountered the dark gaze of Captain Quinlan on her as he oversaw the unloading of his ship. She blushed deeply remembering the strange emotions they had shared during their few moments at the rail. She would never forget him nor his kindness to her. Benoit approached. He picked up her valise and guided her to an open landaulet. He helped her in, casually tossing a coin to a roustabout and giving him directions for the transfer of their luggage to the hotel.

It was wonderful to be home again. Marget breathed in the heavy air of New Orleans happily. The Vieux Carre was cramped and dirty, but it was home. She saw a friend and waved to her.

The friend waved back.

"Must you act like a child," Benoit said sharply. "You are a married woman and a lady. Stop making a spectacle of yourself waving to people on the street. Act with dignity, hard as I know it is."

Marget felt herself shrinking. She imagined she got smaller and smaller until she was so small she disappeared. Helpless tears gathered in the corners of her eyes and dripped down her cheeks. She brushed them away. Was this the way the rest of her life would be? Always the object of Benoit's spite. He complained bitterly of every gesture she used, the clothes she wore and her performance in the intimacy of their bedchamber. He was never pleased and was very verbal about it. Marget felt crushed.

The landaulet pulled up and stopped in front of the hotel. Benoit paid the driver and helped Marget out.

It was a beautiful old hotel, built in the early days of New Orleans. Marget had never been inside and looked about her in wonder as Benoit checked in at the desk.

Their suite was large and airy. Several large bouquets were arranged on various tables, all with little cards tucked away in the leaves. A huge basket sat on the floor. Marget opened the small note and read a greeting from her father.

"What does it say?" Benoit called impatiently.

"It is from my father. Business kept him from meeting the ship. He will see us at dinner in the dining room at eight thirty. He apologizes for the inconvenience."

"Well he should!" Benoit grumbled. "How will it look when word gets around to all my friends that my father-in-law could not spare a moment from business to meet me? Especially after surviving the perils of a dangerous sea voyage. I don't think he much cares for you."

Marget walked away from the grumble of words. She entered her bedchamber and closed the door cutting off the string of words from Benoit. She locked the door and walked across to the bathroom, unbuttoning her jacket as she walked. She dropped the jacket on a chair.

She started water in the huge marble tub and quickly undressed dropping her clothes indiscriminately on the floor. Living on a ship had many inconveniences. One of them was lack of proper bathing facilities. For several days, she had longed for a bath that washed all of her at one time instead of little sections.

A knock on her door sounded, but she ignored it. She stepped into the warm water and lay back with a weary sigh. When the water reached her neck, she turned it off. There was another series of knocks and Benoit's voice shrilling for admittance. She closed her eyes and pretended he didn't exist. The knocking ceased and she drifted to a half-sleep, the tensions of the day draining away from her.

"Hello, my dear."

Marget's eyes flew open. Benoit stood next to the tub clad only in a robe sashed at his waist.

"Are you enjoying your bath? It does look comfortable."

"How did you get in here?"

"You forgot to lock the door from my bedchamber," he said untying the sash of his robe and dropping it onto the floor. "I have always wanted to bathe with a woman. Do you mind? No, of course not. After all, I am your husband. Move over." He stepped into the tub and slid down to sit next to her. He smiled as he ran his hands over her body.

"No, Benoit," she said, struggling to get up. Her foot slipped and she fell back banging her knee on the edge.

"When are you going to learn I am your husband, Marget?" he asked. His voice was soft and sweet. He continued to fondle her, his fingers invading the privacy of her body. "You owe complete obedience to me."

Marget squirmed, but he held her down firmly. He kissed her, his lips a violation of her mouth.

"I owe complete obedience to no one, but God," she protested trying to keep him from sliding between her legs. He forced her knees apart with a firm hand.

"Not God, my dear. Me! Only me!" He laughed as he nuzzled her neck, his hands roaming over her. "Only me!"

Renault had never seen his daughter look so lifeless. She was deathly pale and walked as though her whole body hurt her. She was thin, her clothes hanging limply from her listless body. He had expected a radiant bride. Instead he found a woman with a haunted look in the depths of her dark eyes.

Benoit was enthusiastic in his greetings. He shook Renault's hand eagerly. He had the look of a man well-satisfied with life. He was solicitous of his wife, helping her into her chair and admiring her gown with flowery compliments. She looked up with dead eyes and said nothing.

"Now tell me about Nassau, Marget. Did you like it?" Renault said, not liking the look in her downcast eyes. She looked briefly and then away.

"Nassau was superb," Benoit gushed. He was a fountain of words. They spilled from his mouth with ever increasing force. "It is not much like New Orleans except for the heat and dampness. It is very colorful and even more relaxed than here. The natives wear very colorful clothes and walk about selling exotic birds and animals. I was tempted to purchase a parrot for Marget, but she did not want it."

"What about you, Marget," Renault continued. "Did you enjoy yourself?"

"Of course she enjoyed herself." Benoit said. "We dined with the governor and went to several balls. We even lunched at a plantation. It is a jungle away from the cities. The food is much different and they drink large quantities of rum. I much prefer wine."

"And you, Marget," Renault persisted. He was fast becoming annoyed with Benoit. "What did you do?"

"She shopped and spent a fortune, I can tell you. Didn't you, my love. She took tea with the ladies in the afternoons and walked along the quay in the evening. A lot of people there are talking seriously about war. I told them it was all nonsense. But they are a bunch of provincials. A lot of ships were putting into port outfitting themselves for blockade running. Never saw such foolishness! Blockade running! If there is a war, it won't amount to much. Be over in a month or two. We'll send those Yankees home howling for their mammies."

A waiter approached and took their order. Renault was not pleased to find Benoit ordering without consulting his wife.

"Are you certain you want the shrimp, Marget?" Renault asked.

"Of course she wants the shrimp," Benoit answered. "All the time we were gone she talked of nothing but good New Orleans food. Nassau serves tasty dishes, but not like our food."

Renault could see that conversation with his daughter was hopeless. Benoit was so enchanted with the sound of his own voice, he could not allow his wife to speak. He spoke constantly, making observations about the possible war and about Nassau in comparison with New Orleans. Marget seldom looked up from her plate.

"When do you plan to return to Grandeville?" Renault asked when dinner had been cleared away.

"In a few days," Benoit answered casually. The wine relaxed him. He felt important. "Marget wants to do some shopping before returning home and I have business. It is a pity you are to be delayed here. We could have journeyed up-river together."

"With the loss of the *Lady Marion,* I find myself caught trying to settle all the claims."

"I am sorry about the *Lady Marion,* Papa," Marget said, looking up at him. "I know how you must feel."

"Don't be absurd, Marget," Benoit said impatiently, brushing his wife's words away like an annoying speck of dust. "Who is sentimental over an old hulk like that. The accommodations were terrible. Your father has other steamboats. He will hardly miss the old thing."

Marget looked down at the table. Her face was as stiff as if carved in marble. She did not speak again.

Renault was distressed. She was so listless and uninterested in things. He had thought Benoit would make her a good husband, yet the opposite seemed to be true. He wanted control of Grandeville, but did he want it at the expense of his daughter's happiness? Renault shrugged. What was done was done. There was no going back.

He left the hotel and hailed a cab giving Victoire's address.

"Monsieur, a gentleman to see you," Edmund announced.

"Good morning, Monsieur de Champlain." The man who walked into Renault's office was short and stocky. He had brown hair and pale skin. His eyes were narrow and blue in a plump face.

"May I help you?" Renault asked. The man appeared to be about thirty. He seemed to have a no-nonsense approach to what might turn into a very ugly meeting.

"I am Philippe D'Arcy," he said holding out a stubby fingered hand. "I represent the Criessant family. You do not know the name, but four members of the family perished on your steamboat last week."

Renault picked up a sheaf of papers and flipped through them. "I know the name. The manifest had been turned in to my accountant before the explosion."

"There were two survivors. A boy of eighteen and his sister, fifteen. They are anxious to settle this dreadful business. Their parents and younger brother were dear to them. No amount of money can replace a human life, but . . . "

" . . . but, they are willing to settle for an amount large enough to help them over the shock."

"We understand each other," Philippe D'Arcy said smiling.

"How much are they willing to settle for?" Renault asked wearily. He felt old and tired. Riverboat explosions brought out mulititudes of people claiming damages for existent and non-existent relatives. Renault held claims for seven hundred victims of the explosion. The official death count had been forty-eight.

The lawyer leaned back in his chair smiling amiably. His claim was legitimate and he knew the Criessant family would be satisfied. They argued amiably for half-an-hour before finally settling on a figure.

When Monsieur D'Arcy had left, Renault leaned back in his chair exhausted. Another claimant had been satisfied. He ordered Edmund to prepare the necessary papers.

The mail arrived. A short note from Cole Taggert was in the stack of envelopes informing Renault that all was well at the isolated plantation. He included a list of badly needed supplies which Renault gave to Edmund.

"If you have a few moments, sir." Edmund said at the end of the day. "May I speak to you?"

Renault nodded. Edmund walked into the office with the St. Angele account books under his arm. He lay them on the desk and opened them.

"I have been going through these and I have found something." He pointed to a list of figures and then to a second list in another book. "This is the yield for this past year. This is the yield from the account books for 1858. They are identical. This particular page caught my attention because the notations were exactly the same as the previous year's. Your manager has been copying whole pages from the accounts from previous years and entering them for this year to make the present entries read consistently. Here on this page, he only copied twelve items, but he uses the exact wording your previous man used. I have marked it and several other pages."

"Very interesting," Renault remarked. He looked at the figures for both ledgers frowning.

"He used the back ledgers because he wasn't certain what the proper figures would be. I suspect if you look in his desk you will find a separate ledger with the proper entries."

"Leave this here, Edmund. I want to look it over. I shall have to have Miles dismissed. Start a search for a new man immediately. Check his credentials thoroughly. Make sure he is scrupulously honest."

"Yes, sir."

"I must go. I have a dinner engagement with my daughter and her husband. Thank you, Edmund. You can expect a bonus in your next pay envelope."

Renault spen another uncomfortable dinner with Marget. During the meal he outlined the improvement for Grandeville which Benoit heartily sanctioned.

"We shall repair the outlying buildings first and save the house for later. I have already sent new stock to your mother and some special equipment I purchased in Chicago."

"Interesting! New equipment," Benoit said. "I shall have a look at it and see if it is appropriate. Don't trust Yankee merchandise." He gestured expansively.

"The equipment is already being used," Renault said. "I do not expect you to soil your hands by taking an interest in Grandeville. A good overseer has been provided who knows how I work and how I like things."

Benoit frowned. He thought he would have a voice in the managing of Grandeville. He was finding he was the owner on paper only.

"When I return home, Marget, I hope you will come and visit your mother and me."

"Of course, she will," Benoit said. "We will both come and visit every chance we get. Won't we, my dear." He nudged her and she nodded obediently.

Benoit had been drinking heavily all during the

meal. Renault did not like it. Benoit grew flushed. His eyes turned cloudy and he slurred as he spoke. Renault found him repulsive. Not once did he think his daughter also found Benoit repulsive. He decided it was time to go. He made his excuses and left Marget to struggle with getting Benoit up the stairs to their suite.

"Goin' home to his nigger mistress," Benoit sneered cruelly as he stumbled along the lobby and up the broad staircase.

"What do you mean?" Marget asked when she had closed the door to their suite.

"I told you. Your Papa lives with an octoroon gal. Every year when you and your family are upriver in the country, he returns to the city and lives with some octoroon gal."

"That isn't true. He is devoted to my maman."

Benoit grinned nastily. "I doubt he is devoted to anything but money. If your maman is as cold as you, I can understand why he takes his pleasures with his mistress. Good-looking, too. So are the children."

"Children!" Marget felt faint. "He has children?"

"So you didn't know about your nigger brother and sister. You know now. How does it feel to know your Papa is unfaithful and had children with nigger blood in them? How does it feel?"

"I feel it is none of our business," Marget said steadily. She clenched her hands to keep them from trembling. She was bitterly shaken to think her maman was not the only woman in her papa's life. Did she know about the octoroon woman? She must. Her many friends would never allow a situation like that to remain secret. There was little privacy in the

233

Vieux Carre. It was a separate little world from the rest of the city.

Marget felt sick. She turned away from her husband going into her bedchamber.

"It is our business," he insisted following her.

"No," she said firmly. She pushed him back into the sitting room and closed her door.

"I'm your husband, Marget. Let me in." He yelled pounding on the door.

"I do not feel well."

"You are always ill. I'm your husband. Let me in."

"Go find an octoroon mistress of your own and leave me alone." she snapped. There was silence. Marget ran into the bathroom and locked the door to Benoit's bedchamber.

When he tried the handle, he grew abusive.

"You will regret this," he screamed.

Marget did not answer. She leaned against the door feeling her heart pound with the enormity of what she had just done. She had refused him.

With an angry curse, Benoit flung open the door to the suite and slammed it behind him. He staggered down the staircase unconcerned over the stares he received. Out in the street he found a carriage and got into it, growling the name of Esther Nye's brothel.

Fifteen

The house was very old. It had stood in its cheery glade since before the De Champlain family came to the area. It once boasted four thick walls and two large rooms. Now one end of the house was caved in. The other looked sound enough from a distance, but close inspection showed gaps in the walls and holes in the roof. There were no windows and the rough floor was dirt.

Fleur reined in her horse as she neared the old house. She was always careful of her approach. The tall, unkempt weeds hid an army of insects and poisonous snakes. She almost stepped on one once when in her eagerness she trod unwarily.

Fleur dismounted and tied her horse to a bush. She walked into the house carefully, checking for Michael who had not arrived. She pushed open the sagging door and stepped into the dim interior. The inside was plain and bare. The destruction seemed less. There was a certain tidiness in the room. The floor was swept and the shelves were dusted.

Michael had repaired the bed and Fleur had brought old blankets and sheets with a tick mattress she had found in the attic at St. Angele. She had brought a coffee pot and two chipped cups so they

235

could have hot coffee on cold days.

Fleur knelt down at the fireplace and built a tiny fire carefully feeding it until the chilled room started to warm. When the fire was going well, Fleur stepped outside to the well and filled the pot with water and went inside to add coffee and set the pot in the fire. Soon the aroma of the coffee would fill the air.

She stood up looking with pride at the little room. She worked hard at making it seem homelike. In it she could pretend she was a woman grown with a husband and a home of her own.

There was a sound outside. Fleur flew to the window. It wasn't Michael. She worried. He was seldom late. Normally he would be waiting for her already undressed and propped up in the bed when she arrived.

Fleur blushed at the thought of his smooth, young body. He was so different from Noble who was large and muscular and from Benoit who was too soft. Even his lovemaking was very different. At times he would be gentle and tender. At other times, he would be a violent fury. That was when Fleur was frightened of him. That was when he deviated from the normal ways of making love Noble had taught her. Yet as frightened as she was, she thrilled to that element of strangeness in him and accepted the roles he assigned her with a calmness that amazed her. Some of the things he did, she actually enjoyed, but others filled her with a revulsion for him and for herself. Despite the degradation, she still came back.

Absently she smoothed the blanket over the bed. She looked anxiously out the window. The fire died to coals and she put more twigs on it coaxing it back to life. She filled a cup with coffee and stood in the middle of the room sipping it absently. She had almost made up her mind to leave when Michael walked in the door.

As always, her breath caught in her throat at the sight of his handsome face and virile body. He wore dark colored trousers with knee length boots slightly dusty from his ride. He smiled at her.

"Been waiting long?" he asked. He came to stand in front of her, grasping her chin with one hand and pawing at her breasts with the other. She sighed and leaned against him feeling his hardness against her leg. "Sorry to be so late," he said. He sat down on the bed and held a booted foot out to her. She grasped the heel and tugged it off. Then she tugged the other boot off. "Grandaddy wants everything to be perfect for his new bride. We're all busier than we like."

The whole parish buzzed with the news of Fay Courtland's coming marriage to old Marcus Slaughter. Some people were scandalized, but most were indifferent. With the hysteria of the November elections approaching, few people were concerned with the news of a man wedding a woman fifty years his junior.

Michael stood up and started to unbutton his trousers. Fleur stood back to watch him.

"Well!" he said. His fingers flew impatiently. When he was naked he turned back to Fleur who still stood in the middle of the room fully clothed. His eyes commanded, and she slowly started to unbutton.

When they first started meeting in the old cabin, he had courted her with flowers and sweet words. As time went on, he grew impatient. Fleur missed the gentle

Michael she had first known. She was a little in awe of the impatient man who took less time in arousing her and more time in prolonging his own pleasures.

She fumbled at her skirt, unfastening the buttons and sliding it down over her hips. She tugged at the tapes of her petticoats, aware of his irritation over her slowness. She hesitated at the ribbon which held her pantelets, but the feverish look he favored her with sent her fingers flying to untie it.

Michael watched her avidly. He liked the slim immature body she presented when she stood in front of him a slight blush covering her body. He reached out and touched one tiny breast. He liked exploring her hairless body, so different from the full-blown women he had already known. He reached down to touch the soft swell of her stomach, reaching into the darkness between her legs. She moaned slightly, straining to stand next to him. He gestured at the bed and she obediently lay down. He sat next to her, moving his hands over her, kissing a breast and then her lips.

Fleur shivered. She lay on the bed waiting for him to lay next to her, but he got up and walked to the fireplace and took a small box from the mantle. He looked at her and she immediately spread her legs and her arms while he drew out a stout rope and tied her to the bed.

"It's too tight, Michael," she said a little frightened at the look on his face.

He ignored her and turned around.

"Come on in, fellows," he called.

Fleur craned her neck to see around him. Her eyes dilated in fear as his two younger brothers walked into the room already tugging at their clothes.

"We have a little treat for you, Fleur," Michael said. He sat down again running his hands over her body. "Isn't she a looker. I told you she was beautiful," he said to his brothers.

They both nodded eagerly running pink tongues over thin lips.

"Now, my dear," Michael said, kneeling on the bed. His youngest brother came to kneel by her head. "You will oblige my brothers the same way you oblige me."

An animal whimper sounded in the back of her throat. She struggled helplessly against the ropes. One of the brothers giggled childishly as he looked down at her.

"Be good, Fleur," Michael said. He smiled at her.

Her nightmare had only started.

It was late afternoon when Fleur finally found the strength to roll off the bed and pull on her clothes. She hurt. Every movement of her body was agony. She dressed slowly leaving streaks of blood on her clothes from ripped and torn fingernails.

"I hate him," she whispered through the haze of her pain. "I hate him."

She stopped and rested after a few moments, then continued pulling on her clothes. Never again would Michael Slaughter have her. Never again would she allow a man to use her as he had used her. She wanted revenge, but was wise enough to know, she was only a woman. Her resources were limited.

She moved painfully across the room to the fire. Her skirt overturned the coffee pot spreading a dark stain on the stones. She ignored it as she knelt down painfully and rebuilt the fire. As it grew under her torn fingers, she added larger and larger pieces until the room was a furnace. She walked to the door and dropped a pile of twigs. She dropped another pile on the bed. She picked up a long stick and held it in the flames until it caught. Then she set the small piles of wood on fire, watching them catch and stepping outside as the house exploded in a roar of fire.

The hatred in her grew as the fire grew. She stood outside watching it. No man would ever do to her what Michael had done. Never again would she suffer those indignities. She turned away, stumbling for her horse. She mounted awkwardly wondering how she was going to explain the bruises on her face and body and her torn fingers. She turned her horse toward home knowing the cabin would never again be used by her.

Marget hated Grandeville on sight. As she stepped off the landing to be embraced by her mother-in-law, she stared at the plantation house. The porch sagged like an old drunken sailor. Paint peeled in long strips from the wood to hang from it or fall to the ground adding to the piles among the tall, randomly growing weeds. The marble of the tall white columns was chipped and the chips sat on the ground in forlorn heaps. Did no one care enough to sweep away the trash? Marget began to feel as dejected inside as the house looked outside. She could only imagine the damage within.

"How wonderful to have you home," Monique cried. She embraced her son fondly. He broke away annoyed. He was too old to be treated as a child. He was a married man who did not need to be mauled by his mother.

Monique was gowned in a beautiful gold brocade which clung to her body revealing every sensuous curve. Marget looked at it disapprovingly. Monique was no longer young, yet she dressed herself as though she were still eighteen. Marget turned her eyes away from the low bodice revealing too much of Monique. She felt disgusted. She turned away as Monique reached out to embrace her again. She stepped into the carriage waiting for Benoit and his mother. The carriage was new, Monique's gown was new, but the house was old and tired.

"The house looks terrible," Monique said in a shrill voice.

"It will look better when it is fixed up," Benoit said. He looked at his wife wondering how much longer she would keep her bedchamber door locked against him. He had pleaded and cried with her, but she remained stubbornly alone in her bed. He did not understand this part of her. She had been frightened in the beginning and now she was coldly aloof. He was used to women who fawned over him. It was a blow to him to find that Marget was not soft and tractable and impressed with him.

The carriage pulled up to the sagging porch. Marget jumped out unassisted. Monique continued to complain about the condition of the house.

Marget did not look back as she walked up the tired steps to the front door. She carefully went around the gaping holes in the floorboards. Benoit followed her, piqued that she refused to allow him to even act the part of a gentleman.

The floor creaked under Marget's feet. There was dry rot in the corners along with piles of dust. She wondered why her father wanted her as mistress of this crumbling old mansion. It smelled dirty and damp.

Monique had never claimed much interest in household affairs. The state of the hall was mute testimony to her disinterest.

Cobwebs hung from the ceiling and the massive chandelier which dominated the hall. Two Chippendale chairs flanking a large cabinet on one wall looked old and tired, the upholstery torn beyond repair. Marget tried to conceal her disgust, but it showed in the disdain in her eyes and the slight curl to her lips.

The servants were lined up in the hall. Marget introduced herself to them and they bowed to her. Monique swallowed indignation at her new daughter-in-law's high-handedness. She was secretly pleased when the octoroon wench at the end of the line smiled insolently at the new mistress. Selena dropped into a curtsey, surveying Marget with open arrogance. If Marget noticed, she said nothing, hiding her feeling behind a mask of icy contempt. As the servants turned away, Benoit reached out and pinched Selena on her shapely bottom. She giggled archly and ran down the hall toward the kitchen.

The drawing room echoed the destruction of the hall. Old quilts had been tossed over delicate Queen Anne chairs and Regency sofas to hide torn fabrics or preserve what was left of them. Two petit point cushions had been ripped to shreds. A huge mustard colored cat sat on one of them sharpening his claws and daring Marget to object. She ignored the cat. Piqued, the animal stood and dropped to the floor following her to play in the folds of her hem.

"That is Pierre," Monique said, indicating the cat.

Marget looked at him. The cat passed beyond her, heading for the fireplace still piled high with last winter's ashes. He plumped down scattering the ashes in billowing clouds. He rolled contentedly, then gracefully got to his feet and walked across the carpet leaving gray tracks.

It was disgusting, Marget thought as she surveyed the destruction. Seven servants had stood before her in the hall. Not one of them had the sense to clean. What did they do all day? From the jutting stomachs of two of the women, she could guess.

"Brandy!" Benoit asked her. Her silence worried him. "It is not much, but we'll make a proper home of it." He was pleading and hating himself for doing so. Somehow, the position of master and wife had been turned around. He told himself he was her husband demanding her obedience, but she was no longer giving it. It was as though their last night in the hotel had changed something.

Marget thought it would be kinder to the old house if it were simply burned down and rebuilt. Some of this showed on her face as she stared at Benoit. He shrank from her. Then he stiffened. But she was no longer looking at him.

"Which room is mine?" She did not ask which room was theirs, but mine.

Benoit's heart sank to know her door was still locked against him.

Monique told her and Marget left the room leaving a husband looking like a wounded animal and a mother-in-law convulsed in fury.

Aurore lay on the slope overlooking the river. The grass tickled her chin as she gazed at the Mississippi. She broke off a blade of it and put it between her teeth chewing. In her imagination she could see the other side of the river though in reality it was shrouded in mist. She could picture the landing that led up to the majestic Arundel. She had played there once with a little girl who had pulled her hand and called her crybaby because it had hurt. After that Aurore had refused to play with her because of her meanness no matter how Maman threatened. It was not Arundel that drew her now, but the wild places beyond.

Her father had returned from New Orleans the day before. His conversation had included the hiring of two men from the state of Texas. It was a musical sounding word. Texas! Aurore whispered it to herself, rolling it off her tongue lovingly. Texas! It drew her. She tried to imagine what it was like.

"A penny!" Gayle said laughing, falling down to lay next to her. She looked up at him. "You'll get wrinkles scowling like that."

She smiled, captivated by the sun shining through his blond hair. They had grown close during the long, lazy summer. He made her forget she was only a child verging on eleven. He made her feel grown-up almost.

"I was thinking about Texas," she said turning back to her contemplation of the river. The sun made little diamonds on the waves.

"Why?" he asked intrigued. He had discovered long ago, she did not seem to think about the things that normally occupied ten year old minds. Almost eleven, he corrected himself. Aurore had grown very touchy on the subject of age. He could see the ache in her to be grown, but he wanted her as a child as long as possible.

"I want to go there some day. Papa says it is wild and savage. No place for a woman of breeding. But I still want to go."

"Maybe someday I'll take you," Gayle thought, the words out of his mouth before he really gave them much thought. He gazed at her startled, realizing he meant them. He wanted to take her there. He wanted to take her all over the world and show her the beautiful places he had been. He suddenly wanted to see them again with Aurore.

In some ways, Gayle was like Papa, Aurore thought, watching him. She did not understand the confusion of emotions on his face. He encouraged her to think for herself and to be independent. Yet even he had the stylized ideas of what a woman should be. It confused Aurore a little. As a child, she was indulged. As a woman, she would be expected to conform to a rigid set of rules. She wasn't certain she could.

She's only a child, Gayle told himself savagely. Her dark eyes looked at him trustingly and he wanted to take her in his arms . . . he shied away from the thoughts tumbling over and over in his mind. He tried to look away from her, but he couldn't take his eyes away from the black hair curling about her shoulders or the gentle rounding of immature breasts pressing against her shirt. He pulled away aware of deep pools of feeling which frightened him. She was only a child, he repeated over and over again in his mind. He sat up looking away from her dark eyes trying to control the surge of emotion sweeping over him. He would be glad when she returned to New Orleans though he would deeply miss their friendship.

"I'd like it if you took me to Texas," she said. "I want to know what it's like." She stood up suddenly, brushing dry grass from the folds of her trousers. She had grown over the summer. She was a little taller, a little rounder in the hips. Her small breasts had started to gain fullness.

Gayle dragged his eyes away from the dark circles under her shirt. He found it harder to control the strange frustrations he felt for her. Even the use of Fay's body did not lessen it. Soon there would be no Fay. Within the week, she would be married to Marcus Slaughter.

"How is Fleur?" Gayle asked, standing up and brushing grass off him.

"Better," Aurore said. "The bruises are gone. Papa is furious with her. He says she should never have gone riding by herself. Her horse would never have bolted and thrown her leaving her to walk all those miles on a a hurt ankle. He says we are never to go riding by ourselves without a groom."

"He's right. It can be dangerous around the bayous on foot."

"I'm careful," Aurore said. "I'm a much better rider than Fleur, anyway."

Gayle shrugged. He never let her go home alone anyway. Either he went with her or he sent a man from the stable.

"Oh, look!" she cried, pointing at the river. "Showboat! It's a showboat!"

The showboat appeared in the middle of the river, gaily painted and decorated. Music floated to shore

246

and the people on the decks waved merrily. "It's going to St. Angele," Aurore cried. She ran across the lawn to stand on the shore jumping up and down and waving wildly. She started back to the house, excitement showing on her face. "I have to go home."

"Change your clothes," Gayle yelled thinking of the scandal that would be caused if she arrived home in trousers and shirt. Especially when she had left modestly garbed in a riding habit.

Servants appeared on the veranda. They pointed excitedly at the showboat just disappearing around another bend. Tomorrow would be a day free of work.

Aurore ran up the steps. Mandy was waiting with her clothes rapidly washing her and changing her. Then Aurore was running out of the house to her waiting horse, kissing Gayle as she passed. She jumped on her horse and was half-way across the lawn before her groom was mounted. As she rode away she continued to scream, "Showboat!"

Renault sat opposite John Miles. He looked around the office. It was scrupulously neat. Renault didn't like neat offices. In fact, he didn't like neat homes. Neatness is a compulsion, untidiness reflected the easiness of a person's personality. He liked rooms that looked as though someone lived there. No one lived in John Miles' office. There was nothing in the room to give any indication of the man. There were no personal items strewn about the room. There was no open book. The chairs were hard and uncompromising. For Renault, an open book was as symbolic to him as the coiled whip hanging next to the door was symbolic to Miles.

The single black whip hung coiled ready to strike at

a moment's notice. It spoke of cruelty and desire. Some men considered their whips an extension of their arms. Miles was such a man though he had been forbidden to ever use a whip on St. Angele. The Negroes here were free, they were not subject to the cruelties of any overseer.

On the side-board was a decanter of brandy and one glass. It indicated a need for comfort without sharing it with anyone else. Miles was a man who liked his comfort.

Renault settled in a chair looking about the bleak room, feeling tired. He hated what he had come to do. He looked at Miles who lounged easily in his overstuffed chair contentedly puffing an expensive cigar. He held the cigar delicately between thumb and forefinger gazing at it with rare enjoyment on his face. He liked to think he were owner of St. Angele.

"I like fine cigars," Miles said.

"I know," Renault replied smiling. He had been in the office earlier in the day searching through Miles' desk. He had found a small cache of cigars stolen from the main office in the house. He had also found the ledger that told of Miles' duplicity.

"What can I do for you, sir," Miles asked finally.

"I came to talk about business." Renault said.

Miles was instantly wary. He stood and went to the side-board pouring some of the fine brandy he had taken from the cellars into his single glass.

"Did I make a mistake?" Miles asked. "I apologize for it."

"The books are in perfect order, Mr. Miles."

Miles relaxed slightly.

"Too perfect!" Renault continued. "That made me suspicious."

Miles tensed again studying Renault. His hands shook imperceptibly, but Renault saw it.

"If you had made a few casual mistakes," Renault said. "I might not have taken a closer look and discovered you were cheating me."

Miles turned pale. He set his glass down on the desk with a thud. The brandy sloshed over the sides and pooled on the wood. Miles opened a drawer and slid his hand inside.

"Don't bother looking for your gun, Mr. Miles. I removed it earlier along with your private ledger." Renault took the small gun out of his pocket and pointed it casually at Miles. The desk drawer closed with a snap. "Naturally, you are dismissed. You have two hours to get off my property. If you are not gone in that time, I will contact the authorities and have you placed under arrest. Do we understand each other, Mr. Miles? Good. You were very clever. You almost got away with it. Now I will give you leave to do your packing. Silas has a horse waiting for you. Good day, Mr. Miles. Remember, you only have two hours."

Renault stood and smiled at the man. He opened the gun and unloaded it, tossing it down on the desk. He pocketed the bullet before he left the room. Then with a final nod at the manager, he opened the door and stepped out onto the lawn.

"Papa!" Aurore screamed. She came flying out of the woods on Belle. "The showboat is coming. The showboat is coming."

Sixteen

Showboat! It was a magical word filled with promise and excitement. Showboat! It opened an area of entertainment to people regardless of their class or color. Showboat! It was a magnet that drew families from all the plantations within two hours drive of St. Angele. Before the showboat had even docked at the landing, people were arriving in carriages or on horseback carrying huge hampers of food and blankets to spread on the lawn.

Aurore bounced around, her long hair flying in unruly curls about her shoulders. She laughed and squealed with other children, occasionally interrupted a game to run across the lawn to the landing and check on the showboat.

It was a long, one story barge, pushed by an old paddle-wheeler that had seen better days ten years before. Inside the barge was the playhouse with a huge stage at one end and rows and rows of plank benches for the audience. A gallery around the outside held chairs for the planters and their families.

To Aurore, the old paddle-wheeler was even more exciting than the barge. Inside were brightly painted rooms where games of chance were played. Women threaded their way among the men who thronged the tables and the bar. They coaxed and cajoled the men into spending their money. There was loud music and laughter. Aurore wanted to see. She wanted to creep on board, but men came and went constantly.

She saw Gayle go up the gangplank to be greeted by a tall, red-haired woman in a bright green dress. The dress was too tight and her breasts were pushed high by the tightness. Aurore felt a stab of some strange emotion as she watched Gayle bend down and kiss the woman pressing her tightly to him.

"Ow! That hurts!" Aurore complained as Fleur grabbed her and hauled her to her feet and across the lawn to where the women sat in groups fanning themselves and catching up on gossip. "I want to watch!"

"Maman says you are to come away," Fleur said. She looked around anxiously. Michael Slaughter had arrived with his brothers. She had been careful to stay out of his way, but he seemed determined to speak to her.

"Oh, damn!" Aurore said.

Fleur stopped so suddenly her younger sister bumped into her.

"What did you say?" Fleur asked. "If Maman knew what you said she would be terribly angry."

"Are you going to tell her?"

"I might. You wouldn't be able to go to the show tonight."

"If you do, I'll tell Maman I saw you in the woods with Noble. And you didn't have any clothes on." Aurore said, delighting in her sister's suddenly pale face. "I'll tell on you if you tell on me."

"I won't tell," Fleur said ungraciously. She was so

white the blue veins in her face showed brightly. She started across the lawn pulling her sister ruthlessly by the arm. "Here she is, Maman."

Aurore was deposited at her mother's side.

"I told you to stay away from the paddleboat," Marie-Odile said.

"But all the men are there. I wanted to watch."

"It is no place for a lady," Marie-Odile snapped angrily.

Aurore hung her head in disappointment. She so wanted to see what was going on on the paddleboat.

"Run along and play and stay with the other children," Marie-Odile said. Aurore kissed her dutifully and ran to the edge of the woods.

Fleur was sent to the house on an errand. She didn't want to go, but her maman insisted. She eyed the long expanse of lawn that separated her from the house. She could see Michael watching her. He wanted to talk to her badly. She didn't like the look on his face. It held a threat and a promise. Suddenly, she darted across the lawn, looking behind her and sighing with relief as Bella Moore sailed up to Michael and stopped him from following her. Bella took his hand and pulled him toward a group of young people clustered in the shade of an oak tree.

Fleur grinned. Never in her life would she like Arabella Moore, but right now she could have hugged her. Fleur ran into the house forgetting Michael as she went about her errand.

Aurore joined the group of children and started to play. As soon as her Maman's attention was elsewhere, she slipped away heading determinedly for the paddle-wheeler.

Marget descended awkwardly from the de Ville carriage. The afternoon was warm and she was uncomfortable.

"Watch your step, Marget," Benoit said. He took her arm solicitously, but she shook him off. He said nothing, though his lips stiffened angrily. She showed him less and less respect as the days went on.

The slave woman, Selena, jumped down from the driver's box and hurried to Marget snapping open a parasol and handing it to her mistress. Marget ignored the open parasol and continued across the lawn.

Selena fell into step behind Marget fighting to calm herself. She hated her mistress who treated her as though she were trash. She plotted fruitless revenge knowing she would never get the chance. She could only think up to a certain point, cringing at the thoughts beyond. Even she did not have the courage to lay hands on a white woman, as much as she wanted to.

"Marget," Marie-Odile said, greeting her daughter with a fierce hug.

"Good afternoon, Maman," Marget said. "You do not look well. Are you ill?"

"No, my daughter, I am not ill. Just overworked from supervising the packing. I cannot understand how we go home with more than we came with."

Marget seated herself on the grass, Selena taking up a post several feet away. It had not taken long for Marget to discover the reason behind the slave's barely hidden contempt. It was bad enough finding her to be Benoit's present mistress, it was worse being forced to accept her as a personal maid. Monique had insisted, knowing how it would add to Marget's discomfort.

Marget could not get rid of her without causing a terrible argument. Things were bad enough at Grandeville.

For days, she had scrubbed and cleaned herself, forcing sullen slaves to help her. There seemed to be no way she could make a dent in the destruction of the house. Everyone was against her even Monique and Benoit. They seemed to delight in her discomfort. The only friend she had had turned out to be the mustard colored cat which had taken an unreasoning liking to her even though she spanked him for scratching and clawing. What even surprised her more was that the cat actually did stop his four footed ruin of the house.

"Once we are home in the city, I shall take a week off and do nothing but rest," Marie-Odile was saying.

"You should let Luce do it. It is too hot to work so hard."

"You are sweet, child, but Luce already has much to do. Your Papa is packing away the paintings in the picture gallery and all the silver and good china. He truly believes there will be a war and the North's first order of business will be to take control of the Mississippi. He does not want our prized possessions to fall into their hands."

"Benoit does not think the war will last long."

"He is a fool," Marie-Odile snorted.

Benoit approached her, cutting off their conversation.

"Maman de Champlain," he cried heartily. He bowed low and kissed his new mother-in-law's hand. "How good it is to see you again. As you see, I have brought your daughter back in good health and happy spirits. Is that not so, my love?" He slid an arm through Marget's. He frowned rebuffed as she slid away shifting her position on the grass.

"Madame de Champlain," Monique trilled as she approached. "How well you look. You should always wear yellow, it suits you superbly. Is this not a wonderful day? Where is your enchanting husband."

"I am here," Renault said approaching the group. He had one hand curled around Aurore's arm.

"Renault!" Monique gushed.

"Madame," he said bowing to her. He turned to his wife and thrust Aurore at her staring at his daughter icily. "Madame, I found her on the showboat trying to hide in the gambling salon."

Marie-Odile gasped. She looked down at Aurore who shuffled her feet nervously.

Aurore was frightened. She could not remember the last time her father had been so angry with her. She shifted from foot to foot staring at the ground.

"What shall we do with her, Renault?"

"I suggest a few hours alone in her room will be good for her," Renault replied. He understood her rampant curiosity about the gambling ship. He could not deal too harshly with her. He could only be thankful she had shown no interest for the rows of rooms around the salon officially designated as private parlours.

"And one hour at her prie-Dieu," Marie-Odile added. "You may go, Aurore, Luce will call you when you have thought about what you have done and are properly sorry."

Aurore was certain she would never be properly sorry. She thrilled at the excitement in the salon. The whir of roulette wheels and the slap of cards on a table drew her. She wanted to be a part of that excitement.

She curtseyed to her parents and ran across the lawn to the house. Luce stood in the door frowning darkly at her.

"You have been into mischief."

"I only wanted to see what it was like," Aurore said.

"Did you find what you were looking for."

"Yes," Aurore said, laughing. "It was painted pretty colors like the *Sophie Sutter* and there were exciting pictures on the wall."

Luce hid the smile on her lips threatening to appear. Aurore would never be like other girls. She hungered for a life far from the confines of womanhood.

"What is your punishment?"

"Several hours in my room. One hour at my prie-Dieu."

"You may go."

"I try to be good, Luce," Aurore said looking up at the woman.

"I know, little one. It is not easy. I know."

"How are you, Marget," Renault asked, drawing his daughter away from her husband.

"I am fine, Papa," she answered.

She did not look fine. She had a fragile appearance to her. She had lost weight and there were dark circles under her eyes.

"Is all well at Grandeville?"

Something flickered in her eyes and was gone.

"All is well there," she answered woodenly.

"Papa de Champlain," Benoit said. "May I speak to you about repairs to Grandeville. The roof is falling down and it needs repainting."

"Come, come, Benoit. Today is a day of rest. We will speak business another time."

"But . . . "

"Another time, Benoit," Renault repeated firmly. He steered Benoit away from the ladies across the lawn to the showboat. He was slightly distressed when Benoit threw himself into uncontrolled gambling. He was even more distressed when Benoit disappeared into one of the private parlours with a heavily painted woman in a gown much too tight for her fleshy frame.

"Now tell me," Marie-Odile said to her daughter. "How do you like being married?"

"Forgive me, Maman, but I hate it. I never thought I could hate anyone or anything, but I do Benoit and Grandville. How can I spend the rest of my life there? It is falling down. And Benoit, how can I love him when he treats me like a slave. How, Maman, how?"

"Is it so very bad?"

"It is terrible. Grandville is a slum. I clean and clean and get nowhere. The servants do everything to make it harder for me and Monique and Benoit encourage them in their disrespect."

"You must make them respect and help you."

"Maman, you have always lived among people who love you. I do not. The people around me hate me because I choose not to live with their dirt. I do not like Benoit or his mother. I cannot stand living in his house anymore than I can stand having him in my bed."

Marie-Odile gasped then turned red. "There is nothing so bad in this world a person cannot become

257

accustomed to. When I was your age and had just married your Papa, I often felt that way. But I . . . I . . . grew to like him. I grew to like . . . having him with me at night. It even became pleasurable."

"How does a woman know when she is *enciente?*" Marget asked suddenly.

Marie-Odile hesitated, searching her daughter's face. "Her monthly courses stop," she finally replied. She looked hopeful. Babies were often known to solve marriage problems.

"I have not had one since I was married."

"Are you ill in the morning?"

"Yes, sometimes all day."

"It is possible. You should see a physician immediately."

"I suppose I must," Marget said bitterly. Gayle Courtland was walking across the lawn trying to be polite to Bella Moore. From the look of anguish on his face, he was finding it hard. Marget disliked Bella. She wished her father had married her to Benoit.

Gayle looked her way and she smiled at him. He was so tall and handsome. He was not going to fat around his waist with excess drinking and eating. He would not hurt her as Benoit did at night. Marget looked away guilty with her yearning thoughts. She smiled at her mother.

"You must pray to God for guidance," Marie-Odile said. "He will help you."

Marget sighed. Not even to her mother would she confess that Benoit had refused to allow her to go to church.

"I will pray, Maman, but God has not answered my prayers as yet."

"He will, child. He will," Marie-Odile said sincerely. She truly believed God would look out for her daughter.

Bella finally succeeded in cornering Gayle in the shade of an oak on the edge of the woods. She tossed a triumphant glance at Thomasina Niven who only shrugged and turned away.

"It is hot today," Bella said fanning herself. "Would you walk with me in the cool of the woods?"

"If you wish," Gayle said, shrugging. He wondered how he was going to get rid of her. Her attentions made him uncomfortable. He had long since lost interest in Bella, but he was too much of a gentleman to say so. He simply took her arm and guided her into the cool shade of the woods.

Gayle glanced around for Aurore. She had been released from her room after only an hour. She had immediately joined a group of children on the lawn keeping as far away from the showboat as possible.

Gayle didn't think she looked too repentant. He had witnessed her disgrace on board the paddleboat after her father had caught her sneaking into the gambling saloon.

Bella saw Aurore. She caught the admiring look Gayle gave the child. With an angry tug she guided him into the dark of the woods. She wanted no competition though she couldn't understand why she thought of the child as competition.

John Miles pulled resentfully at his mustache as he stood in the shadows watching the women on the lawn. Their bright chatter irritated him. How could they act so unconcerned when he had just lost the best job he had ever had. He ground his teeth, anger boiling in him. He didn't understand why he had been dismissed for doing what he had always done. None of his other employers had cared what he did as long as the yields were up to their expectations.

In the hours since he had left his office, he thought of and discarded several plans for his revenge on Renault de Champlain. He considered setting fire to the house or stable, but every man on the grounds had been warned against him. He could never get close enough.

The sound of children's voices drifted to him. He stepped away from the tree he had been hiding behind and walked a few yards to find a large group of children laughing and calling.

"Let's play hide and seek," a young girl screamed. There was a chorus of approval and immediately the group was gone, yelling and squealing as they hid.

Miles watched as Aurore streaked by him. Already his mind was in action. He watched as she ran into the woods, then he was after her without being aware he had moved. She hid in a clump of bushes. He stole around her and had clapped a hand over her mouth before she could yell. He slid his other arm around her waist unable to resist a quick feel of her small breasts.

Aurore struggled, but Miles held on tightly. She was stronger than he thought as she kicked him with flailing legs. He almost dropped her when she bit him. When she bit him again, he swung a fist at her face. She went limp in his arms and he picked her and slung her over his shoulder.

"What was that?" Gayle asked frowning. He tried to listen of the inane sound of Bella's senseless chatter.

"It sounds like children to me," Bella said. She pressed her full bosom to his arm, thrilled with her daring. Wait until she told Thomasina this. She allowed the shoulders of her gown to drop lower, causing her bodice to slip slightly. The top swell of her breasts peeked coyly over her gown. She pouted a little when she realized Gayle was not looking at her. He was staring into the shadows. She hoped it wasn't that pesty de Champlain child. It had been hard enough coaxing Gayle into the woods without having that brat show up.

"You are a most exasperatin' man," Bella drawled. She arched her back brushing her breasts against his arm. Was she going to have to take all her clothes off before he bothered to look at her. She seriously considered doing just that. "Here I am talkin' to you, you are not listenin' to a word I'm sayin'."

"Sh!"

"What!" Bella gasped staring at him.

"Be quiet, Bella," Gayle snapped.

"I never!"

Gayle clapped a hand over her mouth to her complete surprise. She wide-eyed at him as he frowned her into silence. She finally understood and nodded. He took his hand away and started walking deeper into the woods. Bella followed him curiously. She was shocked at his treatment of her, but anxious to keep him with her.

There was a cry and distant movement. Gayle stopped trying to focus on the cry. It was a child. He darted forward when it was repeated.

Bella followed as quickly as she could. They pushed through the underbrush, Bella impatiently pushing a

261

branch out of her way as it snapped in front of her face.

Gayle stopped just before he walked into the clearing. John Miles stood over a child lying on the ground. He was busily unfastening his trousers. The child had no clothes. They had been ripped from her and lay in a pile near her head.

Miles pushed his trousers down over his hips. They fell to the ground. He stepped out of them and bent over the child. She cried out and he hit her on the side of the head.

"I'm gonna show you your Daddy can't push me around." Miles hissed. "See what I got here. When I'm through with you you won't be no virgin for some high and mighty planter."

Aurore stared at what he held out to her. She twisted her head away faint with terror. He lay down on her pushing at her legs with his knee.

"Wild cat, ain't you," he growled. She clawed at his face twisting out from under him. He grabbed her and jerked her back pushing his mouth down on hers forcing her lips apart.

"Let the girl go, Miles," Gayle said when he finally broke through the last line of screening bushes.

Miles continued to claw at the Aurore. Gayle stepped up and pulled him away.

Miles got heavily to his feet. He stared at Gayle, his face twisted with hate. Aurore scrambled to her feet and darted to Gayle. Bella reached out and took the trembling child in her arms, pulling a fold of her gown around the small body.

"You are in a lot of trouble, Miles," Gayle said in a deadly voice.

"What are you going to do about it?" Miles asked deliberately taunting. He felt slightly ridiculous standing in only his half-buttoned shirt. He bent over his clothes as though he were going to put them on. Instead he fumbled in his boot and came up with a long knife in his hand.

Gayle's gun went off faster than Miles could throw the knife. For a long moment, Miles stared disbelieving at Gayle. Blood spurted from his chest. He looked down at it in astonishment. He put a hand over the wound, but the blood continued to flow. Suddenly he crumpled to the ground.

Bella screamed. She clutched at Aurore in terror.

Gayle took a step over to Bella who was still screaming. He slapped her hard across the face. She fell silent, staring at him in horror.

"Stop it," he commanded. He took his coat off and draped it around Aurore.

"Is he dead?" Bella asked in a whisper.

"Most likely," Gayle said.

There was crashing in the underbrush. The huge blacksmith, Noble, ran into the clearing. He stopped in astonishment as he stared at the crumpled, half-dressed form of Miles on the ground and Gayle standing over the body, his derringer still in his hand.

"Sir?" Noble asked, bending down to the body. "He's dead."

"Go get Mr. de Champlain," Gayle said crisply. "Hurry up, man."

Noble took off.

Gayle turned to Aurore. She whimpered. It was a low, animal sound. He knelt down and put his arms around her and drew her close cutting off the view of Miles.

263

"It's all right," he crooned holding her tightly. "I won't ever let anything hurt you."

She shivered violently. She clung to him, her dark eyes pools of terror. Then she closed them and started to cry.

"She's finally gone to sleep," Marie-Odile said. She stepped out of Aurore's room, closing the door behind her.

Gayle caught a glimpse of a child's room with frills and dolls. "Is she going to be all right?" he asked.

"She's in shock," Marie-Odile said. "But children are flexible."

"I think she will be all right in time, Madame," the doctor said as he walked out of the room.

In the distance there was laughter and music. No attempted assault on a child could dampen the excitement of the showboat. Except for the group of people clustered in the hall outside Aurore's bedchamber, there wasn't another person in the house. Everyone who could was enjoying the show.

"I hope you are correct, Doctor," Renault said. He held his wife close to him.

"Of course, it is much too early to tell," The doctor continued. "Attacks like this can remain in a child's mind the rest of her life. Other times it has no effect at all. It depends on the child. Aurore has a strong mind. And Mr. Courtland did stop it before anything could happen. She will recover. I am certain. It will just take time. Take her back to the city where she will have school to occupy her mind."

"Thank you for coming," Renault said.

"My pleasure. Anytime." The doctor put on his

coat and picked up his bag. "I've left some laudanum with your woman, Luce. Just in case Aurore has a few bad nights. Luce knows how to administer it."

"Thank you, Monsieur," Marie-Odile said faintly.

The doctor left, running across the lawn to catch what was left of the evening's entertainment on the showboat.

"Thank you, Monsier Courtland," Marie-Odile said. "We will be grateful to you for what you have done, for the rest of our lives."

"I would have done the same for anyone, Madame," Gayle replied. He glanced at the closed door. He wanted to go inside and reassure himself that Aurore was truly all right.

"There is nothing we can do for you except extend our welcome to you whenever you are in New Orleans," Renault said. "Our home will always be your home."

"Thank you, sir," Gayle said, slightly embarrassed. "I must be going." He glanced at the closed door.

"If anything happens, Monsieur," Marie-Odile said. "We will let you know." She touched Gayle's arm in understanding.

"Good evening, Madame, sir."

That night Aurore had the first of the nightmares that would plague her regularly during the next years. Luce tried to comfort her, but she cried out for Gayle.

Seventeen

1861

It was starting. It edged into her mind until she writhed with terror. Sometimes it was John Miles who tore at her body with claw-like hands. Other times it was a strange man, some face she saw on the street and who stared at her. Aurore hated having men stare at her. They always took on large proportions in her dreams.

She groaned, twisting the bed clothes around her. The demon pushed against her, his hands outstretched to tear at her clothes and her flesh. She groaned louder, struggling to wake out of the dream, but her terror held her captive.

With a loud scream, she jerked awake, sitting straight up clutching the sheet to her. She sobbed uncontrollably, her small body drenched in sweat.

She had to leave the curtained bed, the scene of her fear. She swung her legs over the side and stood up, pulling her nightgown over her head and dropping it on the floor. The night air was cold against her overheated skin.

She sighed, trying to still the trembling in her legs

long enough to walk across the floor to her bureau.

"Are you all right, Aurore?" Marie-Odile asked. She held the door open with one hand and a candle with the other. She saw the wet puddle her daughter's nightgown made on the floor. And she saw her daughter clinging to the bed post weakly. "Was it your dream again?"

"Yes, Mama," Aurore said in a slight voice. "But I am fine now."

Marie-Odile went to the bureau and pulled out a nightgown. She set her candle on the night stand and helped her daughter to dress. She threw back the bed clothes and checked the sheets. They were as drenched as her daughter. With as little wasted motion as her bulky body would allow, she stripped the sheets from the bed and got a fresh set from the top drawer of Aurore's wardrobe. She kept a fresh set in the drawer all the time especially since the dreams seem to have increased in intensity.

She remade the bed and pushed Aurore into it. She tucked the sheets around her daughter's small form and sat down on the bed drawing a thin hand into hers. "Are you feeling better?"

"Yes, Mama," Aurore said softly. "I am sorry I woke you. I shall be very quiet now and try not to wake Marget and her new baby."

"You didn't disturb them," Marie-Odile assured her daughter. "Can you go back to sleep now? It will be morning soon."

Aurore closed her eyes only to have them pop open again as soon as Marie-Odile was gone. She stared at the ceiling, then the wall, then the shuttered window. There would be no more sleep for her this night.

Marie-Odile walked silently down the hall. She felt awkward and tired. The baby inside her kicked feebly as though resenting the midnight interruption of sleep and peace. She patted her jutting stomach absently trying not to think how disgraceful it was for a woman her age to conceive and bear a child after her own daughter had made her a grandmother.

She opened Marget's door and looked in. Marget was awake, sitting up and feeding her new little son.

"Is Aurore all right?" Marget asked softly.

"She is fine now," Marie-Odile answered. She went to the bed and bent over her little grandson. His pink mouth worked feverishly at his mother's breast.

"He is hungry tonight," Marget said, smiling at him fondly. He curled a tiny-fingered hand around her thumb tightly.

"They are hungry until they are grown," Marie-Odile said.

"Are you unhappy, Mama, because you are to have another?" Marget asked.

"I don't know," Marie-Odile said with a shrug. She thought of all the tiny bodies in the family crypt she had borne and watched die before they had ever really lived. Losing so many took its toll on a woman. She hoped this new babe would not be another.

"Go back to bed, Maman," Marget said. "You should not have gotten up. I was just going to Aurore when I saw you."

"You belong in bed, Marget."

"It has been three weeks. I am feeling perfectly well."

"You had a hard time. The doctor says you must stay in bed for another week at least. Don't worry about Aurore, I can see to her." Marie-Odile kissed Marget on the cheek and let herself out of the room. She padded down the hall to her own room. Renault was waiting for her.

"Is Aurore all right?" he asked.

Marie-Odile slid her robe from her shoulders and slid into bed, suddenly glad he was there. She curled against his warm body. "It was her dream again. It seems to be happening more and more especially with all this talk of war."

"We must be patient and understanding," Renault said rubbing his wife's chilled feet with his own. "The doctor said it would take time."

"It has been nearly seven months, Renault."

Renault gathered her into his arms, slipping his hands under the folds of her nightgown to caress the proud roundness of her stomach. He could feel the babe moving. It excited him whenever Marie-Odile was pregnant. He always marveled at the complexities of a woman's body. To him, it was beautiful though Marie-Odile thought herself ugly and out-of-shape. He ran his hands up to her breasts feeling them large and firm in his fingers.

"Stop, Renault," she said softly. "It is too close to my time."

"I had no thoughts of that," he said, nuzzling her ear. "I simply want to touch you, soothe away your aches." He rubbed the small of her back where he knew she hurt. She sighed and relaxed against him. He continued to massage tired muscles until her even breathing told him she was asleep.

Aurore was up and dressed long before the house

stirred. Dawn was just lighting the sky as she drew her shawl over her head and hurried down the stairs to the front door. She let herself out quietly, walking swiftly down deserted streets and alleys until she reached the cathedral.

The cathedral was still and silent. It rose against the morning sky like a gothic fortress. Aurore let herself in and hurried to the small corner where she sat down, hiding in the darkness. She found little comfort in God, but she did like the peaceful serenity of his house. She came frequently just to sit and enjoy the peace. It was in this dim corner that she could forget her night terrors.

It was full light when she came out. The streets were beginning to fill with people starting their day. They were too busy to notice one young girl. Aurore ran home.

There was a horse tied in the courtyard. She edged around because it looked at her meanly then went back to cropping Marie-Odile's flowers.

"Who is here, Luce?" Aurore asked, running through the kitchen where Luce briskly supervised the maids, her turbaned head turning this way and that under the stream of her orders.

"Monsieur de Ville," Luce answered absently. She was counting the silver and frowning. Luce always counted the silver before and after each meal. If a spoon or knife came up missing, each maid would be thoroughly chastised and set to searching the house until the piece was found. They were always found, but after each episode, a maid would go around the house for days with the marks of tears on her cheeks from Luce's scolds.

Aurore frowned to hear Benoit was in the house. In the months since Marget had first come to live with her parents bringing along the huge mustard colored cat, they had seldom seen Benoit. He seemed to prefer other amusement than keeping his young wife company during the long wait for the birth of her child.

"I wonder what he wants," Aurore asked. She took a hot roll from a tray and passed it swiftly from hand to hand until it cooled. She broke it open and filled it with honey and stood in the middle of the floor eating it.

Luce shrugged. She had no interest in Benoit de Ville.

Thérèse wandered into the kitchen, her plump thumb deposited firmly between her lips. She wore a nightgown with no slippers or robe.

"Where are your slippers, *ma petite?*" Luce asked gently.

A soft-bodied doll clutched in one hand by its hair was solemnly presented to Luce.

"Kiss," Thérèse said around her thumb.

Luce kissed the doll and picked up the little body. "You will catch a cold, little one." Thérèse squirmed to be let down. "Aurore, take your sister to the nursery and dress her."

"All right," Aurore said agreeably. Normally she hated the chore of dressing Thérèse who jiggled and refused to stand still. She took her sister's hand and led her up the sairs.

Marget opened the top of her nightgown and pushed it to one side. She offered a pink nipple to the open mouth of her son. It was always open, always

271

demanding. She cradled him, awed at the tiny fragility of hands and feet.

Benoit eyed her, his mouth turned down in distaste. He hated the wolfish sounds the baby made against his wife's breast unaware that they were exactly the sounds he made when he was making love to her. He also hated the little bundle of dark black hair and flailing arms. It was because of this infant he had been deprived of his wife's body for so many months. Though Selena was properly adequate, she did not answer a need in him. Only his wife could do that. He stared at Marget greedily, watching the large full breasts, overgrown with the weight of milk. Desire swept over him. Desire for his beautiful wife.

"He is a hungry boy," Marget said, her eyes devouring the babe, soft with love. "He will grow big and strong."

Benoit came close to snarling. She never looked at him that way. He moved restlessly at the foot of the bed where he sat.

"Has a name been decided yet?" he asked. He had been angry when Renault announced that he would choose the babe's name.

"He is to be called Francois Honor Denis Marie de Ville. It is a good name."

"A good name," Benoit echoed. He slid up the edge of the bed until he was close to her. When she shifted the child in her arms and bared her other breast, he reached out and touched the empty one. Milk dropped on his fingers. He thought of the months he had spent without his wife. He felt saintly over his uncomplaining attitude. The child was born now. There was no longer a reason for him to continue to deny

272

himself. He stood up shifting the sash of his new gray officer's uniform. He was a little piqued over her lack of interest in his uniform. After all, he was an officer, worthy of the respect of men.

"I came to tell you, I am leaving," he said. He unbuckled his sword and laid it on a chair.

"Are you returning to Grandeville already?" she asked not looking up. She was totally absorbed in the life she held in her arms. Benoit no longer existed for her.

"No, not Grandeville," he said sharply. "To the war, Marget. Don't you read the papers? Haven't you heard the news?"

"Are we at war?" She asked looking up blankly. Her dark eyes focused on him for the first time.

"We are at war," he shouted at her. What a stupid woman she was. It never occurred to him her family might have kept the news from her in order not to upset her. "Don't you know the new Army of the Confederacy has been gathering itself together. Fort Sumter has already fallen to them. In two days, I am leaving New Orleans under Col. Gladden to join General Bragg in Florida. I am a Lieutenant in the First Louisiana Regiment."

"We are at war!" Marget said. She looked carefully at the uniform finally realizing what it was. She felt scorn rising in her. "So all the little boys are running away from home to play soldiers. Will you be gone long?"

"No," Benoit said, anger rose in him over her lack of interest in his new importance. Her sarcasm stung. He smiled unpleasantly. "We are going to beat the

Yankees into submission and be home before the summer is over."

Francois Honor finished his meal. He gurgled happily. Marget forgot Benoit and smiled down at her babe. He tangled his small fingers in her hair and pulled playfully. She laughed tenderly, unwinding the hair from his fingers. She scolded gently as she put him back in his cradle. Francois Honor contentedly put his thumb in his mouth and stared at the web of sunshine falling across his coverlet.

Marget picked up the ribbons of her gown and started to lace it up. Benoit slapped her hands away. He caressed her breasts with hard fingers. She pulled away.

"I shall not be gone long, but before I go give me a sweet memory of you to carry with me." He brushed the gown off her shoulders.

"Benoit, it is too soon." Marget protested. She twisted away, but he dragged her back, ripping her gown away, staring at her naked body. He fumbled at his clothes. "I am not healed yet, Benoit."

He ignored her, intent only on the appeasing of his lust.

"Do not do this, Benoit," Marget pleaded. He pushed her down on the bed.

Marget tried to squirm away, but he wouldn't let her go. He caught her hands and held them tightly in a cruel grip.

"No matter how short the way, it will be too long without the comforts of my sweet wife."

Marget tried to scream, but he stopped it with his mouth. He bruised her lips, forcing her mouth open.

"Yes, much too long," he whispered, moving over her, pushing her knees apart.

Marget cried silently, huge tears rolling down the sides of her face.

Gayle arrived at the de Champlain house in late morning. Persia opened the door grinning broadly.

"Yah, sar, Master . . . uh . . . Major Courtland. Missy Aurore ain't home from school yet." Persia took the plumed hat Gayle handed him, stroking the feathers gently.

"I came to see Monsieur de Champlain. His office said he was at home today."

"In his study, Major, sar," Persia said. He led Gayle down the hallway. He opened the door to the study and stood aside to let Gayle enter.

"Good morning, Monsieur," Renault said looking up from the pile of papers on his desk. "Aurore is not home from school."

"I did not come to see Aurore, sir," Gayle said quietly. "I came to see you."

"Shall we sit and discuss our business." Renault said, gesturing to two wing backed chairs. The day was chilly and a small fire burned in the fireplace.

Gayle sat down. "As you can see, sir, I have joined the cavalry. We leave in two days for Pensacola, Florida."

"Aurore will be desolate she has missed you," Renault said. He liked Gayle Courtland. He thought the relationship this man shared with Aurore to be one of innocence.

"I don't want to distress her," Gayle said slowly. In truth he knew any farewell with Aurore would be

275

painful. She was such a part of his life. "That is why I have come now, sir. It is going to be a long war. The outcome is far from certain. For myself, I think the South will ultimately lose, but before it does a lot of men will die. I could easily be one of them." Gayle pulled papers from the sash at his waist. He handed them to Renault. "This is my will, sir. I want to give it to you for safekeeping."

"It should go to your banker, Monsieur."

"No, sir," Gayle insisted. "If you will read it, you will find I have named Aurore heir to Grey Lawns if I should die. You are executor with her coming into full control when she is twenty-one."

Renault opened the papers unable to keep his shock hidden.

"You have a sister-in-law," Renault said.

"Fay does not love Grey Lawns the way Aurore does. Since Fay married, she has made it very clear she wants no part of me or our past relationship. Grey Lawns is no prize. I paid off all my debts, but there are no slaves to work the place and there was no money left over. In case anything needs doing to the place while I am gone, I have included a power-of-attorney signed over to you." Gayle stared at the fire thinking of Aurore and the pain he felt at leaving without seeing her.

"What is this?" Renault asked. He held out a paper. Gayle glanced at it.

"That signs over ownership of the slave Jewel to Aurore. There is also a paper of manumission for her since you do not keep slaves. It can be given to her whenever you see fit. Jewel is only a child; you can give it to her when she is grown. Also there is a horse.

A mare who is going to foal soon. The foal was prom-ised to Aurore last summer as a birthday gift."

"Where is the mare and the child?" Renault asked, resigned to the unexpected idea of Aurore inheriting Grey Lawns, a mare in foal and a slave.

"The mare is at St. Angele. The girl is out in the courtyard."

"Persia will get her settled. She will be well-treated."

"Renault," Marie-Odile darted into the study. "Send for the doctor at once. Marget is terribly ill. Oh, the beast? That awful beast!"

"Calm yourself," Renault said. He shook her gently. Gayle ran to the sideboard pouring brandy into a glass and offering it to her. Delphine ran into the room, wringing her hands in her apron.

"I didn't know, ma'am," she wailed. When I took her tray, I thought she was sleeping. I didn't know, she was ill."

"Be quiet, Delphine," Renault said. "What is wrong, Marie-Odile?"

"It is Marget. The doctor must come. Benoit . . . Benoit took her. It was too soon. She is bleeding. Oh! he is a beast, Renault. Why did you marry her to such a beast?"

"I didn't know, ma'am," Delphine screamed hysterically. Her face was gray with terror.

"Delphine took in her lunch tray and thought she was sleeping," Marie-Odile sobbed. "When I went in to check her, I found blood. There is so much blood, Renault."

"I'll go for the doctor," Gayle said quietly. He ran out to his horse and flung aboard. Persia yelled the address after him.

Persia went back to the study. It was empty except for a still screaming Delphine. Persia dealt her a sharp blow across the cheek. He curtly told her to be quiet and go to the kitchen. Then he closed the door and walked heavily up the stairs to await further orders.

Aurore was delighted to find Jewel sitting patiently in the courtyard. She skipped up to her friend crying aloud with joy. "How did you get here?"

"Master Gayle done brought me," Jewel said, looking at Aurore with relief. She had never been so far from home before. She found the city terrifyingly strange.

"Why?"

"Master Gayle is going to the war and he's giving me to you," Jewel explained. Her actual orders had been to watch out for Aurore until Gayle returned, but she did not say it. She already knew of Aurore's confidence in seeing to her own welfare.

"Have you been here long?" Aurore asked, sitting down next to Jewel. Her face was troubled.

"I don't know," Jewel replied. "Master Gayle went in to talk to your papa and he ain't come out yet."

"Are you hungry?" Aurore asked. "I am. Sister Marie-Anne made me go without lunch today because I cried when she hit me with her stick. I couldn't help crying. It hurt."

"You telling me white folks get beaten like us black ones!" Jewel asked incredulously.

"I get beaten at school," Aurore said frowning. "Sister Marie-Anne says I am unruly and undisciplined. She says it is her job to make me into an obedient girl. When I don't obey fast enough, she hits my hands with her stick. I hate her stick. It's long and thin and hurts." Aurore held out her hands and Jewel examined the still red welts on the pale palms. She drew back in horror. "I'm not supposed to cry when she hits me, but it hurts."

Jewel didn't like to think of some old woman hurting her Aurore. She didn't say so, but she glared at the welts angrily. Since it was her job to protect Aurore, she decided she would go to school and watch. Maybe Sister Marie-Anne would let her take Aurore's next beating. She was big and strong and Aurore was so tiny. Jewel sensed that Sister Marie-Anne was someone to be frightened of. Aurore was seldom frightened of anything or anyone, yet she was afraid of this teacher.

"Let's go get something to eat," Aurore said. She ran across the courtyard. Jewel followed more slowly, still thinking about the teacher who beat Aurore.

"What's the matter, Delphine?" Aurore asked. She walked into the warm kitchen following the frantic sobs of the maid. Delphine sat on the floor in a far corner, her apron thrown over her head.

"Missy Marget!" Delphine wailed, "I didn't know she was sick."

"Marget is ill?" Aurore asked. She pulled the apron away from Delphine's face and shook her.

"I'm sorry, Missy Aurore. I thought she was just sleepin'. There weren't no blood then."

"Blood?" A shiver of fear ran over Aurore as she stared at the black face with dark eyes rolled back in terror.

Aurore turned and ran blindly from the kitchen, up

the stairs and through the quiet house. Jewel ran along behind her.

"Wait!" Gayle picked up Aurore bodily and carried her into the drawing room.

"I've got to go to Marget," Aurore screamed, fighting him. Tears tracked down her face.

"You can't go up now," Gayle said. He cradled her against his chest. "The doctor is with her."

"Is she going to die?"

"She's very ill," he said gently.

"Will she be all right?"

"I don't know, Aurore." He dried her tears with his handkerchief and instructed her to blow her nose. "Weeping is not going to help your sister. It would be better if we remain here and be calm. I brought a deck of cards." He held the deck up enticingly, but Aurore was not looking at him. She craned her neck to see up the stairs. At the very top she could see the faint outline of Persia sitting on the top step, his head in his hands. "How about a game of poker? Or would you prefer blackjack?"

Aurore looked at him blankly. After a few massive gulps, she sat next to him and allowed him to divert her from the tragedy going on upstairs.

Eighteen

Marget did not die. The little core of hate which built up around her heart kept her alive. When she opened her eyes to find her mother anxiously hovering over her, she managed a tight little smile. She had not died and she wondered why. If God had been merciful he would have allowed her to lose her grasp on life, but he had not. So the hate grew and grew nurturing her during the long weeks of her convalescence. The only comfort she had was in her infant son who was brought to her twice a day. She mourned over the loss of her milk and envied the wet nurse who put her child to feed.

"How are you feeling today, Marget?" Marie-Odile asked brightly. She walked to the bed and fluffed up the pillows and pulled the blanket up around Marget's shoulders.

"Very well," Marget answered. A breeze swept through the window stirring the ruffled curtains.

"Do you feel up to a visitor today? Pere Buiron is downstairs and asking after you. He says he misses you at Mass."

"I don't want to see him, Maman."

"Oh, Marget!" Marie-Odile cried in distress. She sat down on the edge of the bed and took her daughter's pale hand in her own. "Don't you think it wise to take comfort in God? It would ease the anguish in your soul."

"God did not help me when I needed help, Maman. I prayed to him for guidance and all I received was pain and abuse at the hands of my husband. If God did not help me before, He cannot help me now." Marget slid her hand out of her mother's. She was not bitter. "I will not see Pere Buiron. He cannot help me."

"Please, Marget!"

"I will not see him. Please convey my apologies, Maman." Marget turned her head away to watch the swaying curtains indifferently.

"A person cannot live without God, child."

Marget ignored her mother's words.

Marie-Odile stood up, shifting her awkward body and walking toward the door. There was deep sorrow in her gentle eyes and a helplessness against such hard determination. She sighed. This was not the same Marget of only a few short weeks ago. This was a stranger who frightened Marie-Odile.

"I am sorry, Pere Buiron," Marie-Odile said as she walked into the drawing room and eased her heavy body into a chair. The baby kicked. "She will not see you."

"Do not worry, Madame," he said politely. He delicately took a sugared candy from the tray Delphine offered him. Pere Buiron thanked her with a nod of his head. He was a round, chubby man with greying hair and a cherubic face. The women of his parish said he was a vision from heaven and he approved of their comparison. Only his cool blue eyes were at odds with the rest of his appearance. They were shrewd and assessing. "God walks in mysterious ways, my child." Pere Buiron knew the wealth of his parish. It never failed to gratify him that he was invited to the best homes in the Vieux Carre. If only these proud aristocrats knew they were entertaining the son of a lowly blacksmith. "The good Lord must have a good reason for putting your daughter's faith to such a strenuous test. He will watch out for her. Despite her objections."

"He has not done such a good job, so far," Marie-Odile said more sharply than she intended. "Her husband has treated her shamefully."

"It is a husband's privilege to treat his wife in any manner he chooses. Have you thought it possible that your daughter deserved such treatment?"

"I find it hard to believe God would allow such cruelty to one of his innocent children." Marie-Odile replied tartly, aware of a beginning dislike for Pere Buiron.

"You are only a woman, Madame. You cannot expect to comprehend the mysterious workings of God's mind." The priest leaned forward and patted Marie-Odile's hand solicitously.

Marie-Odile removed her hand puzzled over a feeling of aversion for this man. She looked down at his hand which was thick fingered and stubby.

"I must be going," Pere Buiron said briskly. "Thank you for the visit and please tell your daughter that I look forward to seeing her at Mass again."

Marie-Odile signaled to Delphine to show the priest out. He frowned at her realizing she was showing lack of courtesy at not seeing him to the door herself. It was an insult he would not soon overlook.

Marget spent the afternoon sitting in a chair near the window. She amused herself by counting the people on the street and the carriages that swayed over the cobbles. Two open landaulets passed with giggling girls pressed against the arms of the uniformed escorts. Marget wondered where their chaperones were. Convention had grown relaxed since the start of the war. New Orleans was a different place these days. It seemed gayer and more colorful, yet there was a feverish intensity underlying the laughter. Marget was afraid of this new city. There was an uneasiness in the air that seemed to drive people to frenzied displays of merriment. They lived harder, faster and louder. Maybe it was the tensions of the war. Already lives had been lost. Women in the North and the South were crying over the bodies of their dead. The blood was only beginning to flow.

New Orleans was frantically joyous. The people waved flags and attended ball after ball. Marget was less joyous. She thought of the men dead in the beginning conflict. She was acutely conscious of death because she had come so close to dying herself. She had struggled hard for the right to live. She felt sorry for those men who had not had her chances.

Another carriage passed, its wheels rumbling on the street. A young girl in a green and white striped gown trailed a banner of multi-colored ribbons in the breeze. The young man with her laughed throwing back his head and opening his mouth wide. He was young. He reached out and pulled the girl to him, his mouth hungrily seeking hers and his hand caressing the outlines of her breasts. Marget felt her heart lurch as she watched them. He would die with all the rest.

She fell asleep dreaming of blood and fire. Even her dreams were not free of the horrors of the war. She woke an hour later drenched in sweat and restless.

In the late afternoon another carriage entered the street and pulled to a halt in front of the house. Marget leaned forward curiously to watch the door open and a young man step out. He was vaguely familiar to her. She leaned closer to the window trying to penetrate the darkened shade. He paid off the driver and stood on the street staring at the house. He took off his hat and ran his hands through his dandy-colored hair. He looked up as though sensing he was being watched. Marget recognized Captain Neil Quinlan of the *Inheritance*. She drew back, her eyes wide and shining. Marget was up and walking across the room to ring for Delphine before she realized it. Then she opened the doors of her wardrobe and stood looking at her gowns.

"I shall eat dinner with my family tonight, Delphine," Marget said when the maid ran into the room breathing heavily. Marget held out a gown of peridot green trimmed with silver lace.

"Captain Quinlan," Renault said extending his hand to greet his guest.

"Sir," Neil said. "I called at your office, but they said you had already left for the day. I came straight here."

"Sit down, Captain. Brandy?"

"That would be fine, sir."

Renault quickly poured and handed a large round glass to the young man. Then he rang for Persia and ordered an extra dinner plate set for his guest.

"How did the run go, Captain?" Renault asked when they were seated and sipping their drinks.

"Well enough, sir," Neil said with a frown. "There are a lot of gaps in the blockade right now. Gaps that will tighten when the North realizes how important New Orleans is to the war."

"I suspect they are already making plans to capture the city," Renault said. "When they do, we will shift operations to Savannah or Charleston."

"I've an English buyer in Nassau who is willing to take every bale of cotton he can get his hands on. How much do you have?"

"Enough to fill your hold, Captain."

Neil nodded swiftly calculating. "I'll be unloaded by morning and loaded again by tomorrow night. I suppose you have heard that Jeff Davis has invited applications for letters of marque for privateering on the high seas."

"I heard. I am leaving for Montgomery next week to register all three of my ships."

Neil nodded and their discussion turned to the war.

When Neil Quinlan had been ten years old, his family left Ireland to settle in Boston, the city of opportunity and freedom. It had not taken the young Neil long to discover his family had simply traded hunger in Ireland for hunger in Boston.

There had been little peace in their new lives. The Irish were hated with an intensity that had frightened the young boy. Twenty-five years later he still bore the scars of his fights. He had had to fight his way to school and then fight his way home again. He had had to fight for a better life than the one his family was still leading in a dark tenement in Boston.

"With the war going full steam ahead," Renault said quietly, "are you thinking of returning to the North?"

"No, sir," Neil replied honestly. Nothing could make him give up his position as captain of the *Inheritance*. He'd fought too long for it.

There was a knock on the door and it opened to the rustle of skirts.

"Papa!"

"Marget!" Renault cried. He stood and turned to his daughter, a smile on his face.

Neil also stood and turned. When he faced her he smiled. She returned it shyly. Neil saw that she had changed during the long months since he had seen her last. She was thinner. Her face was lined with suffering and weariness, a look that reminded Neil of his mother.

"Papa, the supper bell has rung twice. Maman is waiting."

"We're coming, Marget," Renault said stubbing out the remainder of his cigar.

"May I, sir?" Neil asked, looking inquiringly at Renault. Renault nodded and Neil held his arm out to Marget. She placed delicate fingers on his arm and allowed him to escort her to the hall.

Neil thought she was still very lovely with her dark hair and dark eyes smiling up at him. But she was much too thin. The remembered softness of her face had sharpened into angular maturity.

"Have you been ill?" he asked in a low whisper as they stepped into the shadowed hall. His eyes studied the sharp ridges of her collarbones against her ivory shaded skin.

"It was nothing," she replied softly. "I . . . had a child and did not recover as I should."

"I should like to see your child," Neil said staring intently into her eyes. She colored and looked away. "I come from a very large family, the fifth of thirteen children."

"That is a big family," she replied, her voice a velvet whisper against his ear.

"The Irish have a fondness for large families."

"How unfortunate for your women," Marget said. The birth of Francois Honor was still fresh in her mind. She could not imagine a woman giving birth year after year after year enduring the pain for little more than another mouth to feed.

"I suppose it would be unfortunate," Neil said remembering his mother's endless toil to feed and clothe them all. "Where is your husband, Madame?"

"Gone to war, sir," she said. They walked into the dining room and she left him to stand at her place. There was a small glow sparkling inside her as she looked at him. She suddenly felt alive and happy. Was this love, she wondered? Was it returned? She stole another glance at him to find his gray eyes bright with her image. She smiled and he smiled.

Marie-Odile waited impatiently. She tapped the table impatiently.

"We've been waiting, Renault," she said when her husband finally appeared followed by Marget and the young captain.

"I'm sorry, my love," Renault said seating her.

All during the meal, Marie-Odile tried not to look at Marget. Her daughter sparkled with an inner glow that made Marie-Odile uncomfortable. Marie-Odile did not like the way her eyes kept straying to the young man nor the look he returned. She sensed trouble, yet was loathe to warn her daughter about this new relationship. Marget deserved more from life than a cruel husband.

"Meet me tomorrow at the St. Louis Hotel," Neil managed to whisper when the meal was over. "Two o'clock." Marget nodded briefly then slipped away.

Up in her room, Marget fought to control the surge of new feelings inside her. As much as she hated Benoit she was still his wife bound to him by the vows of marriage. Yet her duty to him would not keep her from meeting Neil Quinlan though she was deeply troubled by her confusion.

"Normally we go to St. Angele for the summer," Marget said. They sat on a low rise overlooking the Mississippi. It was hard to believe there was a war churning around them when the day was so peaceful and warm. Neil had spread a blanket over the grass to keep her pink and gray gown from becoming soiled. Marget sat on the blanket and Neil lounged next to her, his gray eyes studying her. "But I have been ill and with Maman so close to her time . . ." Marget blushed. It was considered indelicate to discuss such matters with a man, yet Neil seemed to invite such confidences. He nodded in understanding wondering if he should tell her how many babies he had watched being born during his childhood. "My sister, Aurore, is in a fever to go to the country. She loves it there and she worries that Papa is not taking proper care of Grey Lawns."

"Grey Lawns!" Neil asked idly. He reached up and

brushed a long strand of hair out of Marget's face. For a second his sun-bronzed fingers touched the smooth coolness of her skin, then she shuddered and pulled away.

Marget was disturbed by him. He leaned on his elbow next to her, his dark blue coat and hat discarded. His white shirt was open at the throat exposing curly blond hair. Marget was fascinated by the hair. She kept looking at it and trying to resist touching it. She had never seen a man with chest hair since Benoit had none.

Neil felt her studying him, but she blushed and looked away quickly. One would think she was an innocent virgin instead of a properly married woman. No, not properly married, Marget thought. No properly married woman would ever be sitting on the banks of the river with a man who was not her husband.

"Grey Lawns?" Neil asked again, prompting her.

"Our neighboring estate. Aurore is great friends with Monsieur Courtland who owns it. He gave her Jewel who is her friend and personal maid and a beautiful white mare who foaled a few weeks ago. The foal is Aurore's and she is anxious to see it. She is quite a horsewoman."

"Is she?" Neil said. He thought of the raven-haired younger sister of Marget whose eyes danced with secret merriment. "What about you?"

"I ride very gentle horses. I am not like Aurore. I do not run blithely from place to place nor do I have the enthusiasm for life she has. Life is an adventure for Aurore. She loves it. She runs headlong into it."

"What about you?"

290

"I wander through life," she said quietly. "What happens to me happens because others decided for me. I do nothing myself. Aurore will never allow herself to be manipulated as I have been."

"Have you been manipulated?" he asked watching her face intently. There was a longing there.

"Do you think I would have married Benoit of my own free will? I was forced into it because I have not the strength to oppose my parents."

"Don't be sad, Marget," Neil said drawing her down to lie next to him.

"That is the type of person I am, Neil," she said sadly. I am weak and timid. Is that the kind of woman you want?"

"There is strength in weakness," he said touching her face with a strong, large hand. His fingers slid down her cheek to her throat and across the swell of her breasts.

The driver of the carriage walked up to them and coughed discreetly. Neil looked over his shoulder stifling his annoyance.

"You did say to remind you when it was four o'clock," the man said before backing away looking embarrassed at his intrusion on an intimate scene.

"We have to go," Neil said, standing and drawing Marget to her feet. He didn't want their meeting to end. "I'm leaving tomorrow."

Marget bent and picked up the blanket. She folded it and handed it to him. Then she picked up his hat and coat and stood holding them. "I shall be sorry to see you leave."

"I shall be sorry to go." He took his coat and shrugged into it and placed his hat on his head.

"When will you return?"

"In a few weeks."

"I shall be waiting for you." Marget leaned close, tilting her head to him.

Neil's arms slid around her. His lips touched hers in a kiss that was both gentle and passionate. It was like no other kiss Marget had ever received. A strange feeling swept over her. It was a dangerous feeling, but could not be denied.

"We'd better go before your family starts to worry." Neil put her from him firmly.

"Is blockade running dangerous?" Marget asked when they were in the carriage and approaching the city.

"It can be."

"You will be careful. Promise me you will be careful."

"I promise I'll be careful," he said sliding his arm around her and pulling her close.

"I'll pray for you," she whispered.

Neil let her off two blocks from her home. Marget watched him out of sight. She was frightened for him. She wanted to go and share the danger.

"Marget! Marget!" Aurore cried racing up to her stumbling as she came to a stop. "I've been looking for you all over. Where have you been?"

"Walking."

"Hurry home. Maman wants you. The baby is coming."

Marget looked startled. For two hours she had not thought of her family or the problems of her world. She hurried down the block toward home without a thought for Aurore's chatter.

Marie-Odile recognized the slight pain in her back when it first started. She said nothing to anyone. She picked up her knitting and excused herself then went to her room.

It was quiet in her room. She sat in a large chair and continued her knitting while she waited for her child to be born. She hoped this time it would be a boy. Renault so wanted a son. She thought of the family vault with all the tiny bodies in it. She hoped this baby would not end up there.

Another pain hit her and then another one quickly after it. Marie-Odile dropped her knitting, startled. Something was different about this. She gasped in astonishment as a third contraction hit her rapidly. She leaned back in the chair panting and groaning. Beads of sweat popped out on her forehead. She tried to stand, but a fourth contraction doubled her over. She gasped heavily and grabbed the edge of a table to steady her.

It seemed to be hours before she reached the bell pull. It seemed to be hours more before Luce entered the room to find her mistress lying on the floor groaning.

"Where's Marget?" Marie-Odile asked between stabbing pain.

"She is out walking," Luce replied, not adding that Marget was also with the young Captain Quinlan.

"Send someone to find her. I want her."

Luce helped Marie-Odile out of her clothes and then settled her between the cool sheets of her bed. Another pain gripped her, curling her body around her stomach.

"I don't like this," Luce said in an undertone to Delphine who stood in the door with fear on her face. "Send for the doctor immediately and then get my medicine bag."

"Luce," Marie-Odile cried. "Something's wrong, Luce."

"Delphine will bring my medicines and I will brew a tea for the pain. It will ease you."

Marie-Odile writhed on the bed, entangling the sheets about her sweating body. Luce poured water in a bowl and wiped her skin. When Delphine brought her bag, she made a sweet tea over a brazier brought into the room and helped Marie-Odile to sip it. The tea eased her agony and she lay panting in exhaustion.

"Marget!" she called weakly.

"Aurore has gone to find her. She will be here soon," Luce said soothingly.

The doctor arrived, turning away in embarrassment at Marie-Odile's naked body. He draped the sheet modestly over her and carried out his examination under it. Then he drew Luce aside, a worried look in his eyes.

"It's breech," he said in a whisper. Breech! The one word that struck terror into the hearts of all women.

"We'll have to turn it," Luce said.

Marie-Odile gave a half-scream and threw the sheets away from her contracting body. The doctor turned away, averting his eyes from her form.

"This is no time for modesty," Luce said savagely.

"Can't you put a nightdress on her?" he said.

Luce glared at him and he stepped back slightly. Then with a shrug he approached his patient trying to keep his eyes away from the heaving breasts and the opened legs.

Marget did not recognize her mother when she arrived. Her face was twisted in pain and her body heaved and strained.

"Marget," Marie-Odile cried wildly as her daughter entered the room. "Stay with me, Marget."

"Yes, Maman," Marget said. She pulled a chair up to the bed and sat down taking her mother's dry hand in hers.

"It is stuck," the doctor said. "We will have to push it back into the uterus and turn it."

"She is losing strength," Luce said watching the woman's struggle grow weaker and weaker.

"Get me hot water to wash in and clean towels," the doctor ordered. As the situation became more urgent, he had forgotten about his patient's state of undress and actually found how much easier it was to administer to someone who was not encumbered by voluminous nightgowns and sheet coverings.

When the hot water came he washed his hands thoroughly and then his instruments. Marget turned her face away from the sight of the gleaming steel, clutching her mother's hand desperately.

Marie-Odile screamed, when the doctor pushed into her.

"You'll have to do it," he said turning to Luce. "Your hands are smaller. Wash thoroughly and do as I say."

"I want to see my wife . . ." Renault yelled from the hall just before the door was closed firmly in his face.

"I'll be all right, Renault," Marie-Odile whispered. "These things take time."

"Don't talk, Mama," Marget said as she ran a cool cloth over her mother's face and shoulders. "You must conserve your strength."

"This is a stubborn one," she said. "The others were so easy."

"It will be over soon, Maman," Marget whispered. "Soon."

It was a girl. A tiny, red-faced girl with eyes the size of walnuts and lungs as loud as a banshee. Her protest at the difficulty of her birth was voiced in a loud, outraged wail as she entered the world. Her cries were as fierce as a thunderstorm and she would not be comforted until her new mother weakly offered her a full nipple.

When the sheets were changed and Marie-Odile was garbed in a clean white cotton gown, Renault was finally allowed into the room.

"It's a girl," Marie-Odile said in regret. The baby cried angrily at being disturbed when her father picked her up and removed her blanket to look at her. Marie-Odile sighed. The newest de Champlain member had none of the placidity of her other babies.

"I don't care," Renault said handing the baby back and watching his wife open her gown and offer her breast to the lustily crying baby. "It is you I worried about." Renault was surprised to find he meant it. When he thought that Marie-Odile might die, he suddenly knew that having a son was no longer important. It was Marie-Odile he wanted. For six hours he had lived with the fear of losing her.

"Monsieur," the doctor said drawing him from the room to stand in the hall. "I am sorry, Monsieur, but there were many complications. I do not think your wife will ever conceive again. There was a great deal of damage. I cannot tell for sure now, but in a few weeks. Though I am almost certain you will have no more children."

"Thank you, Monsieur, for all you did to save her life. Her life is what is important to me, not the son I will never have."

Renault showed the doctor to his carriage, then went to his study where he opened his safe and took out a long thin box wrapped in velvet. Then he went back to his wife and presented the box to Marie-Odile. She snapped it open to find a necklace of diamonds and sapphires winking at her.

Renault had been saving that necklace for eighteen years to be given to her at the birth of their son.

"It is beautiful, Renault," she said running her fingers over the gems. "I shall treasure it always."

"Come, Papa," Marget said drawing her father to the door. "Maman must rest."

He allowed himself to be shut out of the room. He went down to his study and proceeded to celebrate in his own way by getting quietly drunk.

Nineteen

Marget took Aurore's hand firmly. They neatly sidestepped two young soldiers supporting themselves as they lurched down the street giggling in young, high voices. Marget pressed her lips together tightly as one of the soldiers turned around and said something to her. Aurore did not understand the words, but she did understand the meaning. Marget colored angrily, then jerked Aurore across the street and resumed her fast-paced walk for home.

"Why is everyone so happy?" Aurore asked. Hazily she remembered that a battle had been fought and there had been a great victory. She worried about Gayle. Had he fought in the battle? She prayed he had not. She cried out at the thought.

"They are happy because the victory at Manassas has just confirmed everyone's faith in the supremacy of the South," Marget snapped angrily.

"Don't you think the South is going to win the war?" Aurore asked anxiously. Since Christmas she had grown several inches and was nearly as tall as Marget.

"I don't know," Marget said with a sigh.

"Everyone says we are," Aurore continued. She looked up and down the street at the revelers. New Orleans had grown wild at the news of the victory. It had gone so wild, it had forgotten some of its natural courtesy. Young soldiers, drunk with whiskey accosted young girls and women. Young girls barely out of the schoolroom were seen unchaperoned on the street hanging on the soldiers' arms.

Marget thought the city had lost all sense of propriety. Another soldier lurched into her. She pushed him away, but he caught her hand and held it tightly when she tried to pull back.

"Hello, honey," he slurred, swaying as he talked.

"Let go of my hand," Marget said furiously. "How dare you speak to me? I am not your honey."

He dropped her hand hastily looking astonished. So few of the women acted hostilely. Then anger slipped over his face. "What's the matter, honey? Ain't I good enough for ya?"

Marget stood her ground as he advanced on her. She was terrified. She gripped the handle of her market basket preparing to use it as a weapon uncaring of the hardfound fruits and vegetables in it.

"I suggest you let me pass," she said, her voice so low she could barely be heard. Her words were a mixture of French and English. She repeated herself in English and the man grinned evilly. Suddenly he looked ugly and Aurore was reminded of another man who had threatened and hurt her. She swayed with her memories, her face going blank with terror.

"Listen . . ." the soldier said.

"That's enough." The voice was mild, yet filled with authority. "Let the ladies pass."

"Mister, mind your own business."

Neil Quinlan took the young soldier by the arm and led him to the nearest saloon and shoved him inside.

"Are you all right?" he asked when he returned to Marget.

"I'm fine, but Aurore . . ." Marget held her small sister to her while the girl cowered in fear.

"I'll get a carriage," he said grimly.

"It's all right, darling. The man is gone," Marget soothed. After a while Aurore's trembling ceased and she was able to look up.

"Thank you," Marget said when they were safely in the carriage. Aurore sat next to her staring mutely out the window. She was pale and breathing in heaving gasps.

"My pleasure, Madame de Ville," Neil said formally with a little wink at her. "Is she all right?" He asked in a low voice.

"She'll be fine," Marget answered. "She was attacked by a man once who tried to . . . who tried to . . ."

"Never mind, I understand," Neil said quickly.

"I must remember to write Gayle about this," Aurore said in a high, strained voice.

"Who?" Neil asked curiously.

"Our neighbor, Monsieur Courtland," Marget said.

"I write him everything. He asked me to. I keep a little diary so I don't forget important things. He says I don't bore him."

"I can't imagine why not," Marget said in a bantering tone. Aurore was getting some color back in her cheeks as she talked. "Monsieur Courtland is a grown man and you are just a little girl."

"I'll be twelve in October. That's only four months away."

Marget grinned. Her little sister was in such a fever

300

to grow up. She even knew there was a secret calendar in Aurore's desk with the next five years laboriously figured out and with her birthday circled in red for each year.

"How was your journey, Captain Quinlan?" Marget said turning away from Aurore who seemed to be recovered. "Did you sell your cargo?"

"All of it," Neil said. He watched her thinking how pretty she looked with her dark hair falling in soft curls around her face. In the week he had been gone, he thought of her constantly. An ache had grown in him to be with her. As soon as he had docked he had gone to his hotel, washed and changed in preparation for a visit with her father and possibly a glimpse of her. It had been pure luck to see her on the street and come to her aid in dealing with the drunken soldier.

"I missed you," he said leaning toward Marget when Aurore was caught in fascination with the scenery.

They passed the convent and Aurore turned to look at Marget. "I'm glad I don't have to go back there," she said frowning. "I prefer my lessons with Monsieur Embray. He's much nicer than Sister Marie-Anne."

"He is very nice," Marget said in agreement. She thought of the scene of several weeks ago when Aurore had come home from school crying. The young girl, Jewel, had marched into Renault's study and had been closeted with him for nearly half an hour. When they had come out, Renault had announced that Aurore would no longer go to school.

No further mention had been made of the decision, though Marget had wondered why.

Aurore knew why. The prank had seemed innocent enough. After all, it had only been a tiny tree frog.

But Sister Marie-Anne had become enraged culminating in her stepping on the innocent frog. Aurore had not minded the beating, but she would always remember the sight of the frog after Sister Marie-Anne had lifted her foot. It was then that Aurore had vomited all over the nun's austere habit.

A tutor had been found for her with the new arrangements for her education infinitely more satisfying. Old Monsieur Embray was not interested in the quality of her copperplate or the intricacy of her needlework. He preferred to have her read and study the very books Sister-Marie Anne had announced as unsuitable for young girls.

Fleur was still allowed to go to school, but she was no longer a student. With her fourteenth birthday had come her new status. She had become Sister Marie-Anne's priviliged helper.

Aurore was a little in awe of Fleur knowing that her sister left every morning for the convent school, but only arrived three days out of five. What Fleur did on those two days, Aurore did not know though she felt uneasy. Especially when she knew, but her parents did not.

As they approached the house, Aurore pushed the problem of Fleur away from her mind. She did not understand her restless sister and she did not think she wanted to.

Fleur saw the carriage long before it approached. She also saw Aurore looking out the window. She ducked quickly down a side street and stood in the shadows until the carriage was gone.

That was close, she thought. She had to be careful

on those days when she was not at school. There was always the danger of running into a member of her family or someone she knew who might say something about her not being at the convent when that was exactly where she was supposed to be.

She stepped back onto the street and looked up and down. When she was certain there was no one she knew, she stepped jauntily down the boardwalk.

It had been relatively easy to allow Sister Marie-Anne to think she was needed at home on Tuesdays and Thursdays. The nun believed her and her parents were none the wiser.

"Hi ya, sweetie," a young soldier lounging against a building called out to her. Fleur gave him a long level look and continued on. She knew who had money and who did not. She would not waste her time with someone who did not.

"Not so fast, Sweetie," the soldier said running after her and grabbing her arm. He jerked her to a stop and stood appraising her with knowing eyes. "I ain't so bad. Stay and talk to me. Don't got much looks, but I got the same equipment a better man has."

"Please release me," Fleur said slowly and clearly.

"Don't go gettin' proud with me. I know what you are?"

"What am I?" Fleur asked intrigued.

"You're trash, same as me. You wear pretty clothes and all, but you're still trash."

"Is that so!" Fleur took his hand from her arm. She grimaced in distaste at the bruises his fingers left on her pale skin. "Would you like to see how loud this piece of trash can scream. I guarantee you a dozen gentlemen will come to my defense."

"You think so, sweetie. Go on, try it. I want to see what happens." He grinned showing rotting teeth and breathing whiskey soaked breath at her.

"Senor." A tall slender man in tight-fitting trousers and bolero jacket stepped up to Fleur. "You will remove yourself from this lady's presence."

"Shove off, Mex."

"I am not a Mex. My name is Rico Hernandez and my mother is pure Castillian Spanish. She is very beautiful, my mamacita."

"I'm tellin' ya to shove off, Mex. This piece is mine."

"The senorita does not desire your company."

The soldier turned to swing, but Rico stepped back and the soldier staggered off balance. He righted himself and started at Rico again. Rico stepped back and the man stumbled into the gutter sprawling. When the soldier was on his feet once more, he found himself facing a long, wickedly gleaming knife.

"It is called a Bowie knife, Senor. It is a good knife. It kills well."

Fleur's attacker slunk away, but not without a backward glare at her.

"He will not trouble you again, Senorita," Rico said with a slight bow. He studied the girl. She was very young, but she was a woman in spite of her tender years. "Should you be walking around without your duenna?"

"I have no duenna," she said. "At least, I do not have one now."

"Your family will not worry?" Rico studied the fine cut of her gown and the expensive fabric. This was no ordinary woman of the streets, but the daughter of a rich house.

"They will not worry," she said with a toss of her head. She looked at him through narrowed eyes, feeling the intensity of his magnetism wash over her. She was reminded of Noble in some obscure way. A wave of desire shook her, startling her.

"Would you care to walk a little, Senorita?" Rico offered. He was intrigued with this child. He wondered if she always wandered the street or if she had run away from her duenna. He finally decided she had run away. He understood the strictness of Creole households. They were no less strict than their Mexican counterparts.

"If you wish," Fleur said with a pretty shrug. She watched him from under the fringe of her lashes. He was the most handsome man she had ever seen with his finely chiseled face and elegant features.

"Your city is very beautiful," he said casually, falling into step with her. He admired the beauty of the Vieux Carre. It was so different with its tightly packed homes from the casual sprawl of a Spanish hacienda. He wondered how the Creole families could stand living so close together. Or could they live no other way?

"I suppose it is beautiful," Fleur said trying to see the cramped houses bordering directly on the street with a stranger's eyes. She saw nothing unusual in them. She spied a coffee house and dragged Rico into it with her. It was dark and intimate. She led the way to a shadowed corner.

The waiter came over and she ordered in a low voice for them both. Rico watched her, liking the way her full, sensuous lips formed the French words. He liked the way her small, slim hands expressively echoed the tones of her voice. She was not exactly

305

beautiful, yet there was a firm suggestion of beauty. She was attractive in such a subtle, sensual way that men turned to look at her when she walked down the street.

Fleur stopped speaking and smiled at Rico, open invitation in her bold eyes. He returned the smile aware of the smooth contours of her body. She was young, but already a master at the subtle games played between men and their counterparts.

"Are you going to volunteer for the army?" Fleur asked. "Everyone I know is volunteering."

"I do not fight in this war," Rico said. He was surprised when a look of relief spread over her features.

"What will you do?" His answer pleased her. She was a loyal Southern woman, but the thought of this magnificent man lying dead on a battle field frightened her.

"I return to Texas," he said. "I have plans to purchase land and ranch. I will be a wealthy man someday."

"I like men with money," Fleur said tilting her head up and gazing at him seductively.

"I like beautiful senoritas with something to see. My hotel is not far."

"Is your room nice?"

"It will be even nicer with you in it."

Fleur stood up, pushing her chair back. It scraped the floor, a loud grating sound in the quiet room. "I do not come cheap, Monsieur."

Rico studied her tastefully expensive gown. Had his first impression of her been wrong. Was she indeed a woman of the street?

"But I am not greedy. You say your room is nice.

306

My fee for you is to arrange for me to use that room for one full year."

Rico was surprised, he stumbled as he rose to his feet. Then he started to chuckle. Never in his life had he known a whore with no place to take her customers. "Why do I not give you the money. You can make your own arrangements."

"No. You must make them for me in your name. The management must not know the room is for me."

"You do not have to give your correct name." He was puzzled. Was she a whore or an innocent young girl out experimenting?

"Do you agree to my terms?"

"I agree. Shall we go?" He tossed coins on the table. They clattered loudly. The waiter hurried to the table reaching out avidly.

"My name is Fleur," she said wondering why she gave her correct name.

"It is a beautiful name. I like it, Fleur."

"Thank you, but it is only a name."

When she had dressed and was gone, Rico continued to lay on his bed staring at the ceiling. Where he had thought Fleur to be sixteen or seventeen had been revised after seeing her slim, still developing body. Immature that she was, she still possessed the intensity of any woman. Her knowledge and understanding surpassed that of many women. She had fed his hunger with the expertise of any woman in a brothel. Even though she had left long since, he still hungered for her. She had promised to return on Thursday morning and Rico knew he was anxious for Thursday to arrive.

An idle glance at his watch reminded him of his ap-

307

pointment with Renault de Champlain. He jumped out of bed, washed and dressed quickly. He was still buttoning his shirt as he ran down the stairs.

"Senor," Rico said as he walked into Renault's office. They had met briefly the summer before.

"Please sit down, Monsieur Hernandez," Renault said cordially, gesturing at the chair. He offered a drink and was refused. "I am pleased to meet you again after all these months. You and Monsieur Taggert have done a fine job for me."

"Your warehouses are full, senor," Rico replied. "I have come for our payment."

"Where is Monsieur Taggert?"

"He joined the army last April in Natchez."

"Have you been working the plantation alone all these months?" Renault frowned.

"Yes. Now the job is done, I have come for our money."

"Are you planning to volunteer?" Renault asked as he opened his desk drawer and pulled out his cash box. He looked at Rico remembering that this man was half black.

"I do not go," Rico said. "My padre was a runaway slave, senor. I cannot fight for the people who beat and scarred him, crippling him for the rest of his life. And I cannnt fight for the other side because someday I might sight my rifle on my friend. No matter what my orders, I could never kill him. I will return to Texas with our money and purchase the land we have dreamed of owning. Then I shall pray that he returns to enjoy this land."

"Have you thought of taking another job?"

"With you?"

Renault nodded. "I have a little plantation upriver in need of a firm hand. It is not very far, but it needs someone to harvest and hide the crop."

"Cotton is at its prime right now," Rico said.

"That is so, but when the war is over, it will be in short supply and the price will go even higher. When that happens, I plan to have cotton to sell for that price."

"What will you offer me for this job?"

"I'll double what I have right here and give you three percent of my profit."

"Five percent, Senor," Rico said with a grin. "After all it is wartime and I must hide the crop to keep it from enemy hands. Also, it must be in gold."

"You are a prudent man, Monsieur. It will be in gold."

"I will take the job, but I know nothing of cotton. I know cattle and ranching, but I do not know cotton."

"You'll have someone to help you. He is a good man. It is his job you will be taking over when he leaves for the war."

"Are there horses on this plantation? I grow weary of walking."

"St. Angele has some of the best stock in the state. You may take your pick of all the saddle horses except those belonging to my daughter, Aurore. Old Silas has charge of the stables; he will tell which you may choose from."

"That pleases me. *Gracias.* I have some business to attend to, but I shall be able to leave Friday."

"The arrangements will be made."

Rico stood and bowed gracefully. He flashed a large smile and left whistling under his breath, well-pleased with himself.

Marget met Neil two blocks from her home. She walked swiftly trying to reach their meeting place early. But he was there before her, walking back and forth waiting impatiently. She smiled up at him, breathing heavily from her fast walk. Her hair had come undone and had tumbled into a long wave over one shoulder. She started to put it up, but Neil stopped her.

"Don't," he said. "I like it that way."

She blushed deeply, her hands still smoothing the tangle. "Are we going on a picnic again?" she asked.

"Yes, the carriage is waiting." He took her hand and led her around the corner to the closed carriage. The driver glanced at them incuriously as they got in.

The glade was isolated and remote. Neil dismissed the carriage with instructions to return in two hours, then he picked up the huge hamper and walked Marget to the secluded area they had visited the time before.

"It is so lovely here and peaceful," Marget sighed. She spread the blanket on the ground and sat on it. "There seems so little peace these days."

"War is an ugly thing, Marget," Neil said. He took off his coat and rolled up his shirt sleeves before sitting down next to her pulling the hamper close. He opened it and brought out a bottle of chilled wine and two glasses. "It destroys families and ideals. What do you hear from your husband?"

Marget looked at him curiously. He always seemed interested in her husband. "I hear from Benoit infrequently. I understand he is in Florida and unhappy. He wants to be a captain or major instead of a lowly lieutenant. He considers himself more worthy of a higher rank."

"And what do you think?"

"I hope he gets killed," she said fiercely, then gasped. She stared at Neil in horror. "I . . . I . . . didn't mean that. I really didn't. At least I don't think I did." Marget felt like crying. How could she say such an unchristian thing about her husband. "Please forgive me. I don't know why I said that. I didn't want to marry Benoit." A few tears slid down her cheek. "I'm sorry," she said. She brushed the tears away.

Neil gathered her into his arms and held her tenderly until her sobbing was stilled. He gave her a handkerchief and watched as she wiped her face and blew her nose. Then he kissed her.

Marget pulled away, pushing him from her. She was married to another man and had no right to be with Neil.

"I apologize," Neil said, busying himself in opening the wine and pouring it into the glasses.

"No, I am the one at fault," Marget said bitterly. "I have no right to be here with you. I am married to Benoit and I have given him a child. No power on earth can change that."

"You have the right to happiness."

"I think we should return to the city."

"There's no carriage," Neil grinned. Their eyes met and they laughed. "Let's enjoy our picnic. I promise I won't make any more improper advances." He held out her glass and she took it, sipping the cool wine. He wondered how long he would be able to control himself. Marget was a very desirable woman and he was in love with her.

The dress in the shop window caught Fleur's attention as she walked by. She stopped to admire it, drawn to the vibrant blue velvet. She smiled, appreciating the soft beauty of the gown all the while admiring the rose-colored bloom to her cheeks. Fresh from love with her handsome Mexican, she was sparkling beautiful. He did something to her no other man had done. He evoked a response in her that made her weak and dizzy. Remembering their moments of love caused her heart to flutter.

It was a pity he was leaving New Orleans so soon after his arrival. Fleur would have liked to spend days with him, making love and tasting of his virility. How she wished she had that dress to wear for him. He would like it on her. She half thought of asking her mother for the gown, but immediately put the idea from her. She was only fourteen and girls of her age did not go around in shimmering blue velvet gowns that clung shamelessly to their bodies. Fleur sighed. With one last longing look, she turned away to face a brand new laudelet of bright yellow and brown approaching her. She stared curiously in much the same manner as the other women on the street. Then drew back startled. Fay Courtland and Michael Slaughter looked directly at her.

Fay's mouth was turned down in disapproval. Michael leered openly. Then the carriage was gone and Fleur was turning into a dark alley, running through shadows and garbage until she was certain she was in an area the Slaughters were unlikely to visit.

What were they doing in the city? Of all the people she could have easily run into, it had to be the Slaughters during a visit to New Orleans. Fleur turned down another alley coming out in front of the hotel

Rico Hernandez was still occupying. After tomorrow it would be her hotel. She would have a room all to her own to do with as she pleased. She liked the thought of having it.

Fleur wondered if Rico were still in his room. She thought about joining him, but a swift glance at her watch changed her mind. It was time to meet Luce at the convent. As she walked, her mind returned to the Slaughters and their presence on the street.

"Fleur, darling," Marie-Odile said as Fleur walked into the drawing room. "Mrs. Slaughter was just asking about you."

"Good afternoon, Fleur," Fay said running a swift glance over the girl, a little shocked at the change from girl to almost woman.

"Good afternoon, Mrs. Slaughter," Fleur said, returning Fay's glance frankly. Fay colored a little as she realized she was being as minutely studied as she had just studied Fleur.

"Miss Fleur," Michael said smoothly taking her hand and squeezing it. He bowed slightly, his eyes searching the neckline of her gown. "How nice to see you again." He straightened and smiled down at her fondly. "I was just telling your lovely Mama that Miss Fay and I saw you on the street earlier."

Fleur swallowed her panic. She stared from Fay to her stepson. She blinked, swallowed again and drew her hand from Michael's bone-crushing grip.

"Sister Lisette was sent on an errand to match some silk for the new tapestry Sister Marie-Anne is working on. There was no one free to go with her except me." Fleur was amazed at how skillfully the lie fell from her mouth.

313

"I don't remember seeing a nun with you," Fay said eyeing her suspiciously.

"Sister Lisette was in the shop. I was given permission to look at the gown in the window. It was so lovely, Maman. I wish I had one like it."

"We'll look at it. Did Sister Lisette match her silk?"

"No, Maman. The shop was out of everything. We went to two others, but they had nothing to match either. The blockade is keeping many things out of our shops these days."

Marie-Odile smiled brightly. "Ask your papa to match it. One of his ships arrived from Nassau the other day. The captain can take it with him and look around in Nassau."

"I shall ask, Maman," Fleur said. Her panic disappeared as she realized she was not going to lose her secret life because of a chance remark from the Slaughters.

Michael took her arm and drew her away to the window where the two chattering women would not hear him.

"Are you planning to enter the convent?" he asked grinning wickedly. "Such a waste of good talent."

"I have no plans for doing so," Fleur replied. "I only help during school hours because it is something to do and because Maman approves."

"If you are bored, I know something you could do."

"And what would that be?" Fleur asked innocently.

"Don't play games. I know what you look like under your clothes. Did you have to burn the cabin?"

"I was cleansing my soul," she said. She thought she hated him, yet here she was flirting a little and enjoying herself as well.

"Were you angry over my little joke?" Michael teased. He brushed against her breast suggestively. "My brothers thought it great fun."

"I did not share your appreciation of the situation," she replied drawing away slightly. "It was no joke, Michael. It was deliberately planned cruelty. If you ever try to touch me again, I will kill you."

"Those are strong words for a little girl to use," he said, no longer confident. He watched her uneasily.

"Do you consider me incapable of the act of murder?"

"What would your parents think if they knew you were a whore?" His uneasiness grew at the curving smile on her lips. Any other girl would have been cringing and pleading before him. But Fleur was not acting like any other normal girl.

"Why don't you tell them?" Fleur suggested sweetly. "They will want to know how you found out about me and then what will you say? Such intimate knowledge of my behavior could hardly have come into your possession unless you had first hand experiences with it. They would believe you, but after the first shock, they will start wondering about the kind of gentleman you profess to be. Gentlemen hardly go around seducing children."

"Young men are encouraged to experiment," Michael said. A small knot of fear twisted inside him. Why should he be afraid of her? She was only a child.

"Of course, I would have to bare my soul and tell them about your strange ideas of sex. They are so bizarre that a normal woman would refuse you. Naturally you are then forced to seek young, innocent girls to corrupt with your filth. After that, you would

315

have little chance of marrying into any of the better families in Louisiana. No man would trust you with his daughter. My reputation will be ruined, but you will suffer more than I." Fleur tilted her head and gazed at him fondly. She thrilled at the edge of fear in his eyes. This was the power she wanted over men. She almost laughed when he turned pleading eyes on her. A core of satisfaction grew in her, displacing what was left of the hate she had felt. Her satisfaction turned to contempt. With a slight shake of her head, she left him standing at the window walking back across the room to her mother and Miss Fay.

"What is happening to New Orleans?" Fay demanded peevishly. She twisted her glove in her hands. "All I want is a new fan to match my new gown. My gown is from Paris. But there is nothing in this whole city. Every shop I went into had almost nothing or was totally empty. What goods are available are of such inferior quality that I would never dream of purchasing them. And the prices! They are outrageous!"

"It is the blockade," Marie-Odile murmured. She was less sympathetic than she might have been if it had been someone else. But she had never liked Fay. "Ships won't sail if there is a chance they might be captured and their cargo confiscated as contraband."

"Your husband owns several steamships. Do any of them come to New Orleans?"

"The Heritage docked Tuesday, but I doubt there were fans aboard."

"Are you certain?"

Marie-Odile had no intention of offering to allow Fay to look through the cargo. Too big a fuss was being made of a silly, little fan.

"I'm quite certain," Marie-Odile said firmly.

"What shall I do?" Fay said in distress, wondering how she was going to get her fan. "Marcus did so want to show me off at the Opera tomorrow night."

Marie-Odile found she could not muster the appropriate amount of sorrow of Fay's problem.

"War is so boring," Fay exploded. "A person can't find anything decent. I do hope our soldiers hurry up and win it."

"I don't think it is going to be as quick a matter as they first thought," Marie-Odile said. "If they do not hurry, I expect the women of the South will rise up in rebellion at being made to do without their luxuries."

"Are you implying I am unpatriotic?"

"Not at all," Marie-Odile assured her guest. "Why should I think such a thing? I am certain you are as properly patriotic as the rest of us."

"Of course I am," Fay said through slightly gritted teeth. She stood up abruptly. "We must be going, Michael. Thank you for the lovely visit."

"I was delighted to see you," Marie-Odile replied ringing for Persia to show Fay and Michael to the door. "Come again when times are better."

Fay looked long and searchingly at Marie-Odile, but could detect no insincerity in her face.

"I will," Fay said brightly and flounced out still slightly angry over coming away without a fan.

"You were horrid to her," Fleur said when the visitors were gone. "You knew perfectly well that Papa had a consignment of luxuries on his ship. He gave you first choice."

"And there is a fan that will suit her needs exactly," Marie-Odile said with a rare laugh. "But I could

317

hardly be expected to give it to her for free. Your papa would be horrified."

"Oh, Maman," Fleur said with a throaty laugh. She kissed her mother with a burst of affection and ran from the room still laughing.

Twenty

Sulie Chesterleigh sat on the review stand. She was uncomfortably hot in the afternoon sun. Perspiration gathered in the valley between her breasts, under her arms and behind her knees. The slight shade her parasol offered was barely enough to ease her discomfort.

Why, oh why, did she have to sit here day after day at these silly parades? Sulie hated them. She glanced at her father. He sat on his chair with his back held stiffly and his mouth firmly set. No tantrum on the face of the earth could move him.

"Papa," Sulie said softly. "I am not feeling well."

Colonel Julius Chesterleigh stared straight ahead impassively. The gold buttons of his uniform gleamed in the sun. He was a handsome man with iron gray hair and mustache. He was a hard bodied man molded by the years of military life behind him.

"Papa!" Sulie pleaded. Her snow white gown of crisp organdy had long since fallen into damp folds about her hoops. "Please!"

"Enough!" The colonel said sternly, his mustache barely twitching as he spoke. "You will sit with dignity until the parade is ended."

"Yes, Papa," Sulie said meekly though the look of

dark anger turned her mouth sullen and resentful. I hate him, she thought savagely. She tried to think of pleasant things, but the heat and rising humidity made it impossible. After a while, she truly did begin to feel ill.

"General Bragg, sir," Colonel Chesterleigh said respectfully to the thick-bodied man next to him. "There is the man I told you about."

Sulie followed her father's pointed finger. She saw a tall, blond man on a huge chestnut stallion. She had seen him before, but without interest. Suddenly she was interested. She sat straighter in her chair and vainly fluffed her sleeves and ruffles. She smiled at the man, running a small pink tongue over her narrow lips. He was handsome, she thought. How long had it been since she had had a man she truly liked? Too long.

"His name is Courtland. From New Orleans." Colonel Chesterleigh continued. "He sits a fine horse and his men have a high regard for him. He'd make an excellent addition to your staff. Good Southern man. Plays poker, too."

At the word poker, General Bragg nodded slightly. In the course of a few words, the future of the major was changed.

Sulie's eyes gleamed as the man came closer. She arched her back and smoothed the front of her gown over her breasts. She willed him to look at her, but he saluted smartly and passed beyond the reviewing stand without a glance in her direction. She sank back fanning herself vigorously and frowning. She felt unreasoning pique. How could he not notice her? Every other young officer in the regiment did. Some were her sworn slaves. She was determined to make the young major notice her.

The parade came to an end. Sulie stood up, aware of the beginnings of prickly heat between her legs. Her father nodded his dismissal of her and she started walking across the parade ground.

"Miss Sulie."

"Lt. de Ville." Sulie said with a practiced look over her white shoulder.

"I had to see you, Miss Sulie," he said looking down at her, his hungry eyes searching the aloofness of her face.

"Did you, Lieutenant!"

"It's been so long, Sulie," Benoit said pleadingly.

"So long for what?"

"You know what I mean," Benoit said.

"Lieutenant de Ville, I am afraid you have mistaken something I may have said for something else."

"You said you loved me," Benoit cried. "How could I be mistaken about something as serious as that."

"Lieutenant, can't we discuss this another time. I'm very tired at the moment and it is very hot."

"Sulie," Benoit cried again. "Let me come to your room and we can discuss it civilly."

"I am afraid that cannot be," Sulie said. She stared across the parade ground toward the cool, dark interior of her father's quarters.

"But you said . . ."

"I never said anything. You assumed that I did and then you twisted the meaning. You are a married man, Lt. de Ville. I long ago found there is no future with a married man."

Benoit stared at her, his eyes narrowing angrily. "This isn't the last you'll hear of me, Miss Sulie," he said sharply. He saluted and walked away.

"Don't be a nuisance, Benoit," she said to his back. "If you make things uncomfortable for me, I shall make them very uncomfortable for you. How would you like a transfer to the front lines, wherever they may be at the moment. Somehow I didn't think you would like that. I suggest you leave me alone."

Benoit continued to walk away, though his very body cringed at the scorn in her words. When he looked back she was gone.

Sulie's bedroom was cool and dark. She closed her parasol with a snap, yelled for Mimosa and began to tear at her gown.

"You'll rip it," Mimosa said, pushing her mistress's fingers away from the delicate gown and calmly unfastening it.

"Hurry up," Sulie growled. "I'm so hot, I could faint."

'You've never fainted a day in your life."

"If you don't hurry, I'll faint today," Sulie yelled.

The organdy gown fell to the floor in a sodden lump. Her hoops followed, then whale-boned stays and her silk underclothes. Naked, Sulie stepped out of the pile of clothes and stretched with feline grace. She padded across the floor to her mirror where she pulled pins out of her hair and tossed them on the floor. Her dark auburn hair fell to her shoulders.

"Bring me something cool to drink," she ordered. "Be quick about it. I'm going to nap and then I will want my bath. For tonight, I shall wear the gold gown."

"Yes, Miss," Mimosa said bending over to pick up the discarded clothes. "Will there be anything else?"

"No."

Three days separated the two girls in age, yet they were as alike in feature and shape as two sisters. They were sisters, except for the fact that Mimosa's mother was a dusky-skinned slave and Sulie's mother was the fragile, white-skinned wife to Julius Chesterleigh.

The door closed silently and Sulie was alone. She stood in front of her mirror absently brushing her hair. Someday, she was going to put that uppity slave in her place. It did not matter to Sulie that Mimosa was her half-sister. A slave was a slave regardless of parentage.

Sulie put down her brush and fluffed her hair about her shoulders. She loved the way her hair framed her small face and made dark curls against the whiteness of her shoulders and breasts. She studied herself in the mirror. She loved looking at her face and breasts and rounded hips. She thought her body beautiful. She smiled at herself. As a child, she had spent hours in front of her mirror practicing different smiles and expressions until she knew which ones were seductive enough to make a man swoon at her feet. Even now she still flirted with herself, making little faces at the mirror while her slim hands caressed the firm fullness of breasts and legs. She was a beautiful woman and she knew it. The only thing she liked nearly as much as herself was a well-made man.

She stroked her body, her eyes half-closed and her thoughts full of the tall, handsome major. Instinctively, she knew he was a man who knew how to please a woman. And she was determined he was going to please her.

A movement distracted her. She opened her eyes and watched Mimosa place a tray on the bedside table. The tall, frosted glass of lemonade made her mouth water.

Mimosa turned to leave, a flash of skirts revealing slim, brown legs.

"Not yet, Mimosa," Sulie said sweetly. She glanced at the bed. "Take your clothes off and get into bed dear."

"I've work to do, Miss Sulie," Mimosa said flatly, a look of distaste marring her face.

"Do as I say, or I shall have you whipped. You've never been whipped, Mimosa. There is always a first time. There's a good girl. I do love you and I value your loyalty over anything else." Sulie watched the girl unbutton her gown and drop it to the floor. She stepped out of it, a tall, slim girl who stared angrily at her mistress.

Sulie reached for her lemonade and sipped it slowly while Mimosa climbed into the bed. Then she slid into the bed and took Mimosa into her arms. Her fingers touched the cool, dark flesh. Then she lay back beckoning.

"You know what to do, dear half-sister," Sulie said softly. She drew Mimosa close and pushed her head down to one, already hard pink nipple. "Make it good, darling."

Sulie's gown was inappropriate for a young girl. She knew it, her mother knew and her father knew it. Yet not a word was said about it.

Julius Chesterleigh smiled at Sulie with full approval. She was the bait he used to dangle in front of his fellow officers when he needed their co-operation. Few were immune to his daughter's charms. The more wanton she dressed, the better he liked it. The low-necked gown would cause many of the women present to cluck disapproval, but Julius cared little for how they felt. It was their husbands he wanted to snare.

Tabitha Chesterleigh stared at her daughter in numb servility. She was no match for the powerful combination of husband and daughter. As she stepped into the carriage, she sat in a far corner deliberately removing herself from husband and child.

"Both my ladies look ravishing tonight," Julius said heartily gazing at his daughter. The gold gown was perfection itself. It set off her graceful shoulders and full breasts beautifully. He was a man who delighted in beauty.

From earliest infancy, Julius had taught his daughter to assert herself. He wanted no weak, whining daughter in the image of his weak, whining wife. He watched her grow from infant to child to woman with increasing boldness and seductiveness. He had laughed when he found her in the stable ordering all the little boys to undress and compare themselves with her own white smoothness. He had watched when she first found physical love in the arms of a lusty black buck. And he taught her to use her body to gain power. Power was important.

They arrived at the hall and entered to find the ball not yet started. Tabitha left her husband to circulate among the women. Sulie went with her father to circulate among the men.

Gayle disliked army life. He was a man used to

following his own orders. He had to fight resentment each time he was ordered to do something. As he walked around the large room, he studied the women. For the most part they were officers' wives. There were a few pretty ones though most looked hard and careworn. He ran a practiced eye over the daughters, but they left him disinterested. They were all vapidly pretty or long faced and ugly. Then he turned around and saw the most enchanting creature in the world coming toward him.

She walked across the room with unusual grace. Her belled skirts flowed gently around her. Her dark hair was formed into dozens of tiny ringlets about a tiny face. Her eyes were large and blue. Her figure was generously proportioned under the gown that clung sensuously to her. She was beautiful, but there was a suggestion of raw sexuality in her eyes. As they smiled knowingly into his, Gayle almost chuckled. There were a dozen terms for a woman like Sulie Chesterleigh and Gayle knew them all. He had also met them all during his long years in saloons and brothels.

"Good evening, Major," she said. Her voice was soft and throaty. She flickered a glance at him and put a long, slim hand on his arm.

He was drawn to her helplessly. He was intoxicated with her. She was beautiful and while his mind told him she was dangerous, his senses swam with the intoxicating aroma of her perfume.

"Major Courtland," Julius said. "I see you have met my daughter. A real beauty, isn't she. She will be the delight of my retired years. Sulie, this is Major Gayle Courtland."

"Your servant, miss," Gayle said unable to take his eyes from her.

"Major," she said inclining her head to one side and gazing up at him. "It looks to be a lovely night for a ball, I do hope . . ."

"Miss Sulie," Benoit said, shouldering his way into the group. "How nice to see you tonight."

Julius frowned.

"Good evening, Lieutenant," Sulie said wrinkling her nose at the liquor smell surrounding him. "You do know Major Courtland, don't you?"

"We're old friends, Miss Sulie," Benoit said. He glanced at Gayle.

"Excuse me, gentlemen," Julius interrupted smoothly. "The General has arrived." He took Sulie's arm and led her quickly away from a scene that threatened to turn ugly.

"You're trespassing on my territory," Benoit said in an angry undertone.

"A woman disposes her favors as she pleases, de Ville. I've taken nothing that wasn't offered."

"She is mine."

"What about your wife? I don't think Renault de Champlain will take kindly to having his daughter insulted."

"And you'll tell him. He would be the last to show disapproval when he was his own nigger whore tucked away all safe and proper."

Gayle was unsurprised. What man didn't know about another's discreet affairs. "That doesn't mean what's good for the goose is good for the gander, de Ville. Renault de Champlain has two sets of rules, one for himself and one for you. Don't flatter yourself I would inform him of your indiscretions. He is eminently capable of finding out for himself." Gayle turned away to join another officer, leaving Benoit fuming in the middle of the room.

The orchestra struck a note. Then the music began in earnest. Couples moved toward the floor. Gayle watched as Benoit stalked up to Sulie Chesterleigh and demanded a dance. He was curtly refused. She swung out onto the floor with another officer, her full skirts flying, showing a hint of a slim-ankled foot. She whirled around and smiled at Gayle when she was near him. There was a world of promise in that smile and Gayle was no fool in understanding it.

It wasn't easy making an army out of untried men, but Brigadier General Braxton Bragg set about his task methodically. He was determined to make an army and was succeeding creditably well despite the Federal stronghold at Fort Pickens only a few miles away on Santa Rosa Island.

"I think we should try to take it," Julius Chesterleigh pushed. He had been arguing for thirty minutes and growing angrier with each second that passed. Didn't the old fool know that taking the island would be a real feather in his hat.

Gayle sat back in his chair smothering a yawn. For the last three weeks, he had spent his time listening to these officers talk and he found it boring. He preferred being with his men in the hot afternoons drilling on the parade ground to listening to the constant drone of voices in the constant string of meetings he had been forced to endure since being assigned to Gen. Bragg's staff. He stifled another yawn thinking of the round of arguments to come as General Anderson and Colonel Chesterleigh continued to push for a direct assault on Fort Pickens. General Bragg was indifferent to the capture of the island fort. Colonel Chesterleigh and General Anderson were all afire to capture it and secure Pensacola for the Confederacy. Both were less concerned with the Confederacy than they were for their own personal glory.

"I agree totally, General," Anderson said.

Julius liked action. He was a man of action seething with anxiety that the war was passing him by. He was afraid it would be over before he ever got the chance to show his ability at tactical planning. When the new Confederacy finally established itself as a world power, Julius Chesterleigh did not want to be forgotten on some distant plantation. He wanted to be a part of it, an important part.

"I am here to build an army," Bragg said. "Why do you keep pressing me with talk of glorious battle? We've six thousand untried troops here. Most of them are away from home for the first time in their lives and are still wet behind the years."

Gayle thought the general should introduce those boys to Sulie. They wouldn't be innocent country boys for long. Sulie was an education even for a man like Gayle who had seen and experienced just about all there was to do. He smiled remembering her uninhibited approach to sex. Even he had been startled. She was a demon and a tigress. She knew ways of making love that made a man's blood boil for more until he was too exhausted to move.

"A skirmish with the Yankees will toughen them, sir," Julius said. "A few hand-picked men for recon-

329

naissance and a larger force for strength. Taking that island will boost their morale and show the Yankees we are a force to be reckoned with."

Bragg sighed. He disliked battle hungry officers whose vainglorious attempts were bought with too many lives. Bragg was a cautious man. "The Union forces are dug in prettry well over there."

"We can drive them out, sir," General Anderson said confidently.

"Let me think about it." General Bragg stood abruptly signaling the end of the meeting. He stalked from the room followed by a file of officers.

Colonel Chesterleigh and General Anderson reseated themselves when the room was empty. With a slight gesture of his hand, Colonel Chesterleigh detained Gayle.

"Care for a cigar, Major Courtland?" the colonel asked.

"No thank you, sir," Gayle said annoyed at being kept from his meeting with Sulie.

"You had the best cavalry unit in the regiment before you were transferred here. Do you think you could whip an infantry unit into shape, Major?"

"I'm not an army man of any kind, sir. What I did was just luck."

General Anderson smiled. It was not a pleasant smile. "We are going to need a crack unit for this attack on Fort Pickens."

"General Bragg said he would think about it. What makes you so certain he will give his final approval?" Gayle did not like these two men. He had met their sort before, manipulating to get their own way.

"He'll approve," the General said. He exchanged

looks with Chesterleigh, heavy with meaning. Gayle was puzzled. What did they know that he didn't? "With that in mind, I suggest you start thinking about the men you would like to take with you. You will train them and I do not doubt they will perform as expected. That is all, Major."

Gayle rose. He saluted smartly thinking that if he had learned nothing else in the army, he was learning to salute. He turned on his heels and left the room, the deep sounds of the two men's voices cut off when he closed the door.

"Tell you daughter, Chesterleigh, that the good general is in the habit of taking a short stroll around the parade ground just before he retires," General Anderson said quietly.

Julius nodded. "She is also in the habit of strolling before retiring. She also has a liking for generals."

Anderson laughed. He knew how well Sulie liked generals.

"I've been waiting for hours," Sulie complained as Gayle crossed the veranda and walked into her room. He stopped for a moment to let his eyes adjust to the dimness of the room after the bright afternoon sunshine.

"I couldn't get away," Gayle said. He looked at her appreciatively. She wore a fluttering gown of sheer batiste. It clung provocatively to her breasts.

"I hate it when duty comes before me."

"I do what I'm told, Sulie," he said wearily, a touch of resentment in his voice. There were times when her insatiable clinging wearied him more than the long staff meetings.

"What did you talk about today?" she asked after a long silence. She was helping him undress, her slim fingers moving nimbly over him.

"Nothing important," Gayle sighed. He remembered her father and General Anderson relentlessly relentlessly plotting their own glory.

Sulie hung his coat neatly over the back of the chair and watched as he folded his trousers carefully and set them on the seat. He was a neat man. Sulie liked that. He never came to her smelling of the day's sweat.

"Tell me I'm beautiful," she urged, struggling out of her gown to stand naked before him. He bent his head and nibbled at her earlobe. It sent delicious thrills down her body.

"You're beautiful," Gayle said smiling at her. He ran his hands over her slightly damp flesh. She shivered with desire leaning against him seeking his lips with hers.

The bedding was cool against his skin. Gayle watched as Sulie knelt before him, her lips pursed and her hands moving expertly over him.

"I love you," she whispered when he drew her down next to him. She meant it. She did love him. She loved him with an intensity no other man had known.

"I love you," he whispered in her ear. "I love you, Aurore."

"What did you say?" Sulie demanded, anger sparkling in her eyes. Then she saw that he was asleep. Her anger vanished and she curled next to him forgetting the other name.

The night was cool. Water lapped gently at the boats as men climbed into them as quietly as possible.

As each boat filled, Gayle waved it away from the shore. There was whispering quickly silenced, then the boat was gone caught up in the current and following the dozen other boats making their way to Santa Rosa Island.

General Anderson and Colonel Chesterleigh had had their way. General Bragg had given his final approval to the scheme. The two men were elated. They had made their plans confident of success. Gayle was less certain, but careful not to say so. It was General Anderson's plan to land on the west end of the island and slowly make his way to the fort. Once the western end was in Confederate hands, it would only be a matter of time before the fort fell to them.

Gayle climbed into the last boat and signaled it away from shore. He wished he had the confidence of his two superior officers. He was a gambling man, but for this venture, the odds were all wrong.

"This is going to be the greatest military advancement of my career," Julius Chesterleigh said to Gayle as he ordered the placement of the trenches.

Gayle felt ill. There was only blind ambition and no thought for the common soldier who would bring about this victory. If victory were possible.

The Colonel strolled away and Gayle set about seeing that his men were dug in deeply.

The Union forces were not as surprised to find one thousand Confederates on their doorstep as Colonel Chesterleigh and General Anderson had hoped. Somewhere along the line, the element of surprise had been lost. Gayle said nothing, though he felt the Yankees might have been waiting for just such an attack. After all, what would you do if you held a post completely surrounded by enemy territory?

The Union defenses were better than anticipated. After two days and nights of constant fighting, General Anderson gave the order to withdraw.

Gayle was unaware of being wounded until he sat in the returning boat. He was tired beyond exhaustion. He almost smiled when he thought of General Bragg and the fury the man would show when Anderson returned in defeat. Gayle could almost hear the man saying his piece. But unfortunately, good men were dead.

"Sir!" A dust-covered man sat next to Gayle. "You're bleeding, sir."

Gayle was unsurprised. He watched the rivulet of blood flow down his leg. The soldier fumbled with his neckcloth and tied it around Gayle's leg pulling it tight.

"Thank you, Corporal . . . "

"Corporal Sawyer, sir," the man said. "Second Alabama volunteers."

As though on cue, the leg exploded in pain. Gayle gasped, then moaned. He leaned weakly against the corporal as the man pulled open his jacket where another wound vigorously pumped blood. Several of the men pulled off their neckcloths to hand to Corporal Sawyer who used them to staunch the blood.

For a moment, Gayle's mind wandered and he was once more a younger son forced to support himself. Card playing had come naturally to Gayle. What better profession could he enter.

"Sir," Corporal said. He never finished his words as Gayle slumped forward unconscious.

"Gayle. Gayle, darling," Sulie murmured. "You are safe now, darling. You're going to be all right."

Gayle tried hard to focus on her. Her voice seemed to come from a great distance. His vision cleared, but it was not Sulie he saw sitting next to his bed.

"You're going home to New Orleans," Sulie said gently.

"Aurore," Gayle whispered. Then he fell back on the pillow moaning.

Sulie's lips tightened angrily. There was that name again. She stood in a swish of skirts and stared down at Gayle with less than love in her face.

"What are you doing in here, Miss Sulie?" Benoit said solicitously. "This is no place for a woman with your delicate sensibilities." He drew Sulie away, smiling as she went unprotesting.

"Who is Aurore?" she asked more to herself.

Benoit frowned. It was several seconds before he thought of the half-grown sister of his wife. That was impossible! She was barely out of childhood. He shrugged dismissing the thought from his mind and bent his energies to charming Sulie.

Three days later, Gayle was laid in a canvas-covered wagon by a smiling faced Corporal Sawyer.

"I sure wish I were going along," the corporal said wistfully.

"I wish you were, too," Gayle said. For the last few days, the young corporal had stayed with him seeing to his needs and comfort. "When I get back, I could use a good man like you with me."

"I'd be honored, Major," Sawyer said, his plain face lighting up. "Have a good trip and get lots of rest. I want to have a good officer to be loyal to."

The wagon started with a jerk. Gayle's face whitened with pain and his teeth clenched to keep from groaning. Then he thought of New Orleans and Aurore. Aurore with her fresh innocence and trust. Gayle was going home. Home to Aurore.

Twenty-one

After Benoit's first mention of Victoire Olivier, Marget had felt an overwhelming curiousity about the woman. The day she and Victoire first met was a day of endless rounds and tasks at the hospital. It took only one look at Victoire for Marget to recognize her. Except for the beautiful chestnut hair and cream shaded complexion, Victoire Olivier was almost a perfect double for Marie-Odile. She had the same gentleness of character, the same facial expressions and the same gestures.

"You stare at me, Madame de Ville," Victoire said softly turning an uncomfortable red under Marget's scrutiny. She wore a plain gray gown with a little black velvet collar and matching cuffs. Her hair was wrapped securely into a severe roll at the back of her head and covered with a dark blue chignon.

"I apologize for my rudeness," Marget said slowly. It took an effort not to stammer before the mature composure of the other woman.

"Are you upset?" Victoire asked curiously. Her eyes were full of kindness and understanding. "If you wish, I shall return to my duties and allow you the peace of the nurse's room to yourself."

"Will you join me for coffee?" Marget asked, feeling

terribly shy. She jumped up and poured a cup and placed it on the table before Victoire could protest or leave. "Please. I would like you to join me."

"Thank you." Victoire sat down in a fluid, graceful motion.

"I . . . I . . . imagined you differently," Marget said. It was impossible for her to stop staring. "I have always thought of you as some monstrously evil woman."

Victoire smiled sadly. Her smile was different from Marie-Odile's. It was slower and more cautious.

"How do you see me now?" Victoire asked sipping her coffee quickly.

"I know why Papa has refused to give you up all these years. You are so . . . so like my mama, you could be sisters. Are you?"

Victoire's laugh was deep and husky. "No, child, we are not sisters. I assure you of that. You are very like my little Ursule. She is fifteen and away at school in France. She is very sweet and I think she will take the vows to become a nun. I shall miss her the rest of my life."

"I wanted to become a nun once, long ago," Marget said sadly. Suddenly she started to cry and was surprised when Victoire began to sob as well. Marget rose from her chair and put her arms around the older woman and they cried together.

"We are tired," Victoire said gently. "We should leave and rest. Would you come home and dine with me? It seems as though I have known you always and I would like to know more of you."

"But my Papa!"

"He will not be there. Will you come?"

"Yes," Marget answered simply.

The cottage was small and very neat. Marget was embarrassed when she saw a man's slippers on the floor next to a large chair and a pipe laid in readiness on the table next to the chair. They were her father's. There was that comfortable look to them that said they belonged to this house. Victoire with instant compassion, whisked them away out of sight.

"Is this your daughter?" Marget asked. She picked up the small painting on the mantel and studied it. She saw a young girl with the face of her father.

"This is my son," Victoire said picking up the companion painting. "His name is Etienne. He and Ursule are twins. He is also away at school."

"I have a son. His name is Francois Honor and is like heaven to me. I love him deeply."

"In a way you cannot love his father," Victoire said.

"Is it so very obvious?"

Victoire nodded. "It cannot be easy being married to a man you loathe."

"I would prefer not talking about it now," Marget said.

"Another time, perhaps."

"Another time, perhaps," Marget answered. She wanted to talk about Benoit, but some feeling of loyalty kept her silent.

They ate their dinner in a small, intimate dining room served by a tall, sullen Negro servant.

"Is she a slave?" Marget asked in a whisper.

"No, I do not believe in slavery anymore than your Papa does. I have servants, but it is impossible to keep them with the war going on. That is Mary and she is the third woman I have had this year. I am seriously thinking of not having one any longer. There is so little to do with my children gone, I could easily do it myself. Do you enjoy your meal?"

"Yes." Marget said. She had not realized her hunger until she sat down to eat.

They had wine and made small talk until the long shadows outside the windows announced late afternoon.

"I have been here for hours," Marget cried, suddenly jumping up and going to the window. "I must go."

"I am sad to see you go. Will you come again? I have enjoyed your company so much."

"But . . . " Marget's face was transparent with her thoughts of her father.

"You may come whenever you wish except Wednesday."

"I should like that," Marget said. Impulsively, she hugged Victoire, kissing her on the cheek. Then she was gone, running down the walk and finding a carriage. She turned and waved as the carriage drove away. Victoire waved back then went inside her home and shut the door firmly.

Gayle lay in the huge bed with early morning sun tracing designs on the coverlet through the leaves of the tree outside his window. His wounded leg pained him and the pain seemed to radiate in waves throughout his body. The wound in his side had healed well enough, but infection had set in his leg.

"When are you going to open your eyes?"

Gayle kept them stubbornly shut though a faint smile hovered at the edges of his lips.

"I know you are awake," Aurore said accusingly.

She stirred in her chair impatiently. "I have been waiting for two hours. Mama said I was not to bother you until you woke. Will you please open your eyes so that I am not disobeying my Mama."

Gayle looked at Aurore sitting in the chair. His eyes widened in shock after seeing her. It had been so long and she had changed. The child was rapidly disappearing into a budding young woman exuding a subtle aura of sensuality mingled with innocence.

"I told you you were awake," she said in triumph. She left the chair to sit next to him on the bed. She perched gently, spreading her pink-ruffled gown modestly over her feet.

"You're almost grown," Gayle said unable to look away from her.

"I was twelve years old two weeks ago," she said. "Next year, I shall be able to get rid of these awful pink dresses. Why do Mamans always insist on dressing little girls in pink. It is a stupid custom. I hate pink. But I suppose I shall do the exact same thing when I am a grown-up mother."

Gayle was amused at the tumble of words from her. She was so serious, it was all he could do not to grin.

"I brought you a birthday present," he said when she stopped to breathe. He pointed at his saddle-bags. "Go get them."

She did so and sat down again next to him as carefully as before.

"I thought I was never going to get to see you," Aurore chattered as he dug through the contents of his saddle-bags. "You have been here a whole week. Luce says you have been very, very sick and I am not to stay long."

He found what he wanted with a smile and drew forth a small velvet box wrapped with a coral ribbon. "Open it. I meant to send it weeks ago, but I had been very busy and forgot."

Aurore made a face at him as though saying it was just like a man to forget something as important as a birthday. She took the box from him and sat just looking at it.

"Open it," he prompted.

She untied the ribbon with exaggerated slowness to prolong the suspense. Then she put the box up to her eye and opened it a tiny crack. Then she opened it more and cried out in delight.

"It's beautiful," she said excitedly holding the box out to him revealing the small ceramic locket on a gold velvet ribbon. It was painted with two pink roses and lush green foliage. She bent forward and kissed him on the cheek.

"It opens," Gayle said.

"I must have a lock of your hair to put inside," she said giggling. "Just like the grown up girls. Then I can take it out and show everyone what color your hair is."

Gayle doubted that the older girls used their locks of hair in quite such a manner. But he said nothing, simply taking pleasure in Aurore's childish delight at the gift.

"Let me help you," he said. "You're getting it all tangled in your hair." Aurore bent close for him to fasten it. He smiled at her tracing the line of her lips with his eyes. He wanted to kiss that lovely mouth. He wanted to wake in her the passion he knew was there. Instead he brushed his lips across the creamy smoothness of her cheek and watched as she sat up

342

and pressed the locket to her bosom with her hand.

"Thank you," she said suddenly shy. There was a look on his face that seemed to draw her. As she had done in the past, she cursed her lack of age. She desperately wanted to be older, to sample of what? Aurore frowned wondering what it was that caused all the giggles among her friends. It had something to do with the look of longing in Gayle's eyes.

"I must show Maman," she said, jumping up and running from the room. The door slammed unintentionally behind her.

Gayle relaxed and fell back against his pillows. For the first time he wished Aurore were older. He wanted to hold her and caress her. He wanted to . . . he pushed the thoughts away and in the next moment forgot them as Luce stepped into the room her medicine bag next to her. He groaned at the thought of the pain that was to come as she lanced his wound again.

"Renault," Marie-Odile said walking into his study and standing in the middle of the floor uncertainly. She hated to disturb him at his work, but she could see he was not working. He was gazing abstractedly out the windows. "May I talk to you, Renault?"

"Certainly, my dear," he said, admiring the gentle beauty of his wife.

Marie-Odile wore a gown of blue sculptured velvet. It was cut severely to show off her slim figure and was without adornment to show the beauty of the fabric.

"What is on your mind?" he asked as she came close to him. He could smell the gentle fragrance of her perfume. It made him hungry to kiss her.

"It is Aurore," Marie-Odile said raising worried eyes to her husband.

"Has she been naughty?"

"No, it is not that. It is . . . the time she spends with Monsieur Courtland. He is a grown man, Renault, and no fit companion for a child."

"I see no harm in it. It is an innocent relationship," Renault said.

"But he has been here for three weeks and he does not go out and . . . and visit his men friends or do the things men do when they are bachelors. He spends all his time in the schoolroom with a child. They play cards and do her lessons together. He is a man, Renault." Marie-Odile had seen nothing innocent in the loving look Gayle used with Aurore. Nor was there anything childish in the looks Aurore returned. "He is a man and she is a child."

"It is an innocent affair, Marie-Odile. He likes Aurore because she is no designing female setting her traps to catch him. He is an attractive man and half the women in the city are anxious to catch him. I have even seen our little Fleur casting sheep eyes at him. Do not worry about it."

"But . . . "

"It is an innocent infatuation on both their parts. He will return to the war and Aurore will eventually forget him. She is a dutiful daughter and will marry who I tell her to."

Marie-Odile was not soothed. She was not as certain that Aurore was as dutiful as Renault thought. There was a spark of independence in her missing in Marget and Fleur. Marget was biddable and anxious to please. Fleur was somewhat rebellious, but she always did what she was told. Marie-Odile did not think Aurore would allow herself to be tamely led anyplace she did not want to go.

"He is an attractive man," Renault said.

"I know he is," Marie-Odile said with a faint smile. "Arabella Moore and Thomasina Niven have been to call three times in the last week. He sits with them and they talk to him, but all the while he fidgets and then hurries back to Aurore. We must also speak of Fleur. I want you to know she is not going to the convent everyday as I thought. She goes through the motions of appearing to arrive at the convent, then she sneaks out the side door. I have spoken to Sister Marie-Anne. She says Fleur stopped coming weeks ago. She makes an appearance two or three days, but disappears on the other days. I don't know where she goes, and I am worried."

Renault was not listening. His eyes were on the deep swell of his wife's breasts moving as she breathed. He came to stand near her reaching behind to unfasten her bodice and pull it forward.

"Don't worry about Fleur. I shall see she comes to no harm. The city is an exciting place to be right now. Fleur has always been high-spirited." He dropped her bodice on a chair and untied the ribbons of her chemise to reveal milk-swollen breasts. He pressed his lips to each full tip.

"It is the middle of the day," she protested trying to push him away. He pulled her close and kissed her deeply.

"I shall lock the door," he said.

"But . . . "

"Hush, my love," he said leading her to the sofa and

345

pushing her down on it. He stoked up the fire and unfastened his clothes before sinking down on top of her.

It was pleasant at Victoire's peaceful little cottage. Marget went there whenever she could, often no more than once or twice a week. They enjoyed each other and Marget eventually found herself able to talk about her marriage to Benoit, her confusion, and her attraction to Neil Quinlan. She had not yet given in to his demands for sexual satisfaction. She desired him as much as he desired her, but she was married to another man. Married to him with the seal of the church on the sanctity of the marriage.

"Do you love him?" Victoire asked. They sat in front of the blazing fire. It was unseasonably cold in New Orleans.

"Yes, I do," Marget murmured deeply ashamed. She was bound by her vows to love Benoit, but she did not. "I don't think I can withstand him any longer."

"A woman must take her pleasure when she can," Victoire replied philosophically. So few marriages were bound by love.

"But I am married to Benoit. I owe him my . . ."

"You owe him nothing," Victoire interrupted forcefully. "He has treated you brutally."

"He is still my husband, wedded to him by the sacred vows said in church before God." She turned an anguished face to Victoire who ached with pity for this unhappy woman. She was barely seventeen and caught in a marriage born in hell.

"Your papa is married to your maman, but it does not prevent him from seeking pleasure with me."

"I am told it is different for a man," Marget said miserably.

346

"In order for a man to conduct an affair, there must be a woman who is willing."

"Are you happy like this? Sharing my papa with another woman. Don't you ever want to . . . "

"Marget," Victoire said gently, "I am happy as I am. Yes I share him. But your maman also shares him with me."

Marget had never seen it in that manner. "But I shall go to hell when I am dead."

Victoire shrugged. "I doubt God will punish you so severely simply for seeking love. How long is your captain to be in the city?"

"Another week."

"Eventually he will grow tired and seek another woman."

"I could not bear that." Marget grew pale at the thought. She loved Neil with an intensity that hurt.

"We . . . we have no place to go," she said bowing her head. "You can bring him here," Victoire said. "I will be gone all afternoon tomorrow. Mary will be gone, too."

"But this is your home, Victoire."

"What better place to bring a man than to a cottage built to shelter love. It will serve the same purpose for you as it has for me. Do not look so troubled, Marget. It will work itself out. Follow your heart, my child."

Captain Neil Quinlan of the *Inheritance* waited impatiently for Marguerite de Champlain de Ville to make an appearance. He walked up and down the boardwalk occasionally stopping to search for her. She was not in sight and he began to fear he had frightened her away. She was so delicate and fragile. And he loved her. He could not help but love her. She was so lovely, it was all he could do to control himself when he was with her. He dreamed of her constantly.

"Neil, I'm sorry I'm late. It was hard getting away today."

He had not heard her approach. He smiled away his impatience and kissed her on the cheek.

"I was worried you weren't coming," he said as he handed her up into the waiting carriage. "What shall we do today?"

The nearness of him took Marget's breath away. He was so big and handsome. She felt sheltered and protected when she was with him.

"I have a surprise for you," Marget said shyly. She bowed her head so he would not see her blush. She gave him the direction and listened while he repeated them to the driver. The carriage set off at a fast clip.

"Are you going to give me a hint?" he asked.

"No," she said an impish smile curving up her lips.

The carriage turned a corner, went a few yards and stopped. Neil tossed him his fare and then followed Marget to the partially hidden cottage set back far from the road.

"Do you like it?" Marget asked when they were inside. She could not look at him. She was afraid of what she would find.

No man in New Orleans was ignorant of the discreet cottages on Rampart Street. Neil looked questioningly at Marget, but she was busying herself in lighting the fire. She straightened and turned to him, her face frightened, yet pleading.

"Who . . . " he said.

"Don't ask," Marget said rushing to him and putting her hand across his lips. "It is ours for the whole afternoon."

"I love you," he said, drawing her to him. He untied the ribbons of her bonnet and tossed it across the room. He unfastened the frogs under her chin and drew her cloak away to reveal a cream-colored satin gown edged in brown velvet ribbon. She looked so vulnerable with her dark curls tumbling loosely over her shoulders. He kissed her gently, his lips caressing hers, feeling the urgency springing into her.

"I'm frightened," she said.

"I won't hurt you."

"Benoit always says that," she said bitterly.

"I am not Benoit." His fingers moved over the tantalizing roundness of her breasts under the gown. He had been wanting to touch her there for months. "I want the woman I love to experience the same pleasure I do."

"I have yet to know pleasure," Marget murmured.

He kissed her again. She clung to him. Of their own volition, his hands reached behind her to unfasten her gown. With ease it fell to the floor followed swiftly by the rest of her clothing. He had been waiting so long for this. He stepped back to look at her slim body.

"You are beautiful, Marget."

"Please be gentle," she said in a trembling voice.

"Always," he said. He picked her up in his arms and went into the bedroom. When he came to her, he lay next to her kissing her deeply and passionately. Under the touch of his fingers, he could feel the wild beating of her heart.

"How I love you," he cried. He drew her close and

showed her there was no reason to be frightened.

"You won again," Aurore said angrily. She threw her cards down in disgust. Gayle chuckled. "You always win."

"Luck," he grinned. He gathered the cards and shuffled them. With expert ease, he started to deal them out again.

"No more," Aurore said with a yawn. It was long beyond the time of her normal bedtime. To stay up so late was a treat for her. Luce seemed to understand how desperately Aurore wanted to be with Gayle on his last night in New Orleans.

"You're turning into a pretty sharp card player," Gayle said idly. He turned over the cards he had dealt. "If you keep on practicing, I think you could be better than I am."

"I play by myself all the time. I have to be careful though. Maman thinks cards belong to the devil. She lets me play with you because it passes the time, but when you are gone I must do it in secret."

"She may be right about the evil in cards. I've seen men win and lose fortunes in the course of an evening."

"Why do they wager so much," Aurore started to count the buttons they used for the game.

"Gambling is a disease to some men. He loses control and his ability to think and before he knows it, he's dead broke."

"Do you lose control?" Aurore asked curiously. "Is it a disease for you?"

"I don't think so. I've always set a limit for myself and stick to it. I don't always bet on every hand and I have learned which hands to avoid. You'll understand it more yourself someday."

Aurore touched the ceramic locket at her throat. She had not taken it off since the day he had given it to her. She vowed she would never take it off.

"I shall miss you," she said in a low voice.

"I hate to go back," Gayle said. "My wounds are healed. I have a job to do."

"I have the war," Aurore said vehemently.

"It will end, Aurore. Everything ends someday."

"But you could be killed."

"So can you. You could walk out of this house tomorrow and be run down by a carriage."

There were other words in her mind, but she did not say them. She stood up and put her arms around him, kissing him on the lips.

"Come back. I'll be very unhappy if you don't." Aurore ran from the room closing the door softly.

Gayle felt very alone in the empty room. Slowly he shuffled the cards again, then he put the pack in his pocket. He stretched and yawned, then left the schoolroom for his bedroom.

It rained heavily in the night leaving a heavy mist and damp cold behind. Gayle allowed Persia to help him into his coat suppressing a slight twinge when he put all his weight on his wounded leg. Luce handed him a knapsack filled with food for his journey.

"Good-bye, Aurore," he said gently. "Don't stop writing your letters. I always enjoy them."

"I won't," she said watching him sadly. The childish look was gone from her face replaced by a wisdom too old for her. Her smile trembled on her lips. "I wish you could have stayed for Christmas."

"So do I," he said.

"I made this for you." Aurore held out a package. He took it solemnly. "Don't open it till Christmas."

"I won't. Thank you."

Abruptly he kissed her and turned and left the house. He mounted his horse and gave one last cocky salute before he was gone. He didn't look back.

Aurore stood on the steps for a long time watching the empty street.

"You'd best come in, Miss Aurore," Jewel said. "It won't do for you to catch a chill and take sick."

"I'm coming, Jewel." With a faint shrug she turned and walked back into the house closing the door gently.

Jewel sighed when Aurore came obediently. She had been afraid the young girl would upset herself into one of her nightmares. Nightmares that had ceased with the Major around.

"It's almost time for your lessons," Jewel said casually. It was the beginning of another average day. Jewel tried to show her that life went on. "Mr. Embray's going to be here soon and he don't like long faces."

"I'm fine," Aurore said with a bright, false smile. She ran up the stairs with Jewel following more slowly.

"It's hard growing up in times as unsettled as these," Persia said with a shake of his head. "That's a child with a powerful woman's feelings growing inside her."

"No good will come of it," Luce said sadly. "The master will marry her off quick enough when he can. It will be someone she will not like."

"Do you think she'll let herself be married like that.

352

She's got spirit."

"I think she'll stall as long as she can when the time comes hoping he'll come back. And I hope there won't be any grief in the end." Luce walked off leaving Persia to shake his head sadly.

Twenty-two

"Can you hear the guns?" Fleur asked excitedly. She stood at the window next to Aurore leaning forward slightly. It was Easter Sunday and what had started out as a relatively peaceful day was slowly drawing to a close less peacefully.

Aurore moved away from her sister her nose twitching at the smell of her perfume. It was fragrant and sensual. Aurore did not like it. It disturbed her for some unknown reason.

"I hear the guns," she said moving to another window. The deep booms of the guns in the distance testified to the fact that the war had arrived in New Orleans.

"I think it's exciting," Fleur said. She bent too far out the window and almost lost her balance. She grabbed the sill and pulled herself back in. She had changed in the last few months. The attitudes of childhood had been replaced by a woman confident in herself and her attraction to men. Fleur was very attractive. Every man she met knew it and told her. If a man had money, she was even willing to show them more of herself along with a demonstration of her experience.

"I think it's frightening," Aurore said studying the

deserted street below her. Fort Jackson and Fort St. Philip were strongly enforced, but unlike the people in the city, she doubted their ability to withstand the determined assault of the Northern Navy. She also doubted the South's ability to win the war. Already the blockade was weakening the South. There was a shortage of food, ammunition and medicines. The shortages would grow worse.

"I think it stopped," Fleur said.

The silence was ominous. Aurore leaned her head forward to listen. A lone bird chirped tentatively. The guns started again. Aurore shivered violently. She left the window and sat down at her desk. She picked up Gayle's last letter to her. His regiment was still in Pensacola, but there were rumors it would be leaving soon. Aurore knew it was leaving to join the fight. She said a silent prayer pleading with God to watch over Gayle. Then she put the letter in the bottom drawer of the desk with all the other letters he had written her. She picked up a pen and started an answer wondering if he would ever read it.

The hospital received the wounded and the dead in carts. When the living were separated from the dead, Marget would go among them getting their names if they were conscious or going through their pockets if they weren't. Another woman was doing the same for the dead.

Marget hated her work. She hated the smell of blood and the cries and groans of the men. She hated the way they plucked at her skirts pleading for relief from their pain. There was little morphine to give out. It was reserved for the most serious cases.

Midway through the day, Marget left the horrible area where she worked for a few moments' solace in the nurses' station. She cradled a cup of lukewarm coffee in her trembling hands.

"You look exhausted, Madame de Ville," a long-skirted nun said gently. "Why don't you go home and get some rest?"

"There is so much to do, Sister Madeleine," Marget said wearily. She pushed a lank strand of hair out of her eyes only to have it flop back.

"It will be here when you return," Sister Madeleine said. "Go home and sleep." She pulled Marget gently by the arm. There was no carriage, but an emptying cart was commissioned to take her partway home.

Marget thanked the driver who responded curtly. She pulled her cloak over her shoulders and clambered into the rear of the now empty cart indifferent to the puddle of blood which further stained her already bloody skirts.

She wondered where Neil was. Was he in Nassau reveling with his friends, or was he on the seas playing dangerous games with Federal blockaders? She longed for him and the security of his presence. If New Orleans fell to the Northern forces, it could be years before she saw him again. She ached with the knowledge.

The cart lumbered passed the cathedral. Without thinking, Marget slipped off and went inside, her skirts trailing a bloody path behind her. She lit a candle and sank to her knees to pray. She prayed for Neil, herself and her son. Never once did she pray for her husband.

A worried frown marred Renault's face as he packed ledgers into a box. Edmund took them away and Renault knelt before his safe, opened it and drew out the bags of gold coins he kept in reserve in it. It was Federal money, Northern money, but he had refused to completely convert to the Confederate paper notes. He had changed a token amount, but no more.

"The *Sophie Sutter* is loaded, Monsieur," Edmund said returning to the office. He walked heavily with a weariness that matched Renault's.

"The captain knows what to do," Renault said crisply. "Tell him to take off. Monsieur Hernandez will take charge when the paddle-wheeler reaches St. Angele."

Edmund disappeared, his footsteps ringing hollowly in the hall. Renault shoved the bags of coins into a valise. He would take the money home and hide it in the deepest part of the cellars. No one must know he had so much money.

Holding the heavy valise firmly, he looked around the empty room one last time. Everything of importance was gone from the office. All his records were in his home. The warehouse was empty. The bales of cotton and saleable goods filled the decks of the *Sophie Sutter* to be hidden in the secret warehouses Rico Hernandez had been building and stocking. Even the valuable *Sophie Sutter* was to be decommissioned and hidden deep in the bayous where the enemy would never find her. The day would come when it would be safe to bring her out of hiding, but that day was a long way away.

"The boat is gone," Edmund said heavily. "The

mobs are talking about firing the warehouses and the docked boats."

"Such a waste," Renault said sadly.

"We must go before the mobs get so great we cannot get through," Edmund urged.

"I am coming. Do you have your pistol?"

"Oui, Monsieur."

"Then let us go. In a few days the panic will subside. We will set up our offices in the empty building next to Esther Nye's place."

They left the office. A tendril of smoke curled up around them as they stepped out on the levee. Running people with flaming torches passed setting fire to everything they could reach. The surrender of New Orleans would be a hollow one. All viable materials would be ash by the time the enemy arrived.

"I can't stand it," Fleur cried. An angry mob rushed down the street heading for the levee. "It is so exciting and I am locked in the house. I must get out."

"No," Marie-Odile screamed, but Fleur was already gone, the front door hanging open as she lost herself in the crowd.

Fleur could hardly keep from shouting along with the rest of the mob. She was dragged to the docks where warehouses were already ablaze with fire and piles of burning cotton gave off a horrible stench. It was hard to see with smoke stinging her eyes, but she kept on watching in fascination as steamboats were loaded with piles of cotton and set afire. The whole river was one angry fire.

A barge was being loaded. Fleur was pushed into line as bundles of tobacco were thrown at her. She tossed the bundles to the next person and the barge was swiftly loaded. A torch was thrown on the piles, the line was cut and it was shoved out into the current where the wind caught at the fire blowing it into a raging fury.

A warehouse was broken into and kegs of molasses were dragged out and broken. The molasses ran across the levee catching to people's feet and smearing skirts and trousers.

"It won't stop them Yankees," a voice said in her ear. "Coming upriver will be a mite difficult, but all this isn't going to stop them."

Fleur turned to find a huge, raw-boned man standing behind her. He was naked to the waist showing a mat of dark, curly hair spreading across his muscular chest and disappearing in a narrowing line below the belt of his trousers. He was a massive man standing over a foot taller than Fleur. She had to crane her neck to look up.

"What you doin' here, little lady. This is no place for the likes of you." He took her arm and pulled her away from the burning levee shoving people out of his way as though they were toys.

Fleur thrilled at the sight of his large, paw-like hands with calloused palms as they held her. Her breasts swelled with a strange desire that seemed to match the violence around her.

"Don't leave me," she said when she was clear of the insane mob. A riverboat exploded with a deafening sound.

"You want a man don't you," he said touching her hard breasts with a thick knuckled finger. "I've always wanted a piece like you." He pulled her up to him and kissed her brutally. His excitement matched hers.

When he put her down, his hard blue eyes stared at her relentlessly.

"I know a place," she said. He nodded. Fleur took his hand and led him down a dark alley.

"You're kind of young for this," he said when they were in the privacy of the hotel room.

"I don't think so," Fleur said with a faint grin. She unfastened her gown and dropped it to the floor. She unlaced her chemise and petticoat and dropped them on top of her gown. When she was naked she stood in front of him watching the blaze of passion darken his eyes.

He studied her as he unbuckled his belt and pushed his trousers down over his feet. She was beautiful with a wanton innocence that appealed to him.

"You are beautiful,"Fleur said with a gasp when he stood before her. She threw herself at him and he caught her, swinging her up in his arms and tossing her on the bed. With a growl he fell on her biting at her small breasts.

"Oh, yes," Fleur screamed, matching his violence with her own.

There were no Confederate troops in New Orleans to stop the Union forces from occupying the city. They had been withdrawn despite the city's howling anger. Their orders sent them to protect Richmond.

Fleur didn't care. A man was a man. A soldier was a soldier. The color of their uniforms made no difference to her.

She stood in the window watching the soldier patrol the street. She watched the wildly patriotic women of the city flaunt their Confederate sympathies by boldly wearing little Confederate flags pinned to their hats or gowns. The occupying army was at a loss to control them and helpless with fury as they deliberately taunted and laughed at their uniforms. Fleur thought the women were terribly foolish. Their behaviour was going to bring trouble.

"Come back to bed, Little Flower."

Fleur turned around and grinned mischievously at her brawny lover.

"In a moment, I like watching the soldiers."

"You like watching men," he chuckled. "Come here. I'll show you a real man."

He fondled himself. Fleur watched him wide-eyed. Soon her hands moved to her tightening breasts and stroked them to jutting hardness. This was a man she never tired of. In a few days he had taught her more about her body, herself and men than any other lover she had ever had.

"Come here," he whispered hoarsely. His penetrating blue eyes commanded her. She smiled and remained where she was, her slim hands moving over her body provocatively. She teased and taunted him until he growled and made a move to jump off the bed.

Fleur moved closer still rousing her body. His own was ready for her.

"You're a witch," he said when he finally grabbed her with bruising hands. He pulled her on top of him pushing her head down between his massive thighs. Fleur groaned with pleasure when his moist, probing tongue found the heart of her own passion.

Before their bodies erupted, he jerked her up and turned her around and set her firmly on him. Fleur cried out just as their bodies exploded in a bucking frenzy and left them sobbing.

New Orleans was in an uproar. In response to the open derision of the women of the city, General Benjamin Butler had finally taken steps. In a fit of rage, he issued his General Order 28 which would label him infamous. From now on, women in the city who openly flaunted their loyalties would be treated as ladies of the night plying their trade. General Butler was determined to put a stop to their resistance and their contempt.

Fleur sat in the window in her hotel room watching the scene before her in growing fascination. She had never seen such proud Southern women who prided themselves on their feminine gentility act in such a manner. It was as though a brand new breed of woman had been born in the dark hours of New Orleans' surrender.

A loud knock on her door drew Fleur's attention from the street. She yawned and moved languidly to answer it. If it were her lover, she was ready for him. She wore nothing under the thin gauze of her wrapper.

It was a woman. She was an older woman in a flounced green taffeta with a neckline that plunged below the standard of decency. Her face was heavily painted, but there was no mistaking the hardness in her eyes or the sullen sneer to her lips.

"May I come in?" she asked gesturing with a heavily braceleted arm.

Fleur nodded and moved aside letting the woman into the room. Her contact with the street prostitutes

362

had been very limited, yet they all knew her as well as she knew them.

"I know you're a higher class whore than the likes of me, but I had to come round to talk to you. Doing what we do don't make us unloyal to the South."

Fleur shut the door. She turned and studied the woman intrigued with her low neckline and the heavy breasts that pushed at the fabric.

"I come to tell you, we got to do our part," the woman continued. "Here." She shoved a paper at Fleur who took it and opened it. It was a handbill with a picture of General Butler staring insolently at her. He had had them printed and passed out all over the city to acquaint the inhabitants with his appearance.

"What shall I do with it?"

Me and the other girls are putting them in the bottom of our chamber pots to protest this new order he passed. It's about all we can do."

"How original," Fleur cried, her eyes shining with mischief.

"Will you do it?"

"Of course, I will." Fleur laughed and the woman joined in.

The next morning Fleur left the house in the early hours. She no longer went through the pretence of walking to the convent. Luce no longer accompanied her.

The soldier was young and uncertain. He stared at Fleur with gradual alertness. He walked up to her and took her by the arm.

"What do you think you are doing?" she asked as he pulled her into a dark alley and pawed eagerly at her clothes. She fought at him, scratching and kicking, her screams reverberating down the alley.

Suddenly the young soldier was pulled away and sent spinning. He landed heavily in a pile of garbage.

"Private, what is going on here."

Fleur's rescuer was an officer. He was also an angry man.

"The woman, sir. The General's order."

"Did she offer you provocation?"

"Not . . . well . . . she was . . . just walking . . . sir." The young private stutterd guiltily.

"He caught me and dragged me into the alley," Fleur sputtered, more amused than angry now that the danger was gone.

"Pardon me," the officer said puzzled.

Fleur realized she had spoken in French. She repeated her statement in unaccented English.

"I suggest you apologize, Private."

"But . . . sir . . . the Orders were . . . "

"Only if the subject is disrespectful, Private. Now apologize."

The young soldier mumbled some words and shuffled off after issuing a sloppy salute to the officer.

"You should not be on the street alone, ma'am," the officer said as he escorted Fleur out of the alley to the street. "You're not hurt?"

"I'm fine. Thank you. No harm was done."

"May I escort you to your destination."

"No, thank you," Fleur said with an artful smile. She turned and walked off brushing dirt from her gown.

The hotel looked quiet and inviting. Fleur ran up the back stairs and opened the door to her room.

"Hello, Little Flower."

"How did you get in here?"

"I walked in," her lover said with a grin. He was undressed and lying on the bed. "Ready for action?"

It was on the tip of her tongue to say no, but the familiar rise of passion in her stopped her. She undressed and then stood before him eyeing him.

"After today, it's going to cost you," she said. "I can't give out free time anymore. I come expensive."

"I know, Little Flower. I'll pay for you." He eyed her languidly, his hard eyes running up and down her small compact body appreciatively. It was deliciously mature, yet daintily innocent.

"Next time you pay," Fleur said huskily. She approached him as he beckoned with a thick finger. He ran his hand down her body from breast to knee, then returned his fingers to that secret place between her thighs. Flames spread over her in violent waves. He pulled her closer, his eyes half-taunting.

"If you're going to play the whore," he said in a low voice, "you should learn to act like one." He tossed her on the bed on her stomach and fell on her growling and biting.

When he was gone, Fleur dragged herself from her bed feeling bruised and tired. She ached and hurt with the brutality of her lover's manner. Even Michael who had used her in a similar manner had never been so savage. She pulled her wrapper around her before groping for her wash basin to wash away the feel of him.

When she felt better, she went around her room straightening it with the simple pride she had in keeping it neat and attractive. When the knock on the door sounded, she opened it unaware of the sight she made with her wrapper transparent against her skin and her dark hair tumbling over her shoulders.

"Yes?"

"Good morning, ma'am," the man in front of her said. His eyes widened as he recognized the young girl he had rescued barely two hours before.

Fleur recognized the young officer at the same time. She smiled at him and let her wrapper fall away from her body revealing her nakedness.

He breathed deeply taking in the beauty of her.

"Can I help you," Fleur inquired politely, her gaze going over him and the two enlisted men standing in the shadows.

"I . . . um . . . I came to . . . inspect your chamber pot," the officer said, his face slowly reddening as he gazed at her.

"My chamber pot," Fleur asked puzzled. "You may inspect it if you wish, sir," she said in open innocence.

She stood aside and let the man into her room. He walked to the bed and gestured for one of the enlisted men to look under it. The young soldier bent over and pulled the brass pot into view. He silently handed it to his superior.

"I'll be taking this," the officer said.

"I don't mind," Fleur grinned nastily.

"Good day, ma'am," he said saluting. He closed the door on her.

When the men were gone, Fleur doubled over in laughter. She held onto the doorknob, her laughter echoing through the room.

"Where do you go all day?" Aurore asked as Fleur stripped her gown from her.

Fleur shrugged. She untied her petticoats and pulled off her chemise. She poured water into a basin and started to vigorously soap her skin.

Aurore studied her sister carefully. There was something different about Fleur these days. She was secretive and furtive.

"Maman worries about you," Aurore continued. "She knows you don't go to the convent at all anymore."

"Did she tell Papa?"

"I don't know. Even if she did, he's so busy right now, he has no time for us."

"Does he have a new office?"

"Yes, he owned an empty building on Canal and has taken a lawyer in to share it with him. Monsieur D'Arcy is the lawyer. Papa says he will bring him home to dinner in a few weeks." Aurore turned to the window to watch the street. "We have two officers quartered with us. They came this afternoon. They're aides to General Butler. Isn't it funny what the ladies of the street did putting the General's picture inside their chamber pots. Maman laughed and she hasn't laughed in weeks."

Fleur giggled a little, too, remembering the faces of the men this morning as they looked in her pot. She finished cleaning herself and started to dress pulling silk stockings over her slim legs and pulling on hoops, petticoats and silk chemise. When the dinner bell rang, she was gowned in pale gold silk.

Men's voices came from the drawing room as Fleur walked down the stairs with Aurore. Fleur stopped a moment and checked her appearance in the hall mirror. She added a shy smile to her face and then walked into the room.

"Hello, *cherie*," Marie-Odile said. "Gentlemen, I want you to meet my second daughter, Fleur. Fleur, this is Captain Adam Ross and Lt. Franklin Taylor."

Fleur smiled at them, but it froze on her lips as Captain Ross bowed to her.

"My daughter teaches each day at the convent school," Marie-Odile said, using what she knew was a lie to cover her daughter's mysterious disappearances.

A knowing smile touched Captain Ross's lips.

"I'll wager you could teach those children a thing or two," he said.

"I'll wager I could," Fleur said with a giggle.

"You must let me walk you each morning. The streets are no place for a young, innocent girl." His voice was almost a snicker. His eyes glinted dangerously. He had changed from rescuer of that morning to a man who held Fleur's little secret in his hands. "You lead a dangerous double life," he whispered as he drew her away from the others.

"Yes, I do," Fleur said quietly. The dinner gong sounded again and she turned and walked into the dining room before he could stop her.

Twenty Three

Sgt. Cole Taggert of the Louisiana Artillery stepped sharply up the gangplank of the steamboat, Arkansas.

"Where we goin', Sarge?"

The hollow echoes of the booted feet of his men followed him. The men were all there. Cole could tell. Each one made a noise distinctive of himself, an offending loudness to a man whose life had more than once depended on quickness and stealth. There was nothing quick, nor stealthy about a large, moving army.

"Hey, Sarge! Where we goin'?"

The question was repeated over and over as Cole settled his men in their assigned places on the deck of the paddewheeler. They grumbled and growled their complaints, a further irritation to a man used to obeying orders and having orders obeyed without question. Cole thought of Rico whose silent, good-humored companionship had been his only friend on the long lonely rides on the Texas range. Where it took weeks to get from end to end on the Santa Gertrudis ranch. Where often a man's only companion was a herd of cattle. Where silence was a way of life. What a contrast these men made to the unquestioning Texican. Cole was annoyed with his men's constant questioning.

He had to explain everything from how to load a rifle to the erection of the two-man tents issued them. They knew nothing, understood nothing. They were good-natured Southerners for whom the romance of war quickly grew stale. War wasn't fun anymore. It was hard, dirty work. It was one exhausted step after another. It was short rations and rancid meat. It was torturous agony for a young man reared on the back of a horse.

"How long ya goin' to keep yore secret, Sarge?"

Cole turned icy blue eyes on the men in front of him. He was twenty years old and had men in his command twice his age, yet they were like children to him, ignorant children. They all watched him waiting for an answer.

"Check your ammunition, your rifle, and your side arms," Cole said in a voice which carried over the stamp of other units on the gangway, over the babble of excited voices and the ear-piercing scream of the steamboat whistle.

"We checked them already," Private William Blane piped up in a thin, whiney voice. He was a large, droop shouldered man, hunched over and sloppy. He did as little work as possible. "We check everything a dozen times a day. When will you be satisfied that we're not raw recruits anymore?"

"Do it," Cole snapped. How could he make these men understand that the fine line between life and death depended on their alertness and the condition of their weapons? How could he make them understand that the Federal forces were not going to be a bunch of soft, northern city men, but highly trained troops with a preparedness for war to equal that of the

Confederates? How could he make them understand that their lives were forfeit if their vigilance were relaxed for even a moment?

Heads bent over packs, rifles and handguns. Bedrolls and extra clothing were carefully gone over and repacked. Bolts clicked home, barrels rolled . . .

"Hey! Where's my bayonet?" Willy Blane yelled. He stood up and looked around. His brows were drawn together in a puzzled frown.

There was a stir among the seated men as they looked under legs around boxes of supplies for the missing bayonet. A few heads turned to regard Willy with faint disapproval. A path opened to Cole who stood holding the bayonet in his hands. He had seen it in the dirt just below the gangplank and picked it up.

"Is this what you're looking for?" Cole asked. The bayonet flew through the air and landed on the deck with a dull thud pinning Blane's cuff to the wood.

"That's not funny, Sarge," Willy whined.

"Neither is dying," Cole's voice was hard, "don't lose it again. You won't be so lucky next time."

The bayonet was picked up and slipped into its scabbard. Willy slumped down on the deck out of Cole's sight, but Cole could still hear his grumbling.

"We goin' upriver, Sarge?"

"You'll know when we get there," Cole finally answered. He turned on his heel and walked away.

"He don't know nothin'." Willy taunted.

Cole kept on walking. The Willy Blanes in the world had stopped bothering him years ago.

The gangplank swung away from the dock to be secured alongside the steamboat. The paddle-wheeler eased away from the shore, sluggish with the weight of over three hundred men. It caught in the current, jerked, then gathered speed. In forty-eight hours, the Arkansas would be in Vicksburg. Somewhere behind it, the Federal Navy under Admiral Farragut was steadily crushing the defenses of New Orleans. The gulf city was lost. Vicksburg was to be held at all costs.

The city of Vicksburg was a thriving river community sitting on clay bluffs overlooking the Mississippi River. It was a handsome city of neatly laid out streets, colorfully painted houses and a high-spired church dominating its center.

Cole stood on the embankment built up along the water's edge for the fortification of the city. He studied the city thinking how serene it looked in the morning light. It was different from the dusty Texas towns of his childhood.

"Sargent Taggert!"

Cole looked around to find the Corps Engineer of Defense watching him with a mildly amused look on his face.

"Sir." Cole stiffened. He saluted smartly, cursing himself inwardly for his wool-gathering when he should have been listening to orders.

"Be at ease, Taggert," Captain Kenyon said solemnly. Like Cole Taggert, Kenyon was a Texan. He was a short, squat man with a whiskered face and gentle blue eyes. A short, blunt cigar protruded from between his lips. A cigar he constantly chewed on rolling it from side to side. "Your men are doing a mighty fine job, Taggert. The strengthening of these batteries is going faster than I planned."

"I've got good men for the most part, sir."

"When they're finished have your men position their cannon in these openings and train them on the river bend. That area coming around the turn is going to be where the Federal gun-boats will be most vulnerable."

Cole studied the river. As it approached Vicksburg from the north, The Mississippi suddenly swung east and then doubled back on itself in a tight hairpin turn. Just after this turn, the river narrowed. It was on this narrow neck the Confederate guns were trained. Dug in behind man-high barriers of felled trees covered with packed mud, the Confederate batteries were prepared for a river assault.

"Farragut is going to try and get past us and join with the Northern Mississippi fleet for an offensive attack on Vicksburg. We have to be ready for them." Graves watched the line of men pulling trees into position and covering them with buckets of mud and dirt. He pursed his lips as though the work was not going fast enough.

"We'll be ready, sir," Cole said. He had good men, well-trained men. Men ready to fight for the South. "I understand General Breckinridge is bringing reinforcements."

Ten thousand men, Taggert, to set up a defense around the open area of the city. We're open to land attack from the east, and from what I understand, Grant is in a fever to capture Vicksburg. With this city in Federal hands, it would give Grant control of the river. We can't afford to have that happen. It would cut the South in half and our only major river transport would be closed to us. Vicksburg must be held whatever the cost, or for as long as possible."

Kenyon abruptly walked away still talking to himself.

Cole took up his field glasses and trained them on the open expanse of land, the eastern boundary of Vicksburg. It was hilly, broken land. In some spots, it was open swampland. Already there were soldiers in the hospital complaining of chills and fever. Men who could ill afford to be lost.

"Taggert," Pops Lyttel rolled up to Cole behind a prancing team of horses. "It's Willy Blane. He cut his foot off with an axe."

Cole jumped into the wagon behind Pops Lyttel who drove the wagon like a crazy man back toward a stand of trees swiftly being felled for use on the river batteries. A group of silent, unmoving men stood just inside the shadows. The wagon came to a halt and Cole jumped out, shoving through the group. He dropped on his knees next to Willy Blane who lay on the ground, writhing. Blood welled from the stump at the end of his leg where his foot should have been. It was neatly sliced off just below the ankle.

Cole pulled his belt from his waist. He tied it around Willy's calf and jerked it tight. The bleeding slowed and then stopped.

"Help me get him into the wagon," Cole ordered over Willy's hysterical shrieking. Simmons stepped forward, ashen faced, and helped Cole hoist the man to his feet. "Toss me that blanket."

Cole climbed into the wagon and wrapped Willy in the blanket. The man was white, his eyes rolling back in his head from shock.

"The hospital," Cole yelled at Pops Lyttel. The wagon lurched, the horses surged in their traces. Willy rolled. Cole grabbed him before he rolled off the back, drawing him into his arms. "You'll be all right, Willy."

Willy Blane didn't answer. He'd lapsed into a hideous groaning, his mouth slack and his eyes slitted showing white.

The hospital was two miles away. The wagon did the distance in record time, bursting through the center of Vicksburg scattering soldiers and civilians alike. It left a cloud of dust behind and several hysterical females.

"Easy with him," Cole cautioned the stretcher-bearers who dragged the limp body off the wagon bed. A doctor stood looking at the ankle. He loosened the tourniquet for a second, then tightened it again. A woman stood behind the doctor, a white apron smeared with blood covering a dark gray gown.

"I'll stay with Blane, Pops," Cole said when the stretcher had gone into the hospital, the doctor and nurse trailing it. "You go back to the batteries and keep things going. You're in charge Pops."

Pops Lyttell nodded. He turned the wagon around and started back for the line of batteries on the river's edge.

"How does it look, sir?" Cole asked as the surgeon washed his hands and the nurse laid instruments on a table next to the now silent, unmoving Blane.

"It looks a clean slash, Sergeant. I'll know more in a few minutes. Helen, cut away the boot."

"Yes, doctor," the nurse responded. She had a gentle voice and quick moving hands. She moved toward the table blocking Cole's view of Blane.

"If you would wait outside, Sergeant," the doctor said firmly.

Cole nodded and left the examining room.

It was an hour before the doctor walked out to stand next to Cole. He pulled a long, thin cigar out of his pocket and lit it. Cole looked up expectantly.

"It's too early to tell if he's going to make it or not. He's lost a lot of blood. I cleaned the wound, tied off the artery and pulled enough skin over the stump to make a flap. If the wound heals clean and there is no infection . . ." the doctor shrugged. "He just might make it. It's his ticket home."

Cole said nothing. He pushed himself to his feet, brushing dust off his pants. "Thank you, sir," he said. "I'll stop in in the morning."

"Going back to town?"

"Yes, sir," Cole answered.

"Helen," the doctor said over his shoulder. The nurse walked out of the hospital drawing off her stained apron. "You going home? Give this boy a lift back to town. He doesn't look like he would enjoy the walk."

"It would be my pleasure," she said with a small smile. She was young, but not a particularly pretty woman. She had soft blonde hair and large brown eyes in a pleasantly round face. It was not the kind of face men die for, but there was a steadiness in it, a calmness Cole liked. "My pony and cart are around the back."

"Thank you, ma'am," Cole said feeling awkward with her. He followed her around to the side of the hospital where a small pony stood patiently.

"I'm Helen Jamison," she said with a repeat of her gentle smile. It revealed one slightly crooked tooth.

"Cole Taggert, ma'am."

"You're from Texas," she said. She slapped the pony's rump with the reins. The little animal tossed its head and broke into an even walk.

"How did you know?"

"I was born in Luciusville. It's not far from Houston. I'd recognize another Texan anywhere in the world."

Cole smiled. In a vague way, Helen Jamison reminded him of his mother, soft and warm, comfortable to be with. The way he remembered her being before the crops went bad and she and pa grew old before their time.

"You look like you could use a good meal, Cole Taggert. I just happen to have some sourdough starter that makes the best sourdough biscuits in Vicksburg. My husband and I would be delighted if you would join us."

"Thank you ma'am," Cole responded eagerly. Sourdough biscuits! Already, his mouth was watering.

They pulled up in front of a small, white-washed cottage just inside the city limits. A man stood in the door. An older man with the light at his back. He greeted Cole graciously and invited him in.

"You been gone a long while," Simmons said nastily when Cole walked into the barracks long after dark. Simmons picked at yellowing teeth with a sliver of wood. He eyed Cole with hostility.

Cole said nothing. The room had quieted at his entrance. A few men were already in their cots snoring noisily through open mouths. Others sat around an oil lamp tossing greasy cards down in a sluggish game of poker.

"How is Blane?" Pops Lyttell asked.

"Too early to tell," Cole answered.

"It was no accident," Pops continued. "You may as well know it, Taggert. Blane did it on purpose. He was going to nick himself to get out of work, but his aim wasn't too good." Pops spat a stream of tobacco juice into a spittoon.

"I know, Pops," Cole replied wearily. The angle of the cut had looked too deliberate to be an accident.

Pops nodded and went back to his cot lying down and pulling his blanket over his thin shoulders. He was the oldest man in the group. A mountain man from the West, and the most canny. Cole could depend on Pops for anything.

"You're mighty late, Sarge," Simmons persisted. "Where you been all afternoon. Not at the hospital all this time."

Like Blane, Simmons was a trouble-maker. He was a large, hulking man with greasy, stringy hair and a body that smelled bad enough to choke a person.

"You're so all-fired up for working, I can't believe you took an afternoon off while we were all slaving like niggars." Simmons laughed and looked around for supporters, but his only friend had been Blane and Willy Blane was gone.

"What's on your mind, Simmons?" Cole asked almost too tired to care.

"I hear tell you were with Missus Jamison today," Simmons sniggered. "She's a young woman and got herself a old man for a husband. Must be she's looking for younger blood."

Cole looked at the man. The Jamisons were his friends. They had treated him kindly.

"She's got a soft bed, Sarge?"

"I'm sure she does, Simmons," Cole said flatly. "But I wouldn't know."

"Well I hear tell . . ."

"That's enough, Simmons," Cole said softly. His eyes turned a hard, icy blue. Simmons dropped back and shuffling petulantly back to his cot.

Cole turned around and left the room, preferring to find companionship among fellow Texans who sat around a roaring fire in the compound swapping tall stories.

On the 26th of June, the first of Admiral Farragut's fleet arrived within sighting distance of Vicksburg. When the flotilla was close enough, the Lower Batteries opened fire sending a barrage so heavy at the oncoming fleet that it fell back in confusion. When it was reorganized, a barrage of the city of equal force began. A bombardment of more noise than destruction rained on the city of Vicksburg and was answered with Confederate shelling. For several days the bombardment continued, the people in the city becoming so used to it, they continued about the town doing their business without any fear.

"I hate this shelling," Pops snarled as a mortar shrieked over his head. It landed with a loud explosion several hundred yards away.

Cole shrugged. He hated the constant bombardment, too. His ears hurt and head ached from the noise.

Another shell shrieked and landed with violent force. A house collapsed in on itself as though made of sticks. Cole watched through his field glasses in fascination. His own battery of cannon roared and rumbled with the shells being fired. Lt. Carr ran up and down the line shouting encouragement.

Then the firing stopped. Lt. Carr came racing back.

"What's going on?" Cole asked after the order to cease fire was passed on.

"They've dropped back out of range," Carr said. "No sense wasting ammunition." He ran along the battery.

Simmons commented on yellow-bellied Yankees. Cole said nothing. Simmons made another comment.

"They'll be back," he told the complainer curtly.

Simmons lapsed into silence.

"Was anyone killed?" Cole asked when Carr came running back.

The Lieutenant shrugged.

The stillness continued for the rest of the day. The Federal iron-clads hovered just out of range of the Confederate guns as though trying to entice them into firing again. They seemed to be plotting their next move.

"What do you think they're going to do, Sarge?" a few men asked Cole.

"Don't know. But they'll get back to us when they're ready."

The next morning, the bombardment started again. It grew so heavy, the civilians in the city started to evacuate, taking shelter under clay banks under the bluffs. The Lower Batteries opened fire first. Cole waited with his men at the upper batteries. When the order came for them to start firing, it was because the Federal navy was getting through.

"We hit one," Simmons shouted, jumping up and down.

A few cheers erupted up and down the line. An iron-clad in the middle of the river burst into flames. Cole could see men jumping into the water and swimming for nearby ships. The iron-clad veered off course and headed straight toward the river bank. When it crashed into the shore, a new wave of cheers broke out.

Cole sharply told his men to get back to their firing. He sent a detachment for more ammunition and walked up and down his command adjusting the angle of a few guns or pulling men out and bringing in reinforcements. The noise was deafening. When the bombardment finally came to an end, the last of the Federal iron-clads was disappearing around the bend in the river. It had successfully gotten past the Vicksburg batteries, but at a cost. Two large iron clads sat on the shore burning and several gunboats in the middle of the river were gradually sinking even as their crew fought to control the boats.

"We got wounded," Pops Lyttel yelled. He ran to a fallen man and turned him over.

A wagon was brought from the rear and the wounded men loaded into it.

"You're bleeding, Taggert," Pops said.

Cole wiped his hand across his face. It came away clotted with blood and dirt. "I'm fine," he said fingering the long gash down the side of his face.

"You're not fine," Pops ordered. "You get yourself in that wagon and have that seen to. It looks like it could use a little sewing." Pops steered him toward the still loading wagon. "Go on, I can take care of things here."

"Got yourself a little scratch, Sarge?" Simmons asked walking up to Cole and grinning. "It's goin' to ruin your looks. Missus Jamison won't be likin' too much after this."

Cole ignored him, climbing up on the seat of the wagon and clutching the side. He felt a wave of dizziness.

"Get a burying detail going, Pops," were his last orders as the wagon pulled away.

The hospital was crowded. Civilians, as well as soldiers, had been wounded. A pile of dead bodies lay outside waiting burial. Cole felt ill looking at the pile of dead bodies. Wrecked bodies with limbs gone, the aftermath of war.

"Let me look at your face," Helen Jamison said. She turned Cole's face toward her, her hand under his chin. Her fingers were cool. Her touch light. "You need a few stitches. I'll find the doctor."

"I can wait until the more seriously wounded have been cared for," he replied.

"Most of them have already been done. Dr. Russell, I have a man here with a bad gash on his face."

The doctor who had cared for Willy Blane bent over Cole. He pushed the ragged edges of the wound together. Pain shot through Cole. He gasped. "Wash it out, Helen. We'll have to trim the ragged edges down a bit so that when it heals you'll have a nice straight scar. You'll be one hell of an attractive young man then, Sergeant. I understand ladies like romantic looking scars." The doctor chuckled.

Cole could only wonder at him. After a week of death and surgery, the doctor was still thinking of making the scar as unobtrusive as possible.

"I'll be right back, Helen. Feel up to a little surgery, young man?" Then he walked away.

Cole wasn't up to a little surgery. The doctor snipped at the jagged edges of the wound with his scissors, evening it out. Then he proceeded to sew it. "Sorry, I can't give you an anesthetic, Sergeant, but the morphine is reserved for the really bad cases. Hard to get morphine these days. That damned blockade is getting to be pretty effective." The doctor sewed and Cole clenched the edge of the table with his hands. When it was done, he rolled over with relief and vomited into a pail.

"You look a little pale," Helen said when it was over. "You go on out and take my pony cart and drive up to the house. Tell Paul I said to put you to bed and wash the wound with carbolic every couple hours. Tell him I'll be home when I can get there."

"What about you?"

"I'll find my way home. Been doing it for months," she replied cheerfully. "Now go on, I've others to tend."

Cole managed to keep the pony heading toward the Jamison cottage. He stabled it haphazardly, and walked into the kitchen swaying on his feet.

"Evening, Mr. Jamison," he said pleasantly and pitched forward on his face.

In the morning, he felt better. Helen served him breakfast and sent him on his way back to his unit. Paul Jamison drove him, dropping him off at the batteries.

Pops Lyttel stood next to the cannon, Cole's field glasses in his hand. He had them trained on the hillside. He handed them to Cole and pointed in one direction. "Take a look. The people from the city have decided to get themselves new dwellings. They're hollowing out caves in the clay."

Cole watched in amusement. In its own way it was a logical thought. The clay banks at the back of the city were almost impervious to the mortar shelling unless it was a direct hit. The people would be a lot safer there than in their own homes. He turned away and searched the river for the Federal boats. At that moment, the order to commence firing came through. The bombardments had started for another day.

"This has been going on for two weeks," Helen complained. She washed Cole's cheek with carbolic and opened the small infected area to let the pus drain. "I told you to keep your face clean."

Cole decided not to tell her how difficult such an order was to follow. She finished cleaning the wound and held a clean cloth to his cheek. The carbolic stung.

Another shell whistled overhead. Helen ducked and then looked up at the roof of her cottage as though expecting it to come crashing down on her.

"I don't think I can take much more of this. I have a headache all the time."

Cole who had gotten used to the constant bombardment said nothing. He was amazed he wasn't deaf.

"I understand the northern Mississippi fleet has joined Farragut north of us and joined in the bombardment."

"They dropped anchor yesterday," Cole said. He decided not to inform Helen how truly harmless the shelling was. They hit almost nothing. The real irritation was in the noise. A few people had died, but that in itself was inevitable.

"What happens next?" she demanded.

"The Colonel was telling me that Federals are trying to build a canal across the neck of the river south of the city in order to bypass us completely. Not working too well I understand."

"A canal. That area is nothing but swamp. How does the enemy plan to clear it?"

Cole shrugged. He wasn't an engineer and didn't understand the mechanics of canals.

"You are full of interesting conversation today," Helen snapped. Her husband walked into the cottage, a newspaper under his arm.

"Evening," he said with a friendly smile. "I'm hungry, Helen. Anything to eat?"

"I'm hungry, too," Cole announced. He followed her to the kitchen.

"How is Missus Jamison?" Simmons asked as Cole walked along the batteries checking the guns.

Cole ignored him and walked on.

"How's it going?" he asked Pops Lyttel.

"Quiet for the moment. There's talk the Federals are going to pull out. Heard anything from Lt. Carr?"

"Not yet," Cole said. He leaned over a cannon and check the sight. It was sighted on the right target. He straightened, then clambered up on the battery to look down on the river. The mortar boats were anchored among the heavy iron-clads.

"I wonder if they ever get tired of the noise?" Cole mused as he studied the boats.

"Maybe," Pops said. He spat a long stream of tobacco juice at the ground. "Maybe. This has been going on for near to five weeks. You'd think they'd run out of patience."

"Well we got work to do," Cole said sliding down to the ground.

The next morning, the Federal fleet was gone. The river was empty of any sign of the enemy.

"Think we scared them away?" Pops asked half-jokingly.

Cole shook his head. He was looking at a large hole in the battery where a direct hit had scattered trees and mud. "We got repairs to make," he announced later in the day. "Captain Kenyon says we're going to extend the batteries another five hundred yards beyond us. So let's get busy."

The men turned away from the big cannons, organizing into forest details.

"By the way, Simmons," Cole said as the man passed him. "I thought you might want to know that Willy Blane died yesterday."

"Naw! I don't believe you. He went home," Simmons said shuffling past. He picked up an axe and continued on his way.

Twenty-four

The war was over for the city of New Orleans. It was humiliating, but the humiliation had only begun. General Butler was determined to make the people understand who was in charge. He ordered every person over the age of eighteen to take an Oath of Loyalty to the Federal government or risk confiscation of property. Renault de Champlain, in an effort to preserve his extensive holdings in the city, quietly took the oath and urged his friends to do so.

"What are a few words?" Renault argued with Edmund Vernay. "A piece of paper signed under duress has no legal binding. It is what is in your heart that is important."

"I am a Southerner, Monsieur. I cannot compromise my ideals."

Renault kept his temper firmly checked. He considered Edmund's stand stupid and rash, but there was no arguing with such single-minded patriotism.

"What of your family? Your wife is *enceinte* and near her time. A move now would be dangerous. Your property will be confiscated and you will be homeless."

"My wife is as loyal as I. She will go where I go. I must do as I feel I should," Edmund insisted stubbornly.

Renault sighed in frustration. "You will no longer be able to work here, Edmund. I shall give you six months' pay. That should be enough to settle you in your new home."

"You are very generous, Monsieur," Edmund said stiffly. "I shall clear my desk and be gone in an hour."

"What will you do now?"

"I plan to send my wife to her brother in Natchez and I am going to volunteer for duty. I only stayed out this long because I felt I owed you enough time to settle your affairs."

"That was very kind of you, Edmund," Renault replied a trifle sarcastically. He knew Edmund had stayed out of the army for his own private reasons and not because of loyalties to Renault. "You may go."

For awhile, Renault watched his former accountant thoroughly cleaning his desk, then he turned to the pile of work sitting on his own desk. Where was he going to find someone capable enough to understand the complexities of his vast organization and who understood the meaning of discreet.

"The young idealist is gone," Philippe D'Arcy said as he walked into Renault's office and sat down. "Have you anyone in mind to replace him?"

"No one."

"Do you mind employing a woman?"

"Is she capable?"

"Her name is Helen Williams. She is my neighbor and has been left a widow with several young children to support. She is very clever and discreet. Shall I bring her around in the morning?"

"She is not sensitive?" Renault asked thinking of the separate set of books kept on Esther Nye.

"I don't think so. Work is work and when one is desperate . . . " Philippe shrugged eloquently.

"I shall see her tomorrow at ten, Philippe." Renault looked at Edmund's now empty desk. "And thank you."

Marget stood in the administrator's office and listened to his dry voice drone on and on. Behind him stood two Union officers who nodded occasionally in approval of his words. The status of the hospital was changed. Since the city was now in Federal hands, they would be required to accept the Union injured. Marget did not care. A wounded man was a wounded man regardless of his loyalties. For her it was a job. A job that helped ease the aching loneliness in her. There would be no return of the *Inheritance*. There would be no return of Neil. It had been weeks since the city had surrendered. The blockade operations had been shifted to another port. Marget chewed her bottom lip nervously. She sent a swift, silent prayer to God for Neil's safe return.

The administrator concluded his speech and dismissed his nurses. Marget turned and went back to her ward, already overflowing with the helplessly wounded.

"Hello, sweetheart."

Marget stopped and smiled down at a young boy hardly older than herself. She smoothed the blanket over his gaunt body and checked the dressing over the stump of his left arm.

"Did you get a letter from your mother today?" Marget asked cheerfully. She held a glass of water to the boy's parched lips and ran a cool rag over his fever-flushed face.

"Not today," he said. "Maybe tomorrow."

"New Orleans is a long way from New York. It will take time, but you will get it soon."

He smiled up at her, his dark eyes reflecting loneliness. They were all lonely and young and tired of war. Marget had special smiles for all of them.

"Ma'am," a weak voice called.

Marget hurried to the next bed, the man in it bright with fever and his face twisted with pain. She rinsed her cloth and wiped his face and neck.

"Is that better?" she asked softly.

"I hurt, ma'am," he whispered.

"I'll get the doctor," she promised and signaled for a nurse to take over. She hurried down the hall, but the only physician she could find was Major Saul Prescott, a short man with huge whiskers and a graying beard.

"What can I do for you, beautiful?" he asked in a soft, intimate whisper. His eyes lingered on Marget's bodice.

"I have a patient in severe pain," she said, carefully staying just beyond the reach of his filthy, blood-encrusted hands. There was blood on his apron and some in his beard. Marget disliked him.

The major spat a stream of tobacco to the floor perilously near the hem of Marget's skirt. She stepped back trying to control the contempt in her eyes.

"Is he a Northern boy or one of your Confederate dogs?"

"Does it matter. The boy is in pain and in need of help."

"It make a difference to me," he said and spat

another stream of tobacco to the floor.

Marget started to turn around, but Major Prescott caught her arm and dragged her back.

"You're a mighty fine lookin' gal," he said softly. "You must be missin' that husband of yours bad, by now." He ran a hand over her breasts, chuckling when Marget struggled to get away. "For a little kiss, I'll go look at your sick soldier-boy and I won't grumble if his uniform is the wrong color."

"Let go of me, please," Marget cried.

"Not yet, little lady." He unfastened the top button of her bodice. "Let's see what that gown is hiding."

"Let me go," Marget twisted, trying to elude his powerful hands.

"Major Prescott, release the lady! At once!"

"Colonel Norton!"

Marget jerked away, brushing at her tears with the back of her hand. She fastened her gown.

"Major Prescott, there's a young man in bed no. Twelve in Madame de Ville's ward who is in need of attention. I suggest you attend him instead of trying to force all the ladies in this hospital."

"She's just a Southern whore, sir."

"She is a lady, Major, something I doubt you would recognize. Please attend your patient."

The major stamped away angrily.

"Are you all right, Madame de Ville? He didn't hurt you?"

"I'm fine, Colonel Norton," Marget said. She was trembling and frightened, but did not show it.

"I think it would be better if you discontinued your work here, Madame de Ville. You are a fine nurse and I will hate losing you, but I cannot be around to protect you and Major Prescott will try to take advantage again. He is notorious for his womanizing."

"There will always be someone else."

"Sister Madeleine has been kind enough to assign her nuns to this floor. That should stop him temporarily."

"I could work another floor, Colonel," Marget said. She hated the thought of being dismissed. All the lonely days spread out before her with aching regularity.

"I am sorry, but you are just too pretty to keep around here."

"I shall leave immediately, sir," Marget said meekly. She left him standing in the middle of the floor watching her hungrily as she went to the nurse's station and picked up her cloak. Marget seeing him still standing there realized that her danger came not only from Major Prescott, but from the other doctors in the hospital who were just as woman-hungry as the major.

"What is wrong?" Victoire asked in concern. She made Marget sit and poured her a cup of coffee.

"I have been dismissed," Marget said heavily. Suddenly she burst into tears as she told Victoire of the scene with Major Prescott.

"It is for the best. I have been asked to leave as well."

"But why you?" Marget asked in amazement forgetting her own misery.

"I am Negro, no matter how weak the strain is, my blood is black. I am not considered good enough to wait on all the white soldiers."

"But . . . " Marget was dumbfounded. She had long ago stopped thinking of Victoire as Negro.

Victoire burst out laughing. She reached out and hugged Marget fiercely. "Now, we shall have time for those long, cozy visits we keep promising ourselves as we nod with weariness," Victoire said. "And I shall teach you to cook all the dishes you have been wanting to learn to cook for months now. And we shall shop at the French Market when food is available and we will do all the things I have wanted to do for a long time with you."

Marget smiled. Victoire would plan their days together and they would be together. Some of the ache inside her eased.

"I worry about Neil," she said finally.

"He is a man totally capable of caring for himself," Victoire said. "Come along, let's find a carriage for you. You look exhausted."

Victoire fastened Marget's cloak about her chin and led her from the room. Outside, she found a carriage and settled Marget into it.

"Come Thursday, Marget."

"I will," she promised as the carriage started to roll away.

For a long time, Victoire watched the street. When the carriage turned around a corner and rolled out of sight, she turned back into the building. She looked up and felt a shiver of fear. Major Prescott stood in the window watching her. He turned away, but Victoire still felt cold.

For several days, Fleur left her house only on errands for her mother. When she was in the house, she took careful pains to avoid Captain Ross when she could. But the captain was a determined man. Finally, Fleur grew tired of her enforced boredom and left the house for the sanctuary of her hotel room.

"May I come in?" Captain Ross asked. "I followed you."

Fleur stood aside. He walked into the room and looked around as though he had never seen it before.

"What do you want?" she asked ungraciously. She was gowned in a cream-colored gown bordered in dark green satin.

"Don't you know?" he asked surprised. He reached out and pulled the pins from her hair. "What were you planning to pay me for keeping your little secrets." He touched her face, allowing his fingers to wander down the length of her neck and across the swell of her breasts. "I'm an easy man to please."

Fleur stepped away and turned around. She unfastened the buttons of her gown and stripped it away. When she turned back to him, she was naked, her dark hair flowing to her waist outlining her small face and huge eyes.

"Is this what you want?" she asked in a low voice.

"You're very lovely," Captain Ross said in a hoarse whisper. He fumbled frantically at his clothes. "You have an unusual career for one so gently raised. Your parents do not know, do they?"

"They don't know."

"What will you do to keep your little secret?"

Fleur raised dark, veiled eyes to him.

"I'm waiting, little Fleur," he said.

She went to him, pressing her body to his feeling his warmth. His eyes widened in appreciation as she dropped to her knees in front of him. Fleur knew exactly what to do and she did it expertly. When he left,

Captain Adam Ross was a well satisfied man.

"Did he talk to you, Little Flower?"

Fleur's unnamed lover studied her frankly. She was still flushed with another man's loving as she stood in front of him.

"Do you mean Captain Ross?" Fleur asked with a frown.

"Yes, I mean him," her lover said impatiently. She looked so desirable, he was tempted to pull off his clotes and have her on the floor. But he didn't. This was business.

"He said his office was very busy," Fleur said, her face puckered into an engaging frown as she thought. "There are plans to go upriver to Vicksburg. But he said nothing that isn't already generally known."

"When he comes back find out how many ships and troops are being sent." Fleur reached out to him. She had been left unsatisfied by Captain Ross. "Not today, Little Flower. I have business. Will you do as I ask?"

"How much?"

"You're a bold baggage," he chuckled. He eyed her with rising desire. She was a thorn in his smooth life, but he could not live without her.

"How much," Fleur asked again. "I'm not going to spy for free for you or anyone."

"Most of my people do," he said wryly.

"I'm not most people."

"I can see that," he said, his eyes moved over her hungrily. It was torture to see her standing there wanting her.

"I'll be back tomorrow," he said. He named a figure and Fleur nodded in agreement. He went to the door then turned back to her. "Find out what he knows."

"Do you have a name?" Fleur asked before he left.

"You can call me . . . you can call me, Pewter Piper," he said with a chuckle. He stepped from the room and closed the door a last glimpse of her standing in the middle of the room totally naked almost sending him back to her. Then he remembered his next appointment and frowned ominously.

Aurore settled at the upstairs window watching the street below. There was traffic on the street, mainly of women in carriages going about their shopping. New Orleans had all the appearances of a normal daily routine except that the women were the wives of Union officers.

"Here she comes," Aurore said over her shoulder.

Marget ran to the window, her eyes dark with anger.

"Have you ever seen anything so . . . so arrogant?" Aurore asked with a giggle.

The woman in the carriage was too old for the corn-yellow ringlets that framed her fleshy face. She wore a bright green taffeta gown that was two sizes too small for her. Rolls of fat ringed her waist while her breasts seemed to threaten escape from her tight bodice.

"Do you know her?" Aurore asked curiously as Marget's face darkened with anger and twisted into a bitter frown.

"That is Major Prescott's wife," Marget said. "He's a doctor at the hospital." She did not add that it was because of him she no longer worked there.

"They say she confiscated Madame Balfour's carriage simply because she thought the silver candles were pretty." Aurore did not like the fat woman in the

396

Balfour carriage.

"That happens when a person refuses to take the Oath of Loyalty."

Aurore said nothing. She watched the carriage out of sight, then left the window to wander aimlessly about the room. The tragic realities of war were just beginning to be understood by her. She was nearly thirteen with a young, budding body that drew the gazes of men when she walked through the streets. She was frightened of the men. Her dreams started and Marget moved into her room to be with her at night.

"Maman!" Francois Honor de Ville plucked at Marget's skirts as he pulled himself unsteadily to his feet.

Marget picked up her son and cuddled him against her chest. He was her anchor in the hellish world she was forced to endure. He was so sweet and lovable. His innocence helped Marget to forget her loneliness and aching love for Neil Quinlan.

Luce walked into the room and Francois Honor immediately called to her and held his arms out for her to take him. Luce smiled and held the infant in her arms, his light face nuzzling her dark one.

"It is time for his nap," she said. "And this came for you." She held a piece of paper to Marget who took it.

The note was from Victoire asking that Marget come immediately.

"I have to go out," Marget said. "I'll be back when I can."

Luce clucked her tongue in disapproval. She knew who the note was from. She did not like her master's daughter being friendly with her master's mistress.

Marget ran from the room and changed from her

day dress into a gown of pale blue silk which rustled gently as she moved. It was one of the few good gowns she had left.

On the street she could not find a carriage and had to walk to Victoire's cottage. It was a long walk and she hated the way the soldiers would stop her and demand to see her pass. The soldiers seemed to delight in subjecting decent women to their rough behavior and foul language.

Marget turned on Rampart Street and walked quickly towards Victoire's discreet cottage. In the weeks since they had left the hospital they had spent much time together. Marget wondered why the urgent note when she was to see Victoire tomorrow. She ran up the walk and burst into the cottage with a clatter.

Neil stood at her entrance. He seemed to fill the room with his presence.

Marget slid to a stop and stared at him speechlessly. Then she flew into his arms.

"I've been so worried," she cried. "It's been months."

He soothed her, holding her tightly and caressing her face.

"Are you all right?" she asked, drawing back and studying him.

"I'm fine, puss," he said fondly. He kissed her, his lips moving over hers urgently.

"How did you get her?" she asked drawing away again to look up at his face. She touched him almost fearfully.

"I went to your father's warehouse, but it had been burned down. Then I came here and asked Madame Olivier to send a message to you."

Marget laughed. As she laughed she started to cry. She leaned against him savoring the feel of his lean, hard body. Her months of loneliness vanished. She was with Neil. She could touch him and love him.

"I've missed you so much," she said. "I lie awake at night and pretend to talk to you. I dream I'm with you on the bridge of your ship and we're sailing across the sea and filling each other with our love."

"You are with me wherever I am," Neil said. He drew her close to him, kissing her. His love was a sweet, wistful yearning of his need.

"I love you," Marget said letting him pick her up and carry her into Victoire's bedroom.

They lay side by side in Victoire's bed. As always, Marget tried to imagine her father in this room, loving Victoire, touching her body as Neil touched hers. But she couldn't. It was Neil who filled the room with his masculine smell of the sea.

Her flesh quivered at the touch of his hands on her. Her breasts ached to be fondled, but he did not touch them. Instead his fingers wandered over her stomach and down the outside of her legs. He teased her. He touched her. He roused her body into a fever of desire until she panted and cried for release. Then he moved over her and covered her body with his. He filled her and she moaned with pleasure.

Have you heard from Benoit lately," Neil asked casually when their fury had abated and they lay peacefully near each other barely touching.

"I have heard nothing from him in nearly a year. The army in Pensacola left for Mississippi in May, but that was in the paper. I don't even know if he went with them."

"He didn't. I saw Benoit in Savannah with a woman named Sulie Chesterleigh."

"There was a Sulie Chesterleigh at the convent school when I was about eight. She was thirteen and there was a terrible scandal and her parents removed her. I don't remember what happened anymore. But it was all very hushed."

"It might not be the same girl."

"It probably is. Sulie was always less than discreet."

"Will you come to Nassau with me?"

Marget turned to stare at him, her mouth open in astonishment.

He repeated his question, feeling her hesitation. The months away from her had been torture. There was no peace in him knowing she was in occupied territory.

"I don't know," Marget said slowly. She rolled on her side to look at him. "I have my son to think about. I can't just leave him. I love him deeply. And my parents! My father would never allow it. You could lose your command."

"You can bring your son with you. I found this very attactive house. It is small, but there is room for a child. We would be alone. You don't have to tell your father the truth. You could say you want to visit some friends you met while on your honeymoon. Or you need to get away. New Orleans is not a good place to be right now. It is no place for a growing child."

"He would know," Marget said softly.

"This may be the only time we will ever have, Marget. The war will end and Benoit will return home."

"Benoit . . . could . . . get killed." Marget's words came slowly. Would God in his heaven ever forgive her. But how easy it would be if Benoit died in the war. She would be free to marry Neil and be cherished and loved the rest of her life.

"I could get killed, too, Marget," Neil said soberly. "Come with me. Please."

How could she not go? She went into his arms, tears clouding her eyes. But what about Benoit? She had vowed to love him. But she didn't love him. She loved Neil. And Benoit was far away.

"If my father will give his permission, I will go with you to Nassau." Why not, she asked herself. Why not take this time to be with Neil? What could Benoit do? He was in another city chasing another woman.

Neil kissed her long and deeply stirring the flames of passion in her. It was a long time before they left the cottage for Renault's office.

Marget did not anticipate her mother's violent reaction to her decision.

"It's so far," Marie-Odile wailed.

Marget stopped her packing and went to embrace her mother.

"I must go, Maman," Marget said gently.

"These friends. Will they take proper care of you?"

"They will," Marget said with shining eyes.

Marie-Odile did not like that look on her daughter's face. It filled her with foreboding.

"How will you get to Nassau?"

"Captain Quinlan will take us overland to Savannah where we will meet the *Inheritance*. It is not such a difficult journey. The trains are running through most of the South."

"But why, Marget?" Marie-Odile cried.

"I can't stay, Maman. It will be so much easier for you with two less mouths to feed. Do you think I don't know how you and Luce agonize over the little garden you planted? Do you think I don't know how you plan and measure each little meal? Things will not get better. Already there are thousands of ex-slaves pouring into the city with the promises the North makes them. They will have to be fed. Food is going to become very hard to find. Let me go, Maman. We will be safe."

Marie-Odile had to let her go. There was something different about Marget. She seemed surer and more firm in decisions.

"It will be all right, Maman. Trust me."

"I will see that Papa gives you enough money to live. I understand it is very gay in Nassau. You will need ball gowns and a place to live and enough money to hire a nurse for Francois Honor. Will you be happy, Marget?" In that one sentence Marie-Odile acknowledged her daughter's relationship with the young sea captain.

"He will take good care of me."

"Will you be happy, Marget? I mean truly happy."

"Yes," Marget said firmly.

"What about Benoit?"

"Benoit will have to take care of himself," Marget said indifferently. The huge, mustard colored cat Marget had brought from Grandeville so long ago rubbed against her foot. She bent and scratched him between the ears. "You are not going to like where we're going, Cat. But I found the largest basket I could because I am not leaving you behind."

The cat glared at the basket, but obediently got inside and sniffed. Marget closed the basket over his head ignoring his plaintive whine.

"It won't be long, Cat. You'll be in a new home. And so will I."

Marget and Neil watched Nassau come into view from the privacy of his cabin. It was gay and colorful with hundreds of foreign ships in the harbor and the scents of exotic blooms filling the air.

"I have to go on deck," Neil said. "You'd best get dressed, Mrs. Quinlan and greet the city properly."

"Mrs. Quinlan," Marget said in wonder. She gazed up at him, her large dark eyes filling with tears.

"That is who you will be while we're here," he said stooping to kiss he swiftly. "You're my wife, Marget. My most beloved wife."

"You are my most beloved husband," Marget whispered. He smiled at her and left closing the door firmly behind him. "My most beloved husband," Marget murmured. She got up slowly and dressed watching the harbor come smoothly into view.

When Neil returned for her, she was modestly dressed and the cabin was cleaned. The nurse engaged to watch Francois Honor during the voyage tapped briefly at the door and turned the squiggling child over to Marget. She was as anxious as Marget to leave the ship and left immediately.

"Are you ready for your new life?" Neil asked. He held the door open for her.

"I'm ready," she said softly. She smiled up at him, all the love she had shining on her face.

Twenty-five

1863

"Senor," Rico Hernandez walked into Renault's office flashing a broad smile.

"Monsieur," Renault said genuinely glad to see the man. He offered his hand and Rico shook it warmly. "It has been two years since you went upriver to St. Angele. How is everything with you and the plantations?"

"With me, all is well," Rico said pulling a long, slim cigarillo out of his pocket and lighting it. "With the plantations, all is not as well as should be. Grandeville burned to the ground last week. Yankee raiders. Pah! Yankee pirates is more the truth. Not that there was much of value at Grandeville to save, it is a pity to burn down so fine a house. St. Angele has been raided, but all your possessions had been packed away and taken to the swamp warehouses so they are safe. But the house." Rico shrugged. The destruction of a beautiful place like St. Angele had been hard for him to accept. He had been raised to value other people's possessions. "To destroy beauty is a desecration. There is no exterior damage, but inside. They have ripped the beautiful draperies from the windows and torn the

404

furniture apart. I could do nothing to save your home."

"What about Grey Lawns?" Renault asked heavily.

"Nothing. It escaped totally." Rico said. He did not add that Monique de Ville was presently living at Grey Lawns because Rico refused to let her live at St. Angele. "The warehouses are unharmed and the supplies you wanted are on the packet which brought me to New Orleans."

"Is Madame de Ville all right?"

Rico shrugged again, eloquent in his silence. Renault nodded. He had known Monique many years and knew how difficult she could be.

"Madame de Ville is not the easiest person to understand," Renault said slowly. "She has had many disappointments in her life."

Rico's eyes darkened with amusement. This was no time to discuss with his employer the difficulties of Monique de Ville. "She wishes to come to New Orleans," he said with a sigh. He rolled his eyes to the ceiling. His two years at St. Angele had been spent eluding the woman who had grown enormously fat with discontent.

Renault said nothing. The last place he wanted was Monique to come was New Orleans. His life was complicated enough with Marget gone and Fleur involved in some unusual activity.

"The senora says the country is boring and she wishes some excitement. I have told her it is dangerous here at the moment, but she refuses to believe. She desires new clothes and parties and trips to the opera."

Renault looked down at his own threadbare suit. He thought of his wife wearing the same gowns for the last three years. He had plenty of money to replace their clothes, but there were no clothes to be bought. Trade was almost at a standstill in New Orleans. What little goods brought by the packets were delivered, they were usually food stuffs for the starving city.

"The best thing to do is to let her come and see for herself what a humble city New Orleans has become."

"She is an unhappy woman, Senor. I shall tell her, but even then she will not be content."

"Monique is never content," Renault replied. "Let's forget about her. Tell me how your young friend is. Does Monsieur Taggert like being in the army?"

"He hates it," Rico said with a hearty laugh. "No Texan ever walks when he can ride. Cole complains that he has not seen a horse since they ate them all at the beginning of the siege. He is at Vicksburg and things are desperate there."

"The city will fall soon. They are low on food and ammunition. There seems to be little hope that General Lee will send reinforcements. He has his own problems in Pennsylvania right now. It looks like the two armies are getting ready for a big battle near some town called Gettysburg."

"This war is sad, Senor. Once the Mississippi is in Union control the South will slowly be crushed. Already we suffer. There is not enough of anything and the soldiers go barefoot in the winter. It is very sad indeed."

"War is stupid," Renault exploded violently. He calmed immediately. "Enough of our problems. Come to dinner tomorrow night and we will continue our conversation."

406

"Thank you, Senor, but it is impossible. I must return upriver and my packet leaves in the morning. I do not want to leave the plantations unattended though I have able men to help me. Very few of your people left after they were 'liberated' by the Union. They see to the guarding of all the plantations and do so well. I am training a man to help me. I cannot see all the plantations so Noble, your blacksmith offered his help. He is very loyal to you."

"I always liked Noble. It is good to know my people value the ownership of their properties more than they value this so-called freedom the northern politicians promise them. Tell Noble I am pleased with him and he is to have that ten acre meadow he has been saving to purchase these last five years. I will deed it to him immediately. How is Old Silas? He is still alive, isn't he?"

"Si, but he grows more feeble with each passing month. He can barely get around, but he sees to the comfort of the Senorita Aurore's horse. Silas has trained the animal well and hopes she will come soon to see how beautiful the animal is and how well trained. He sends her a present." Rico took a carving from his pocket. It was a high-stepping mare with flowing mane and tale. It was beautifully executed and highly polished.

"Aurore will be pleased to get this," Renault said admiring the handsome carving. If the carving was any indication, the mare herself must be magnificent.

"Before I leave, have you any orders for the plantations? The crops are in and stored. I have abandoned the cotton crop at Grandeville, the fields were burned and could not be replanted. But the sugar and corn at

St. Angele and Grey Lawns look well. There will be a good harvest this year."

"Have you enough people for the harvest?"

"Si, there are enough, but the work will be hard."

"Do what you can."

"The deserted plantation where Cole and I first worked is now empty of all the hidden supplies. What is on the packet today is from Grandeville."

"Thank you, Monsieur. You have done a good job."

"And you have become a rich man."

"Some of the wealth is yours when the war is over and you return to your home. What money I have does me no good. There is nothing to buy in the city and what there is is at too inflated a price to purchase. So we make do with what we have."

"It is bad all over the South," Rico said standing preparing to leave. "Send me a list of what you need and I shall prepare it for the next South-going packet."

"Thank you, Monsieur."

Rico bid farewell to Renault and went out the door grinning. He still had a day and night left to him to do as he pleased. His step was cocky and sure as he walked down the hall and the stairs. The street door slammed and the hall was silent.

Philippe D'Arcy walked into Renault's office and sat down. Like Renault he was threadbare. Business had not been good for him and he did not have the diversity Renault had. He was a lawyer, plain and simple. There was little need for a lawyer in a city under martial law.

"Have you thought over my proposition?" Renault asked.

"It has been on my mind since you first mentioned it," Philippe said. He had lost weight. His clothes hung on him loosely. "Fleur is a very beautiful woman, but I have no attraction for her. She is too bold for all that she is only sixteen. I much prefer Mademoiselle Aurore."

Renault was astonished. "Fleur is a lovely and intelligent woman. She will make a fine wife."

"She is too intelligent and too lovely. Women like her invite trouble. The younger girl is the one I want."

"Aurore is only thirteen."

"I will wait for her. This war will not last forever. Peace will return and when it does I shall once more be in a position to support a wife. I hope you will reconsider and allow me to have Mademoiselle Aurore."

"It makes no difference. Aurore is a fine girl. I shall just have to find another husband for Fleur. I will draw up the agreements and when the war is over, Aurore will be your wife. She is young, but easily managed."

"Yes, she is," Philippe said thinking of the young girl growing to womanhood. There was a look about her that made him want her. She would be the ideal wife for a prosperous lawyer. "Shall we drink on it?"

Renault opened the bottom drawer of his desk and drew out a bottle three-quarters empty. He poured a small amount of the liquid into two small glasses. "Another commodity in short supply," he said recapping the bottle and carefully putting it away again. "Enjoy, Philippe and welcome to my family."

"Almost," Philippe said. He raised his glass to Renault's and then downed the fiery liquid in one gulp.

Fleur sat on the open window frame of her hotel room. A faint breeze lifted the ends of her long hair and cooled her face. She wore nothing, but an organdy wrapper nearly transparent as it clung to her sweaty skin.

"Senorita," a voice called.

Fleur looked down at the street to find an old familiar face looking up at her. It was the Mexican-Spaniard, Rico Hernandez.

"Is it truly you?" Fleur asked leaning out of the window. Her wrapper fell open affording him a tantalizing view of her gleaming breasts.

"I will be right up," he said blowing her a kiss.

Fleur ran to her dressing table and drew a brush through her hair. She shook with barely contained excitement. When he walked in the door she was ready for him, the hastily applied perfume dabbed on wrists and ears swirling fragrantly about her.

"You are still here," he said joyfully, picking her up and swinging her around the room. He set her down and kissed her deeply sensing the growth of experience in her. Before she had been a girl experimenting in the ways of men, but two years had matured her into a woman experienced in love.

"I'm glad you came," Fleur said, bubbling with delight. No man had ever stirred in her the pleasure Rico had once done. She stepped back and looked him up and down critically. Life had left its mark on him as well. He looked older and more tired. Some of the arrogance was missing from his face.

"I was afraid you would be gone," he said smiling down at her. She had grown older. Her figure had filled out to a voluptuousness that appealed to him, though she was still slim and elegant. There was an earthy sexuality about her that made him eager to see how well she had learned. He opened her wrapper to look at her white flesh, bending down to kiss the tips of each breast. "You have grown more beautiful than I could have imagined."

Fleur slid her wrapper off her shoulders and stood in front of him posing. "Have I?" she teased. She held her full breasts in her hands offering them to him.

"Yes," he whispered throatily.

She came to him, unbuttoning his shirt and running her hands over his smooth chest lovingly.

"You have grown more handsome," she whispered. Her eyes smoldered with desire as she unbuckled his belt and unbuttoned his trousers sliding them down over his slim hips. "You are as I remembered," she said running her hands down his thighs before coming to rest on his maleness. She caressed him until he groaned. Then she led him to the bed, pushed him down on it and showed him what she had learned in the two years since she had seen him last.

"I worry about Fleur," Marie-Odile said looking up. She sat back on her heels and watched Luce still bent over the patch of ground she was weeding. They worked constantly in the little garden to produce enough food to feed ten people.

Luce sat back and looked at her mistress, perspiring heavily in the afternoon heat. Marie-Odile was not made for such labors. She was small and frail, yet insisted on helping with the work. A chicken strutted past her picking up seeds lodged between the bricks.

Luce wondered if she should tell her mistress about

411

Fleur and her activities. All the servants knew. They also knew there was no controlling her. She had decided on her course in life. Luce shrugged and kept silent. She would not tell Marie-Odile, the one person Luce loved more in the world than her own children.

"And Marget has not sent a letter in months." Marie-Odile continued unhappily. "I wish I had never let her go to Nassau."

"She will return," Luce said confidently. She had looked in her bowl one dark night and saw her returning on a large ship. Her face had been unhappy, but it had looked with concern at someone just beyond the edge of the bowl whom Luce had been unable to see. There had been something different in the set, older face of Marget. It had been sadder, but more at peace than Luce had ever seen before. And she had grown, grown beyond the limits of her family and the cruelties of an unfaithful husband. There was great trouble in the future of the family Luce had been guardian to for over twenty years. She feared the future and what it would bring.

"And I worry about Aurore," Marie-Odile said looking across the courtyard at her daughter seated in the shade with Jewel next to her. Jewel sewed while Aurore read out loud to her, her sweet voice drifting across the yard in lilting tones. "This is no place for a child to be growing up. I have seen the way the soldiers look at her when she goes out. Her nightmares have been worse than ever. Jewel has been moved into her room to sleep with her. Jewel is the only one who seems able to cope with her night terrors." Marie-Odile's voice ended on a sob. The war was destroying her family. Marget was a thousand miles away on

412

some little island. Fleur was a growing woman with dark secrets. And Aurore was a child haunted by terror. And what of Therese and the baby, Clotilde. What did the future hold for them? Therese was seven years old and there was a maturity in her dark eyes that frightened Marie-Odile. How could any child look at the world in such a weary way? Clotilde was two and a cheery child, but the depression and gloom of war had its effect on her as well.

"Renault is working himself to death. He is no longer a young man."

Luce put her hand on her mistress's shoulder. There was little she could say to ease Marie-Odile's worries. But she could offer the natural compassion that was part of her.

Marie-Odile looked up seeing the friendship and concern in the other woman's face. They had long since gone beyond the mistress-servant relationship. They were friends, women of equal status suffering the same fears and tragedies brought to them by a war beyond their control

"And now Renault tells me, Monique de Ville is coming. What does she expect to find?"

"She will not stay long when she realizes there is no opera to go to, or new clothes to purchase," Luce said.

"But she is another mouth to feed."

"We will kill one of the chickens," Luce said.

"But we need the eggs."

"We will kill the old red. She has stopped laying."

"She's going to be tough."

"Food is food," Luce chuckled, not mentioning she had eaten worse in her life.

Delphine came skidding around the corner of the

yard waving her arms. "The packet has arrived. Madame de Ville is here." She came to a stop breathing heavily, her dark cheeks flushed with exertion.

"Oh no," Marie-Odile groaned scrambling to her feet and walking to the pump to wash her hands and face. How informal her life had become, she thought as she wiped her hands on her skirt. Three years ago she would have rushed to her room and ordered hot water and a total change of clothes. Today she was washing from the pump and going in to the drawing room in her old, faded day gown.

In the house, she stopped before a mirror to tuck a few strands of stray hair back into her chignon. She looked old and tired. Her face was brown from hours of working in the sun and her hands were rough and red. Where was the elegant Marie-Odile de Champlain? Where was the pampered lady of wealth and society?

Marie-Odile looked at herself hardly recognizing the worn face and clouded eyes. Would she ever go back to the person she had once been? She doubted it. She had done too much growing these past years. She smiled at herself wanly, pinched her cheeks and wet her lips with her tongue. Then she went into the drawing room to greet Monique de Ville.

"Monique!" Marie-Odile gasped in astonishment at the grossly fat woman sitting on a sofa and leaving no room for another person.

Monique rose shaking out layers and layers of flounces decorating an absurdly large hooped gown.

"Hello," Monique said a shade from sullenness. She fluffed out a ruffle across her enormous bosom and paused to admire the lay of the fabric. "You look well, Marie-Odile. A touch too thin perhaps, but then everyone in the city appears to be hollow with starvation."

"You are not," Marie-Odile answered dryly. "There seems to be no shortage of food in the country."

"There is always food in the country. There has always been food here."

"Where are we going to grow it when we can't get deliveries from our plantations?"

Monique shrugged. Except for the burning of her home, Grandeville, she seldom troubled herself about trivial problems. "I hope you are planning to show me a good time while I am here," she said, turning to admire herself in a mirror primping as though she were still a slim, young girl instead of the huge monstrosity she had become. She wore a gown of pale lavender edged in ecru shaded lace. The design was far too girlish for a woman of her years and size. She pinched her cheeks and bit her lips before turning back to her hostess with a fatuous smile on her face. "Where is Renault?" she asked fluttering her lashes childishly.

"At his office."

"He should be here to greet me," Monique pouted. An expression less attractive on her than it would have been on a younger woman.

"We did not know when the packet would arrive. Travel is so uncertain these days."

"Now that I am here," Monique settled back more comfortably in her chair. "I should like to see Marget and the child. I have not seen him since his christening. Why he is nearly two years old."

"Marget is not here," Marie-Odile said uncomfortably.

Monique frowned at Marie-Odile's words. "Where is she? Is she shopping?"

Marie-Odile could see that this was going to be a disagreeable visit. She sighed and looked down at her hands.

"Well, where are they?" Monique demanded irritably.

"Marget and Francois Honor went to Nassau last year to stay with friends."

"What!"

"She felt it would be safer for a growing child." Marie-Odile sent a fervent prayer to heaven hoping Renault would be home soon. She did not think she could cope with Monique.

"Why that little strumpet!" Monique finally exploded. "How dare she go running off to live a gay life filled with parties and shopping while her husband is risking his life to defend her honor."

"You don't understand. New Orleans is a dangerous place to be right now and Marget is a young woman. You have no idea the indignities the women of this city are forced to endure."

"Then she should have stayed and endured them. It was the least she could do to show her patriotism. I knew Benoit should never have married her. She's nothing but a . . . but a . . . tart."

"She is not," Marie-Odile said in a rising spasm of anger. "She is my daughter and a good girl."

"She deserted my son. My poor, poor son."

"She has done nothing of the sort," Marie-Odile replied sharply.

"She has. I knew she was no good. I can't think why I ever allowed the marriage to happen."

"Possibly because you needed the money she brought in her marriage settlement," Renault said dryly as he walked into the room. He bent politely over Monique's offered hand fighting to hide his astonishment over the change in her. It was hard to believe he had ever found her desirable.

"Which I have yet to see," Monique half-screamed. "She's a bold hussy, your daughter. She has deserted her husband in his hour of need. And after all he has done for her."

Marie-Odile rose in her chair alarmed at the increasing red stains on Monique's face. She looked as though she were going to burst like a balloon in a fit of apoplexy.

"Marget has not deserted Benoit," Renault said trying to calm the woman. "It was decided that New Orleans was not safe for her and Francois Honor. It is dangerous here for a young woman whose husband is gone. I thought Marget might feel safer if she were away from here."

"She has deserted my son," Monique screamed. "She is a slut and a . . . a . . . "

"Calm yourself," Renault said sternly. "I will not allow you to malign my daughter. If you do not control yourself, I shall take you back to the packet and have you returned upriver immediately."

That threat sobered Monique as no other ever would. She sank back in her chair, the redness draining from her face. She fanned herself lethargically managing a tight smile.

"There, I am calm," she said finally in a tight, tense voice. "I will give you the letters my son sent to Marget through me and you may send them on to her. I assume you have some communications with her."

"Infrequent, but yes there is communication," Renault said, relieved that the disaster had been averted.

"I assume that man who is your manager told you Grandeville burned to the ground. There's not a stick standing. I thought while I am here, we could discuss the rebuilding. Your man has been kind enough to install me at Grey Lawns. It has grown very lonely in the country and Grey Lawns is more isolated than I realized."

"I have never known you to be at a loss to entertain yourself, Monique," Renault said, amusement lighting his eyes.

"There aren't many people who feel sociable with all those Yankee pirates scouring the parish. The Slaughters see no one, especially since all their slaves ran off when that intolerably stupid President Lincoln issued that silly paper freeing all the slaves. There's hardly a black face left there. Not that I mind. I never did like Fay Slaughter. It makes me feel good to see her humbled."

"How horrid," Marie-Odile gasped.

Monique ignored her and continued with her gossip. In a quarter of an hour, Renault excused himself and went back to his office unable to stand listening to the flood of words from Monique's malicious mouth.

Marie-Odile with tact she did not know she possessed convinced Monique to rest until dinner in her room and then sought refuge in her own room where Luce sat on the rocking chair holding little Clotilde in her arms.

"I don't think I can stand it," Marie-Odile cried sitting down across from Luce and looking at the other woman with huge unhappy eyes. "Six weeks with that woman in my home. She's horrible."

"She will not stay," Luce said quietly, her large capable hands patting the sleeping child gently.

"She has grown so . . . so coarse. You should have heard the things she said about Marget."

"I heard them," Luce said with a gentle chuckle. "The whole house heard her."

"She has grown so fat! Why, Luce, I hardly recognized her."

"Madame de Ville is a very unhappy woman. We must all be kind to her."

"Oh, Luce. What are we going to do."

"We shall continue as we have always done. She will either fit into our routine or she will go home. It will not take her long to find there is no opera or theater except for select engagements to which we are not invited to attend. It will not take long to realize there are no Paris fashions in the shops and no yard goods to purchase. Our lovely city is a ghost of her former self. Just as Madame de Ville is a ghost of her former self. She will not stay long."

"I hope you are right," Marie-Odile sighed.

"I am right," Luce said smiling. "Here take Clotilde and I shall go down to the kitchen and tell everyone they can come out of hiding now."

Marie-Odile laughed suddenly. It transformed her face from a care-worn woman to youth and vitality. She took her tiny daughter and sat back down in the vacated rocking chair.

As Luce walked down the hall to the back stair, she

heard the faint strains of a lullaby coming from Marie-Odile's lips. She smiled to herself, then went down the stair to the kitchen.

Twenty Six

1863

"Hey, Johnny Reb, you still there?"
"I'm here, Yankee."
"What you doin', Johnny Reb?"
"Eatin' my dinner, Yankee."
"What ya eatin', Johnny Reb?"
"A fine, tasty mule, Yankee."
"I hear your short on ammunition, Johnny Reb."
"You hear wrong, Yankee."

The pickets along the Confederate and Federal lines called back and forth to each other in the dark of the night. Each soon grew familiar with the sounds of the other, not only talking, but occasionally passing food to the starving Confederate army. Back and forth they went the long lonely, night only to find at daybreak they were enemies again.

Major General Ulysses S. Grant was a determined man. From October of 1862 to April of 1863, he mounted three massive expeditions against the city. His objective was to surround it entirely, cutting Vicksburg off. His first expeditions failed, but in April, 1863, he finally achieved what he had first set out to do. Vicksburg was now totally surrounded with Federal gunboats on the river and 70,000 troops all dug in on the land side. The siege had begun.

"I sometimes think I'll go mad," Helen Jamison said. She sat on a camp stool in front of the cave her husband had hollowed out of the hillside for them when it became too dangerous to stay in Vicksburg anymore.

It was dark. Cole could barely see her. Paul sat on the ground, his pipe in his mouth, indulging in a smoke with some carefully hoarded tobacco.

"It will be over soon," Cole said wearily. He leaned his head back against the clay. In the distance he could hear the bantering tones of the pickets. A shell, landing closer to the cave than normal, brought him to his feet.

"I can't stand it," Helen screamed. Her husband rushed to her and soothed her drawing her into the cave.

"I'd better go see if that one did any damage." Most of the damage of the shelling was in the city, but the shells did land on the caves. The last time had been a direct hit. Cole had helped to dig out a family of five all hideously dead in the cave. He could still see the tortured look on their faces. He shuddered. "I'll be back later," he said moving away anxiously in a quick, determined stride.

There was no damage. A tree toppled in front of a cave trapping a couple of children in it. He helped drag it away. Then he went back to Helen and Paul Jamison's cave, sat a while longer, then went back to the batteries.

"They're slowing down some," Pops Lyttel commented. The bombardment had eased slightly, but not for long. After a few minutes, the heavy shelling increased again.

"I'm beginning to really hate this place," Simmons complained. He had grown gaunt with everyone else, emphasizing a feral look to his face. He looked around, his eyes darting back and forth furtively.

"We all hate this place," Pops said.

"I hate it more than you do," Simmons screeched. He ran off into the darkness.

"Dangerous going around in the dark like that," Pops commented calmly. "Right dangerous."

Cole sat down. He was tired, but too tired to sleep. He gazed up at the night sky, distant stars twinkling brightly. Then his head fell back and he slept.

"Hey, Johnny Reb, how's the mule?"

"Even the bones are tasty, Yankee."

"I'll bet they are. How's the ammunition holding out?"

"I got enough left, Yankee."

"Glad to hear that, Johnny Reb. When you run out, let us know. We promised President Lincoln we'd give him Vicksburg for a Fourth of July present."

"Over my dead body, Yankee."

"It just might come to that, Johnny Reb."

Lt. Cole Taggert stood in the warehouse carefully counting the cases of ammunition. There were too few cases in the huge warehouse. He counted them again. A third time. No matter how many times, the answer would always come out the same. He reported to Colonel Ogden who passed the report on to General

Pemberton who did with it whatever generals did Cole did not know and he didn't really want to know anymore. He was too tired to care. Long hours at the batteries with too little rest and rations down to a quarter share was getting to be too much for any man. He was hungry. He was tired. And he wanted the damn war to come to an end.

He spent his twenty-first birthday sitting in the mud thinking about Texas, the Santa Gertrudis ranch and the farm he had grown up on. Cole had come a long way from the green eighteen year old who had agreed to work for the wealthy plantation owner, Renault de Champlain. He'd come a long way from the West Texas kid who'd tried to take on the world all at once. The Cole Taggert of today bore little resemblance to the Cole Taggert of a year ago or two years ago. If he went home now, Rico Hernandez would not recognize him.

Cole had not heard from Rico in nearly a year, not since the Federal navy had captured New Orleans and cut off all communication from it. His last letter from Rico had been filled with Renault de Champlain's offer to manage St. Angele. The salary was good, far better than expected and when the war finally came to an end, they would have the money they would need to buy their own ranch in Texas. Their own property with cattle grazing on the rich prairie grass. Land and cattle were always good investments.

The explosion of a shell near Cole woke him. He had not known he had been asleep, but alertness came immediately. He scrambled to his feet and made his way up the side of the Batteries to look at the river. Like everyone else on the line, he sensed that the siege was slowly drawing to a close. But like every other Confederate soldier, he would go down fighting.

"If we could push our way through the lines, we could fade into Mississippi like ghosts and come back to fight again."

Cole sat down in the mud again and looked curiously at Simmons. The man had wonderful plans for a retreat of all Vicksburg forces. If they had been workable plans, Simmons would have been a general. But it wasn't a real retreat he was talking about, but desertion. Too many men were tired of the weariness of the siege and were quietly fading out of the picture. Simmons would have gone if he could, his loyalty to the South was diminishing more rapidly than their ammunition, but he didn't quite have the courage.

"Remember Willy Blane. He cut his foot off and got sent home." Simmons continued. "Wish I'd thought of that. I'd be home right now sitting in my woman's kitchen smelling fresh bread baking in the oven, and eating from a meat stew so thick I'd be full in bites."

Nobody was listening to Simmons. They never did. Pops Lyttell turned away with a snort of disgust and several other of the men moved away from Simmons. Cole did not correct him on Willy Blane's supposed ticket home. He'd gone home all right, but in soul only. Infection had spread and killed him. Simmons refused to believe it.

"What about it, Sarge?" Simmons asked. He persisted in addressing Cole by his old rank as though his field commission to Lieutenant had never happened. "Let's ay you and me . . ."

"Keep it up Simmons and I'll report you for insurrection in the ranks and treason," Cole responded sharply.

Simmons fell silent. He moved off by himself and sat against the mud battery studying the field around him. Occasionally he would mumble to himself.

"He's just talk, Taggert," Pops said, spitting tobacco juice at the ground.

Cole grunted. He didn't like Simmons. Didn't trust him. He leaned back against the mud and fell asleep again.

"Hey, Johnny Reb, how's your mule tonight."

"Ain't mule, it's horse, Yankee, and it's right delicious."

"Getting might close to the Fourth of July, Johnny Reb, you ready to let us in?"

"I'm ready, Yankee. You just come ahead and see how ready I am."

"Just might at that, Johnny Reb, just might at that. See you on the Fourth."

"We're going to lose Vicksburg," Pops said a little mournfully. He gazed over at the city half standing and half fallen into the ground from the shelling from the Federal gunboats.

Cole sat next to Pops, their meager rations in the tin cups in their hands. They'd been on quarter rations for a week. It wasn't much food for a grown man, but there was no food, no ammunition. Very shortly the war would be over for them.

"What do you think will happen?" Cole asked curiously. The gruel was thin and watery and smelled distinctly of horse. One winter on the range when one of the mares had died, Cole and Rico had cooked her instead of killing a steer. Horse didn't taste bad, but it didn't taste great either. At least it was meat. Cole's stomach growled long and protestingly.

"What can they do with us. There's 30,000 men here in the city. That's a lot of paperwork. They'll probably parole us and send us to our lines in Tennessee or Virginia."

"Sometimes the waiting bothers me. I've spent all my life waiting and learning patience, but I feel like I've forgotten everything I ever knew sitting here and waiting." Cole finished his ration in one long gulp. He thought of Helen's sourdough starter lost when a shell had landed on her kitchen. Thankfully she and Paul had not been in it. But he was still a little saddened at the loss of that sourdough starter. It had been good. And she'd kept it for so many years.

A shell whistled overhead. It embedded itself into a clay bank. It didn't explode.

Pops looked at that shell disinterestedly. It was amazing how a body could get used to the constant day and night shelling. It made a person realize, a man could get used to any unpleasantness no matter how uncomfortable.

"Maybe I should go over and take a look at that. It might fit one of our guns," Pops commented. "I hear tell, the troops in the outer trenches go around at night and picked up unexploded shells to reuse in our own guns."

"The noise bothered me at first," Cole said scanning the sky. Another shell went overhead. "You'd think they'd run out." Another shell whistled and exploded into the hillside. The earth rolled and jerked, then quieted again.

"They have an inexhaustible supply." Pops pushed himself to his feet. He drained the last of his ration as he walked. Leisurely, he approached the shell. Just as he reached it, it exploded.

For a long second, Cole continued to sit staring at the spot Pops had been standing. He was gone. There was nothing left of him. One second he had been there and the next, he was gone.

Cole felt numb. He'd seen so much. He thought he should have been upset over Pops death, but no emotion seemed to come. Pops had been a tough old bird, too tough to die like this.

Slowly, Cole got to his feet. He hooked his empty cup over his belt. He thought he ought to go and report the death to someone, but he couldn't think who he should go to.

He started walking. His foot hit something. It rolled along the ground with a clank. Cole looked down to see a hand still clutching a tin cup.

Cole stared at the dismembered hand. A new horror gripped him. He started to shake and shiver. Then he fell to his knees and vomited.

"Helen," Paul said softly as Helen walked into the cave, her skirt rustling. The afternoon light was going, but he could still see the two small cans she held in her hand. She smiled at him.

"What luck, Paul. I found two cans of tomatoes in our pantry. I can't think how I managed to overlook them."

"Helen!"

She looked at him curiously. Then he nodded at the

corner of their cave. Helen whirled around to find Cole Taggert sitting in the corner on her little camp stool. He was trembling, his eyes blank. His mouth was slightly open, but he made no sound.

"He showed up about an hour ago," Paul said. "He hasn't said a word to me, just sitting in that corner and kind of rocking back and forth."

Helen set the cans down on the table and went to Cole. She took his hand in hers. His skin was cold and clammy, his eyes were dilated and slightly rolled back.

"He's in shock," she said turning and pulling a blanket from her cot and draping it around Cole's shoulders. She picked up a small brazier and set it near Cole. Gently she set several tiny pieces of precious timder into it with hoarded coal on top. She lit the brazier, then hung a kettle of water over the heating coals.

"I need to get something warm into him," she said, tossing a few bits of coffee grounds into the water. Coffee grounds used so much that the taste was bitter and rancid. "Did he say what happened?"

"Not a word," Paul said. He came to stand next to her, putting an arm around her shoulders, "but it must have been pretty bad."

"This whole thing is pretty bad," she said bitterly. "Children are dying, Paul. All those children we could never have, they're dying, and for what?" She leaned her head against his shoulder. "He's just a boy."

"I know," Paul said sadly. He shook his gray head and held his wife tightly to him.

After a long while, Cole's convulsive shudders stopped. For the first time, the blankness left his face and eyes. He looked at Helen and Paul hovering anxiously over him. "I'm tired," he said, his first words in hours.

"Lie down on my cot and rest," Helen said gently.

He moved awkwardly, like a child, as he stood up and walked to the cot. He settled himself down with a sigh, closed his eyes and fell asleep.

"I'll sit up with him, Helen," Paul said. "You rest. You've worked all day at the hospital and I know you're tired."

"I'll share it with you," Helen said with a slight smile. "Wake me at midnight and I'll take over. You're a working man too and I know you're tired."

"It's all right. Go lie down."

She settled on his cot. He tucked the blankets in around her and kissed her lightly on the forehead.

Paul didn't call her at midnight. He sat until dawn watching the sleeping young man toss and turn in his sleep, mumble at dreams brought on by the horrors of the war. Paul soothed him several times by touching his face and stroking it softly. When morning came, Paul watched as Cole woke to another terrible day.

Cole shook his head and stood up. Helen offered coffee but Cole refused mutely. He left the cave without saying anything. When hostilities broke out in the trenches, Cole joined them and killed his share of Yankees. All the while, he felt dead inside.

"Hey, Johnny Reb, we're comin' to dinner tomorrow. What ya havin'?'

"Not much, Yankee."

"Rabbit stew sound might nice, Johnny Reb."

"You best bring your own rabbit, Yankee."

There was no firing of guns or mortars that day. The city was oddly silent, sitting hushed waiting expectantly for the next move to be made. From where he stood on the bluffs overlooking the rear trenches, Cole could just make out General Pemberton under a flag of truce negotiating the surrender of Vicksburg to General Grant. Grant had won. The city had fallen. The Federal army now controlled almost all the Mississippi River.

"I think the war is over for me," Colonel Ogden said in a hushed voice that matched the expectant waiting of the city. He stood next to Cole watching the two men in the distance. General Pemberton looked crushed and defeated. Like all the men in his command, he had aged a great deal during the long weeks of the siege. "Think I might go home and see my family for awhile. Haven't seen my family in over two years. Then maybe, just maybe, I'll go see General Lee and see if he has any use for my services. I'm a good artilleryman. What about you, Taggert?"

Cole didn't know. All he did know was that the war was not over for him. There was a new savagery in him. A new savagery that demanded sacrifices of blood. He'd go and find Lee's army in Virginia and join up with a cavalry unit. He was damned tired of walking.

The negotiations were complete. The two generals parted with friendly handshakes. Cole squinted to catch their movement.

"We're surrendering because we're out of food and almost out of ammunition. We couldn't possibly repulse a strong offensive attack right now. Grant knows it. Pemberton knows it. This way, Pemberton

431

saves lives."

Cole said nothing. He understood Pemberton's strategy. The more lives he took away with him from Vicksburg, the more lives he had to offer to General Robert E. Lee for future hostilities.

"Going to hate giving up my rifle," Cole said quietly patting his old rifle. He watched Pemberton stride back to Vicksburg a proud, beaten man. "This piece has come a long way with me." Cole turned around, scanning the trenches until his gaze came to rest on his artillery unit standing next to their silent guns waiting with everyone else. They were all good men and had done a good job trying to keep Vicksburg out of Federal hands. But it was over now, Vicksburg had surrendered.

One man sat apart from the others. As Cole watched him he seemed to inch further and further from the body of the unit. Inch closer and closer to a thin grove of trees. Without really knowing why, Cole knew it was Simmons.

Simmons, the man who'd been wanting to desert for a long time. Simmons, the man who had lost his enchantment with war when he found out how much work it was.

Cole straightened. In a fluid motion he raised his rifle and sighted on Simmons just as he reached the edge of the trees. The range was long, almost too long, but Cole fired anyway.

The shot echoed and re-echoed through the silence. Men turned to look at him, but he stood poised ignoring them all. Then the figure at the edge of the trees slowly crumpled.

"What was that all about?" Ogden demanded unsure on whether to be angry or not.

"Deserter," Cole replied and walked back toward his unit.

Twenty Seven

They called it Gettysburg. A peaceful, little Southern Pennsylvania town where Confederate and Federal forces clashed in one of the bloodiest battles of the war. It was also one of the worst defeats for the Confederacy. A blow they would never recover from.

"Colonel Courtland!" General J.E.B. Stuart said as he paced back and forth in front of a pitched tent. It was night. The battlefields were silent after three days of death.

Inside the tent, an oil lamp flickered throwing grotesque shadows of the two men inside onto the tent walls. Two hunched men, silent and brooding. One of those hunched figures was General Robert E. Lee, a man whose bright horizon was facing a bleak future.

"I am detaching you from my brigade to accompany General Imboden in transporting the wounded back to Virginia." Jeb Stuart stopped his pacing. The moonlight cast long shadows on his face. He was a tired man. The years of war were aging him as they were aging others. "General Imboden is short a company and will need you. Have your men saddled and ready to go at first light." Jeb Stuart turned to look at the tent. Separated from the other tents that formed staff headquarters, it looked lonely and alone.

"Dismissed, Colonel."

Gayle saluted, but Jeb Stuart did not see. He had re-entered the tent and stood over one of the hunched figures. Gayle saw him put a comforting hand on the stiff shoulder, then Gayle, too, turned away.

"Let's round them up, Sawyer, and find General Imboden."

"He's camped two miles south of here, sir," Sawyer said. He and Gayle had been together since Florida. In a way, Sergeant Sawyer considered himself responsible for the welfare of this man whose life he had saved. It made him Gayle's constant shadow. He wasn't the young, freshly recruited boy anymore, either. He was a hard, seasoned soldier. Aged to a man twice his age.

"Fine, get Captain Russell and send him here."

"Captain Russell was reported missing, sir," Sawyer replied. They all came and went so quickly. So many men were dying. So many officers who got field commissions to replace those who were gone.

Gayle closed his eyes. One by one, his gallant men fell in battle. He felt alone and tired.

"Find Lieutenants Smythe and Churchill. They should still be around. The snipers don't aim for the junior officers." His voice was pained and harsh.

"Yes, sir," Sawyer said. He caught his horse and climbed wearily into the saddle. His horse moved along with dispirited gait. It was as tired as its master.

Gayle moved away from the tent to find shelter under a huge oak tree. He sat down, his back to the tree and drawing his knees up, he leaned his arms and head on them and allowed himself to fall into a light sleep.

"Our men behaved magnificently today, Colonel."

Gayle woke. He scrambled to his feet rubbing his tired eyes. He'd had little sleep in the last three days and it looked as though he would get little more in the days to come.

"We put up one hell of a fight," Robert E. Lee continued. "But we lost. Too bad! too bad!" He walked away, an old gent growing bent and tired with the weight of his command. His shoulders were slumped, his footsteps slow.

Morning dawned to gray clouds and damp air. General John D. Imboden sat on his horse shouting and trying to put order into the confusion of wagons, ambulances, walking wounded, and frightened animals in front of him.

"We'll never get this column moving by noon," Imboden yelled at Gayle over the hysterical braying of a team of mules. A horse screamed and backed up into the mules, hind legs coming up to kick the soft underbelly of the other animals. The mules screamed and lurched in their traces. The wagoner in the seat of the wagon brought up his whip and lashed at the luckless horse's hindquarters. A wounded soldier, his arm in a sling and a large bandage around his leg ran up to the horse's head, calmed it, and moved it away from the braying mules. The animal went reluctantly, the whites of his eyes rolling back in terror.

Hundreds of wagons lined the fields along the road from Gettysburg to Cashtown. Hundreds of wagons filled with as many wounded men that could be rounded up and transported from the battlefields. Most of them had not yet had even the most rudimentary of medical attention.

"We need to be on our way before dark," Imboden

436

continued. "Get that wagon forward." He shook his head in despair. Nearly a thousand wagons filled with wounded. How did one go about bringing order of such chaos?

A man in a ragged, torn uniform approached Gayle and plucked nervously at his spurred boot.

"Sir!" he croaked looking up. "I've a wounded young boy, sir. The Sarge said to bring him along to you."

"Find him a spot in a wagon, soldier," Gayle ordered. A team of horses in front of him stood to their knees in mud. They floundered helplessly while their driver lashed them with whip and curses.

"It's my son, sir," the man continued still plucking at Gayle's boot. "You will keep an eye on him?"

"I'll do the best I can," Gayle said leaning over to look at the man, his eyes full of sympathy. The soldier was grimy with gunpowder, his stubble of beard was alternately gray and black. His eyes were tired and haunted by three days of vicious fighting. "You'd best get back to your outfit, soldier."

"I promised his Ma I'd watch out for him. He's our youngest."

"I'll do the best I can," Gayle said gently, seeing and understanding the man's exhaustion.

The soldier sighed and shuffled away. Gayle saw him later with a small body wrapped around his shoulders looking for an empty spot in a wagon.

Shortly after noon, the threatening storm of the morning broke. Gayle slid his slicker over his shoulders to shelter him from the cold rain feeling guilty that he was protected when so many of the wounded had little more than the wagon canvass over their heads.

It was a furious storm, shrieking and howling with a fury that defied man's understanding. It was as though the very heavens were conspiring to keep the wagon train from getting under way. When the first wagon finally was put on the road to Cashtown, Gayle felt like cheering, but he was too tired. He simply turned and shouted for the next wagon to get into line and then the next.

"I'm going ahead to Cashtown," Imboden told him when the train was finally moving. "You keep those wagons on the march and bring up the rear with your cavalry. Keep a sharp eye out for the enemy."

"Yes, General," Gayle shouted over the fury of the still raging storm. He turned back to the column and signaled the next wagon into line. As it went past its canvas sides flapped frantically with the storm. The mules brayed piteously and the wounded moaned.

The next wagon got stuck. Even Gayle dismounted into knee deep mud to help pull it free. An extra team was finally hitched to it and when it finally rolled out of the mud with a sucking sound, Gayle went down into the mud on hands and knees, panting. Despite the hard, cold rain, he was drenched with perspiration.

"Get that wagon moving," he screamed as he remounted his horse. Another wagon rumbled past.

It was midnight before the last wagon was finally pulled into the column. It was midnight before Gayle got his cavalry into formation and fell in behind the last wagon cantering on exhausted horses who slipped and slid through the slippery mud.

"Lt. Smythe, take a detachment of men and fall back to see what's coming up on our rear."

"Yes, sir," Smythe wheeled his horse around and called out a patrol. Men dropped out of the line and fell into formation behind the Lieutenant who was heading back toward Gettysburg through the sheeting rain.

Gayle was so tired, it was all he could do to keep his seat on his horse. The rocking motion finally allowed him to fall into a very light doze.

The rain stopped just before dawn. The sound of its fury was replaced by a new sound. The sound of thousands of wounded men moaning and crying. The sound of thousands of men lying on the hards beds of the wagons without even a layer of straw to cushion them, or a blanket to cover them. They were hideous sounds. Screams mingled with prayers, fierce curses mingled with stony-faced stoicism.

"Can't we at least stop and aid the men, Colonel?" Lt. Churchill was newly assigned to the unit. Young and inexperienced, the cries of the wounded in their horrible need pained him.

"Our orders are to push on to Williamsport without stopping," Gayle snapped. "There's no time for pity, now fall back into formation."

The young lieutenant dropped back to his position, but his horse pranced nervously under his trembling hand.

Gayle did have pity for the wounded, there just wasn't time to indulge in it when the enemy was hot on their back and the darkness, a fleeting time of safety.

The last of the column passed through Cashtown and was winding up into and over the mountains.

"We're not going through Chambersburg," General

Imboden said falling into step next to Gayle. Like Gayle he was gray with exhaustion. "We'll leave the main road at Fairfield and go across country to Greencastle. That will put us closer to the Potomac. We're to meet supply trains there. Hopefully, they'll have blankets." Not even Generals were immune to pity.

Gayle nodded wearily and watched as the General coaxed his exhausted mount into a shambling trot heading toward the head of the column.

"Colonel," Lt. Smythe was back leaning wearily over the lathered neck of his straining mount. "There's a small band of Federal cavalry behind us. They're following at a slow, but steady walk. Don't seem to be in too much of a hurry to catch up."

"They will, once it's light," Gayle replied. "Sawyer, take fresh men and fall back to prepare a defensive."

"Yes, sir," Sawyer called. He wheeled his horse and rode down the line. Men dropped out to follow him.

It started to rain again. A fine misty drizzle which seeped into men's clothes and chilled already cold bodies. The wounded soldiers in the wagons cried for blankets and hot food. Gayle ignored them, hardening his heart as he moved up to urge the wagons into a faster pace.

Dawn broke the sky, its light a thin sluggish light moving over the long columns of the wagons. With the dawn came a new menace. Bands of Federal cavalry descended on the train to harrass and annoy.

At mid-morning, the wagons ahead of Gayle came to a sudden stop. He called out half his company and raced ahead to find out what was wrong.

What was wrong was a Federal unit blocking the road and firing on the wagons. The foremost wagon was on its side, the driver sprawled in the mud dead and the horses staggering in the traces. The wounded were flung out over the mud and crying in terror.

"We'll charge them," Gayle cried. "We've no artillery." Before the Federal unit could set up a defense, Gayle and his men broke into a ragged charge, hair-raising rebel yells on their lips. The Federal cavalry broke and scattered.

"Churchill, take twenty-five men and follow them. The rest of you start getting these wagons moving and caught up. Get them going, or we'll be captured."

The men scattered and rode back to the train. Wagons were already pulling around the downed wagon, the wounded being divided among those wagons with space.

"But the wagon, sir."

Gayle glanced at it. It was caught in the mud up to its axles.

"Leave it," he shouted and moved back down the column assigning two guards to each wagon.

Gayle rode up and down the column urging them on until the lead wagons were once more in sight of the main column. General Imboden was there watching anxiously for him.

"I was beginning to worry," he said.

"So was I," Gayle responded wryly. He dropped back again to find his men engaged in a skirmish with Federal cavalry.

"We're getting low on ammunition," Sawyer said pulling up to Gayle.

"Supply wagons are to meet us in Williamsport."

"When will we be there?"

"Before dark," Gayle said, hoping his guess was close.

The last wagon moved into Williamsport shortly after dark. Gayle dismounted stiffly, patting his shuddering animal. A woman walked out of the nearest house with a cup of hot coffee in her hands. She handed it to Gayle, her sullenness unnoticed as he gulped it down.

"Thank you, ma'am," he repled courteously.

"Damned southerner," the woman murmured as she walked away.

"Not too friendly, hereabouts," Sawyer said watching the woman walk back into her house.

Gayle shrugged. He handed his horse over to Sawyer and went to see Imboden.

"The supply wagons aren't here yet," Imboden said as Gayle walked into the town hall. The town hall was an imposing structure with fancy letters emblazoned across its portico saying Williamsport. Surgeons were inside busily setting up surgeries in the room to get back to their grisly business of tending to the wounded.

"The river's swollen with all the rain we've been having and there is only two flats going across river. Those men who think they can walk on to Winchester will be provisioned and ferried across the river now. It's going to be days before we can get all these wagons across. What about those supply wagons," Imboden snapped at Major McNeal walking into the room.

"Nothing, sir."

"Take a detachment across the river and see if you can find them, McNeal. We've ten thousand animals and nearly every wagon from Lee Army filled with wounded. We need food and ammunition."

"Yes, sir." McNeal stepped smartly away despite his

442

weariness and walked out of the door.

Gayle sat down. He didn't know how long he sat there, head nodding, eyes partially closed. A scout, running into the room woke him.

"General, there's a large party of Federal cavalry coming this way."

Imboden sighed and closed his eyes.

"Courtland, take your people and see what you can find out. Colonel Black let's start organizing the walking wounded who can handle a firearm or command a unit. Captain Hart, set your artillery up on the hills around this town. Let's try and keep the battle away from here. Get moving, all of you."

Gayle got stiffly to his feet, dragging his heavy body out of the room and into the street with slow steps. Not even a battle could excite him to alertness.

"Sawyer," he yelled. The sargeant straightened up from where he had been sitting. "Find Lt. Churchill and get back to me immediately."

"Yes, sir."

Thirty minutes later, Gayle was back in the saddle riding out of town at the head of half his company. Lt. Churchill sat just behind him on his right and Sargeant Sawyer on his left. They crested the hill around the city and went down the other side.

"Lieutenant, take half the men and circle south around the Federals. I'll go north. Find out how many guns they have, how many cavalry regiments and foot infantry." The men parted going their separate ways.

It was dawn when Gayle stood once more in front of General Imboden trying to give a coherent report. He had been in the saddle without stop for over forty-eight hours.

"They have three batteries of rifled infantry, twenty three units of cavalry and eighteen guns. The force appears to be about seven thousand strong. They should be here about noon."

"Very good, Courtland, I can understand why General Stuart values you so much. Now get a few hours sleep and be at the lines by noon."

"Yes, sir." Gayle stumbled away no further than the grass outside where he lay down under a tree next to his sargeant and fell asleep.

The first sighting of the enemy column was made at one o'clock. Gayle stood next to General Imboden surveying the Federal troops through field glasses.

"We'll fire all our guns at once and keep up heavy firing until we're out of ammunition," the General said. His artillery commander nodded and moved down the line of artillery with the orders.

"Are your people ready?" Imboden asked Gayle. Gayle nodded. He was as ready now as he would ever be. "Good, Colonel, you've a good outfit."

In half an hour the firing started. Thirty minutes after that, the first of the Confederate guns fell silent. Another gun fell silent.

Major McNeal came running up to the General panting breathlessly. His horse fell to its knees and was unable to rise. "I found them. Ammunition."

The General clapped the Major on the shoulder and sent the wagon up and down the line handing out the ammunition.

Little by little the Federal troops fell back, but did not retreat. The heavy fire rained down on them, but they stubbornly held their lines knowing how weak Imboden's defenses were.

Gayle saw the messenger at the same time General Imboden saw him. The man galloped a lathered horse up the hill and dismounted, saluting smartly. He held out a message to the general who read it quickly.

"I'll be damned," the general laughed. "It's Fitz Hugh Lee. He'll be here in less than an hour with 3000 reinforcements. You may pass the word along. We're saved."

Gayle grinned and nodded at Sawyer who raced to his horse and ran down the long line screeching the news.

"Here, Colonel, you'd best read the rest of it," the general handed the note to Gayle who read it and felt a creeping numbness spread over him.

Vicksburg had fallen. Their last port on the Mississippi was in Federal hands. The first feeling of foreboding swept over Gayle. Then he handed the message back to the general and mounted his horse to join his cavalry.

The battle was over by dark. The Federal troops were gone, the wagon train safe. But there was no joy. The news of Vicksburg's surrender went up and down the line like fire to be greeted with total silence. It was a subdued army that finally crossed the Potomac back into Virginia.

Twenty-eight

Fleur did not feel well. She had not felt well for some days. Rising each morning was a chore. She dreaded it, yet she could not stay in the house. Monique de Ville drove her mad with her constant eating and non-stop gossip. But it was the eating which bothered Fleur the most. It made her ill.

"Where are you going?" Monique asked as Fleur descended the stairs pulling her shawl about her shoulders. She wore a pale green gown that grew older and paler with each passing month.

"Don't you know. I help at the convent every day," Fleur said hating to have to explain herself to Monique.

"You must be very devout," Monique said drily. She popped a piece of candy into her cavernous mouth while she studied Fleur. "You look ill. Are you feeling all right."

"I am bored," Fleur said.

"You could stay home a day and keep me company."

"No thank you. I prefer the convent to watching you eat."

"I don't think you really go to the convent," Monique said, her small eyes glinting maliciously.

Fleur shrugged. She marched to the door trying to control the uneasy rolling of her stomach. Monique smelled of last night's dinner, boiled chicken and potatoes. Fleur resisted her desire to gag as she opened the front door to be assailed by the humid morning air. It was going to be hot. July and August were always hot.

"Why don't I walk along with you," Monique suggested.

"If you want," Fleur said nonchalantly hiding the sudden fear leaping into her eyes.

"I'll just get my shawl. I'll only be a moment," Monique said. She huffed her way up the stairs and started down again her shawl over her arm only to find Fleur gone and the front door firmly closed against her. With a shrill curse, she flung her shawl down on the stairs and left it for Persia to pick up.

"What does she do every day?" Monique demanded of the patiently suffering Marie-Odile.

Marie-Odile bent over her sewing. She was hemming a gown for Aurore who seemed to be growing taller and taller lately.

"She teaches at the convent," Marie-Odile said. It was a lie. They both knew it was a lie, but Marie-Odile did not retract it. She bent her head further ignoring Monique's determined munching of cookies.

"You don't look like you're enjoying yourself."

Fleur's unknown lover rolled away and lay next to her his head propped on his hand.

"I don't feel well," Fleur said. She sat up and drew her wrapper around her looking at him with tired eyes. All she wanted to do was sleep and she wished he would go away so she could.

His eyes studied her knowingly. He pushed her wrapper away from her breasts. They were swollen and blue veined. Her small stomach was slightly rounded.

"You're pregnant," he announced with a chuckle. "I never knew a whore like you before. Don't you even know when you're pregnant?"

"What!"

"With child. *Enceinte*."

Fleur's mouth dropped open in astonishment. She stared at him unbelieving. She was sixteen years old. Marget had borne Francois Honor by that age. Fleur stood and dropped her wrapper to the bed. She padded across the floor to the mirror to study herself. No wonder her gowns felt tight and uncomfortable.

"What am I going to do?" she asked turning around and staring at him. There was a strange horror in the depths of her eyes.

"How would I know," he shrugged. He left the bed grabbing his trousers as he rose. "Go talk to one of the street girls. Or better yet, go see Esther Nye. She's pretty knowledgeable about these things. She runs the cathouse off St. Charles. It isn't mine, is it?"

"No, you haven't been here in weeks. There was only Colonel Bickley and . . . " Her voice trailed away as the thought of Rico Hernandez sitting on her bed smiling at her. She had spent a day and night with him. It had been a glorious night. He was a tireless man. Even as she thought about him a strange smile came over her. She ran her hands down her body thinking of the strange fulfillment he instilled in her. He was the best lover she had ever had.

"And the Mex," he finished for her.

Fleur looked startled.

"Didn't think I knew, did you?" He grinned at her confusion. "I came to see you, but he was here. He sounded like an old, old friend."

"He is an old friend," Fleur said.

"You service him for free, don't you."

"It's none of your business," she replied wondering why she felt hot and uneasy. She pulled her wrapper back around her tying it tightly at the waist.

"Listen, kid. I don't care who you entertain in this room and whether or not you do it for money or for free. Just so long as I get the information I want when I need it.

"I got what you wanted from Colonel Bickly didn't I."

"You got it. The best information today. I get the best information from you. You have a flair for spying, Little Flower."

"Do you have more than one spy?" Fleur asked, suddenly curious.

"It's none of your business," he grinned. He dressed and then stood in the middle of the room watching her. She moved restlessly about occasionally pressing her fingers against her stomach. "I think I know someone who can help you," he said finally.

"Who!"

"She'll be here tomorrow." He went to her and took her hands in his. "You're beautiful. Even when you're angry." He kissed her, bruising her lips and then with a smile. "I may not be a Mex, but I know what a

449

woman wants, too," he said walking to the door.

Fleur glared at him, but he closed the door and walked down the hall whistling. Then she lay down on the bed and stared at the ceiling. What was she going to do? She never thought about becoming pregnant. It had never occurred to her that this was how babies were made. She grinned wryly. She had been thinking about herself as a woman of experience only to find out how truly naive she was.

"Hello," the woman said. She stood in the room elegantly gowned in gray taffeta with exquisite black lace about her throat and wrists. "My name is . . . ah . . . Sulie." She had beautiful auburn hair gathered into a cluster of curls about her lovely face and large blue eyes. "A mutual friend told me of your problem. He thought I might help you."

"Can you?"

"I think so," Sulie said with a faint gleam in her eyes. She stared at the lovely, disheveled girl before her. She seemed so young and vulnerable. "How far along are you?"

"I don't know," Fleur said thinking of Rico and of the tiny life inside her. She felt a strange sadness.

"Let's take a look."

Fleur unbuttoned her gown and stepped out of it, then stripped down to her skin and stood in front of the elegant woman feeling faintly self-conscious. The woman's blue eyes studied her and there was more than a normal interest in them.

"About six weeks, I suppose," Sulie said touching the rounded stomach with cool gentle hands.

"There's a woman in the bayous who can abort the

450

baby. But it will cost you."

"I have money," Fleur said a little vaguely. She was aware of the gentle hand still on her stomach. The hand seemed to circle around and around until the long fingers dipped slightly into the dark-covered mound between her thighs. Fleur sighed feeling a strange desire come over her. The hand moved to her stiffening breast and circled the nipple.

"You don't look like a whore to me. How old are you?"

"Sixteen," Fleur said. She looked up into the deep blue eyes that were so close to hers. She wet her lips.

"Does your family approve of your activities?" Sulie asked. Her hand wandered to the other breast and circled it. This was no ordinary street walker. This girl had the blood of generations of Frenchmen in her veins.

"My family is of no importance to you," Fleur said calmly.

"You do have one. Our friend tells me, you leave in the afternoon and return the next morning. I presume you go home. If this abortion is to be successful, you must be in a quiet place for several days."

"I have a place to go. Get me what is needed and tell me what to do and I will do it. After that, it is no longer your affair," Fleur said aware of a growing tide of desire in her as the other woman's gentle fingers massaged her breasts. "Can this woman of yours fix it so I never have children."

Sulie drew back in surprise. "I suppose so. I never asked. She simply gives me something which I take every day to prevent a pregnancy. But I'll ask her. I can't promise anything."

451

"I would appreciate it."

"Do you spy for John, like I do?" Fleur asked suddenly.

Sulie smiled. "Let's just say, I help out on occasion."

"Does he pay you?"

"After a fashion," Sulie grinned.

"What would you do if you got caught?"

"I don't know. I guess I would try to escape. The Yankees are a bit reticent about arresting women, though they have sent a few to prison. Are you worried about getting caught and being hanged as a spy? Don't be. I don't think the Yankees would hang a woman."

It wasn't very reasssuring, but Fleur was no longer thinking about being caught. She could think of nothing, but Sulie's gentle hands moving over her body.

"You're beautiful," Sulie said with a sigh. Her jacket came off, then she unbuttoned her blouse, all the while Fleur watching her as though she were in a dream. "I never could resist a truly beautiful woman. Though you're still not more than a girl."

Fleur had never seen another woman unclothed before. She stared at Sulie who held long white arms out to her.

"Come to me, my pet," Sulie said gently. "Let me show you how beautiful love can be."

Fleur went to her feeling the slender arms close around her and the full lips touch hers. They tumbled back on the bed, the cool sheets making them shiver.

Sulie moved her mouth over Fleur's fullness. It had been so long and she was tired of men.

"I just cannot believe you go everyday to the convent just to teach children," Monique declared loudly at the dinner table.

"I don't," Fleur said with more calmness than she felt. "I'm a spy for the Confederacy. I spend my days prowling the streets searching for unwary soldiers to tell me the next step in the Union campaign to control the Delta." Fleur looked at Monique who flushed with sudden anger. She glanced at her father who stared at her making her uncomfortable.

"Monique," Renault interrupted. "Let the child be. Eat your dinner."

"Boiled chicken and potatoes," Monique wailed. "Isn't there anything else to eat besides this?"

Marie-Odile shrugged. There was little pleasing Monique who grumbled about the slightest inconvenience. They had taken Monique to the theater the week before only to find the place filled with Union officers and the haughty wives. They had not been actively attacked by the men, but the wives had a more subtle approach to make the unwanted leave. Marie-Odile hated these haughty women who strolled the streets of her home as though they owned it. She hated the way they looked at a woman's gown or her jewels as though appraising the value for their own purchase. Marie-Odile dared not wear her many beautiful jewels for fear of having some Yankee woman confiscate them as war spoils. Renault had locked away her jewels in the vault in the cellar along with anything else of value. Somehow her home did not look the same without her silver service on the sideboard, or her Sevres china in the cabinets. They ate off plain white plates which Marie-Odile prayed no one would recognize for what they truly were.

"Beggars can't be choosers," Renault said with a faint twinkle in his eyes. He met Marie-Odile's gaze and suddenly his wife had a streak of amusement in her face.

"I don't understand how you can eat this trash day after day," Monique continued to complain.

"We eat to survive," Marie-Odile said.

"May I be excused?" Fleur asked.

"You have not eaten, ma cher," Marie-Odile said.

"I am not hungry, Maman."

"Neither am I," Aurore said with a sniff.

"Then you are both excused," Marie-Odile said softly. She understood their desire to escape from the dining room. Even on her best days, Monique was no fit companion for two young girls.

When the meal was ended, Renault went to his study while Marie-Odile helped Luce clear the table.

"Don't you have servants to do that?" Monique demanded angrily. "I cannot stand the way you demean yourself like a common drudge."

Marie-Odile looked at Luce who merely smiled. Then she picked up her tray and left the dining room.

"May I come in?" Monique asked as she walked into Renault's study closing the door firmly behind her.

"You are already in," he said looking up from the book spread across his legs. "Brandy?"

"I should love some. You always did keep the best cellar in the city. It has been years since I had a decent brandy."

He handed her a glass which she took and sipped greedily.

"I'm sorry for my outburst at the table."

Renault shrugged. He was uninterested in her apologies. She said it every night and he was tired of listening to her.

"Renault, I said I was sorry."

"No apologies are needed, Monique," he said smoothly. He glanced up at her with a half-smile. She had lost weight during the month she had been with them. It wasn't much, but it was enough to make her gown hang a little looser.

"I don't know what is wrong with me," she said after a long silence.

"It is the war. It affects us all this way."

"I hate it here, but I hate it more in the country. There are marauders and scavangers all over the parish. They burned my beloved Grandeville and now you won't rebuild it."

"There is no one to rebuild it for me, Monique," he said wearily knowing they had been over this time and again and still she refused to believe him. "There is no money and no labor. Once the war is over and we return to normal, I will rebuilt. But not now. You will have to continue living at Grey Lawns until something better comes along."

"Or until Monsieur Courtland comes home," Monique said. "Renault."

He looked at her and then rose from his chair in surprise. Monique stood in the shadows, her gown pooled on the floor about her feet. Her undergarments were tossed on an untidy pile near her. Her flesh was white and opulent against the darkness.

"You loved me once, Renault," she said stepping forward. The illusion of opulence was gone. Rolls of fat were evident normally concealed by the drape of

455

her gown. Her stomach distended grotesquely under long, bulbous breasts. Ironically, her legs were still slim and shapely except for the tops of her thighs which bulged.

"You were beautiful then, Monique."

"Aren't I still beautiful."

"If you think so, you're a bigger fool than I ever knew."

"Love me, please. I need you, Renault."

"Cover yourself," Renault said harshly.

"You . . . you bastard," she screamed. "Aren't I good enough for you. You liked me well enough once."

"That was a long time ago when we were both young, Monique. Put your clothes on and go back to your room. In the morning, I shall make arangements for you to return on the first packet."

"No, I won't go back. It's so lonely there."

Renault looked at her, pity clouding his face.

"Put your clothes on, Monique," he said gently.

She looked as though she were going to fling herself at him, but then changed her mind. Dully, she bent and picked up her discarded clothing and pulled it on sluggishly. When she left she walked as though she were a puppet. As though someone controlled her on invisible strings.

Renault watched the door close behind her. Never in his life had he felt as sorry for her as he did then.

Fleur took the vile medicine Sulie gave her in one nauseating gulp. Then she lay down on her bed and waited for the liquid to do what it was supposed to do.

Outside in the hall, she could hear Aurore chattering to her tutor as they walked down the hall to the nursery. Small Therese's voice was added to the conversation. There was swift laughter, then the door to the nursery closed cutting off the sound of the friendly voices.

Luce walked heavily up the stairs and stopped for a moment puffing. When she regained her breath she walked slowly to the linen closet. Fleur heard her fussing about the closet, then the door closed with a snap. When she walked back down the hall, Luce's steps were lighter and she hummed a curious little tune Fleur had never heard before.

Later, Marie-Odile came up the stairs and talked to Jewel in a quiet voice who answered her back with a slight laugh. Jewel and Marie-Odile walked down the hall to the nursery and opened the door. Therese giggled and ran down the hall, freed from her lessons for the day. Aurore followed more slowly still debating something with Mr. Embray the tutor. Then there was silence once again.

Just before she drifted into sleep, Fleur felt a strange loneliness and longing come over her. It had been a long time since she had been a part of the everyday sounds of this house. Then she lost the thread of her thoughts as she fell into a deeper sleep.

Late in the afternoon, Fleur woke. She was uncomfortable, sweating profusely. She struggled to sit up only to have a cramp hit her. She was unprepared for it falling back on her bed and gasping. She clenched her fists and tried not to scream. When the cramp subsided, she breathed in short whimpers. Then the next cramp hit her. She curled into a ball, thrusting her fists in her mouth to keep from crying. When it was gone she lay back panting staring glassy-eyed at the canopy.

There were other cramps. She stood them stoically determined to keep silent. No one must know what was going on in the privacy of her room. She had told everyone she was not feeling well. Marie-Odile had been solicitous, but Luce had stared at her suspiciously.

Another cramp hit and she moaned louder than she wished. In a moment, the door opened and Luce stepped into the darkened room.

"Go away," Fleur ordered weakly.

Luce examined her swiftly. Then she went to the wash basin and poured water into it, dropping a cloth into the water and wringing it out. She placed the cool cloth over Fleur's forehead and went to the door to call Jewel.

"Miss Fleur is ill," she said in a low voice. "Go to my room and bring me my medicine bag."

Luce went back to Fleur and sat down on the bed taking her hot dry hand into her own.

"What did you take, Fleur?" she asked urgently.

Fleur stared at her unseeing. It was hard to concentrate on the wavering figure of Luce. The room spinned and Fleur groaned as a spasm of nausea swept over her.

Luce looked around the room and saw the small bag on the dressing table. She opened it and took out the bottle sniffing at the open neck. She returned to Fleur a worried frown on her face.

"Why didn't you come to me if this is what you wanted?" Luce asked gently.

Fleur did not hear her. She was curled into a ball

drowning in her pain.

Jewel returned with the large bag Luce called her medicine bag. She opened it and found a small bag of black satin.

"Drink this," Luce ordered when Jewel returned with the hot water and she had brewed a bitter-tasting tea. "It will ease the pain." She told Jewel to return to her chores and to remain silent about Fleur.

Jewel nodded, her eyes wide with fear. She slipped silently away, running down the back stairs quickly.

The warmth of the tea spread through Fleur's tortured body. She lay back, smiling at Luce.

"It will be easier for you now," Luce said softly.

The life in Fleur clung stubbornly, but after an hour, it left Fleur's body in a pool of blood.

"There. It is over," Luce said hurrying to clean Fleur and strip the bed of its bloody sheets. "Rest now. You will be weak for several days."

"Are you going to tell Maman?"

"I will say nothing," Luce said. "Now rest."

"Is she all right?" Marie-Odile asked anxiously after being told of her daughter's illness.

"She is fine. She will be up in a few days."

"I'll go sit with her."

"No, she sleeps now and needs the rest. I will summon you when she wakes."

"Very well, Luce," Marie-Odile said worriedly.

Luce went back into the room.

"Next time, little one," Luce said softly to the sleeping girl, "Come to me with your problem. I can do it with less pain than that stupid woman in the swamps."

Twenty-nine

"Can I get up today, Luce?" Fleur asked when Luce threw back the draperies and let the morning sun into the room. "It has been a whole week."

"I think it would be good," Luce said. "You should take a short walk in the Square. You will feel better for it."

"I wanted to thank you, Luce."

"There is no need, little flower. But I want you to promise me to come to me first if you get pregnant again. It can do it easier and with much less pain.

"I promise," Fleur said privately hoping there would never be any need to go through this again.

By the time she was dressed, Fleur felt good. She walked down the stairs to the drawing room where she kissed her Maman.

"You look so much better today," Marie-Odile said.

"I feel better. Luce says I am to take a short walk in Jackson Square."

"I'll find Aurore to go with you."

"Thank you, Maman, but no. I prefer to go by myself."

"But if you should feel ill . . ."

"I am fine now. I shall be back soon."

Fleur went out into the sunshine and down the busy

street. She had missed the activity of the city.

"Hello, little flower," John Doe greeted her when she walked into her room. "I've been waiting five days for you. From the look on your face, I assume the abortion was successful."

"It was," Fleur said with a coy toss of her head. "Though I shall have to confine my activities to the less arduous for a week or so yet."

"That is all right, I am well satisfied," he grinned.

"Sulie should be very skillful," Fleur said with a knowing smirk.

He laughed at her and agreed heartedly. "She is almost as skilled as you, but her heart isn't in it. You my darling are made for your profession."

"Is there anything else," Fleur asked suddenly wanting him gone.

"Not today. But be careful. An informant tells me, the military governor is concerned about spy activities in the city. They are talking themselves into a manhunt, or womanhunt, as the case may be."

"I'll be careful," Fleur said confidently.

"See that you do," he said. "You're the best spy I have. Take it easy for awhile and the whole mess will blow over when our esteemed military governor forgets it."

He left her kissing her on the cheek as he went out the door. It was a chaste, non-passionate kiss that left her feeling curiously unsatisfied. She went to the window and watched him come out of the hotel. He smiled up at her and she blew him a kiss.

"So this is where you come," Monique said walking into the room still puffing from her three story climb. She sat down on the bed and smiled nastily at Fleur.

"This hardly looks like a convent."

"I should have thought you'd be on your way home by now."

"The packet hasn't come yet."

"That's a pity."

"Tell me who the handsome young man is who just left."

"A friend," Fleur replied noncommittally. "Have you taken up spying?"

"Just curious. I didn't think you looked innocent enough to want to bury yourself in a convent. I know a slut when I see one. What would your parents say if they found out?"

"Probably lock me in my room and marry me off to the first available offer," Fleur shrugged. She sat down across from Monique, strangely unafraid of the huge woman.

"What would you do if I told your parents?" Monique asked. Her eyes roamed the room admiring its neatness. She saw the flowered wrapper of sheer lawn hanging on a hook and imagined Fleur greeting men at the door wearing it. She felt a flash of jealousy for this girl who dared to be something not only totally alien to her upbringing, but unacceptable to society.

"What would I do?" Fleur asked half smiling.

"You're not afraid of me, are you?"

"No. I don't think I'm much afraid of anyone. Not any more. I know men and their weaknesses and I know women and their vanities. What do I have to be afraid of? You could go to my parents and tell them your tale, but then I would have to go to my friends and tell them my tale. I would tell them I want a man killed and it would be in their power to do as I ask."

She caught her lips with her teeth. In reality, she did not think she could ever carry through with such a threat, but Monique would never know that.

"You wouldn't dare."

"I would," Fleur said softly watching the color drain from Monique's face. "Your son is a monster and the world will never miss him."

Monique stood and stumbled to the door defeated. In her life, she prized her son above everything.

Aurore was in heaven. After nearly a year of silence, she had received a letter from Gayle. She took the envelope and ran up the stairs to her room, trembling with excitement. It was a short letter telling her he was all right. He had been transferred to a cavalry unit under General J.E.B. Stuart and was doing reconnaissance work.

"It doesn't say much, does it," Jewel said reading the letter quickly. For the rest of her life she would be thankful she had been allowed to sit with Aurore during her lessons with her tutor. She had learned to read and figure and felt great pride at her accomplishments.

"It's long enough," Aurore said happily. She carefully smoothed out the letter and read it again. When she was through with it, she opened the top drawer of her dressing table and put it with the few others she had received from Gayle. She wondered if he treasured her letters as much as she treasured his. But then again, a man on the move did not have the space to keep memories. She sighed and closed the drawer.

"Good evening, Monsieur D'Arcy," Marie-Odile said when the lawyer walked into the drawing room. "It's been months since we last saw you."

"I have been busy," Philippe said, bowing over her extended hand.

"So has my husband," Marie-Odile said. "Here is Aurore. My dear, Monsieur D'Arcy has come to visit."

"Good evening," Aurore said politely, dropping into a curtsey. Then she turned to her father and kissed him on the cheek. "I got a letter from Monsieur Courtland today," she announced.

Philippe frowned. Who was Monsieur Courtland and why was he writing to the child he was going to marry?

Monique waddled in. She was pale and unhappy looking.

"How was your walk today?" Marie-Odile asked without interest.

"I went too far," Monique answered sitting with a small breathless groan.

"You should be careful on a hot day like this."

"The packet arrives in the morning," Renault said. "I trust you are packed."

"I am." Monique's voice was tight with anger. She resented being packed off home like a sulky child.

"Good," he said not looking at her. He took up Aurore next to him on the sofa and smiled down at her. "Tell me what Monsieur Courtland said in his letter."

"He's with General Stuart," Aurore said with bubbling excitement in her eyes. She looked very pretty with her long black hair looped into braids on either side of her face. Her dark blue gown was one of

Marie-Odile's cut down for her. It was trimmed with a paler shade of blue lace that set off her creamy white skin to perfection.

"Your daughter looks very beautiful this evening," Philippe said approaching them. He stared at her tracing the outline of her figure from her swelling bosom to her narrow wrists folded sedately in her lap.

"Thank you, Monsieur," Aurore replied looking at him searchingly then looking away. Her father stood up and allowed Monsieur D'Arcy to take his place. Aurore shifted away not liking the smell of his clothes.

"Is this Monsieur Courtland a friend of yours?" Philippe asked. He admired the curve of her long neck under the coil of her hair. She was a proud child who returned his look uncomfortably. He took her hand, but she twisted her fingers out of his grip instantly.

"He is our neighbor at St. Angele," Aurore said not liking the bold, intimate look in his eyes. She felt as though he could see through her clothes to her naked skin. She colored in embarrassment.

"Do you like him?"

"He is a good friend," Aurore said her voice cool and indifferent. Some instinct told her not to reveal her true liking for Gayle to this man. "When I was younger, I had a fawn that he helped me nurse when its leg was broken. But it grew up and went back to the woods where it belonged. He said all wild things should be allowed to remain wild."

"He sounds a wise man," Philippe said leaning back in relief. He had half been afraid there was more to this relationship than just friendship. But she seemed to think of this man as nothing more than a neighbor who had saved an animal's life once.

"My husband has invited you to stay for dinner, Monsieur," Marie-Odile said drawing Philippe's attention to herself. His look at Aurore was too intimate for comfort. True, Aurore had grown into a very pretty young woman constantly drawing the looks of men in the street, but she was still a long way from the beauty that she would soon become. There was too much immaturity in her oval face and innocent eyes.

"I am honored, Madame," Philippe said to his hostess. And afterwards, the announcement of his betrothal to Aurore would be made and she would be his. He glanced back at Aurore wondering how she would take the announcement.

Dinner was pleasant. Monique did not add to the conversation. Her normally loud complaints were silent as she studied her plate with elaborate concern. Occasionally she would glance up at Fleur with fearful questioning looks.

Renault was pleased with himself. He smiled at Philippe and Aurore even allowing Aurore a tiny amount of wine with such good spirits his wife began to wonder what the gaiety was all about.

"Before you ladies leave the table," Renault said when the meal ended, "I have an announcement to make. I have come to an agreement with Monsieur D'Arcy. He has asked for Aurore for a wife and I have given my permission."

There was silence at the table. Marie-Odile smiled and Aurore's mouth dropped open in surprise.

"To my future bride," Philippe raised his glass in a toast to his intended who gaped at him unbelieving.

"To a happy future," Renault said with equal fervor.

466

"No!" Aurore burst out. "I won't marry him."

Everyone's smiles were replaced with frowns at her interruption.

"You are to marry Monsieur D'Arcy, Aurore," Renault said firmly. "The arrangements are made."

"I will not," she said with equal firmness.

Father and daughter glared at each other across the length of the dining room table. Philippe shifted uncomfortably in his chair. He found it hard to believe a well-brought up Creole woman would dare to defy her father, yet he had expected some sort of reaction. It was her boldness and pride that made him ask for Aurore. There was nothing timid about her and he wanted nothing timid in a wife.

"Marget's marriage is a farce. I do not want a like one."

"You have no opinion in the matter. You are to wed Monsieur D'Arcy when the war is over. I will hear no more on the matter."

Aurore stood scowling fiercely. Even in her anger she was lovely. Her breasts pressed against her bodice as her chest heaved in anger. Suddenly she stalked from the room slamming the dining room door behind her.

"There is nothing to worry about, Philippe," Renault assured his future son-in-law. "She will marry you."

Marie-Odile said nothing. She looked from the determined face of her husband to the lusting face of Philippe D'Arcy. She felt a faint schill come over her, a feeling of foreboding.

"May I be excused?" she asked looking questioningly at Renault. He nodded curtly, his face full of annoyance for Aurore. "I shall go talk to her."

"She will come to realize this is for the best," Renault said when his wife and Fleur were gone.

"I shall woo her," Philippe said. "She is very beautiful. She will be a wife any man would be proud to own."

"Of course," Renault said. "To a happy future and a secure marriage."

"To me," Philippe said softly his eyes gazing at his wineglass reflectively. "To me."

"I will not marry him," Aurore cried.

"You have no choice," her mother said gently. "It is your duty to marry where your father wishes."

"He is old and fat," she said, her eyes glittering with stubbornness.

"You have no choice," Marie-Odile repeated.

"There are worse things than a loveless marriage," Luce said walking into Aurore's bedroom.

"Are there no secrets in this house?" Marie-Odile asked with a faint smile.

"Not when I can hear the shouting in the kitchen."

"What can be worse than marriage to one man while in love with another," Aurore asked cautiously watching her mother from under the black veil of her lashes.

Marie-Odile was shocked. Who could her daughter love? She was only a child, but a child verging on womanhood.

"Are you speaking of Monsieur Courtland?" Luce asked.

"I suppose so," Aurore said. Suddenly huge tears rolled down her cheeks evidence of her confusion.

"How can you be in love with that man?" Marie-Odile demanded tightly. "You are only a child."

"I am old enough to be pushed into marriage with Monsieur D'Arcy. Doesn't that make me old enough to love another man?"

"Not now, Aurore," Luce said softly pulling the girl away from her mother and sitting her down at her dressing table. Expertly, Luce pulled the pins from Aurore's hair to let it fall about her shoulders while she picked up a brush and started to pull it through the lustrous blue-black hair.

"Monsieur D'Arcy will be your husband. You must put all thoughts of Monsieur Courtland from you. He is not for you, nor will your father ever consider him. He is not suitable. He is a gambler and a . . . a killer." Marie-Odile could not prevent the shock from entering her voice. She stared at her daughter who was suddenly a stranger. The thoughts of Gayle Courtland had softened her face and brought a strange light to her eyes.

"Child, child," Luce murmured, "It will do no good to say these things."

But Marie-Odile was gone, her skirt snapping around the corner of the open door and her footsteps sounding a swift staccato in the hall.

"I can't marry Monsieur D'Arcy," Aurore said, two huge tears rolling down her cheeks.

"You will do what you must," Luce said gently. She undressed Aurore and slipped her into her nightgown. When she was in bed, Luce kissed her good-night and turned out the lamps.

"Good night, Luce," Aurore said to the shadow in the doorway.

469

Luce closed the door and stood in the hall staring at the wall. A murmur of voices from the drawing room drifted up the stairs. It was a mistake, she thought. No one was going to force Aurore to do anything she refused to do. Renault was beginning a second tragedy for this little family.

In her room, Luce closed the door and locked it. With the grace of her indian ancestors, she walked to her bureau and opened the bottom drawer feeling for the familiar lines of her bowls and jars wrapped in their black cloth. She drew them out and sat down in the middle of the floor to unwarp them. One copper bowl, two candles and two firmly sealed jars were set carefully on the floor. She murmured a chant as she shook out the cloth and smoothed it across the floor. She opened a jar, swirling the sacred water around a few times before pouring it into the copper bowl. She opened two soft pouches and took a pinch of the aromatic contents and threw the dust over her shoulders. Then she lit the candles and set them on either side of the bowl.

Luce was ready. Her chant changed to a steady, hypnotic murmur. In her mind, she saw her mother teaching her the meaning of the chant when Luce had been small. How beautiful her mother had been in life and how horrible she had been in death. Luce's great sadness overwhelmed her as she sat on the floor, sadness for her lost youth and for Aurore's empty future.

She opened two more pouches and breathed in their startling fragrances. The fragrances mingled with the incense of the candles swirling around and around her head. She smiled dreamily leaning over the copper

470

bowl with its clear water slowly changing to mist.

Luce held the copper bowl in her hands, swirling the water gently and staring into it. Her lips moved as she called up long abandoned gods begging them for a glimpse into Aurore's future. The water rippled faintly as she held the bowl.

The picture was hazy. The outlines blurred. The longer she stared the more the outlines moved into and out of focus. Then the mist cleared and Luce saw the street outside the de Champlain home.

Aurore stood on the street across from the house. She wore a simple gown of dark green, her hair pulled back from her face and tucked into a neat roll at her neck. She stared at the house with a mixture of longing and dread. She looked behind her and spoke, then a man stepped next to her. A man who looked down at her with blazing love in his eyes. A man who was a stranger to Luce. A man who was neither Gayle Courtland or Philippe D'Arcy. He was young with dark hair and blue eyes. His face was deeply chiseled and lean. Aurore looked up at him, her face radiant with love. She opened her mouth to speak. The picture faded.

Luce almost dropped the bowl from weak fingers. But she managed to set it carefully on the black cloth, then she shut her eyes and breathed deeply to regain her strength. Absently she rubbed her neck to ease the pain of her unnatural angle.

Who was he? she cried silently. Who was this man whom Aurore stood with? Luce frowned. Whoever he had been, he had also been Aurore's husband. A bright gold wedding band had shone on her finger.

Luce sighed and began to clean away her ritual

returning her wrapped bowl, candles and jars to her drawer. It was not in her to question what she saw. She simply knew Aurore's future was beyond the scheming of her father. It would happen in spite of him.

The union officer who knocked at the door was a pleasant looking young man with sandy brown hair and a matching beard and mustache.

"Is Mr. de Champlain at home?" he asked. Persia nodded briefly wondering if this was another meddling soldier trying to free a man who had been free for most of his life. "Can I see him? I'm Capt. Marshall."

"Come in," Persia said standing aside to let the young officer in. Only then did he see the four soldiers on the street who moved to stand in front of the steps.

"What can I do for you, Captain Marshall?" Renault said looking up from his book as the young man walked into his study.

"Don't be long," Marie-Odile said as she left the room. "I should like to finish my household accounts today."

"Brandy, Captain?"

"This is not a social call, sir," Captain Marshall said gravely. He looked about noting the fading elegance of the room and felt a slight contempt. This is what the South's noble cause had brought its people to. They were beggars and refused to admit it.

"You have a daughter, sir?"

"I have five daughters, Captain," Renault said, grinning in wry amusement.

"You have a daughter named Fleur."

"Yes." Renault frowned at the man.

"I have a warrant for her arrest." The Captain held out a document to Renault who took it and read it swiftly.

"The reason, Captain?"

"Espionage," Captain Marshall said flatly.

Renault looked so startled, the Captain decided not to add that his daughter was also a notorious prostitute in the city.

"I don't believe it. It's ridiculous. She's only sixteen."

"We have been watching her activities for weeks."

"But she only goes to the convent to teach," Renault said while in the back of his mind he remembered his wife's uneasiness over their daughter's activities.

"Even teachers can be spies," Captain Marshall said softly aware that this man had no idea who or what his daughter was. It was not his place to enlighten him.

"Hurry," Luce said to Fleur, pulling her from the kitchen and up the back stairs. "Come with me."

"What's the matter?" Fleur asked scrambling after the tall woman anxiously. There was fear in her voice.

"There are soldiers here to arrest you for spying."

"What!" Fleur stopped in the middle of the hall to stare wildly at Luce.

"There's no time. You have to leave immediately or you will be arrested. Do you want to be sent to prison?"

Fleur sprang after Luce who headed for her bedroom and dragged a valise out of the wardrobe and shoved some clothes into it. Fleur grabbed her

473

cloak and then reached into the darkened depths of the wardrobe to bring out a bag heavy with gold coins. She shoved it into the valise and walked to the window. Luce tore it open and pushed Fleur out and into the spreading magnolia tree.

"Climb up into the leaves and hide," Luce ordered. "There is a shelter up further Persia built for Aurore's use when she was little. When it is safe I will come back for you and help you out of the city. You can't stay here any longer."

Fleur scrambled up the tree, her feet automatically searching for the old steps nailed into the trunk. Her dark cloak hid her effectively as she climbed into the small shelter and crouched among the leaves.

"I'll be back," Luce promised. She closed the window and looked about the room cleaning away the signs of Fleur's flight. Then she went out the door and down the stairs, her hands folded sedately at her waist.

"Search the house," Captain Marshall said to his soldiers. The men thundered into the hall and started throwing open doors and looking under and around furniture.

Marie-Odile clung helplessly to Luce. She stared at her husband in fear.

"What is it?" she asked in a quivering voice.

"Fleur has gotten herself involved with an espionage group working here in the city. These men are here to arrest her."

"Oh, my God," Marie-Odile wailed half fainting in shock. "She's just a child."

The Captain looked at Marie-Odile. He started to tell her just what her daughter was, but changed his

474

mind at the deathly pallor of the woman's face. It would serve no purpose to enlighten these people on their daughter's choice of profession. As for being a child, Fleur was old enough to understand a lot of things. Captain Marshall knew only too well what she knew. He had spent a lot of hours in her hotel room sampling her merchandise.

"The girl is not here, Captain," one of the men said as he clattered down the stairs.

Aurore stood at the top of the stairs with Therese clutching at her skirts. Delphine's white face showed behind them, her eyes rolling in terror.

"Do you know where she is?" Captain Marshall demanded harshly. Only bewildered faces stared at him.

Only Luce could not quite hide the grin of triumph. The Captain stared hard at her, then dismissed her as an ignorant negro who would hardly understand what was going on.

"She's only sixteen. How can you arrest a child?" Marie-Odile cried.

"A spy can be sixteen just as easily as thirty," the man retorted.

"Extended the search to the outside," one of the soldiers said at the Captain's nod.

"Order more guards," Marshall said. "Cordon off the house and arrest anyone who tries to leave. When you find the girl, bring her to me."

"Fleur," Luce said softly to the dark tree. A few early night stars twinkled lazily in the sky.

There was no answer. Luce called again. Again there was no answer. Fleur was gone.

Luce eyed the tree anxiously. She hoped Fleur had enough sense to leave the city immediately without stopping at her hotel room.

Fleur walked down the streets wondering what to do next. She had started for her hotel room, but a light in the window told her there were soldiers there. She hoisted her valise and started down a dark alley carefully avoiding sentries.

How to leave the city was a problem. She could hardly walk away or hail a cab. She had to think of something soon, it was nearly curfew. She started walking aimlessly, her feet dragging in satin slippers not made for outside hikes.

She stopped in surprise to see that she was at the levee gazing at six ships tied up at moorings. She bit the inside of her lips trying to think. Would they search the ships? Instinct and commonsense told her yes. But then again . . .

The nearest ship was dark. Fleur studied it a moment, holding grimly onto her valise. She thought of the money in it carefully saved for the last two years. She thought it was a lot, but compared to what she needed to keep her in comfort the rest of her life it was precious little.

The next ship was dark. She passed it. The third ship had a light, but it was a river packet preparing for a journey upriver. The next ship was also dark, but the last one had a light and several sailors straggled on board holding each other up. It was an ocean going ship. With a slight shrug, Fleur walked up the gangplank.

"Identify yourself," a voice barked.

"Fleur jumped startled. "I want to see the Captain," she said to a tall, dark figure.

"Who are you?"

"Do you take passengers?"

"This is a navy vessel, ma'am. We don't take passengers."

"Can I see the Captain anyway? Please. It's very important."

"Just a minute," he said and disappeared down the gangway. In minutes he returned and beckoned her to follow.

"Here's the lady, sir," the sailor said opening a door to show a lighted cabin and a man sitting at a desk. The sailor saluted smartly and stepped back to allow Fleur entrance.

"Come in, ma'am." The Captain stared at Fleur fuzzily. An overturned glass on his desk and an empty decanter told its own story.

"I need passage out of New Orleans," Fleur said with a sultry smile. She closed the door behind her and stood in the lamplight studying the man. He was middle aged with gray streaked hair and beard. He wore a dark coat over a white shirt opened at the throat.

"This is not a passenger vessel."

"You carry cargo. Can't you just think of me as cargo," Fleur said. She dropped her valise on the deck and opened up her cloak. His eyes wandered over her slim body hungrily.

"It's a matter of life or death," she said arching an eyebrow and running a hand lightly over the underside of her breast.

The Captain stared at her. She was a pretty baggage even if she was a Southerner.

"We're going to Texas," he said thickly.

Fleur began with her top buttons. He watched in hypnotic fascination as she stepped from her gown, revealing her petticoats and chemise.

"I do have to leave the city," she said softly, dropping her undergarments. The candlelight gleamed on her skin. She smiled as she stroked her breasts, the nipples hardening under her expert fingers.

"I sail in two days' time," the captain said hoarsely unable to take his eyes from the small, jutting breasts. He reached for his buttons to release his swollen manhood. He licked his dry lips.

"You will take me, won't you?" Fleur pleaded. She walked to him and placed his hands on her breasts.

"You'd have to stay hidden here."

Fleur slid his coat off and swiftly unbuttoned his shirt. She ran her hands over the hair of his chest. Oddly, it was still a thick, silky black. Reaching for his trousers she found the buttons already undone and the root of his desire protruding rigidly.

"I don't mind staying in your cabin."

She smelled of a deep, arousing perfume. He pressed his lips to her breasts and ran his hands down the shapely curves of her back. He sucked at the hollow of her throat and the red tips of her breasts, running his hands down her belly to the secrets between her thighs. He brought her to the floor.

"I'll take you to Corpus Christi, he said.

"It's far enough," Fleur said, her dark hair spread over the floorboards. She ran her hand down the length of his body. With a groan he enveloped her.

Thirty

1864

There's a loss of humanity in war. It is a time when men are urged to fight, told to kill. They organize themselves into armies with intent to devastate the enemy. Kill! Destroy! Win the war! Preserve the South! Preserve the North! It was bloodlust, hatred, disease, and death.

Death was everywhere. It sickened Gayle. It changed him. There were times when he no longer knew himself. As a gambler, he had accepted death on a personal level. But war was not death, it was slaughter. It made him hard and callous. Yet he killed and would kill again while a small part of his mind grew sick with it.

"Colonel, are you going to stand there all day staring at that tree?"

"Sorry, General." Gayle roused himself from his grim and dismal thoughts. His attention returned to the collection of maps strewn across the table before him. General J.E.B. Stuart watched him, waiting patiently.

Jeb Stuart was not ordinarily a patient man, yet neither was he impatient. He regarded Col. Courtland with understanding eyes and waited.

"There's Union canon here and here, sir," Gayle said, his voice strained with effort. He moved his gloved hands across the map pointing out positions. Occasionally, he looked at his own small map with hastily written scrawls across it. Each Union position was carefully pointed out until dozens of scrawls covered General Stuart's map, as well.

This was a part of war, too, Gayle thought even as his voice calmly continued. Spying on the enemy, or as it was more politely called, reconnaissance.

"Very good, Colonel," Stuart said. He bent over the map studying it.

Gayle was pushed away as the rest of the General's staff moved in for closer looks.

Gayle waited for several moments in case he was wanted again, but then he wandered away heading for the small group of his best men sitting on a grassy knoll watching their horses grazing.

"Was he impressed," Sergeant, formerly Corporal Sawyer, asked.

Gayle shrugged. He sat down on the grass accepting a tin plate of cold beans and hard bread from Sawyer.

"Saved it for you," the Sergeant said.

Gayle looked at it with resignation. After a week in the saddle being cold and hungry, he would have liked a little warm food. Visions of feasts being held at Grey Lawns and Aurore on her mare with cake and candy glued to her face swept over him. He wished he were home, warm and comforted. He thought of Aurore, almost grown to womanhood, and another ache filled him.

"Meade's army is moving this way," Sawyer said,

leaning back and filling his pipe. The tobacco was old and sour. But he lit it anyway ignoring the stale cloud that rose from the bowl. "Looks like the North is going to push to Richmond. Only logical place left to fight over."

"There's not much of the South left," Gayle mumbled around his bread. Vicksburg fell in '63, New Orleans in '62. The Union army controlled the whole of the Mississippi River, most of Louisiana, all of Arkansas, Tennessee, Kentucky, Mississippi and Florida. There wasn't much South left to defend anymore. The war would be over soon. The South was on the run, preparing for its last gasp, short on everything. The North had an unlimited supply of food, medicine, clothing and men. Especially the men. The South was running dry of men.

"Picked up a letter from the Quartermaster for you," Sawyer said when Gayle was finished with his meal. He drew an incredibly dirty envelope out of his pocket. He handed it to Gayle.

The writing was almost totally obscured. His name was faintly readable along with part of his regiment number. It was a miracle the letter had arrived at all.

It was from Aurore. For a moment, Gayle felt a thrill of excitement lift his lethargy. He lived for the few letters that reached him from her. They were an anchor in a world gone crazy.

He read the first page, then went back and read it again. The handwriting was small, difficult to read. Suddenly he felt a spurt of anger mixed with fear.

The letter was two pages long. It was not chatty, or newsy. It was a stark letter, from a child whose illusions were long gone. Aurore described the conditions in the city, the lack of food and medicines. She wrote angrily about the treatment of the women in the city by the soldiers. She mentioned Fleur's disappearance and the reason behind it. She told of Philippe D'Arcy and her engagement. The strain she was under showed in the precise wording of the letter, the careful rounding of her letters. And the fear she felt for Philippe on one line where her hand trembled too much to write. There was desperation and pleading in her words.

"I love you," ended the letter. In that moment Gayle came as close to deserting as his honor would allow.

"Bad news, Colonel?" Sawyer asked in sudden concern. Since their first meeting in Florida, he had seen many different sides of the man he had come to admire, but the dark, bleak look in Gayle's eyes were different from any other.

"It's nothing," Gayle said, his voice taut with strain. He folded the letter with elaborate care. He felt dead inside. If he was dead, why didn't he fall over? Why didn't the sounds stop, his vision cloud? Aurore! She was the one hope he still clung to. The last hope he allowed himself to have. And now, she was being taken away. He was half to his feet unaware of the tortured, furied face he showed.

"Colonel," Sawyer said, one hand restraining him drawing him back to sit on the grass.

Gayle thought nothing, said nothing. He sat back and stared, a man possessed.

Shouts sounded in the distance. Gayle looked up as a squad of men rushed by, their rifles ready.

"Find out what that is all about," he said.

the men asked jokingly. "A real, honest silver dollar?"

"To buy meat and clothes with," a younger voice called. There was thin laughter as the men rolled to their feet.

"We're going on recon," Gayle said, "Draw three days supply of food. Sergeant Sawyer, there's a Lt. Taggert with General Stuart right now. Go over and wait for him. He and his men are joining us."

In an hour the horses were saddled, fresh supplies in bulging sacks and worn blankets were being tied to the saddles. The men were ready.

Gayle stood in the center as his men grouped around him. Tired men, ragged men fighting for a dying cause. Yet, they would fight on because there was nothing left to do. A few were from Louisiana, most were from Georgia. Lt. Taggert, a tall hawk-featured man and his dozen men were Texans.

"Sheridan is east of us about three miles," Gayle said, his voice loud during a lull of stillness. "He's moving his army South toward Richmond. General Stuart needs what information we can get, artillery, mounted troops, foot soldiers. We are to harass Sheridan, but not to engage in any major entanglements. I will set up our command post here." Gayle pointed to a crudely drawn map in the dust. "Report to me as soon as possible. Let's ride."

The men mounted and fell in behind Gayle as he spurred his horse to the head of the group. Lt. Taggert followed him, his deep blue eyes missing nothing, his heels dug into the sides of a bony gelding who pranced nervously.

"I was in New Orleans once," Taggert said softly. "Pretty place. I liked it there."

The sergeant nodded. He pointed at two men who got to their feet wearily and followed him.

"Deserters, Colonel," Sawyer said when he came back, his voice and eyes reflecting his derision and contempt. "Trying to sneak off to Richmond. Someone told them there was food there."

Deserters! More and more men were deserting, going home. Not because they were cowards, but because they were tired of war, cold and hungry.

"It will be over soon."

Gayle looked up to find General Stuart standing a few feet away. Together they watched the armed guard come back with several young men in their midst. Not men, boys. Homesick little boys, who wanted to go back to Mom and Dad, brother and sister, warm fires, and fresh clothes.

"They are just boys, General," Gayle said wearily. The urge to desert died in him. He pushed himself to his feet and stood next to the man who commanded him.

"I know," the General said softly, compassionately. "I know."

"Rouse the men, Sergeant," Gayle said in the early morning yellow. He pushed at Sawyer with his foot. The other man rolled smoothly to his feet already alert. There was the sound of firing in the distance, cannon booming. The acid smell of gunpowder hung in the still air.

"Another day, another dollar," Sawyer grumbled as he moved among the ragged group on the ground clutching threadbare blankets to patched uniforms.

"When was the last time you saw a dollar," one of

Gayle shrugged indifferently. New Orleans would never be the same once the war was over. Aurore would be married, his home probably destroyed. There would be nothing there for him.

The task of recognizing the units composing Sheridan's army did not take long. Proud banners waved in the breeze, laughter and talk floated to Gayle as he squatted on the ground marking his map. The column was thirteen miles long and moving quickly toward Richmond. The war could end today. If Richmond fell, the heart of the South would be gone. There would be nothing left. Lee would be cut off from retreat.

"We have quite a party," Lt. Taggert said conversationally as he stared at the swiftly moving column of Union cavalry.

Gayle said nothing. He was thinking about the letter in his pocket. The letter that would remove Aurore from his life.

"Colonel!" Taggert said sharply.

Gayle looked at him, half-smiled, then went back to his contemplation of his map. Sheridan's manuever was bold, but if Jeb Stuart could get in position in time, he could be stopped.

"I played cards in Galveston a long time ago," Gayle mused. "It was pretty dull there."

"Not anymore," Taggert said wryly. "The union held it for a few months in '62, but lost it. They've been tightening the blockade around it ever since."

"Been with Stuart long?" Gayle asked after a slight silence.

"Was in Vicksburg with my Texas outfit. When the city fell to the North a few of my men and I slipped

485

away and re-enlisted with a Mississippe outfit. Good thing it was cavalry. In Texas, no man walks when he can ride even if it's just across the street."

"We'd better be getting back to Stuart with this information. You stay here, group the men and bring them back."

It was after midnight when Gayle finally left General Stuart's tent. Sergeant Sawyer lay outside the tent, their horses picketed nearby.

"Let's go," Gayle said, rousing him gently.

"Lt. Taggert's picketed the men about a half-mile down the road."

Gayle nodded wearily.

Cole Taggert was still up waiting for Gayle. He sat in front of a fire so tiny it was barely visible. A battered coffee pot sat in the middle.

"Want some," Taggert asked when Gayle sat next to him. Sawyer led their horses away and picketed them with the rest.

"Pretty bad," Gayle commented. He didn't really care. It was warm. It filled up the hollowness in his belly.

"In Texas, we call it hogwash," Taggert said wryly.

"You have a name for everything in Texas."

"Yep!"

Gayle sat for a time staring at the flickering fire. Finally it went out. He picked up the coffee pot and poured the coffee over it carefully preserving the dregs for the next pot. He lay down, wrapping his blanket around him and fell asleep.

He woke to cold rain and black skies. The hard ground had turned to mud. He was soaked through to the skin.

"I hate rain," Sawyer spat as he walked over to Gayle leading his horse. The animal sank into the ground, pulling its hooves out of the mud with little sucking noises. "I hate mud, too."

"Save your hate for the enemy," Gayle said grimly. There were a few gunshots. "We're to hold this position."

"Strange morning," Taggert said pulling his horse to a sliding stop next to Gayle's. Gunfire sounded in the dark distance.

"One of my men saw a white owl this morning," Taggert went on. "Swears it's an omen of some sort. Truth is, he doesn't know a good omen from a bad."

Gayle said nothing. He felt as grim and foreboding as the darkness. A mist was revealing with the coming light. A swirling mist, ghostly and frightening. The rain seemed to add to the mist instead of dispelling it.

A man ran out of the mist toward the line of horses. His blue uniform invisible until he was close to Gayle. Sawyer calmly sighted his rifle at the man and fired. The man went down, twitched, then lay still. Blood spurted from a gaping hole in his chest.

"Damn Yankee," Sawyer said grimly.

Other men were breaking across the field toward the line of Confederate cavalry.

"Fire at will," he said hoarsely. Rising nausea forced him to swallow convulsively.

A volley of shots thundered through the mist. Men stumbled, fell, and died. Men who had been alive with families awaiting their return and who would now mourn their deaths.

Who will mourn my death? Gayle mused as he fired. His horse trembled under his legs. A man in the

Confederate line screamed, went down. His horse bolted, stumbling across the field where dead bodies were twisted grotesquely under the runaway hooves.

Gayle fired again. He thought of Aurore, lost to him now. He would welcome death.

Then the battle was on them, and Gayle ceased to think.

"We're dropping back and forming a new line," the tight-lipped messenger said.

Gayle already knew Stuart's force was not strong enough to stop Sheridan. But it was strong enough to make his advance to Richmond difficult.

Gayle signaled his men.

"We're retreating," Cole Taggert said.

"We're setting up a second line of defense. We're not defeated, yet."

"We're outnumbered," Taggert said grimly.

"But not defeated," Gayle repeated stubbornly.

Night fell. The battle slowed, but not much. Gayle caught a few hours of sleep to wake to a steady pouring of rain from the black sky. Daylight came, chill and damp making men and animals shiver. An infantry troop was dug in ahead of Gayle's unit. They lay on the damp ground, rifles pointed at a clearing and line of trees beyond.

A ripple of excitement ran through the Confederate lines. No matter that war was a frightening hell. It was still exciting.

"They're coming," someone shouted.

Richmond was less than six miles away. The line had to be held at all costs.

Rifle fire drew closer. Confederate cavalry burst

into the clearing. Followed by Union cavalry. Gunfire, the clash of swords, the screams of the dying shattered the peace of the little clearing.

Gayle looked left and right. Other units were preparing for the fight. Gayle felt no excitement. He felt sick.

"Prepare to fire," he said, his voice hoarse. "Fire."

The fleeing Confederate cavalry burst past them. A barrage of gunfire sent Union horses and men to the ground. Riderless horses milled confused around the field.

"Fire at will," Gayle screamed. The second barrage erupted. The oncoming enemy stopped, fell back, and regrouped. Then the war continued.

Gayle fired his pistol until it was steaming when rain hit the hot barrel. He fired point-blank at a grinning mouth. The mouth exploded blood and teeth, curling into a silent scream of terror.

"Colonel, behind you."

Gayle turned to find a bayoneted rifle aimed at his throat. He fired again. A youth fell silently from his horse, his face blown away. He sat heavily on the ground and fell back. His terrified horse rearing and planting two huge hooves on a face already dead.

Another soldier lunged at Gayle. He pointed his pistol at him, fired and the man fell back clutching his arm. He pulled his horse back.

His revolver empty, Gayle had no time to reload. He drew his saber. A boy hardly older than Aurore reached for him. The saber sliced through his body as though it had been a loaf of bread. Blood spurted soaking Gayle.

He turned and slashed again and again. Men fell,

groaned, and were still. The rain became a downpour.

Abruptly the Union cavalry pulled back across the clearing. Gayle watched, his bloodlust drained.

"Colonel!"

Gayle swung around. The flash of a young face and a blue uniform dashed at him. Gayle brought down his saber. The hurtling body impaled itself on the tip. The young face stared at Gayle in astonishment mixed with terror. Then he sagged, falling to the ground, the saber slipped out of him. He was so young. Gayle bent over him. The boy's mouth opened. Blood, not words, spilled from him. The eyes pleaded with him. Gayle took the boy's hand and held it while he died.

He wasn't aware he was crying until Cole Taggert pulled him to his feet and led him from the body.

"He was only a boy," Gayle sobbed. "What kind of war is this?"

"But old enough to want to kill you," Cold said.

Gayle wiped his face of the blood, and dirt.

"We're pulling back again," Cole continued. He signaled Sawyer, who led Gayle's horse to him. Gayle could not remember when he'd dismounted. "And . . . General Stuart was badly wounded today."

"The General! He's indestructible!"

"He's not expected to last the night."

"We're all going to die," Gayle said looking around at the day's carnage. What had once been a small forest clearing was now a place of death and destruction. "If we're falling back, assemble the men. Taggert, and let's get going."

"Yes, sir," Cole said, watching Gayle regain his poise.

Gayle took one last look at the field, feeling an infinite sadness for himse.f, Aurore, and the future.

Thirty-one

Every Sunday afternoon promptly at two o'clock, Philippe D'Arcy presented himself at the de Champlain home. His hair was slicked down, he wore his best broadcloth suit. Sometimes he brought a small bouquet of sad little flowers. Other times, he would bring a small, preciously rare, box of candy.

"Good afternoon, Monsieur," Aurore said politely as Philippe bowed to her. She was conscious of the frayed hem of her gown, the tired lace around her wrists which concealed cuffs too short for arms grown long.

"Good afternoon, Mademoiselle," Philippe answered with stilted politeness. He studied the thin, oval face hungrily. This enchanting creature would be his one day. The elfin face, the wide eyes, and the exquisite body would belong to him and him alone. She was perfection, she was beautiful. The most beautiful of her sisters. But she was so cool to him, so aloof.

He took her hand, squeezing it feverishly. She raised large, distant black eyes to him. She withdrew her hand firmly and backed away. Philippe swallowed his anger. He would allow her this small bit of independent revolt. She would be his regardless.

"How nice of Monsieur to visit when he is so busy,"

Marie-Odile chatted inanely to cover the silence. "You work very hard, Monsieur."

"It is always a pleasure to take time to visit a beautiful woman," he purred, his eyes never leaving the small shadows on her chest cast by her breasts.

"Sunday is the Lord's day," Aurore said gravely. "It is supposed to be reserved for him and not for work."

"But in these confusing days I must tend to my business when it presents itself." Even he was conscious of the shiny patches on his suit. He did not like being poor. "Of course, when we are married, I shall do my best to leave Sunday strictly a family day. You will find I am a devoted husband and father, Mademoiselle."

"Aurore is very religious," Marie-Odile said. It was not exactly true. Aurore obediently went to Mass every day, but she did little more than give lip-service to the traditions.

"That is good in a wife," Philippe said approvingly. He beamed at Aurore and was piqued when she looked away.

"Why," she asked turning back to him, her dark eyes alive with mischief.

"It is improper for a woman to have any other interests other than her church and family," he answered promptly. He stared at her envisioning her pale body writhing in passion beneath his. She would be a passionate wife. He could see it in her. He was in a fever to be married to her, but she was barely fifteen and the decision had been made to wait for the war's end.

"Oh!" Aurore said distantly losing interest. She glanced at Jewel who rolled large eyes to the ceiling in mock despair. Then she looked away stifling a giggle. Like Aurore, she found the Monsieur to be laughable.

"I think I shall check on Luce in the kitchen. You will stay for dinner, Monsieur?"

"It would be my greatest pleasure."

Aurore muffled a groan. She hated it when he stayed for dinner which was most Sundays.

Marie-Odile rose with the grace of a queen and swept from the room with dignity. Outside in the hall, she looked at her watch, and sat down on the stairs to wait out the required ten minutes before she returned to the room.

"Will you walk with me in Jackson Square after dinner?"

"It is up to Maman, Monsieur," Aurore said looking down at her hands. There were times when Maman would forbid the outing, Aurore hoped today would be one of them.

"I've a surprise for you," Philippe said. He moved to sit next to her taking her dainty hand in his. There were callouses on the slim hands. He frowned when he touched them.

"The day will come when you will not have to ask your Maman for permission to do anything." Philippe hinted broadly. He glanced at the door wondering how long he had before Madame returned. When he looked back at Aurore he was disconcerted to find Jewel standing next to her mistress her own dark eyes taunting and bold. He wondered what the mulatto body looked like under the simple calico gown.

"Do you wish coffee?" Aurore asked.

"Yes," Philippe said and was disappointed when she jumped up and went to the urn steaming on the sideboard. She poured him coffee and returned to him with the cup.

Aurore sat down again on another chair not quite facing him. She was afraid of Philippe. She did not like it when he touched her, or watched the rise and fall of her bosom as she breathed.

"You are not listening to me, my dear."

Aurore was brought back from her thoughts by a sharp rap across her knuckles. She glared at Philippe. "I am not a child to be punished."

"When I am speaking to you, you will listen to what I am saying," he responded delighted with the look of anger in her face.

"What were you saying?" Aurore asked politely.

"I have engaged an apartment. It is very nice. You will like it. I am also planning to engage a new maid for you." He glanced at Jewel who stared insolently back at him. "As you can see, I am planning your future perfectly."

Aurore focused her eyes on him. They were cold, indifferent. "Plan what you will, Monsieur. But I am not marrying you. I have my own plans for my future."

Philippe stared at her, fury making the veins in his neck pop out. She watched him, daring him to shout or hit her. He almost did, but sense prevailed. He relaxed with an amused, superior smile. Let her have her moment of rebellion. The time will come when she will know who is her master.

Marie-Odile walked back into the room. She radiated charm and warmth. The tension dissolved around her and Philippe could sit back and relax.

"Someday, you will go too far," Jewel cautioned Aurore when they were alone.

"I am not going to marry that . . . that ass."

"You may end up doing exactly that," Jewel said grimly.

Aurore erupted into tears. She covered her face with her hands and sobbed into them.

Jewel put her arms around her young friend, soothing her, holding her fiercely. "If I could, I'd snap my fingers and end the war to bring Master Gayle back to you. But I can't. No one can."

"I love you, Jewel," Aurore said simply. She dried her eyes and allowed Jewel to help her out of her clothes and into her nightdress.

"Read awhile," Jewel suggested when Aurore was settled in bed. "I've some chores to do and then I'll bring up some hot cocoa."

"I'd like that," Aurore said. She inclined her head listening to the patter of rain against the windows. "I wonder where he is tonight?" She slid down into the blankets thinking of Gayle.

Jewel puttered about the room for a few minutes putting away clothes and pulling her trundle bed out from under Aurore's and turning down the blankets. She lay her own nightgown neatly across the pillow.

When Jewel was gone Aurore closed her eyes. She wanted to dream about Gayle, about being mistress of Grey Lawns. Slowly she drifted off to sleep.

Aurore was running. She looked behind her and saw two shadowy figures pursuing her through long twisting corridors that led nowhere. The two shadows called to her, their voices echoing eerily through the dark corridors. Aurore ran faster. She stopped at a door and tried to open it, but it was locked. She tried another and another. They were all locked except one tiny door that was too small for her to get through. She peered through the door panting with exhaustion. Philippe D'Arcy grinned back at her evilly.

Aurore woke up. For a moment she stared at the dark room trying to remember where she was. Then the thunderous pounding sounded again.

"Jewel!" Aurore slid out of bed and touched Jewel's bed only to find it empty. She found her robe and pulled it on. She ran out into the hall without realizing the pounding had stopped and there were voices in the hall.

She ran down the stairs only to meet Jewel running up.

"What's happening?" she asked curiously.

"Someone at the door," Jewel answered. She pushed past Aurore and ran down the hall to knock at the mistress's room.

Persia walked into the hall holding his candle high. He peered out into the dark, his candle a feeble light against the darkness.

Renault came into the hall drawing on his robe. "What's the meaning of this," he demanded as he went to the door to stand next to Persia. Persia shook his head.

"Some man . . ." Jewel began.

"Here, I need a hand," a voice called from the street. Aurore shrank back against the wall staring out the door. She trembled. There was a grunt and a moan.

A strange man walked into the house. An arm

dangled about his shoulder. He stepped into the light with Persia following, supporting the other arm, a bundle of rags dangling between them. Blood dripped onto the floor.

Aurore's heart seemed to stop. Then it started beating again erratically. For one long moment she thought it was Gayle. But then the man raised his head to give a hideous groan. It was Benoit de Ville. Benoit, the cocky soldier who had gone to play at war. He was home, but he had left a part of himself behind. Benoit de Ville had no legs!

"Is he dead?" Marie-Odile asked in a hushed voice. She stood in the doorframe watching the still, half-figure on the bed. His sunken chest barely moved as he breathed.

Dr. Laboutierre leaned over Benoit checking his pulse, heartbeat, and breathing. Then he laid back the sheets to expose two bloodied stumps.

Marie-Odile gasped. She swayed, but Renault held her steady.

"He is not dead, Madame," the doctor said curtly, "But he will be if we do not move quickly. Hot water, woman, lots of it," he said to Luce. "The blood has dried bonding the dressings to his stumps. We will have to soak them off."

Luce hurried away and returned with steaming water.

"Start soaking the bandages," the doctor ordered.

She applied wet, warm cloths to the dressings. Benoit screamed. He open a toothless mouth and let out a scream so hideous Aurore fell to the floor and cowered in the hall.

"You're hurting me! You're hurting me! Stop! Please!"

Luce looked up to encounter the doctor's troubled gaze. He bent over his patient again.

"Will he die?" Aurore asked when Marie-Odile turned around to find her daughter behind her on the floor. Her face was as pale as Benoit's.

"Go to your room, Aurore. This is no place for you."

Aurore left reluctantly. Once in her room, she knelt at her prie-dieu to say a prayer. But the prayer would not come. She thought of Gayle instead. She thanked God, it wasn't Gayle across the hall crying and screaming. She crossed herself and got into bed trying to sleep.

"Marget will have to come home," Renault said.

"How? We can't even get a letter to her."

"I will leave as soon as I can arrange a passage. There's a British ship in port, they might drop me off in Nassau if I pay them enough."

"It was at Spotsylvania," the young man who had brought Benoit home said.

Marie-Odile jumped. She had forgotten the boy who looked hardly older than Aurore. "You must be hungry."

"Yes, ma'am," he said politely.

"Come along. What little we have we can share. I'll see you have a warm place to spend the night."

"Thank you ma'am."

"It doesn't look good," Dr. Laboutierre said shaking his head over the mangled stumps. "It was a damn poor job of surgery. There isn't even enough flap to go over the wound."

"You must do the job properly," Luce said firmly.

"I didn't bring enough morphine for a long operation."

"I will put him to sleep while you prepare."

The doctor nodded. He ordered a frightened Jewel to bring more water, then he laid his instruments on the night table.

"No!" Benoit screamed. "No more! I beg you! No more!" He whimpered, tossing his head from side to side. "Where are my legs? What have you done with them? I can feel them. Why can't I see them?"

"Look at me," Luce commanded in a gentle voice. She took Benoit's head between her palms and turned it to look at her. "Look at me." Her voice was compelling, hypnotic. After several minutes murmuring, she turned to the doctor. "You may begin now."

Dr. Laboutierre looked at the calm, sleeping man, and went back to the cleaning of his instruments.

Hours later, he packed his case. He looked down at his patient. "I've done the best I can. I cut out the putrid flesh and shortened the bones. The flap is sewn on properly. It's in God's hands now."

"And mine," Luce whispered.

He looked at her. "And yours. You're a remarkable woman. I should like to talk to you sometime about tonight's work."

"Sometime," Luce said with a smile.

"I'll look in later in the day." He put on his coat as he left the room. As he left the house, the first rays of morning brightened the sky. It was going to be a hot day, he thought. He moved his shoulders to relieve some of the fatigue and then set off for his home.

Thirty-two

Marget sat on the second story veranda watching the street through the branches of the tall magnolia tree. The magnolia was in bloom, the sweet scent of the large, cream-colored flowers wrapping itself around her. For the rest of her life she would remember these moments of peace and contentment.

She leaned her head against the fanned back of her wicker chair. She closed her eyes listening to the street sounds below. For the rest of her life, she would love Nassau with its vibrant beauty and soft-spoken people. There was such a mixture of peoples on this island from the prim wives of the British delegation to the swaying mulatto women. Nassau was gay and beautiful. Marget loved it.

There was movement behind her. She craned her neck to see Neil walking into their bedroom muttering angrily. He tugged at his shirt and pulled at his neckcloth. He looked harried, but handsome.

"I wish you were coming with me," he said walking out onto the veranda. Mammy Juno followed him fussing as she straightened his neckcloth and brushed lint from his shoulders.

"The governor wants to see you, not me," Marget said smiling up at him lovingly. How handsome he was. How much she loved him. "Besides, I can't go."

He bent and kissed her, the ends of his new, sandy-colored mustache tickling her nose. "I love you," he whispered. "Damn this coat. It just doesn't fit right. I'm a sea captain, not a fashion plate." He tugged fitfully at his cuffs.

"You look extremely handsome. Now stop fidgeting and let Mammy Juno brush you off."

Mammy Juno lifted her broad, black moon face with a look of appeal in her eyes. Marget laughed. The other woman allowed a brilliant, flashing smile to part her thick lips.

"You'll rest while I'm gone," Neil said anxiously.

"I will, I promise. The doctor is coming by to check me though Mammy Juno swears I don't need him because she is the finest midwife on the island. I believe her and trust her."

"The doctor is certain you have two babies in there," he said running a hand over the great mound of her belly.

"I've always wanted twins," Marget said. The babies moved sluggishly. "Feel that? They know their Papa is here waiting for them as anxiously as their Maman."

"And me," Francois Honor cried running across the bedroom to touch his mother. "I'm waiting, too."

"Scamp!" Neil laughed, scooping the boy up into his arms and swinging him through the air. The three-year-old squealed with delight.

"You'll crease your coat," Marget said with a chuckle. "Put him down, Neil. You two can play later."

Neil put the boy down reluctantly. Francois Honor grinned.

"I've got to go, Scamp. Take care of Mammy Juno and your Maman for awhile."

The child nodded gravely.

"Neil, you're going to be late. You know how the governor likes punctuality."

Neil kissed Marget again, patted her belly one last time and left the room.

"It's time for your nap," Marget reminded Francois Honor.

"No!" he cried. Mammy Juno expertly swung him up in her arms.

"I'm going to take one, too." Marget watched the frown leave her son's face. She spoiled him. She knew it, but Mammy Juno and Neil added their share. "Kiss your Maman and go with Mammy Juno."

Francois did as he was told and went off to his nap without further protest.

"You lie down now," Mammy Juno said when she returned to the room.

Marget nodded agreement. She allowed the woman to help her to her feet and guide her to the bed. Mammy Juno slid Marget's peignoir off and helped her into bed pulling the cool sheets over her swollen body.

"It's so hot today," Marget said leaning back with a sigh.

"You sleep," Mammy Juno said. Expertly she massaged Marget's shoulders until she drifted off to sleep.

Mammy Juno tiptoed into the darkened room and watched her mistress a moment before reaching out a plump hand to touch her shoulder.

"What is it. Is the doctor here?"

"No doctor. Man here. He say you daughter." Mammy Juno helped her mistress up slipping her peignoir over her shoulders.

"My father!"

"Yes, mistress." Mammy Juno combed the tangles out of the long black hair and pulled it back from Marget's face. She tied a ribbon around the hair. "He say Madame de Ville. I say, no Madame de Ville. Madame Quinlann live here with man, boy-child."

Marget sighed. She pushed herself out of bed and stood awkwardly. "He had to know sometime."

Mammy Juno nodded agreement. She was sad that things would end now. She treasured the great love that existed between mistress and master.

"Show him up, Mammy Juno. Bring lemonade out onto the veranda. Then see if Francois Honor is awake. Get him ready to meet his *grand-pere*."

"This I do."

Marget walked slowly out onto the veranda and lowered herself into her chair. She felt so huge and ungainly. Why should her father choose now to visit her?

"Well, Marget. I hardly expected to arrive in Nassau and find you living openly with Captain Quinlan. I expected more discreet behavior from you." He walked toward her and stopped his eyes widening in astonishment.

"If you'd waited a little longer, Papa, you would have met your new grandchildren. Now you will have to wait."

"Marget!" His voice shook with horror as he stared at her.

"You are shocked?"

503

Renault was speechless. He glared at her. "How dare you bring disgrace to my name," he said coldly. "I came to bring you home and what do I find. You live openly with a man and call yourself wife to him and you shamelessly flaunt a big belly. You bring dishonor to your house. You have betrayed your most sacred vows . . ."

"Enough, Papa," Marget said holding out her hand. "You can say nothing that I have not already said to myself. And fought, yes fought, with myself and my conscience. Yet I decided to do what I have done."

"Why, Marget?" His eyes pleaded with her for understanding.

"Because I love Neil," she replied simply. "And I hate and fear Benoit. I need happiness and love to live. I have Neil now. I can't go back to Benoit. I love Neil, and I shall always love him. My little Francois Honor was conceived in hate. These babies I carry were conceived in love. Love, Papa. The true love of a man and woman for each other. Not greed or lust, but love. Now please sit down, here is Mammy Juno with our lemonade."

"I think I prefer brandy," Renault said eyeing his daughter as though she were something loathsome.

"You said you came to take me home. Why? Is Maman ill? Is it Aurore? We have had no letter for months from you."

"It is not your Maman. It is Benoit. He was severely wounded in a battle and was brought home. I came to get you to nurse him. He is still your husband and you owe him some loyalty." Renault was thinking of how he was going to avert a scandal. Especially if Benoit

504

should prove hardier than predicted. "Benoit lost his legs and is seriously ill. When I left New Orleans it was uncertain if he would survive."

"So you came to take me home to ease his last days. As you can see, I am in no shape for a journey. My time is too near and it will be weeks before I can travel with two small babies."

"Two!"

"It is to be twins."

"Have you thought how you are to explain them?"

"Since I have no intention of returning to my husband, there will be no need to explain them. Here I am Madame Quinlan. Here I shall always be Madame Quinlan."

"No, Marget." Renault shook his head sadly. "It would never work. Benoit is still your husband and he needs you now, more than ever."

"Papa!"

"I am sorry, Marget."

"Marget," Neil strode into the bedroom. "You were to rest and I . . ."

"Papa is here from New Orleans. He has come to take me home."

The two men eyed each other warily.

"Marget stays here."

"Are you two so wrapped up in yourselves that you have lost all sense." Renault finally exploded. "She is a woman married to another man. A man who needs her . . ."

"And abuses her," Neil finished.

"She has no choice, Captain," Renault said patiently.

"Stop, both of you," Marget cried. Her voice

trembled, and she was pale.

Neil went to her. He wiped the sudden trickles of sweat that popped out on her forehead. Then her nightgown was suddenly soaked with a burst of liquid. She groaned and bit her lip. Neil swung her up in his arms and curtly sent Renault to find Mammy Juno.

"Hello," Francois Honor said when Mammy Juno had deposited him into the arms of a strange man.

Renault studied him. This was the boy, the son he'd always wanted. His arms tightened about the small body. This child was his heir, the person who would come after him.

"Would you like to play in the garden. Captain Neil gave me soldiers."

Renault nodded agreement. He put the child down and allowed him to lead him into the garden.

Marget strained and pushed against the pain. Mammy Juno murmured soothingly to her. Neil wiped her face with a cool cloth.

An evening breeze stirred the warm air of the room. Marget turned her face toward it. It felt good on her hot, moist skin.

How different this was from Francois Honor's birth. She was not being piled under heavy blankets while the doctor examined her under them. This time she wore a light nightgown to soak up the perspiration and there were cool sheets instead of hot blankets. She smiled up at Neil who held her hand and gripped them tightly at Mammy Juno's directions.

"It goes well," Mammy Juno said in satisfaction.

A clenching contraction eased and Marget sank back in relief. Neil wiped her face, neck and shoulders. Mammy Juno took a fresh nightgown from the chest and swiftly stripped Marget of her soaked one. When Marget was gowned again, Mammy Juno patted her shoulder and left the room to prepare what she needed.

"Have you any preference for names?" Marget asked. She was comfortable reclining against mounded pillows.

"I like Ann. It was my mother's name. And maybe Matthew." He sat down next to her and held her hand.

"What happens if it is two of each," Marget teased.

"We'll think of something." He grinned at her then swiftly took her hands as another contraction gripped her. When it eased, he shook the cramps from his fingers.

"That's quite a grip you have, lady," he sighed lightly.

"I'll have to go back. Papa says Benoit lost his legs. He may die. He may be dead already. I have to go back."

"I know. Neil smoothed her hair away from her face. "But you'll always be mine."

"I love you, Neil."

"I . . ."

Another contraction hit. More powerful than the others. Marget cried out as Mammy Juno walked back into the room. She dropped her pile of towels on the chair and went to Marget.

"Babies want out," she said with a chuckle. "They fight, who be first."

"I hope they settle it soon," Marget whispered.

"It be soon."

"I don't think I should be here," Neil said.

"Don't leave," Marget said clinging to him. "This is a precious thing happening. You had a part of its beginning. It is only right you stay."

Neil smiled down at Marget. He would have hugged her, but she was holding his hands too tightly.

At two minutes to midnight, Neil Quinlann's son was born. Then minutes later, his daughter was born. Neil looked at them in astonishment as Mammy Juno laid them on the bed next to Marget. They cried little mewling sounds like newborn kittens.

Mammy Juno helped Marget through the last stages of her labor, then showed Neil how to massage her stomach. A small mouth was put to her breast sucking and searching until she found what she wanted.

Mammy Juno washed the boy while the girl-baby fed. Then she exchanged the two. When the twins were clean and fed, they drifted off to sleep. Mammy Juno then turned her attention to Marget, stripping the soiled nightgown from her, washing her, and remaking the bed.

"Rest now," Mammy Juno ordered.

Marget smiled. She drowsily watched her two infants, satisfaction and contentment washing over her.

"They're beautiful, Neil," she whispered. Her hand still gripped his.

"A boy and a girl," he replied. He kissed Marget, smoothed her hair away from her face. She was asleep.

"She sleep. You sleep," Mammy Juno ordered again pointing at the dressing room with made-up cot.

He dropped off to sleep listening to the quiet

sounds Mammy Juno made as she cleaned up the room. He heard her gentle murmur in answer to a quiet question from Marget. Then all was still.

Mammy Juno stood for a long moment watching the infants stir in their sleep. A blanket slipped away. She bent forward and replaced it, her black hands moving lovingly over the newborn skin. She had helped many babies into the world. Some lived a few hours, some a few years. But many grew to strong adulthood. She was determined these two would grow to adulthood because she was going to stay with them. Mammy Juno had no idea what had caused her youthful mistress to desert a husband and take another man in his place, and she didn't care. But she did remember the lines of pain and sorrow which had creased the face when she had first arrived in Nassau. Lines long gone through the tender care of Neil. Now she had to go back, back to what she had fled from, and Mammy Juno was going, too.

The old witch woman sat in her hut over a smoking fire. Mammy Juno looked timidly into the hut. She worked to control her trembling.

"You bring the afterbirths of the white woman," the old witch woman said flatly without looking up. She reached to a pile of tinder and tossed small bits of wood onto the fire.

"Yes," Mammy Juno said humbly. She walked into the hut, the smoke stinging her eyes, the unwashed smell of the woman gagging her. She held out a small bundle to the woman.

"You do right." The old witch took the bundle and laid it in her lap. "The woman leaves. You go with her."

Mammy Juno nodded in surprise. The decision to leave had only been reached within the last few hours. How had the old witch woman known so quickly?

Black eyes, deep and fathomless, were turned on Mammy Juno. She resisted the impulse to cross herself against bad magic.

"It is good you go. The white woman needs much protection. There is one who will do her harm." The witch put a thin, scrawny hand into her bodice and drew out a sack. She handed the small sack to Mammy Juno who took it and then carefully placed a gold coin into the withered palm.

The bag smelled peculiar, but not unpleasant.

"That is powerful magic. Put it near you mistress."

Mammy Juno mumbled awkward thanks and backed out of the hut.

"All will be done that must be done." The witch woman said.

Mammy Juno nodded again, then turned and ran away.

"I go," Mammy Juno insisted loudly, her voice reverberating throughout the house.

"You've never left your home in your life," Marget argued. "Your friend and family are here. You'll be lonely."

"I go." Mammy Juno stood in the middle of the bedroom arms on hips glaring alternately at Neil and then at Marget. "I go. No more talk."

Neil chuckled. In fact, he felt relief. Whether Marget knew it or not, Mammy Juno was a friend, and Marget would need her.

"But . . ." Marget said one last time.

Mammy Juno glared and then turned back to the packing.

"Kitty!" Francois Honor cried. A streak of mustard colored cat raced across the room for the darkness of under the bed. Francois ran after, wriggling down and crawling as far as he could.

Neil grabbed him and hoisted him to his feet. "Kitty doesn't want you," he said hugging the child.

Marget watched in bittersweet pain. She loved this man more than she could ever tell, and she had to leave him.

Neil received a sloppy kiss on the cheek. The cat ran from under the bed and out into the hall again with a squealing child giving chase.

"That poor cat," Marget said shaking her head. Tiny Anne began to cry with little Mathieu joining in. She bent and picked up Anne. Mammy Juno reached for the boy. Having two babies with an identical set of needs presented Marget with a unique set of problems.

"Don't you believe it," Neil said, "that old tom loves every minute of it."

Anne's cry turned to a bubbling gurgle.

"She smiled," Neil cried with delight.

"Gas," Mammy Juno said, dismissing him with a shrug.

Suddenly Marget began to cry. Huge tears poured down her face.

"I can't bear it," she said with a husky whisper looking at Neil with huge eyes gone bleak with sadness. She put Anne down in her cradle and covered her face with her hands. The cheerful sounds of the street drifted into the room as though mocking her sorrow.

511

Neil took her in his arms and drew her into the dressing room away from the sounds of crying babies. Mammy Juno caught his eye and nodded.

"We've had two good years," he said closing the door and drawing her to sit on the cot with him.

"I don't want it to end," her sobbing grew. He drew her to him cradling her in his arms.

"It isn't our time yet, Marget," he soothed gently. He stroked her hair, her face, her neck. His hands drifted to the swell of her breasts under her blouse. It was a loose blouse. She wore nothing under it. His hand moved down the smoothness of her flesh until he cupped the roundness in his palm. She was warm and slightly sweaty. Her hair tickled his nose. "It will come for you and I, it just isn't now. Trust me, darling. We'll be together again. I promise."

"Once the war is over . . ." She swallowed convulsively to check her tears conscious of his palm on her.

"I'll come. I have an interest in you, our children. They bind us together."

"I'll miss you," she said wearily. She dried her tears on his shirt.

"We've two days left. Two whole days. It's been six weeks, Marget, since the babies were born. Do you think . . ."

She smiled reaching for him and drawing him down on the cot.

Renault waited impatiently. He walked back and forth occasionally glancing at the ship. She promised he thought, she promised.

For six weeks, he'd been waiting for today. Six

weeks of uncomfortable days spent with two people who loved each other so much it hurt him to watch them. In a way, he almost wished Benoit would be dead when they arrived.

A carriage clattered up to the dock. Neil stepped out and turned back to help Marget, Mammy Juno and Francois Honor. It was painful for Renault to watch these last moments of parting. In all his life, he had never seen such a love, never felt it.

"It's getting late," Renault said stepping forward. "The captain is getting impatient."

"Yes, of course," she said, matter-of-factly. She smiled one last time at Neil, then turned and walked onto the ship, Mammy Juno and Francois Honor following.

"I'm sorry," Renault said to Neil.

"You've got what you came for, sir," Neil said grimly.

Renault studied him a moment. This man who was more than Benoit would ever be. This man who captained Renault's blockade-runner and deposited the profits in a bank in New York.

"Thank you for not making a scene."

"I don't want to lose my job." Neil turned abruptly and walked away. He stopped a few yards down the dock and stared up at the ship. Marget stood at the rail.

Renault mounted the gangplank. As the ship made its final preparations for sailing, he dismissed Neil Quinlan from his mind and turned instead to the problem of getting Benoit to accept his wife back again. If he were still alive, that is. If not, well, he had another marriage in mind for Marget. He was not going to waste her on a common seaman.

Long after the island had disappeared from view, Marget continued to stand on the deck, hands clutching the rails, dried tears leaving streaks on her cheeks. Already she ached with loneliness.

"Babies hungry," Mammy Juno said joining Marget at the rail.

With a deep telling sigh, she turned away and started for her cabin.

Benoit opened his eyes. A large, mustard colored cat sat at the foot of his bed regarding him with inscrutable feline aloofness. If Benoit had been a superstitious man, he might have shuddered and made a quick sign to ward off any coming evil. Instead, he snarled savagely at the animal. He kicked at it. Still the animal did not move. For a moment, Benoit stared before remembering he had no legs.

No legs! Disgust and revulsion poured through him. He reached for a pillow and flung it at the cat. It missed and still the cat studied him unmoving.

"Kitty!"

The door opened and a small, sleep-flushed boy peered into the room. On seeing the cat, he walked in a smile splitting his face. He dragged a long blanket with him.

"Kitty!" he cried and flung himself at the bed, his three-year-old hands opened. The cat turned and licked a hand. His long tail curved caressingly about the boy's wrist.

Benoit recognized his son immediately. Not because he had known the child was in the house, but because he was slim and small with Marget's fragile features.

There was no de Ville in the child and that caused Benoit to growl in anger.

"Get the hell out of here, damn you."

The pleased smile dropped from the child's face to be replaced by fear.

Benoit repeated his statement. The cat stiffened and hissed at him.

"What is going on here?" Marget walked into the room, her slim body enclosed in a wrapper of fine silk which clung to her curves. Her black hair fell into a long flowing cascade down her back, and her face was flushed with sleep.

Benoit studied her. For the first time in months he felt the heat of passion in him. He wanted her. He desired her.

"Maman!" the boy ran to her burying his face in the folds of her wrapper further accentuating the roundness of her bosom. "He yelled at me."

"You shouldn't be in here." Marget gently soothed the child even as her dark eyes warily watched Benoit.

"Kitty." Francois Honor pointed at the mustard-colored cat still sitting on the bed.

Benoit was becoming a little unnerved by the cat.

"Bad man, Maman. Go home. Captain Neil."

"Hush, child. Go find Mammy Juno and tell her to get you ready for breakfast."

"Go home, Maman." Francois Honor insisted.

"Sh! Go on and find Mammy Juno." Marget urged him toward the door. At the last second he pulled away and held his hands out toward the cat.

"Get that brat out of here," Benoit snarled. All the hatred he felt for her poured out. "And come back, I want to talk to you."

Marget picked up the cat and drawing the boy with her withdrew, the door clicking on finality.

She did not come back. For hours Benoit lay on his bed and fumed. Silent servants washed him, fed him and left him alone.

"Marget," he screamed. "I want to talk to you."

Three years was a long time to do without the services of a wife. He wanted her with a passion that grew and grew in him until he moaned with the unrelieved intensity of it.

It was late the next day, when his anger was exhausted that she finally came back. She opened the door and came to look at him, standing at the foot of the bed. She looked freshly washed with her skin still slightly damp and her hair darker than normal. His desire for her re-awakened. He patted the side of the bed smiling at her. When she didn't move, his smile vanished.

"Aren't you going to give your husband a kiss?" he asked when the silence stretched before them. "After all, three years is a long time to be without the comforts of a loving wife."

Amusement lit her eyes. She almost smiled, but the smile never quite reached her lips. Benoit was reminded she had two good legs left her.

"Well."

"No, thank you." Marget said politely.

He fancied there was a touch of derision in her eyes. He almost broke out in a rage again, but contained himself.

"I fancy Nassau was pleasant enough for you."

"I suspect Sulie Chesterleigh was even more pleasant for you."

"A man is allowed his indiscretion, my dear. You know that."

"Do I?" Her inquiry was polite. Benoit felt himself growing angry again.

"I'm a man. I'm allowed. I don't have to give excuses."

"Neither do I." Marget agreed sweetly.

For the first time Benoit was aware that he didn't like Marget. The patient, cringing wife was gone. A woman, sure and confident, stood in her place.

"What about your shame," he exploded drawing himself up on his elbows. He glared at her.

"My shame!" She sounded surprised.

"What kind of woman are you to flaunt your bastards in public. You'll never be received in decent homes again."

"I don't much care," she said with a shrug. "I'm here because my father insisted you were dying and needed the comforting touch of a wife to ease you into the afterlife. It's a pity you didn't die."

"So you could go back to your bastard lover."

"Yes," she agreed calmly.

Benoit was stunned. He glared at her. This was no shrinking woman, no wary wife. She was a stranger to him.

"I don't care about my reputation," she continued, "or yours for that matter. I don't care who knows about my children. I don't even care about you anymore. I was prepared to accept you once. If you had shown half the kindness Neil showed, I would never have left you. As it is, we are two people caught in a very unpleasant situation. For the moment, I will accept this situation, but only for now."

Benoit was chilled. He fell back staring open-mouthed at this strange woman. "Is this the way you treat your husband, honorably wounded in battle."

Marget laughed. "Honorable! Papa did a little checking about you. I find it hard to understand how any man can be honorably wounded when he's running away."

Benoit turned pale, then an ugly red. His eyes popped with the onslaught of his rage. Had she no mercy? He was a pitiful wreck of his former self. How could she treat him this way?

"Papa found out a great deal about you." Marget said with a second laugh. "His picture of your military career is extremely accurate. Honorable! You coward."

She bent forward smiling at him.

"Get out!" Benoit snarled.

"Gladly." Marget's voice shook with wry amusement. She left without another word.

Benoit lay back on the bed. He searched the room until his eyes rested on the wooden atrocities the doctor had called legs. For the first time in weeks, Benoit knew he was going to live. His anger and his hate would make him live, if only to make Marget regret her actions. He clawed himself into a sitting position and reached for the legs. By God, he would learn to use them. And then she'd better watch out. He would make her suffer. He would make her so miserable she would break and he would toss her aside like a dog's chewed bone.

He strapped the ugly wooden things onto his tender stumps and levered himself to a standing position.

They were partners in a marriage made in hell. And hell is what is was going to be.

Thirty-three

1865

It was over! Just like that! How simple! One minute the North and South are fighting like savages, and the next moment—peace. What had started in boundless confidence and hope was ended in tragic defeat. The war was over. Ended. The South had lost. Now it was time to get on with living.

Marget walked down the damp early morning streets amidst shouts of triumph and sporadic gunfire. She hugged her shawl close to her body to cover the worn spots in her gown. She stepped in a puddle. Dirty water seeped through the thin soles of her slippers.

"It's hard to believe the war is ended," Victoire said embracing Marget.

"Yes," Marget replied. She carefully folded her shawl and laid it over the worn arm of a chair. The lovely little cottage so elegant at one time was now as worn and weary as its owner. As shabby as its guest. Two women dulled to lifelessness by starvation and exhaustion. "Now the real war starts."

"What do you mean," alarm coursed through Victoire's voice. She looked at Marget fearfully. Nervous fingers plucked at hair once rich auburn now threaded with gray. She glanced at the pictures of her two small children who were no longer small. They were eighteen, grown to adulthood during the years of their exile. She had hoped for a better world for them. A world where they wouldn't be stigmatized by the black blood that ran through their veins.

"Do you think the North is going to let us forget the insult we offered to the sovereign unity of this country?"

"The war is over. President Lincoln says . . ."

"The wounds are still raw," Marget said ruefully. "It will be years before they heal no matter what Lincoln says about treating us with dignity and friendship."

They sat down in the chairs looking at each other bleakly. Victoire thought of her children faraway in France. Marget thought of Neil separated from her for nearly a year. She longed to have him with her. Longed to feel his arms about her neck. Longed to ease the ached in her heart. If only he were near, maybe then she could endure Benoit.

The city grew more boisterous with each passing hour. The cathedral bells rang long and loud. Men and women laughed and cried as they danced in the streets. Soldiers shot off their guns. Little boys lit firecrackers and tossed them under the wheels of passing carriages. New Orleans was a city gone wild. It was drunk on the cries of new freedom.

Not everyone rejoiced. Aurore sat in the upstairs window of her bedroom overlooking the street while Jewel watched Marget's twins. Aurore viewed the celebrations with dismay.

"You'll be marrying Master Philippe now," Jewel

said. Anne, just learning to walk, fell and started to cry. Her brother content to let his younger sister lead the way, sat placidly on the floor chewing the end of a blanket.

Aurore nodded. The wedding would be planned now and she would be given away, no—sold, like Marget had been sold to a man she did not love. Aurore shuddered.

She was a beautiful fifteen with the first cast of maturity appearing on her small oval face. Her eyes were large and dark, her nose straight, and her lips firm. Her skin was fashionably creamy with a hint of duskiness to it. Her body was firm and graceful. Aurore was enough to make any man lust after her. Because of this, Jewel feared for her.

Aurore's attention was drawn back to the window. A man on horseback appeared. A tall man, thin and straight. For a moment, her face lit up with a glow that Jewel knew could only be love and anticipation. Then the man passed on. Aurore's face crumpled into disappointment. It had not been Gayle.

He had to come home now. The war was over. Maybe her father could even be persuaded . . .

"Don't go getting your hopes up," Jewel cautioned seeing the turn of her thoughts cross her face. "Your Papa will never let you marry him."

"But he might." Aurore said with a backward glance over her shoulder at Jewel. "He really might."

Jewel kept silent knowing it was a fruitless hope.

Renault and Philippe sat in Renault's office and toasted the ending of the war. The brandy was good, a carefully preserved bottle kept hidden over the years. From below them came the sounds of laughter. Esther Nye's place of business was busy today.

"We survived," Philippe said. Business would increase now. There would be money. He thought of Aurore who deserved the best.

"Yes, we did," Renault said. He listened to the sound of the cathedral bells mixed with the street noises. It was a rejoicing city, but he was less jubilant. The war had made him rich, but at what cost. Fleur, gone, disappeared on a dark night never to be seen again. Marget, intractable and stubborn, refusing to go back to her husband, mother of two illegitimate children. Benoit a legless man consumed with a bitter hatred for his wife. And Aurore, who had always been Renault's favorite, still haunted by a nightmare four years old and showing no signs of going away. Even now he could hear her screaming of the night before and her frantic crying for another man. Philippe would never understand her night terrors, nor her feelings for Gayle Courtland. He would have no patience with her.

"When things have calmed," Philippe began then stopped.

"We'll set the date for the wedding." Renault finished. Aurore would do as she was told. She was a good child. Renault needed this marriage. His plans had been made for years. He needed Philippe, because one day Renault was going to be governor of Louisiana.

"To the future," Renault said raising his glass.

"To the future," Philippe echoed, pleased with himself and the years to come.

Marie-Odile put Clotilde down and sharply told Therese to stop mumbling and pick up the toys. Therese, less biddable than her older sister, flatly refused.

"I didn't make the mess," she complained standing in the middle of the room throwing dark looks at Clotilde who regarded her older sister with a blank look on her face. She sucked her thumb and watched her little world go by from innocent, uncomprehending eyes.

"Clotilde has fouled her pants again, Maman," Therese wrinkled her nose at the drifting odor.

Luce bent down and lifted the child into her arms. Clotilde giggled and smiled sweetly at Luce.

"When is she going to learn to walk and talk?" Therese demanded. "Look at her, she's still sucking her thumb."

"Go to your room," Marie-Odile ordered. Scalding tears threatened to overflow from her eyes. With each passing day, it became harder and harder to pretend that Clotilde was normal, only a little slower than the rest. She did nothing, but sit where she was put and play odd games with her fingers and toes while she watched life around her with huge, incurious eyes. She was four years old and destined to remain four years old the rest of her life.

Marie-Odile grieved privately for her child. The time would come when it would be increasingly difficult to ignore her strangeness, to pretend all was normal with her.

Clean once more, Luce set the child back down on the floor. Clotilde reached for a doll and drew it to her to hug it against her chest. Then she smiled, rolled back and curled into a ball. She closed her lovely baby eyes and went to sleep.

"What am I going to do?" Marie-Odile asked helplessly.

"You will take each day as it comes," Luce said taking the other woman's hand and gripping it.

Marie-Odile returned the pressure of the grip and wondered how Luce had managed to grow from less servant to more friend. She thought of how nice it was to have her. Marie-Odile was thirty-seven years old and looked and felt twenty years older. The shining black hair which had always been her pride was streaked with early gray and dulled from malnutrition. She was thin to the point of emaciation, and haggard with the weight of countless worries.

There was Clotilde who would always be a child. And Fleur, missing for two years. Where was she? Was she alive? Dead? And Marget, a woman grown into a mysterious stranger defying custom and tradition. Benoit, a man grown malicious and hating. And Aurore, about to be given in marriage to a man who frightened her.

Of them all, it was Benoit who worried Marie-Odile the most. She had watched him learn to use his hated wooden legs and crutches. His new mobility frightened her. She'd seen the looks he'd given Jewel and Aurore. She'd seen the naked hunger of his face, the unhidden lust as he studied the growing Aurore. She wasn't safe. Marie-Odile and Luce knew it and took care to be with her whenever Benoit was in the house.

"There are times when I wish I could be a child again," Marie-Odile said sighing wearily. "Life was so simple then. Maybe my precious Clotilde is not so stupid, after all."

"You're tired," Luce said. "Why not rest? You will feel better later."

"Maybe," she said distantly. She laid her head back against the chair back and closed her eyes.

Benoit thumped out of his bedroom, his crutches balancing him. The house was silent, yet there were people about. He glanced down the hall and noticed the door to Aurore's bedroom standing open. He looked in seeing a frilly girl's room, grown shabby. It was empty, yet he could still feel her. She drew him, excited him. She was an innocent.

The table drawer was ajar. He thumped across the room to her bed and opened the drawer more. A packet of letters wrapped in a fading ribbon lay in the drawer. He wondered who had written her letters that she should treasure them so? Did she have a secret even her family knew nothing about?

"What are you doing in here?"

Benoit turned. Aurore stood just inside the room watching him warily. There was a faint alarm in her dark eyes.

Benoit waited to see if Jewel would follow her into the room. In a moment he knew she was alone. Alone for the first time in months. Benoit licked dry lips.

"Looking," he said. He waited for her to come nearer, but she did not move. He took a step nearer and she back away bumping into the wall.

"I think you should leave," she said watching him warily.

"Of course," he said. He was staring at her. Staring at the rise and fall of the roundness of her bosom. She was fuller, more voluptuous, in a way that had always attracted him.

"You're beautiful," he said moving close to her smiling at her.

"I think you'd better leave," she said, her voice rising in panic. "Jewel will be here in a moment."

Benoit had no legs, but he was still a man. A man with needs, desires. Marget had refused him his satisfaction until he was frustrated to a frenzy. It was only right, that Marget's sister help him to relieve his needs.

He reached out and touched her. She tried to jerk away, but his grip was tight. She opened her mouth to scream, but he clamped his other hand down on her lips. He pressed against her, leaning, pushing her hard against the wall.

Aurore tried to free herself. She struggled. She jerked her head back and banged it against the wall stunning her for a moment.

"So lovely," Benoit crooned. He touched her, fingered her breasts, caressed her neck. He wanted her to feel him, to touch him. He guided her hand to the bulge in his trousers. He remembered Marget during the first nights of their marriage, her fear. And he remembered Fleur on the steamboat and her boldness. Now he would sample the last one.

He fumbled awkwardly at the buttons of his trousers, tearing some away in his haste. He grabbed Aurore's shoulders and pushed her down, blind to the insane terror in her face. He knew nothing but the need to satisfy his raging lust.

"Go on," he said thickly. He buried her face in the opening of his trousers. He pushed and pulled until he climaxed. Then he sighed in relief.

Benoit let go of Aurore. She slid to a sitting position, her eyes empty, her face vacant.

"Go clean yourself," he said. She did not answer. Her hands jerked spasmodically in her lap. "You keep this to yourself. Not a word to anyone. If you tell, I'll say you seduced me. Remember, not a word." He fastened his buttons. Two were missing, he looked down at the floor but could not see them. "Remember, tell no one." He left her thumping awkwardly out the door and down the hall to the stairs.

Aurore twitched. Her whole body shuddered. Her lips parted and a strange, eerie moan came from them.

Marie-Odile carried Clotilde up the stairs. The child smiled and tugged at Marie-Odile's hair. She murmured nonsense words in a language only she understood.

Marie-Odile saw the fold of a skirt on the floor spilling from the open door of Aurore's bedroom. She looked in curiously and saw her daughter sitting inside against the wall. She saw the jerking hands, the twitching body. And she saw the hideous, twisted caricature that was her daughter's face.

Marie-Odile screamed. She screamed again, unaware that the answering wail that lifted and filled the room came from her daughter.

"What's wrong?" Renault ran up the stairs. The odd, strange wailing came from Aurore's room. Shivers ran up and down his spine. His hair stood on end. He ran into the room to find Aurore sitting on the floor rocking back and forth, screaming and cry-ing. Her face a blank.

"What's wrong?"

"We don't know," Marie-Odile said. She crouched on the floor next to Aurore, holding her, trying to comfort her. Jewel held one hand trying to still the horrible twitching. "Luce has gone for Dr. Laboutierre. They should be here. Help me lift her."

Renault reached for Aurore, but she shrank away, her wail increasing to a tortured scream. Renault tried to touch her again, but a nightmare shriek from the depths of hell, stopped him.

"Can you tell me what happened?" Renault demanded staring at his daughter in puzzlement.

Jewel held out her hand. On the palm lay two small buttons.

"Has she been . . ." He couldn't finish his question.

"Raped?" Jewel said. She indicated the stains on the front of Aurore's dress. Renault felt ill. "I don't think so."

"He's been after her for weeks." Marie-Odile's voice was flat, disbelieving.

"Benoit? Where is he?"

Marie-Odile shrugged. Jewel dropped the buttons into Renault's outstretched hand. He pocketed them with grim precision.

The front door opened and closed. Shoes rattled on the stairs. Luce flew into the room with the doctor behind her. Dr. Laboutierre took one look at Aurore and reached into his bag drawing out a small, dark bottle. He leaned close to Aurore and tipped the open bottle into her mouth.

After a few minutes, the tension drained from the

small body, the empty eyes closed. She slid sideways to lean against her mother.

"Let's get her on the bed," the doctor ordered.

Renault watched as the small body was placed on the sheets. A blanket was drawn over her. She looked so tiny, so frail. What horror could Benoit have inflicted on her?

"I want you out of this house," Renault said to Marget who stood in the middle of his study, her face drained of all color. "I want you and your monstrous husband out of this house by tonight."

"Monstrous!" The contempt in Marget's voice made Renault wince. "You chose him for me. Now he is a monster! How selective your memory is!"

"I've a house on North Billere. You will be comfortable there."

"And money?" Marget asked dryly. "My 'monstrous' husband has none."

"Everything will be taken care of for you." He wanted her to leave him, but she stood in the middle of the room mocking him. His words of praise for Benoit's worthiness were dust in his mouth. Yet he refused to believe this tragedy was one of his making. His pride forbid him to acknowledge it. He would blame Marget instead.

"We'll be gone tonight," Marget said bitterly. She turned and left the room, walking heavily up the stairs to stop briefly at Aurore's closed bedroom door. It was silent in the room beyond. Somehow ominous, deathly silent. Marget shivered. She wanted to go in, but somehow she knew she would be no more welcome there she was had been in her father's study. She went on, her heart heavy, her step, the step of an old woman.

St. Angele! Marie-Odile stood on the drive and stared up at it. She had the feeling of having come home.

"Senora," Rico Hernandez, the manager, walked up to her hand extended. "Welcome home."

"Thank you," she said taking his hand and smiling up at him. He was a handsome man. She felt an odd thrill race through her.

The horses in front of the carriage stomped restlessly. Marget alighted. Marget, banished from New Orleans, because Neil Quinlann was there, and she had had no strength to resist her father's plan.

Rico smiled at the pale haggard woman. Marget acknowledged it briefly. Aurore followed from the carriage with Jewel. Rico smiled at her, was disconcerted to watch her eyes slide away from his as she edged past him as though terrified of him.

"It is good to be home after so long," Marie-Odile sighed. She did not see the shabbiness of St. Angele. She avoided any glance at the burned out shell of the south wing. The war had come to St. Angele, as well.

"Everything is ready for you inside," Rico said.

"Thank you."

The second carriage spilled out with children and Mammy Juno laughing and shouting at the sudden freedom of the outdoors. Marget laughed as she caught up her tiny stumbling daughter and held her tightly. Marie-Odile went into the house pretending it still shone with its former glamour.

"I'm sorry about the state," Rico said. "We saved

what we could from the fire and piled it in here."

"Don't apologize," Marie-Odile said dreamily. She didn't see the clutter of scorched furniture, bed linens, or draperies. She saw four years into the past.

The long line of servants curtsied to Marie-Odile's unseeing eyes. There were gaps here and there. Some of the younger men and women were gone, lured by the promises of new life in the North.

Suddenly, Marie-Odile started to cry.

"Stop yore cryin', missy," Cook said gently. "It's all over now. Yore home."

"Let's get her to her room," Luce said, taking Marie-Odile by the shoulders and leading her upstairs. "Delphine, you see to the luggage. Jewel, you see Miss Aurore to her room. She looks like death."

Delphine scurried from the house. Jewel took Aurore's flaccid hand and led her upstairs.

Aurore sat in a chair staring at nothing. Jewel sat across from her, her sewing in her lap.

"It's mighty pretty out today. Would you like to go and sit on the veranda?"

Aurore did not answer. Jewel chatted on. She had not expected an answer from Aurore. She never spoke anymore. She did nothing at all except sit and stare at nothing.

"We could have fresh made lemonade and some of Cook's delicious gingerbread cookies. She made them just for you. She knows how much you like them."

Aurore looked at Jewel blankly. Sometimes it unnerved Jewel to sit hour after hour keeping up a one-sided conversation and pretend nothing was wrong. Often, she thought Aurore had gone insane. Occasionally there would be the faintest glimmer of madness in those dark eyes. A madness that threatened to overcome and control Aurore.

"Would you like that, Aurore?"

No answer. Jewel gathered up her sewing with a sigh and stood up. Obediently, Aurore also stood. She always did exactly as she was told. She was a puppet. She walked, ate, and slept at Jewel's commands.

Jewel led the way down the front staircase, stopping once to ask a maid to bring lemonade and cookies to them. The little maid, a young girl, gazed at Aurore with huge, fascinated eyes.

"Is it true what they?" the maid asked boldly.

Jewel looked at her willing her to go on.

"Is it true she's gone totally mad?"

"No." Jewel answered curtly and walked swiftly away pulling Aurore with her.

They sat in the cool shade in wicker chairs, a gentle breeze from the river washing over them. Jewel bent studiously over her sewing occasionally glancing furtively to her right. After a few minutes, she heard the halting, shuffling sound she'd been waiting for. Old Silas walked the length of the veranda and sat down heavily.

Aurore was a stranger to him. He studied her, seeing the traces of the child and the suffering of the woman.

"Nice day," he said. His voice quivered with age. "A bit hot, but then my old bones don't keep the warmth the way they used to. I like the heat."

Aurore was a small, withdrawn doll living in a secret place. Yet Jewel was almost certain she was listening. She glanced at Old Silas who sat back easily and filled his pipe. He nodded at Jewel and smiled encouragingly.

Silas kept up the light chatter of his words. He watched Aurore knowing that her unthinking, unfeeling mind was only healing itself. He knew a day would come when that mind would emerge again and take up life where it had left off. Silas came to help.

A stableboy walked across the patchy lawn pushing a cart. Silas watched him out of old, red-rimmed eyes. At several points, the boy stopped and tossed boards to the ground. Then he went back and set up the hurdles. He left, pushing the cart.

"Yes sir, it is a right nice day for my old bones." Silas puffed contentedly on his pipe. He smiled at Aurore as though saying it was time to come back and live.

The boy reappeared leading a prancing black mare with three white stockings and a long blaze down the head. The animal walked with rippling grace, her high-stepping gait telling of breeding and unquenched spirit under control.

The boy grabbed a handful of mane and vaulted aboard the smooth back, his bare feet dangling. He walked the mare around the lawn, leaning forward and whispering in her ears. The mare tossed her head playfully.

"I call her dancer," Silas said, breaking the tense silence.

He watched Aurore intently. Was there just a faint flickering of interest in her dead eyes? Silas nodded at the boy. The mare was urged into a trot, then a loping canter. The horse circled the lawn twice before turning to the first hurdle.

Aurore's body tensed as the mare went around the lawn, taking the hurdles. She leaned forward with sweet longing in her eyes as the boy trotted the horse around the lawn one last time.

Silas nodded at the boy again. The mare trotted, then, slowed to a walk, disappearing around the house.

Aurore's interest subsided. She withdrew again, but both Silas and Jewel were satisfied.

"Well, got to get back to my chores," Silas said. He pushed himself out of the chair and walked slowly back. The stable boy reappeared, pushing the cart.

"When is the wedding to be?" Philippe demanded.

Renault read his wife's letter again. It said their daughter was better, but shouldn't be wed.

" . . . Aurore fears men." Marie-Odile wrote, "I cannot allow the marriage to go ahead while she is in this condition. She will never let Philippe near her."

"I'm tired of waiting for my bride." Philippe said slightly peevish. "The Delacourt girl is attractive."

Aurore will be sixteen in a few months," Renault said heavily. "I'll write and have my wife make the arrangements for the wedding to be that day."

"Good," Philippe said satisfied. He grinned.

Aurore laughed. Jewel heard the laugh and looked up. Aurore stood near Dancer patting her lovingly. The young stableboy stood near her laughing, too.

"Do you hear?" Luce asked.

Marie-Odile stood at the window. "I hear."

"We're going to get her back."

"Yes, yes, we are."

Thirty-four

Marget sat on the shaded veranda, eyes closed, head back against the chair. The fragrance of bougainvillea swirled around her bringing other memories of happier times. She could almost pretend she was in Nassau again.

Neil! Oh, Neil, she mourned. Was she never to see him again? Her body craved him, his love. And he was in New Orleans.

Her father had been firm. She would go to St. Angele and not see him. Already there was speculation about the origins of the twins. Speculations explained by the lie that Benoit had visited Marget while she was in Nassau resulting in the twins. Marget hated the lie. They were Neil's children, just as she considered herself his wife.

"Missy," Mammy Juno said softly.

Marget opened her eyes. For a woman as large as Mammy Juno, she could move with amazing silence.

"I think I was sleeping."

"Yes, Missy." Mammy Juno agreed solemnly as though knowing the direction Marget's dreams had gone. She glanced around furtively. Then she leaned close to Marget and slipped her a folded note. She stood up and smiled oddly.

Marget opened the note and read it quickly. She smiled, refolded it and handed it back to Mammy Juno.

"Destroy it," she said in a whisper. Then she stood and in a normal voice announced she was going for a walk.

"Nice day for a walk, Missy," Juno said in shared conspiracy.

"I'll be back for dinner."

Marget strolled nonchalantly down the stairs. She waved at Aurore and Jewel who walked across the lawn arm in arm giggling over girlish secrets. She smiled pleasantly at Rico Hernandez who went by on his tall, big-boned gelding. He nodded and tipped his hat. He was ever the gentleman, his manners charming, his smile a dazzling flash on his dark face. She approached the woods and stepped into their coolness. It was dark amid the trees. Dark and private. She hesitated to get her bearing and let her eyes adjust. Then she started briskly for the pond.

"Neil," she said in a husky whisper.

Arms came around her. Strong arms, bronzed by years in the sun and roughened by sea air. She turned and looked at him, all her love for him in her eyes. He kissed her tenderly.

"You got my note."

"yes, I got it." He smiled at her. Blue eyes and brown eyes studied each other. The months of loneliness and despair echoed in each face.

"Papa won't consent to a divorce. I asked him."

"I know. He discussed it with me."

"I'm frightened, Neil."

He tilted her face up to his and kissed her again.

536

Tears came unbidden to her eyes. He wiped them away.

"He'll spend the rest of his life fighting to keep us separated," Marget said with almost fatalistic calm.

"It won't be forever."

"I can't live with Benoit anymore."

"A little while longer, Marget. Just a little while."

"How long? A year? Two years? Forever?"

"No, not forever. But it will be soon. I have almost all I need for my own ship, Marget. And if I do one last thing for your father, I'll have the rest of it."

"What? What are you doing for him?"

"Not now, later." He led her to a blanket made soft by a pile of last years leaves. He pulled her down with him, his hands moving over her bodice, undoing buttons rapidly.

"Love me," she begged him. Her own hands flew over him loosening his clothing, touching him, aching with a need that matched his own.

"Riverboat coming," a child screamed, jumping up from play and running toward the big house.

Aurore and Jewel ran to the water's edge to watch the riverboat angle up to the levee.

Marie-Odile came to stand out on the veranda. She shaded her eyes with her hand and watched the riverboat pull closer. She shook with dread.

"Renault and Philippe will be on it," Luce said calmly.

Marie-Odile nodded. Next week would see Aurore married to Philippe. Next week she would be sixteen.

Philippe's first picture of Aurore was of a thin, strained face turning deathly white as he smiled at her. Dark eyes filled with such a terror that he drew back and stared at her. Then she turned and ran away. Jewel looked at him strangely and then hurried after Aurore.

"What did I do?" he asked looking at Renault who stared at his fleeing daughter.

"Nothing."

"That girl needs a little discipline."

Renault sighed. "She's been ill."

"So ill she forgets her manner."

Renault knew he would have to tell Philippe of the attack on his daughter and hoped he understood.

"She needs a strong man to show her how silly she's being," Philippe said at the end of Renault's narrative. "There's no reason to persist in this irrational terror."

"It isn't irrational," Marget said sharply. She had heard the last words of her father's talk.

Philippe looked at her sharply. He noticed what Renault did not. Her hair was down and snarled with dried leaves. Her gown was crumpled.

"She should be married and made to understand how foolishly she is acting," Renault said in annoyance.

"You can't do that to her," Marget replied hotly. She glared at her father wanting to remind him of the disaster of her own marriage.

"All she needs is a proper husband to take her in hand and get rid of these fears." Philippe did not like Marget. He wondered who she had been dallying with in the forest. He could even smell the staleness of spent passion about her.

Marget bit her lips to prevent anymore words from escaping. This man would be no proper husband for

Aurore. She needed compassion and understanding, not a rude awakening to womanhood. She needed to be a child for awhile yet. She turned and walked abruptly away.

"Aurore is in need of compassion," Marie-Odile said having watched the exchange from the veranda. She did not greet her husband for Marget's feelings were her own.

"Compassion is best left to silly women," Philippe snarled.

"Enough of this bickering," Renault interrupted. "I am newly home, Madame, have you no greeting for your husband?"

Marie-Odile turned on her heel and went into the house leaving him standing there.

"Let me in, Aurore," Jewel pleaded. She scratched gently at the door, but it remained stubbornly closed. "You can't stay locked in there forever."

Jewel leaned against the door fighting tears. The polished wood was cool against her face.

"Please, Aurore, let me in." Jewel whispered. There was no answer. Jewel sank to the floor still crying. She leaned against the door, her knees drawn up to her chin. She drifted to sleep unaware that Mammy Juno was down the hall keeping vigilance at her mistress's door for a far different reason.

It was early when Marget woke. She opened her eyes lazily and turned her head to watch Neil. He was different when he slept. His face was smoothed out into the innocence of childhood, he smiled a little in his dream. She felt a small breath on her arm and turned to find a pair of warm brown eyes regarding her steadily.

"Wake up, Maman," Francois Honor said. His face rested on the heels of his hands. His elbows sank deep into the mattress. It was a sweet face that smiled at Marget. A tiny face, elfin with mischief. "Can I wake Captain Neil?"

Francois Honor did not wait for her answer. He clambered up onto the bed and bounced exuberantly.

"Captain Neil," the boy cried. "Wake up."

With a growl, Neil grabbed the child and swung him up.

"I want to be a sailor when I grow up," Francois Honor cried. "Just like you. A real sailor."

"You've done some growing since I saw you last."

"I'm four."

"Francois Honor," Marget said gently. She smiled at the child who regarded her with merrily dancing eyes. "Do you remember what I said about secrets?"

"Secrets! I know a secret, but I can't tell."

"You're a good boy," Neil said tickling his sides. Francis Honor squirmed giggling.

"Captain Neil is a secret," Marget said urgently. "You can't tell anyone about him."

"I won't tell." He kissed Marget solemnly and slid off the bed. "Can we play today?"

"We'll have a picnic near the pond."

"I'd like that."

"Go find Mammy Juno and tell her to get you ready for breakfast. And remember what I said about secrets."

The boy nodded and skipped happily away.

"You'd better go," Marget said turning to Neil. "It's getting late."

"Not just yet," he said eyeing her lazily. He reached

for her and brought her close, his arms circling her drawing her down to his chest. He ran his hands over her until she pressed into him moaning softly.

"Please, Neil?" She trembled with desire, but her fear for his safety was stronger.

"Since you insist." He rolled out of bed after one last lingering kiss and fumbled for his clothes. "Meet me at the pond as early as you can. Don't forget the twins."

"I'd never forget them. Now hurry, you'll be seen."

He dressed hastily, then bent one last time over her kissing her lips, caressing her breasts until she pushed him away.

"I love you," she whispered as he disappeared out the window. He walked swiftly across the roof to the tree and dropped to the ground, rolling to his feet.

Marget closed the window watching him walk across the lightening lawn.

Marie-Odile knocked. There was no answer. She knocked again and then opened the door to find her daughter standing dreamily at the window, her naked body gleaming in the early morning light.

"Marget!"

Marget turned and smiled sweetly. She reached for her robe and slipped it on.

"Why, Marget?" Marie-Odile asked fearfully. "Don't you fear for your soul? For yourself? Adultery is a grave sin."

"I've done nothing terrible, Maman."

"He is not your husband."

"But he is, more so than you will ever understand."

"I know this will lead you to disaster."

"Possibly, Maman." Marget walked to the bed and

541

touched the pillow where his head had so recently rested. "You and Papa could have let me enter the convent as I wanted. I would have brought greater honor to this family. But Papa decide otherwise."

"But Benoit! If only you could learn to love him."

"I tried to love him, but he mocked and abused me. Now we must accept the consequences of our actions, even you and Papa."

Marie-Odile saw a stranger before her. A woman who bore no resemblance to all Marie-Odile thought womanhood stood for.

"Will you tell Papa?"

"No," Marie-Odile said turning away defeated. "I won't interfere."

"After tomorrow you won't have to worry about me for a long while. Papa is very clever. Neil goes to China to open trade negotiations there. Papa has promised him the rest of the money he needs for his ship, if he does this. He will be gone a long time. A very long time." Marget was bitter. Papa had defeated them all.

Jewel was stiff and sore when she woke. She still sat on the floor in front of Aurore's closed door, but sometime during the night she had rolled to her side curling into a ball. Someone had covered her with a blanket.

"Wake up, child," Luce said gently. "You'll catch your death sitting on the drafty floor all night."

"Aurore wouldn't let me in."

"She's not trying to keep you out, child. She's trying to hide from herself."

"She'll never get better married to him."

Luce patted Jewel's face. "You're the best friend she has. She'll need you when she's wed."

Jewel got to her feet. She tried the door only to find it open. When she walked in, the room was empty.

"It's all right," Luce said seeing the fear on Jewel's face. "She left an hour ago. She rode North toward Grey Lawns."

"Will she come back?"

"Yes, there's nothing for her there."

Aurore sat easily on Dancer. The mare flowed in graceful motion as they rode through the woods. There were no thoughts in her mind, only a vague, fearful longing.

She approached Grey Lawns quietly. In the early morning light, she could almost feel Gayle standing on the front veranda waiting for her, laughing over her disheveled state. She could almost picture the mornings they had spent eating their meals on the cool veranda while Fay had hovered disapprovingly about them. She had been a child, and he had been a man. She was a woman now, and he was gone. Aurore wept.

"Aren't you going to say hello?" Benoit asked Marget noting the reddened eyes, the rumpled gown as she walked into her bedroom.

She brushed past him without seeing him. Neil was gone. She had seen him off on the early morning packet and spent the next hours wandering through the woods crying.

"Those tears aren't for me, are they?" He mocked her.

"Go away and leave me alone."

"He was here wasn't he?"

"Leave me alone, Benoit." Marget turned to him.

He started for her, but she backed up fumbling at her night table, drawing it open and bringing out the small handgun. She pointed it at him. "Please, leave. If you don't I'll do what the war failed to do. I'll kill you."

Benoit believed her. He moved away feeling the first twinges of fear. How could he be afraid of his own wife, he asked himself? She was only a woman!

The gun did not waver.

"We're married, Marget," he whined, his eyes never leaving the gun. Would she really kill him? He already knew the answer in the steady aim of the gun and the calm look in her eyes.

"Only on paper," she said softly. "Don't you ever dare approach me again. When the wedding is over and we have returned to the city, I shall expect you to remove yourself from my house."

"Where will I go?"

"Wherever you will." Marget answered indifferently.

Benoit backed toward the door. "Your father won't like it. He'll cut you off without support."

For the first time Marget smiled. Benoit gaped at her in horror. She had a secret, he thought.

"I won't want for anything," she answered sweetly. "Now, I suggest you leave."

Benoit fell out the door and stumbled down the hall.

"Good morning," Philippe said forcing a note of cheerfulness into his voice. He glanced quickly around to see if anyone was near. There was no one. He and Aurore were alone for the first time since he had arrived. Tomorrow was the wedding. It was time he had words with her. It was time they came to an understanding. Once they were wed it would do no good for her to act so oddly, so withdrawn. He would not tolerate it.

Aurore did not hear him. She sat in the shade of the arbor looking north toward Gray Lawns as she did everyday. In the back of her mind she vaguely thought that if she concentrated hard enough, Gayle would come home. She prayed he would come home. She pleaded with God to let him.

"You can't continue to act this way," Philippe said. He sat down next to her. "We'll be married tomorrow. I will be your husband."

Her silence was maddening.

"Aurore," he pleaded, "you can't treat me this way."

She was so still, so quiet. He took her limp hand in his. He traced the blue lines of her veins along the narrow, too narrow wrist. She was so thin.

"I know what happened to you," he said. "This foolishness of yours must end."

She did not even glance at him. His fingers moved almost clumsily up the length of her arm.

"I know you've been cruelly treated. Such attacks can be a shock on young women of such tender innocence as yours. But it has nothing to do with the ways of men and women. There is nothing sinister in marriage. Let me show you." His fingers touched her breast. She shivered. "I can't wait forever. I'm willing to allow you certain exemptions from the marriage

545

bed, but I am still a man. I must have my needs attended to."

She shuddered, but Philippe did not feel it. She turned wide, staring eyes on him. She tried to draw her hand away, but he held her fingers tightly. He felt a certain satisfaction that she was aware of him at last. He dropped an arm around her shoulders and pulled her close to him. Her struggles increased. Her eyes were filled with a horror, he did not recognize.

"I love you," he whispered. He pressed her tightly to him. He took her hand and forced it down to the bulging under his trousers. "Feel me. Feel my hunger for you."

She was screaming. Her mouth was opened uttering screams that set the hairs on his arms to standing straight up. He stared at her, his arms falling away. The girl was demented.

In the next instant, Philippe was given a huge shove and he lay on the ground staring dumbfounded into the furious face of Jewel who pummeled him with her fists.

"What did you do to her?" Jewel screeched. She scratched at his fave, bloodied his nose.

With a huge shoce, Philippe hurled her off him. But before he could get to his feet, she was on him again, a wild animal, clawing and screaming.

Then she was lifted from him bodily by a pair of huge black arms. Noble set her on her feet, alarmed at the dark fury in her face.

"You damn niggar," Philippe shouted.

Aurore screamed and cried. She rocked back and forth hugging her arms to her. Tears tracked down her cheeks. She shook her head back and forth.

546

Philippe watched Jewel go to Aurore, take her gently and rock her. Her voice was soothingly gentle.

"Get Luce," she said to Noble who nodded and hurried off. "Get out of here, you animal."

Philippe stared at her. He made no move to leave.

"She's mad, insane," he cried.

"She's frightened," Luce said calmly walking into the arbor. "You'd better go."

"She's to be my wife."

Luce ignored him. She looked at Noble. "You'd better go for the doctor."

Aurore's shrieks had calmed to heart-rending sobs.

"Gayle," she whispered, and only Jewel heard the tortured plea.

"Sir!"

Renault looked up from his books to find a tall, ragged man standing in the door. He blinked and frowned trying to recognize the scarecrow man.

"Monsieur Taggert!"

"Good afternoon, sir," Cole said stepping into the room. He bore little resemblance to the nineteen year old who had gone reluctantly off to war. The indecisiveness of youth was gone. The unformed planes of his face had hardened to maturity. A maturity that had been sorely tested.

"I will send for Monsieur Hernandez." Renault said.

Cole dropped into a chair and looked curiously about the room. It was very similar to the office where he had first met Renault de Champlain years ago. It was a comfortable man's office.

"The war has been over for months," Renault said

when he walked back into the room. He stopped at the sideboard and poured a generous helping of brandy into a glass.

"It's a long way to Louisiana from Vicksburg, sir. Even longer without food, a horse, or a rifle." He was weary. He was weary of fighting to survive, weary of war. He looked down at his ragged uniform, cracked boots.

"Amigo!" Rico ran into the room and lifted Cole from his chair and hugged him vigorously. Then he stood back to study his old friend, to see what kind of a man he had become.

"I have been worried, compadre."

"I'm here," Cole said simply.

Rico nodded in understanding. He was back. He was alive. They could go about the business of living again. "Come," Rico said. He took Cole's arm and led him from the room. In his small cottage in the shade of the forest he closed the door firmly on the world.

"She'll sleep now," Luce said pulling the light blanket over Aurore.

Jewel pulled the drapes closed, shutting off the light. She sat down next to the bed.

"What about tomorrow?"

"I don't know," Luce said sadly. She felt as great a dread for tomorrow's wedding as she had once felt for Marget's. No good would come of this union. It would end in greater disaster then Marget's.

Jewel glanced at the wedding gown on its form in a corner. It was like a sly ghost in the shadowed room.

"He'll kill her," Jewel said flatly. "She'll be dead in a month."

548

"Hush, talk like this won't help her."

Jewel stared at Luce, thinking quickly. How could she save Aurore. If only Master Gayle had come home from the war. He would know what to do. But deep in her heart, Jewel felt he was dead. Nothing, but death would keep him from Aurore.

"Don't waste time on dreams," Luce said after a long silence. "It is in the hands of the good Lord."

Jewel shook her head violently. It wasn't in the hands of God, it was in her hands and she was going to do something.

It was late, when Jewel woke cramped from sitting so long in the chair. It was time now, she thought, going to the window and looking out at the dark, moonless night.

She went to Aurore's wardrobe and dragged out her old valise. With planned actions, Jewel swiftly packed everything they would need for a journey. Then she slipped quietly from the room and ran down to Renault's study. She knew where the strongbox was. And she knew where the key was kept. Without further thought she opened it and took everything that was there. She was stealing, but did not care. Aurore's safety was her foremost thought.

She was stealing across the front hall toward the stairs when the knock came. She stopped, frozen in fear. The knock came again. It was almost timid, light. With sudden curiousity Jewel moved across the hardwood floor to silently open the door. She stood for long seconds while the great hall clock behind ticked loudly.

"Master Gayle!" It couldn't be him. This was not

the same man she had once known. He was thin and haggard, weary to exhaustion.

"It's me, Jewel," he said.

"Out!" she said, pushing him suddenly. He fell back from the urgency of her hands. She pushed back down the stairs and as far away from the house as she could and still remain within the shelter of the oaks. She looked back at the house. It was quiet and dark.

"Here," she handed him the sack of money. It was heavy in his hand.

"What is this?"

"Money," she answered curtly. "We have to get away, Aurore and I, tonight."

"Away!" He felt stupid. His mind would not work. He had not slept in days, such was his urgency to get home.

"Yes, away, all of us. As far away as we can get."

"But, Aurore's husband."

"No husband, yet. Tomorrow, and we must get her away before she dies. You'll see. Understand. Wait here." Jewel was gone leaving him to stare stupidly after her. All he could understand was the Aurore was in some kind of danger. He shook his head trying to clear it. The thought of Aurore marrying someone else had tortured him for months. For months he had been caught in a mixture of emotions. Desire to see her one last time, and the need to disappear forever from her life. To not complicate it by returning. He was suddenly clear-headed. He had come back, the need to see her again winning. To see what kind of woman she had become. He was here and startled by the announcement that she was unmarried and planning to run away. New excitement coursed through him. She was not gone, lost to him.

Aurore slept restlessly. She tossed and turned in the huge bed, moaning under her breath.

Jewel shook her until her dulled eyes opened.

"Wake up. We're leaving. Master Gayle is here."

There was a long moment of clear lucidity in her dark eyes. Then she lapsed back into blankness.

Jewel half-dragged her from the bed. She forced her into riding clothes, pulling boots on unresisting feet, tying lackluster hair back with ribbons.

"Quickly, quickly," Jewel urged, trying to hurry and make as little noise as possible.

This wasn't Aurore, this blank-faced stranger. Gayle was frozen with shock. Suddenly she looked up at him. Her eyes cleared briefly. She saw him standing there. She smiled sweetly, hauntingly.

"You came back," she whispered. Then she withdrew once more leaving him stunned.

"Those are the first words she's spoken in months," Jewel said softly.

"But . . ."

"Later, I'll tell you all later." Jewel urged them toward the stables.

Old Silas was waiting for them, whittling at a stick.

"Knew you was coming," he said softly. "Here tell the *Silver Slipper* is tied up for the night at Shay's Landing. You got plenty of time to get there."

Gayle swung Jewel up on Dancer's back. He started for Aurore and hesitated, but she put her hand trustingly in his. He swung her up in front of Jewel and took the other horse. There was no time to saddle a third. He breathed easier when they reached the shadowed darkness of the forest and turned north.

Thirty-four

The carriages started arriving shortly after dawn
They pulled up to the side of the house and turned th
reins over to a host of stable boys under the directio
of Silas. Then the guests strolled up to the house t
chairs placed on the veranda and in the shade of th
oaks. There was no resemblance in the guests to thos
who had attended Marget's wedding. They were
defeated people, their gaiety gone. Many faces wer
missing.

Marie-Odile stood at the window in the upper hal
that overlooked the lawn. There was so little laughter
so little friendship. Most of the guests sat dully o
chairs and stared at people who had been friends an
neighbors for years as though they were strangers. I
was a sad assembly.

"Should I wake Aurore?" Luce asked coming up t
stand behind Marie-Odile. She looked down on th
lawn. So many people were missing.

"Let her sleep," Marie-Odile answered. "It will d
her good."

Luce nodded and left thinking of dozens of littl
things left to do.

Renault stopped. He kissed his wife absently on th
cheek. He looked out over the assembly. "Isn't tha

Thomasina Niven with that Union officer?"

"It's her husband, Major Stanton. He's a physician at the hospital in New Orleans."

"Hm!" Renault said, all the contempt he felt for one who had sold out to the enemy in his tone.

"Don't judge her, Renault," Marie-Odile said sadly. "She had to live her life the best way she could."

"She went to the enemy."

"She fell in love."

"And sold herself . . ."

"For security," Marie-Odile finished gently.

Renault said nothing more. He saw nothing wrong in selling his daughter to achieve his own desires, but for Thomasina Niven to do it . . . that was different.

"Where is Philippe this morning?" Marie-Odile asked. She searched the group. She could see Benoit sitting in a chair and drinking heavily. Things were not good between he and Marget. Something had happened to cause him to suddenly drink so heavily. Marie-Odile wondered what it was.

"He's introducing himself to our friends." Renault directed his wife's attention to a small group just inside the shade of the nearest oak. Philippe's stocky figure was amidst a group of admiring guests who smiled politely over his new suit while trying not to draw attention to their old, patched and turned gowns. Arabella Moore was one of his admirers. She flirted and smiled with him.

"Aurore is still sleeping," Marie-Odile said. "I hope the noise is not disturbing her."

Renault shrugged. He had not thought of her all morning.

"I'm going down to join the party." His voice was

heavy with sarcasm. It was anything but a party.

"I'll be down later."

People Renault had not seen in years approached him as he stepped from the house. A few commiserated with him over the loss of the South wing. He did not mention that all his silver had been saved buried in the garden with other family treasures. Rico Hernandez had been surprisingly effective in keeping St. Angele in as intact a condition as possible. There had been no vandalism here.

"Did your people all run off?" Marcus Slaughter asked. He was stooped and gaunt. The loss of two sons and three grandsons had left him without joy. The loss of his plantation had broken him.

"A few," Renault said. "Mostly the younger ones. Those who had their own land stayed." He did not add that he had never owned a slave. He had never believed in slavery. He believed in good business practices. Few of his people had left because they had always been paid for their work. Always rewarded. For his own foresight, Renault was also rewarded. He still had a working plantation where others had nothing. He felt a certain smugness settle over him. A smugness that allowed him to be generous with his less well surviving neighbors. He thought about the land which would be available soon. He thought about expansion. He had the money they did not have.

"Monsieur!" Arabella Moore smiled at him, slipping her hand through his arm. "How good to see you again after so long."

He smiled politely at her. Despite the shabby gown she was still a pretty woman. Starvation and deprivation had honed her full features down to a sharp

554

beauty. She would not be single for long.

"I don't see Monsieur Courtland here. Have you seen him?"

"He hasn't returned yet."

"Is he dead?"

Renault shrugged. He saw a fading hope leave her face drained and desperate. "I haven't heard anything. It's possible he's been delayed."

"But it's nearly November. The war has been over for seven months. Surely . . ."

"If he were alive," Renault said cruelly.

Her face crumpled to despair. "I had hoped . . ." she fluttered away looking lost and wilted. A young man in an Army uniform stepped up to her. Arabella brightened briefly. She allowed him to lead her to the punch bowl. From the look of avid hunger on her face, she would allow much more before the day was over.

"Good morning, Monsieur," Philippe said formally. "Where is my lovely bride this morning?"

"Resting," Renault answered. "She wants to look her best."

After the scene yesterday in the garden, Philippe doubted she cared how she looked. But then again, they would not send her to the altar looking like an orphan.

"Nice day for a wedding," Renault said.

"Yes," Philippe answered absently. He wandered away toward a group of silent men.

"Senor!"

Renault turned. Rico smiled at him. Renault was glad to see him and Monsieur Taggert looked refreshed and at peace.

"It's a nice day for a party," Cole said, his eyes drifting from one somber group to another. His cold eyes were unrevealing. He felt a certain contempt for the array of wealth being presented about the lawn. Tables were laden with food, the house looked well despite the burned wing.

"We are leaving," Rico said almost apologetically. He had worked here for a long time. The plantation had become as close to a home for him as it could.

"I'll be sorry to see you go," Renault said and was surprised that he meant it.

"I have trained Senor Noble as my replacement. He is a quick intelligent man. He will serve you well."

"Thank you. Have a good trip home."

Rico nodded and turned away. He saw Marget come from the house. Again, he felt the faint familiarity he had felt when he had first met her. He had the strangest feeling he should know her, or someone like her. But he couldn't place it. He and Cole drifted away availing themselves of the food-laden tables. Cole ate as though he would never eat again. Rico watched him in sympathy.

"Renault," Marie-Odile whispered. There was an urgency in her voice he could not ignore.

"What is it?" he asked.

"It's Aurore," said his wife drawing him away from the assembly and into the privacy of the house. "She's missing."

He stared at her, going numb. Then he raced up the stairs to Aurore's room.

It was empty, the opened wardrobe and the scattered clothes about the floor mute testimony to her flight.

"Jewel?" he asked already knowing the answer.

"Gone." Marie-Odile spread her hands helplessly. Tears started down her cheeks. She watched her husband grow stiff with anger.

Renault was angrier than he had ever been in his life. He looked at the untidy room. Blood pounded widely through his temples. His pulse beat frantically in his throat. He left the room, slamming the door so furiously, it jumped back and swung open again.

"They can't have gotten far," he told Rico and Cole when they stood in his study. Renault walked back and forth. His anger contorted his face until he was barely recognizable. "I want you to find them."

"Do you keep money in the house?" Cole asked.

Just picking up the strongbox told Renault it was empty. He picked up the box and threw it across the room.

"Calm down, Renault," Marie-Odile begged. Luce held her tightly trying to give comfort. But Marie-Odile would not be comforted. Her face was ravaged. Her looks had disappeared in the period of an hour. She would never be a beautiful woman again.

Renault cursed steadily.

"I'll take a look outside," Cole said. He motioned for Rico to follow him.

They checked the stables. Old Silas sunned himself on his stool looking at them vacantly when they questioned him.

"There's two horses missing," Rico said eyeing the elderly man suspiciously. Silas avoided his look.

Cole started looking at the ground. He circled the barns over and over again until he found the tracks of two horses in a dusty patch of ground. He looked toward the forest, went toward it and found more tracks in the shadows. He stared at them puzzled.

"What is it?" Rico asked. He squatted and looked at the tracks.

"For two horses carrying women, those animals are cutting mighty deep tracks," Cole said.

"For two women on one horse and a man on another, the tracks make more sense," Rico offered.

"Who would the man be?" Cole frowned.

"It is said . . ." Rico stopped. "It is said the young senorita has been in love with a neighbor for many years. A Sr. Gayle Courtland."

Cole looked startled. He stared at the tracks thoughtfully. He'd fought at the Colonel's side for over a year. The Colonel would have had a darn good reason for kidnapping a woman about to become the wife of another man.

"It is also said he was very fond of the senorita. He once killed a man because of her."

"So she ran away with him."

"No, she did not run away," Rico said. "The young senorita was a much troubled girl. It is said the husband to the Senora de Ville hurt her in some way. It took away her reason. She was . . . she was much sick in her head."

Cole looked back toward St. Angele. For the first time he wondered what kind of man Renault was who would force a daughter who was ill to marry someone she did not love.

"For someone who listens to rumors, you're pretty well-informed about the family," Cole said dryly.

Rico shrugged. He watched Cole with a glint of humor in his eyes. "For someone who has been told to find a runaway bride, you are being very slow about it."

"So I am," Cole said. For the first time since he'd arrived the day before, he smiled. It was not a pretty smile.

"Yesterday, something else happened. The husband-to-be was seen running away. I saw the girl later. She was in deep shock."

"I'd say she's had some pretty nasty shocks."

"The girl lives in another world. One of her making."

Cole looked back at the tracks. "Maybe she's better off with the man she loves," he mused. Then started back toward the house.

Renault was so furious he was speechless. He stared at Cole when the young man told him there was no sign of his daughter other than the missing horses. She was gone, vanished without a trace. He stamped around his office in blind rage. He threw precious figurines to the floor. He screamed at his sobbing wife. Renault de Champlain was a man gone mad.

Philippe came in. Marget arrived. Philippe took the news with unusual calm. It had come to him recently that he did not want a demented wife. He was almost relieved that she was gone, yet angered that she should shame him.

"Calm down, Renault," Marie-Odile pleaded between sobs.

"It is all your fault, Madame," he said icily. "I wanted sons, all you gave me were puny, destructive daughters." He glared at her. "What good are you?"

"Renault!" she gasped. In all her life she had never

seen him like this. So angry, he was purple.

"Bitch!" he suddenly screamed. "Get out, you treacherous viper."

Marie-Odile paled to transparent whiteness. She swayed against Luce.

"That's it," Marget said with a laugh. "Blame us for your failings. You're a coward."

There was complete silence in the room. Renault walked to her stiff-legged and struck her across the mouth. "I've had enough embarrassment from you."

Marget fell back. Rico caught her as she stumbled. He righted her and she stalked toward her father and hit him back.

Father and daughter stared at each other. Suddenly, Renault paled. He clutched at his chest, his body sagging. As he collapsed, he continued to glare at his daughter.

"Someone get a doctor," Cole ordered, reaching the man first. "Hurry."

"It doesn't look like there's going to be a wedding today," Philippe said wandering out of the room. "I guess I'd better tell the guests."

Gayle stood at the rail of the riverboat slowly winding its way North. It was a gambling boat. From the main saloon came the sounds of loud laughter.

Behind him the open door of the cabin showed Aurore on her bunk tossing restlessly, fitfully. He looked at her. They were both shadows of their former selves, he thought bitterly. The war had taken its toll. Neither of them would ever be the same again.

Aurore called out troubled. Another burst of laughter came from the saloon. He wanted to go in, to forget his troubled future. His hands itched to touch a deck of cards again. Instead, he went into the cabin and closed the door.